SCARLET & MAGENTA

LINDSEY DAWSON

outLOUDpress

First published in New Zealand in 2016 by OutLoudPress
Updated and reissued 2025
Copyright © Lindsey Dawson, 2016

978-0-473-34142-8 (print edition)
978-0-473-37618-5 (Epub)

The moral right of Lindsey Dawson to be identified as the author of this work has been asserted. All rights reserved. No part of this book may be reproduced, stored in a retrieval system, or transmitted in any form or by any means — electronic, mechanical, photocopy, recording or scanning — except for brief quotations in reviews or articles, without the prior written permission of the author/publisher.

This is a work of fiction. All characters portrayed in this novel are either used fictitiously or are the products of the author's imagination.

Text Design: Smartwork Creative Ltd
Cover design: Bevan Tonks

www.lindseydawson.com
www.amazon.com/author/lindseydawson

For all our ancestors, without whom our own stories could not have come to pass.

CHAPTER ONE

'Advice to Wives: Don't be too prodigal in the use of kindling wood. There is no fruit of his toil that man guards as jealously as he does his kindling wood. Just because you have free access to it, don't burn up in one day enough to last a week.'
— *Ladies' Column, Bay of Plenty Times.*

January 17, 1886

Summer heat had fled in the face of a westerly gale that sliced over the Kaimai Hills. It scudded through the coastal town of Tauranga, whipping at the flimsy lettuce leaves and carrot tops set in rows behind the thinly scattered homes.

If the wind kept up, at least the laundry would dry swiftly tomorrow. *Kindling,* thought Anna Hamilton. *Soap.* She thought she had enough of both. But her hands would suffer. She made a fist and felt the dry scratch of her skin against the fabric of her gloves.

The wind snatched at her skirt as she walked with her husband, Thomas. He whisked off his hat before it went flying. They quickened their pace. Anxiety rose within her, as it so often did. Even this brief stroll home from church was turning into a trial. Would life ever deliver up any rest? There was no ease, no time to sit, unless one was being harangued at church or driven to distraction by gossip over sponge fingers. 'We play at being ladies over the teacups,' she suddenly said out loud. 'But we're no better than skivvies most days.'

'Pardon?' said Thomas. He'd been thinking of the work waiting on his desk at the bank, of loans and interest rates, of all that potential investors needed to create good farms on the wild Bay of Plenty land being opened up for farming.

'I was just thinking of my dreary social life. And of tomorrow. Monday. The laundry. The weight of it, wet.'

Their last lazy maid had recently run off to Napier, where the pay was better, or so she'd heard. She'd not been of much help but had at least been another pair of hands. Anna sighed. 'There are simply no spare servants in this town.'

'Well. it's the rub of living here. New territory, fresh fields, brave starts. There's always a shortage of domestic help. But my love, you did know that before we came down from Auckland.'

Anna felt like dragging her toes the way four-year-old Jamie did when he was reluctant to obey. Unwilling to concede, she made no response.

They turned the corner to walk the seafront. Three ships were in port, tugging at their mooring lines. 'Mr Hamilton!' someone shouted from the stern of the *Albion*. 'How would you be this fine Sunday?' The man looked at the darkening sky and grinned. 'Or by the look of that, maybe not so fine at all!'

Thomas gave him a wave. 'It's someone I need to talk to, Anna. I'll not be a moment.' He strode along the wharf to the gangplank, leaving her stranded just as huge drops began to spatter the dust at her feet. Anna turned to see the approach of leaden curtains of rain and dashed for the nearest shop veranda. She paused, looked back. Thomas gave her an apologetic nod and ducked below decks. The squall whipped her along the street. She let it take her, knowing that in the lee of the building was a deep doorway leading into Horne & Reid's drapery. Darting into it, she bumped hard against another body, saw startled blue eyes, heard a gasp. 'Oh, pardon me,' she said. 'Did I hurt you?'

The woman shook her head, fists white-knuckled as she held a silk shawl around her shoulders. 'No, no, do join me, please.' She shuffled closer into her corner to make more room, pressing against the green door.

A flash of white light cracked overhead, followed in an instant by an explosion that thumped down like an iron hammer. They both flinched.

'It's only thunder,' Anna said, to soothe herself as much as her accidental companion. The rain was sluicing down now.

Anna touched the woman's elbow and turned to the window, away from the storm. 'Look, we can pick out our next purchases while we wait.'

Another leaping glare flung blue-white light on the reels of braid and racks of trousers. There were rolls of tweed, serge, wincey and calico, cabinets brimming with chemises and pantaloons, drawers packed with trays of buttons and a Chinese vase on the shop counter that held an arching display of albatross feathers. In the mirror behind the shop counter, they could see themselves for a blazing second as black silhouettes against a mercury backdrop.

After the next flash it took a little more time for the thunder to crash over them. 'See,' Anna said. 'It's already moving on. Trouble always seems to come swiftly here, does it not — storms, illness, flea bites, boils.' They both smiled then. 'We've not met properly. I'm Anna Hamilton.'

'I know. I've seen you in your garden with your little boy. My name is Violet Sutton.'

There was a small pause. They eyed each other curiously and then — staring being intrusive — looked back out to the soaking sky.

Anna already knew her name. Mrs Sutton's husband Henry was a big noise up and down the Bay of Plenty, full of ambition for its future. He had been away in England and recently returned with this young and pretty wife. Few had yet met her but her elegant clothes had fuelled much gossip. She had sleek dark brows and what appeared to be a sooty mark on her cheekbone.

Anna felt obliged to fill the awkward pause. 'Of course, not everything happens quickly. Letters take an age with everywhere else being so monstrously far away. I wrote to my brother in India and it took five months to get there via heaven knows how many ports. Five months! And while we wait, all else seems to dawdle. Water won't boil. Washing won't dry. Fruit takes for ever to ripen so you can treat yourself to apple pie.'

'I have orders to turn some of ours into cider,' said Violet.

Anna did not make cider. She and Thomas rarely took a drink. She remembered her father-in-law, the old missionary, speaking against the evils of alcohol at their wedding breakfast. They had sipped at a mild fruit punch. 'I'd scarcely know where to begin, Mrs Sutton,' she said.

'Violet, call me Violet. It's not difficult. Buckets of apples, bags of sugar, lots of boiling and bottling and tying corks down with string. And then waiting. Actually it's not so long, that delay, just two or three weeks in hot weather. I'll have a batch ready soon and am looking forward to how it prickles the nose. Would you like the recipe?'

'Thank you, but I doubt my husband would applaud.'

'Ah, husbands.' Violet Sutton rose lightly up on her toes, tapping her heels down on the shop's wooden doorstep. 'Applause from husbands is most often issued in small measures, don't you find?'

Anna pinked up a little, feeling disloyal. 'Not exactly. Thomas is the most moderate of men. I'm not exactly reined in.'

'But even the kindest of coach drivers knows how to bring the team up short,' said Violet. 'And even if the horses are trotting gently they are still in harness, heads forced to point the same way.' She looked up. 'Sometimes I long to sweep up the reins and canter off into open fields, to roll there and smell the flowers and take my ease.' She laughed. 'Drinking cider all the while, of course. Even the horses might take a draught or two.'

'Do they like such a tipple?' Anna was smiling too, intrigued and slightly shocked by Violet's vision of intoxicated languor. The clouds were beginning to shred apart, releasing small exhausted blots of blue. Now that their nook was more brightly lit, she thought the mark on Mrs Sutton's face might be a bruise and not a smut.

'Oh yes, a little idle play does them good. But I think it's wild flowers they probably most enjoy. I miss them, don't you? Well, I miss so many things, but flowers especially. There are so few of them here. Just those tea-tree bushes with tiny white blooms and spiteful prickles. I would so love to see bluebells and forget-me-nots and meadowsweet.'

'I'm slowly creating colour on our small patch,' said Anna. 'You're welcome to cuttings.'

Violet's smile was warmer now. 'Only in return for my cider recipe.'

'We were just on our way home from church,' Anna said. 'The Reverend Larkin took care to berate us all this morning for lack of thrift.'

She had barely been able to contain a roll of the eyes as his sermon rang out over Sunday hats and dandruffed shoulders. What else could a woman do in the colonies but practise all the thrift she could muster? Only yesterday she had been struggling to make a jacket for Jamie from the remains of a cape of her own. She had carelessly slung it on a chair too close to the kitchen fire, scorching one side beyond repair.

Anna had treasured that cape. As the ship wallowed over mirror-bright tropical seas on the long voyage to New Zealand, she had hung it on nails above the open cabin door so she could have privacy as well as a waft of breeze. Then, down in the Roaring Forties, it had given her comfort during freezing, howling storms. More hurtfully, it was a lost link to her old life in Northern Ireland. She'd worn it to stroll the promenade at Warrenpoint, where she'd been able to chat with neighbours she'd known all her life. Now she had few good friends and no cape.

After the service, Larkin had stood, beaming, at his door, his cheeks damp with the sweat that ardour had driven through his pores. They shook his plump hand. 'Capital!' he cried. 'Thank you!' as if they'd praised his preaching to the skies.

'I've not met the Reverend,' said Violet, 'but if the size of his belly is any indication, there is little parsimony being practised in *his* household.' The rain had eased back to a sulky drizzle and they stepped out onto the street. 'Do you like to walk, Anna?'

'I have little spare time but occasionally, yes. If Jamie is off playing at a neighbour's, like today, then I can.'

'Do take a turn with me sometime. It's nice to share the path and talk awhile, don't you think?'

CHAPTER TWO

'Woman's one notable invention — perpetual emotion.'
— Ladies' Column, Bay of Plenty Times.

ANNA HAD NO TIME THAT WEEK FOR ANYTHING SO LEISURELY
as a walk. On Monday, Jamie was feverish and miserable. The laundry
had to wait but there was still all the dusting and sweeping to do. She'd
been doing that herself after finding her former servant girl moonily
pouring puddles of tea on the floorboards and dabbing at them with a
broom.

'Tea *leaves*,' she cried. 'Not tea! You sprinkle damp leaves for the
dust to stick to. Give it me.' And she'd grabbed the broom to finish the
job, seething with irritation.

Tuesday was washing day, which began with lighting and stoking
the fire beneath the copper. Jamie was out of his cot now but clinging to
his mother's skirt, his nose needing constant wiping.

On Wednesday he was better, but there was sewing to tackle and
letter-writing long overdue. On Thursday, boxes of fruit were delivered
and she stood for hours in the kitchen, and right through Friday too, to
put up preserves and make jam. And the dairy ran out of butter, so she
had to buy cream and churn it herself. That day was so hot it was

impossible, so she rose at 5 a.m. on Saturday when it was cool enough to try again. And by then the cream had soured.

There were times when she felt like weeping. And sometimes did.

She seldom, however, showed Thomas any tears. He had never seen his own mother weep — she who'd borne children in draughty huts with oiled calico tacked up in place of window panes. She had kept her first children fed in trackless, appalling places, until at last the church allowed the doughty missionaries to fetch up in the relative civilisation of Auckland where there was an actual doctor on hand for the arrival of Thomas, her ninth and last baby. The doctor had little to do. Mrs Hamilton had endured childbirth so often that she knew how to be simply carried along by the effort of it until another bundle of squealing warmth was placed into her exhausted arms.

Crying never helped anything, Thomas's mother always said. And so Thomas was confounded by any tears produced by his wife. 'Buck up now,' he'd say awkwardly.

If Anna couldn't buck up he felt helpless and wretched, unable even to calm her shudders with a stiff, appalled embrace. Her tears had been endless when Rosa, their first-born, died from some form of poisoning before her first birthday — bad food or water, they'd never know which — racked by vomiting, her little nightgowns stained with a vile, watery effusion that drained her tiny frame dry.

After they'd buried her Thomas had been able to cope only by removing himself from the room. And the house. And the town. Sometimes he hired a horse and rode it hard far back up the coaching route into the Kaimai Hills, returning hours later. By then Anna, pale and emptied of tears, would be plastering over her pain with chores — chopping meat with a rigid fist, polishing glasses with a knuckling whirlwind of bunched-up rags, or sewing seams with her Singer as fast as she could go, her knee bobbing at the treadle, the sharp needle blurring a savage path through weft and warp.

* * *

MRS VIOLET SUTTON, companion-less, with Henry engaged in a meeting about plans to push a railway through to the Hot Lakes, laced up her boots and set out on a Friday morning walk along the sea front. First she took the shell-strewn Strand, past the line of shops and the Post Office and Victoria Wharf. When Tauranga's slight attempt at grooming petered out, she set out on the sandy path that skirted dreary swathes of mangrove. Soon she'd left the town behind.

The day's empty, eye-squinting shine offered no sound but the wind whickering at tawny blades of sedge grass at her feet, the nagging squawk of squabbling gulls, the rustling of her skirts. How she envied men their freedom to stride unhindered. Long skirts caught on every thorn. It meant hours of repairing rips and torn lace edgings. Henry could not abide his wife to look less than perfect. Their housemaid, Hester, was a deft cook but so clumsy at sewing that she couldn't be trusted to mend even a dish cloth. It was Violet who wove tiny restorative stitches with her shiny needle.

She felt that all the townsfolk must see her wardrobe as ridiculously elegant for so provincial a place, but Henry thought that if a man had built some wealth over the decades there was no point in being modest about its display. Merely glancing at his house, his horse and his wife would bring the word 'quality' to mind. Paths had to be well raked. Brass had to gleam. Hester was required to labour at their shiny doorstep every day. His wife's mending drove him to distraction, however. 'For God's sake woman, it's only a petticoat. Let Hester have it. You have an account at the draper's — use it.'

But Violet clung to her quiet times with her sewing basket. In the evening she would hunch close to a kerosene lamp, the wick wound up high so she could see, listening to Henry slurping at his port as he bent over the latest papers from London. She would pour him generous glassfuls, hoping he'd precede her to bed and fall into a wine-deep sleep. After he'd lumbered to the bedroom she would sit for a long time, hoping to hear him snore. But there were nights when he would call out, 'Violet, come now.'

Once their door was closed he would wait for her to go from window to window to ensure the damask curtains were pulled tightly closed. Then he would watch as she undressed, insisting that she face him and unhook her corset slowly and lift off her chemise, revealing long marks where tight whalebone had pressed creases into her flesh.

Then she would take down her hair and brush and brush and brush until it crackled and rose, alive with electricity, around her naked shoulders. Sometimes that was enough. She would be permitted then to don a nightgown, douse the candle flames and make her way through the smoky reek to their bed to lie down and gaze into the gloom as he fumbled and groaned and exhausted himself.

At other times he would require her to dance or at least, in the absence of music, to strike various poses. She had taken ballet lessons from some French artiste in London, he had learnt. Henry had molten memories of Paris. The dance made a girl so graceful, *dontcha know*. So he would require his young wife to keep the candles burning, disrobe completely and do her exercises, one hand on the iron finial at the end of their bed to act as a barre.

She would follow her girlhood routine — first position, second, third, fourth, fifth, her slender arms rising, her breasts lifting, exposing the tender hollows in her furred underarms. Then pliés he always wanted, the exercise where the knees must bend and spread wide. He liked to watch her from the rear as she did this, enjoying the straightness of her back, the tautness of her buttocks and thighs, and the dark smudge just visible in between the pale half-moons of her derrière.

Derrière. It was Henry's opinion that the French language contained such excellent words.

Occasionally he would require her to open the chest beside her wardrobe and take out the filmy ballet skirt that lay inside. He had wheedled it, years before, in exchange for cheap perfume, from one of his favourites at the Paris Ballet.

One of his friends had known an artist who painted those dancers obsessively. Henry had even met that girl. Fifteen years later she still lingered in his life, twirling in the small oil sketch that hung on the wall just inside his front door — her filmy skirt a blur of apricot on a luminous blue ground. Though just a small picture, he'd paid that moody artist, Edgar Degas, a stiff price for it.

Now he had Violet slip on just such a skirt and tie the frayed satin ribbon at her waist before stepping to the oval of fine Persian carpet at the foot of the bed, clad in only that one garment. Floor exercises would begin. Her movements would make the transparent bell lift and drift around her thighs and calves.

He would want to see her pas de chat — springy, foot-crossing steps named after the lightly elegant stepping of cats — and if she faltered he would tell her she leapt like a cow. Or: 'You have knees like a camel's. It should be softer, softer.' Always, she would be required to finish with an arabesque, balancing with the arms and one leg arched upwards, holding the pose for as long as she could, until her whole body shook with the effort.

He sometimes liked to stand alongside her to train her in this, his broad hands enforcing the arch of her spine. Then one of his palms would knead her breasts while the other ran up and down the flesh of her straining thighs, ending each stroke with a grunt and a thrust of fingers between her legs. Violet had learnt rigid passivity on these nights. She knew not to make a sound and not to fall out of the pose, to maintain balance at all costs, until he allowed her to stand on her two feet. She knew how those meaty hands could become fists. She also knew the time was coming when she would never, ever, submit to them again.

* * *

VIOLET ROUNDED a corner and approached a small curving beach overhung by shady pohutukawas. The blood-coloured Christmas blooms had died, but the ground was scattered with darkened filaments from the flowers. 'Mrs Sutton!' someone shouted.

She stopped. A blue dinghy appeared from behind the gnarled trunks, carving through calm water ten yards from the shore, two men in shirtsleeves, one at each oar.

It was the banker boys — stolid Thomas Hamilton, manager of the local Bank of New Zealand agency and his friend Rupert Beckford from the National Bank, foolishly hatless. Beckford broke his rhythm and the boat slewed as he waved to her. Men with hair so bright always had the palest of complexions, liable to painful burning. His wavy, blazing mop was a russet so intense that in certain lights it threw off an almost purple halo. She knew that around the town they called him the Magenta Man. She was not sure if he knew that.

'Good afternoon,' she called.

'Stop, Tom, wait,' Beckford told his partner. Digging in his blade and swiping deep, he swung the bow out so as to back the dinghy in towards the beach. She could see the name *Iris* painted on its stern. Thomas had no option but to ape his choppy strokes as he nodded a greeting.

'Come boating,' Beckford said with a sweep of his hand. Their sweat-damp shirts clung to them. 'There's room. We can ferry you to town.'

She smiled, indicating her long skirt. 'First build me a wharf, gentlemen, or a gangplank.'

The dinghy grounded on sand with a soft crunch. Five yards of shallow water stood between them. Beckford grinned. 'I could play the knight and carry you to our galleon.'

'Yes, well, best not, I think.' People were approaching through the tea-tree acres — Maori women with woven flax kits for collecting seafood. She dimpled a little. 'What would the neighbours think?'

'Oh, what do we care about them?' Beckford looked at his shipmate and gave his shin a careless kick. 'Don't look so worried, Tom. We are all being *fraightfully* proper. Are we not, Mrs Sutton?'

She took a step or two back, leaving her boot prints filling with brine. A crab scuttled at the sea's quiet lip. Women's laughter drifted to them. 'Indeed yes,' she said. 'And I do appreciate the invitation.'

Thomas pulled at his oar and Beckford reluctantly matched his stroke to shift the boat's keel. It rasped over the sand into deeper water. 'Farewell then. But allow me to organise dry access and we'll do it another day,' Rupert called to her. 'It would be my pleasure.' His voice tilted up a little at the sentence's end, as if to leave space for a positive reply.

She stood still, lifting her shoulders with a wry shrug and said, 'Perhaps.'

'My compliments to your husband,' Thomas shouted as the dinghy pulled away. She nodded, raised her hand and turned away.

* * *

THE MEN WORKED their oars once more, leaving small, eddying whirlpools in the wake of each stroke. 'Would you really, Rupert?' Tom asked. 'Take her boating.'

Rupert gazed for a moment at the rise and fall of his blade, drops sliding off its wet lower edge as it lifted from the surface, each globule glittering in the sun before rejoining the sea. 'Why not? She's a pretty bit o' jam. Intriguing, too. Looks like the ice maiden but I sense something volcanic underneath. Dissatisfaction, too. When you see the Suttons together it is as if they are apart.'

Thomas snorted. 'But she's a missus, not a maiden. She is rather married, Rupe. To a powerful man.'

'Who is at least fifteen years older. I can't begin to reason why she said yes to him. How can an old warhorse make such a filly content?' He grinned. 'Such a spirited filly, too.' He looked sideways to his friend's broad face. 'Good Thomas, so upright in all things. "Compliments to your husband", indeed. You're just after his business.'

'Better his business than his wife.' Thomas purposely flubbed his next stroke to rattle his partner. 'You're slowing, Rupe. We'll never win the race at this pace.'

'Who says? Three more weeks of this and there'll be no one who can beat us.' They rowed on steadily. 'What of his schemes, anyway? Do you think he can raise the funds for the railway?'

Thomas shifted a little on the thwart. He and Rupert worked for rival banks, so there were things they did not discuss. Both were looking for business that would please their masters in Auckland and Australia. The colony needed railways, roads, farms, buildings, schools and industries. The plan was to grow and grow. This land was wide open for a man with vision and capital.

Henry Sutton gave little away about where his wealth had come from, but Thomas had been pleased to inform head office that Sutton had recently deposited fifteen hundred pounds with him. He did not know if Sutton had spread his risk by doing the same at Rupert's bank. He couldn't ask.

Much as Thomas enjoyed Rupert's reckless dash and lively sociability, he thought that banking was an odd choice of profession for his friend. Rupert enjoyed a drink too well and tended to gamble on the horses more than he should. He was the sort of man many saw as a chancer. He did not think Rupert would hover too long on New Zealand's eastern rim. 'Would you return to Melbourne?' he had once asked him.

'Lord, no,' he'd snorted. 'What, back to my mother's beady gaze and beastly preachings? She's as relentless as the Reverend Larkin. But Sydney, now that could be my kind of town. A more roistering sort of place, don't you think? Full of curious dives and loose ladies. We should sail off there one day, Tom, just you and me — away from our ledgers, two braves off on an adventure!'

'Ah, I'm too fond of my domesticity to join you. I am a man well roped and tied.'

'Anna's a sweet lady, Tom. I understand. But life can never take that path for me. I'm a roving sort of cove.' He had flashed his broad smile then, with which (Anna had once said) he could charm the feathers off a hen.

The oars clicked in unison in the rowlocks now. Lacy bubbles trailed from the stern as they considered the question of laying iron tracks into the country's interior.

'It's all about politics for now,' Thomas said. 'Wellington is so slow to pay attention. And it would take a lot of capital. But, oh, how we need it. That coach road is interminable. Nine hours of lurch-and-jiggle! But look at the steady stream of visitors willing to endure it. The Pink and White Terraces are a wonder of the world. Everyone says so. Even that writer fellow, Trollope.

'Tell you what, Rupe, let's try it for ourselves! Here we are, living so close by and I've never seen them. And I do actually have some business over there. What do you say? Can you think of a good excuse to be absent for a few days.

They bent their backs and rowed so hard that salty froth boiled behind the transom. 'Never a problem for me, dear boy,' grunted Rupert. 'I've a book full of excuses.'

* * *

When, two days later, Rupert set out for a foreshore walk and happened to meet Mrs Sutton there seemed to be no reason for them not to walk together. They rounded a corner at the same time and stopped still. Rupert swept off his hat and grinned. 'We seem fated to encounter each other,' he said.

'Indeed,' she replied. 'Are you setting out or heading back?'

'Very much setting out.'

Violet smiled. 'I've been walking for a while, but extended exercise can only be beneficial.'

She turned and they went on together, keeping a respectable distance. He began to tell her a silly story about a horse race up the coast where a mare had come close to buckling under a corpulent jockey. Rupert talked with his hands. She glanced sideways as his arms shaped a wide ball in imitation of the rider's girth. She noticed the shape of his jaw and cheekbone, the way his bright hair flopped with each stride.

Viewed straight on, his face had its own identity, but side on, as she saw him now, there were echoes of another face she'd once loved deeply. She became aware that as she matched his pace, her hand had risen to cover her heart. And she realised that here, now, with laughter rising, there was a lightening of the habitual weight she carried inside.

CHAPTER THREE

'A cynical sailor has given his reasons why a ship is called " she". It is because the ships are useless without employment, they bring news from abroad, they wear caps and bonnets, they are often painted, and a man never knows the expense until he has got one.'
— *Bay of Plenty Times.*

JANUARY 23, 1886

The next day, Anna went out to tea. Her hostess, Fanny Bell, was eager to share news of Mr Beckford. 'I understand he and that Violet Sutton were seen together yesterday, walking the shoreline path. Just the two of them.' Her spoon made a regular chime — tink-tink-tink — as her plump hand spun an astringent disc of lemon in clear brown tea. 'She is a married woman,' said Anna mildly. 'They hardly need a chaperone.'

'But she is not married to *him*.' Fanny's voice slid deep into her fleshy throat, tremulous with outrage. An ardent follower of human foibles for all of her fifty years, she tended to hear quickly of any event that might cause outrage — her husband was the town's newspaper editor.

'Well, I suppose an accompanying maid would tend to allay the flapping of tongues.'

'Indeed, yes.' Fanny licked a tiny dot of cream from the tip of her little finger. 'Mind you, we all know how difficult it is to get good help.' She darted a look at Anna. 'Have you found anybody yet? Surely one of Mr Hamilton's needy clients might have a useful girl you could take on?'

'We keep asking,' said Anna. An itchy film of sweat bloomed on her neck, under her arms, between her thighs. She longed to be out on the veranda where at least they could take advantage of the sea breeze, but Fanny always preferred to be inside. Her windows were a bulwark against dust, pollen and the infernal insects. Besides, at her age, she said, it was best to avoid draughts of any sort.

On the far side of the lace curtains a blowfly battled to break through the glass. Fanny picked up a small brass bell and rang it furiously. Her cook trudged from the kitchen wiping her hands on her apron, laced shoes loud on the wooden floor, strong dark hair pulled back in a bun. She had been plucking a chicken. A few feathers stuck to the apron's coarse hem. 'There's a fly,' Fanny told her. 'You know how I hate them.' The cook slipped in behind the curtains and flailed at the insect with the stained end of her apron. The buzz was silenced, the corpse carried away within the folds of fabric.

'Mind you change that!' Fanny sighed. 'Training these native girls is such a business. I've told her time and time again that when I have company she must wear a clean apron. But over and over again, she forgets. What happened with that Welsh lass of yours?'

'Oh, she gave me more vexation than assistance. Restless, too, always complaining she wasn't meant for this place.'

'None of us are meant for this place, Anna,' snorted her hostess. 'And yet that sea, that never-ending sea!' She waved her bulky arm at her window. The house was close to the shore but the bulk of Mount Maunganui and its peninsula meant she could not see the endless ocean, so huge that if one were to sail eastward there'd be nothing to stop a puny ship until it fetched up against the alien cliffs of South America. She was close enough to smell its taint.

'So much emptiness. Pitiless, lifeless, sterile,' she moaned. 'How I long to go Home, my dear. But I shall never set foot on a ship's deck again.'

'I met Mrs Sutton recently. She was very pleasant. She gave me the impression she'd like to go Home, too,' said Anna.

'But that can't be! Her husband's ambitions are here. She can't be entertaining any such fantasy.'

Anna looked down at her napkin and felt a small pang of guilt. It was spotted with bright strawberry jam as if fresh blood had dripped there. The cake fork was slightly mottled with dark tarnish. The cook had not yet, it seemed, been taught to rub clouded silver with a baking-soda paste. 'It's just my impression.'

Fanny's ample shoulders twitched. 'Foolish girl. She has one of the largest homes in Tauranga, a grand piano, those lovely rugs all the way from Oetzmann's in London, more fancy clothes than any woman living here has a right to, and a substantial husband to boot. Have you been inside the house?'

'No,' said Anna.

'Oh, my dear, do wheedle an invitation. So few of us have gained entry — Mr Sutton has not been the most sociable of men. Perhaps that will change now he has a wife. I believe he has Parisian art on the walls — an extraordinary daub of a half-dressed dancer by some French dandy. Oh!' she whooped. 'The scandal of it! I wonder that a young wife like her is happy to have such a lurid picture before her eyes every day. But then, there's no knowing, my dear, what goes in the head of an idle woman.'

* * *

ANNA'S KNEES thrust crossly against the cotton of her skirt as she made heavy weather of the walk back home along Willow Street. Workers from the town board had just laid down another layer of shells and its glare was fierce. Horses' hoofs and cartwheels would eventually crush the shells flat, but for now they were a slip-siding swathe of sharp edges.

The shells were of some help but in heavy rain the road still became a sticky quagmire that caked the stoutest shoes and pushed creeping stains up skirt hems. Anna yearned for gravel underfoot. Like so much else, however, this was not a luxury the colony could supply.

Thomas had never in his twenty-nine years felt the reassuring crunch of gravel beneath his feet. In this, as in so many things, his life experience was different from hers, for he was colonial-born. Anna had come out at twenty with her widowed mother, Amy Vincent. They had arrived only eight years earlier, following in the footsteps of Anna's adventurous older brother. But mere months after their arrival he had cut his foot with a spade. Though it was just a small injury, it became swollen and foul. All his youth and vitality had not saved him from infection, fever and death. Having made the huge journey around the world, neither Anna nor Amy was keen to go back, and so they reeled with grief, did their crying and then resolved to make the best of things.

Anna met Thomas then and his solid affection had warmed her heart. She was tolerably happy in Tauranga but still yearned a little for the comforts of civilization. She tried not to use trifling examples to point out to Thomas how limited his experience was. But today, she'd have welcomed gravel.

She stepped into their domestic quarters alongside the bank, turned into the parlour and found him bent over ledgers and chequebooks. He had retreated there to get away from his customers. His time was too often worn away with idle conversation. Letters demanded his attention too, always such a flow of paper — pleading, cajoling, grovelling, apologetic, demanding, importunate. There was little peace to be had even in his own house. Thomas was also supposed to be keeping an eye on Jamie and could hear the boy babbling to himself as he played with blocks on the kitchen table.

'My dear,' he said as Anna swept in and sank onto their small sofa. Half-circles of damp showed beneath her arms, inking her sage-green bodice. Into the parlour she brought a vaulting waft of perspiration, salt, horse dung, and the tang of some pungent plant she must have brushed past on her way home.

She tugged off her straw bonnet with a sigh.

'Come, come,' he said, 'surely it wasn't so trying.'

She pushed sticky strands of hair back from her forehead. 'You'd have such a mood as well if you had to listen to that gossip and keep smiling.'

Thomas dropped a blob of ink upon a stern note he was writing about the size of a store owner's overdraft. 'Damn and blast,' he said, and blotted too fast, making a smear. 'I'm sorry, Anna, but my reputation depends on attracting a healthy flow of deposits. We must keep relations congenial here and the Bells are so well connected. This town is too small to allow enmities to develop.'

'I know, I know. I shall have Fanny here next week and Louise Archer, too. But it is so,' she spread her arms to encompass the room, 'cramped in here.'

'Our home is no smaller than those of most of our acquaintances. I could push my desk into the alcove to make more space.'

'It will do little for the space between their ears,' said Anna. Her face softened as Jamie ran in, arms spread wide for a hug. 'Hello, darling boy, have you had a good afternoon?' She kissed his round cheek. 'I suppose you are right, Thomas. I must play my part. But I suspect what Fanny really wants is to deliver more gossip about Mrs Sutton. "How unfortunate that tongues are flapping," she says, even while her own is as busy as a cormorant's wings.'

'Anna, now you are being unkind. One can't help people being curious about their neighbours in a town as small as this. If people behave unwisely, perhaps it's no wonder if there's a little talk.'

'You've heard rumours too? It's said she and Rupert Beckford are seen together rather too much.'

Thomas shifted in his creaky chair. 'Hardly likely, I'd have thought. We saw her on the shore path last week when we were rowing, but she was alone. He said nothing about accompanying her. Though there was, now I recall it, a certain familiarity in her manner. Far be it from me to make assumptions, of course but with no children in the house she must have time to fill.'

Anna sighed. 'Well, how favoured she is. If I could find some time I'd go strolling with her too.' She squeezed her son, making him giggle. 'Now, it must be time for your supper soon.' She could smell the sheep's-head broth she had left on stove, congealed by now no doubt. It would need reheating. 'In a few minutes we'll go get a treat — some fresh bread from Mr Ward's bakery. Off you go now and brush that messy hair of yours. We'll leave very soon.'

Thomas cleared his throat as Jamie scampered away. 'Are you sure that would be wise?'

'Pardon?'

'Going arm in arm with Mrs Sutton. It could be seen as somewhat declarative, could it not?'

'Of what?'

He stood and went to the window. A stately line of clouds was blocking the sun and so the glare had eased somewhat. He squared his jaw. Thomas liked neatness in all things, whether in his accounts or the emotions that so often roiled the air in his small household. 'That you'd be allying yourself with a woman whose reputation is, well, a little suspect.'

'So you *have* heard talk of her, then.'

'Not in any way that needs repeating.'

'Don't then,' said his wife airily. 'And until I have proof of wrongdoing, I for one do not intend cutting her in the street. This is a hard and lonely place, Thomas, for women much more than men. You have your business. We women have only our friendships to keep us going. And our work, which never ends.' There came a shriek from the kitchen. 'A rat!' yelled Jamie.

Anna scurried to the panic. Thomas stayed put. There was no need for three of them to take alarm all at once. 'Hush, Jamie, it's just a tiddler,' he heard her say. She had become adept at dealing with rodents. He heard a thud and a squawk from James. 'Got 'im!' he cried.

A minute later Anna walked past the window at which Thomas sat. She held a fire shovel level before her and he could see the rat's slack tail hanging over its edge. At the back of their plot of land she used an awkward, two-armed throw to send the rodent sailing off into the knee-high grass of the empty lot next door.

Thomas grunted with irritation. Burying the corpse would have been better. Left to rot in the undergrowth it would provide feed for even more vermin. He went to the kitchen and was calming Jamie down when she returned.

'It was by the flour bin,' she said as she dropped the shovel by the stove. 'I'll need to check it for droppings. And scrub all the shelves.'

Thomas shook his head. 'Throw it away.' He didn't like waste but he hated rats. Every ship that came in brought more of the vile things in their cargo. Like so many ailments and pests, rodents flourished in this mild climate. 'We don't want sickness in the house,' he added. Then he felt abashed by the burning look his wife flashed him as she washed her hands. There was, he knew, no need for him to caution her on the matter of sickness.

CHAPTER FOUR

'Stout people, be they tall or short, should remember that they require almost no trimmings or puffings. They look handsomely dressed in quite a plain garment, if it be well cut and rich in texture. Thin people, on the contrary, take any amount of trimming and puffing to give them a sufficiently clothed appearance.'
— Bay of Plenty Times.

JANUARY 28, 1886

A week later, waiting at the baker's counter, Violet and Anna filled the warm, yeasty air with confidences. 'Tom's away off up at the Hot Lakes,' said Anna, tucking two loaves into her basket. 'Business, he says, with a hotel owner there. But Rupert Beckford's gone too. I suspect it's more a case of men on an adventure.' Jamie jumped up and down alongside her as they stepped outside. 'Jamie, stop that.' He ran off at speed, shirt flapping.

Anna sighed. 'He's been so difficult lately. I heard chopping sounds yesterday and found him hacking at fence posts with my kindling axe. I was terrified. I can still see the flash of light on its edge. One slip and. . .' She shuddered and peered ahead. 'Jamie, wait!' He had reached the next corner and seemed about to scamper on, but then hesitated, kicking at stones.

'A modicum of obedience, I see,' observed Violet.

'Only because he felt my hand a few times, and then was soundly chastised by his father as well. Jamie!' she yelled, for suddenly he took off again. Grabbing at her skirt, hampered by her full basket, she ran after him. Then, turning the corner, she was suddenly off-balance and tipped over, her basket tumbling. She was still sprawled, skirt hiked to her knees, when Violet caught up with her. Jamie ran back too. 'I'm sorry, Ma!' he wailed.

Slipping in a slew of shells, Anna struggled to rise. The right sleeve of her dress was ripped. Blood dribbled rapidly from a cut below her elbow. Jamie was wide-eyed at the scarlet trickling down his mother's wrist.

'Come home with me,' Violet urged as she helped her up. 'You need a bandage.'

Hester looked up from scrubbing her table as they came in. Blonde and broad, with brows and lashes pale as fish scales, she slowly raised her broad palms and said, 'Dearie me, what have we here?' Hester was not a fast mover. The only lightness about her was her pale hair, so abundant and electric that it constantly sprang out into a frizzed halo no matter how ferociously she screwed it into a bun.

Violet found clean cotton to tear into bandage strips and dabbed Anna's wound with clean water as Hester put the kettle on the range and jiggled the embers with a poker.

'We'll have tea in no time at all,' she declared. 'And young fella, you can help me make some girdle scones. Are you good at stirrin' milk an' flour?' He nodded. 'And at taking the lid off a pot of Hester's jam?' Even more avid nods. 'Well, then.' She bent over to squint at Violet's ministrations. 'They say honey is good for cuts 'n' scrapes. Here, try this, straight from the next door's hives.' She lumbered to a cupboard, fetched a jar of amber goo and put it on the scrubbed table.

'You're sure?' Violet asked.

'Yes, ma'am. My own ma was a healin' woman. She reckoned honey was good for just about anything that could ail a body.'

Anna was soon sitting in Violet's drawing room sipping sugared

Darjeeling. Jamie stayed in the kitchen, shelling peas for Hester and, Anna had no doubt, scoffing a measure of them along the way.

Violet regarded the bandaged arm. 'You'll have to be kind to that for a while. How will you cope? Especially with Thomas away.'

'I'll make do. No doubt a new body will turn up. Though how useful they'll be is an entirely different matter. You're fortunate to have Hester.'

'She came through Mrs Elsmore's office in Auckland. They list all sorts of domestics — even a smattering of butlers, they say. But it's hard to persuade people to come all the way down the coast. Being so dull and provincial, we have to pay them mightily.'

Anna was too proud to admit that over-generous wages were beyond her means. She looked ruefully at her torn sleeve.

'Let me mend that,' said Violet. 'I have more time than you. In fact,' she added, standing swiftly, 'why don't you leave your dress with me today? You can borrow one of mine.'

In her bedroom, Violet flung open a huge closet to reveal a mass of garments. From the rack of bright silks, crisp lawns and rich velvets she drew out a skirt and jacket in creamy cotton, trimmed with cord sewn in elegant loops across the shoulders. 'It's nun's cloth — so smooth to the touch, yes? And *so* becoming when properly tailored. This military look has been all the rage in London, you know, and I think it will fit you better than me.'

The fit was indeed perfect. Violet patted Anna lightly at the back of her waist. 'Of course, to look really duchess-like you need a *tournure* under here.'

Anna grimaced. 'I detest bustles. Even with a chemise worn underneath they still prod at you.'

'In the evening, if we have guests, then a lady must suffer a little to create a comely impression.' Violet smiled a little grimly. 'Or so they say.'

She insisted on hairstyling as well. 'Sit!' she ordered. 'Let me play.' And so Anna perched on a stool while her hostess set to work.

'It's no wonder you fell,' Violet said. 'Such foolish skirts we wear, down around our ankles. Did you stop at any tropic isles on the way out here?'

Anna shook her head. 'We came the hard way against the wind, round the Horn to Valparaiso and then to Tahiti. The women there, so beautiful, so free.' Violet flung hers arm wide. 'No corsets, Anna, not even a bodice. So much brazen skin and bare teats that one hardly knew where to look. Though of course the crew did all the looking they possibly could. How I envied those women! They looked so cool while I was drenching every piece of clothing I possessed.

'Imagine how easy that life must be. To get up at sunrise, twist a little cotton around your waist, put some flowers in your hair and go out free as air. I declare, dear Anna, we were born into the wrong society. There,' she said, fixing a pin in place. 'How is that?'

Anna gazed at herself, attention scattered by Violet's frank talk (for teats and sweat were rarely mentioned in polite company) but also quite impressed by her newly groomed self.

'At least we're now not hampered by crinolines,' said Violet. 'Even after Florence Nightingale declared them hideous, still our mothers wore them. Ladies who were short and thick-waisted looked like a plum duff atop a mushroom.'

Anna giggled. A photograph of her own mother-in-law, round as a pudding, hung in her hallway.

'The saddest story I ever read,' said Violet, 'was about how Longfellow's wife died. The poor woman was putting locks of her children's hair into envelopes, sealing them with hot wax. Somehow her crinoline caught alight. Can you imagine?' She shuddered and stood up. 'We should be grateful to be whole, hmm? And alive.'

Anna departed in some splendour in her nun's cloth attire, Jamie trotting happily alongside, full of girdle scones and peach jam. Back in her bedroom, she checked her reflection again and was rather sorry that Thomas was away. He had never seen her in anything this grand. But then she felt foolish. *Too grand for the likes of me*. She changed into a plain, loose dress and apron. Enough primping. Wounded arm or not, chores did not wait.

* * *

Immersed to his collarbones in hot water at the Pink Terraces, Thomas wished he could be here with Anna. How primal this place was! His lassitude was so deep that he could almost block out the rowdy banter of his companions. Although he would never have shared such a tender thought with the grizzled men around him, he wondered if unborn babies lay like this in their mother's wombs, wallowing within rosy walls. The water's clarity was spritzed with bubbles that gently prickled at his skin.

At the foot of the slope below him the shallowest pools were the purest blue. The land all around was rugged, the vegetation inglorious. Only tough scrub thrived here amid the pungent drifts of steam. Across the lake yet more terraces spilled down to the shore in gleaming white steps, a larger array than the confection of pink shelves suspended on his own hill.

The basin he wallowed in was deep enough to allow him to float about like a lazy frog. Everyone in his party had let out a deep 'Aah' as they eased into the warmth. It could almost turn a man insensible with pleasure, he thought. He turned on his front to run his hands along the pond's pink silken skin, trying to think of the words to tell Anna how the slow spillage created fantastic crusts on the outside of each rounded level. The terrace was like a giant, bow-fronted chest of drawers with each drawer dispensing never-ending hot water to the layers below.

Down on the dark emerald lake were the whaling boats that had brought his party to the pools, the Maori rowers talking together as they waited for the next load of passengers. Thomas wondered how they felt about the daily influx of visitors. Once this place would have been exclusively theirs. They showed no sign of resentment, but then, pleasure could always be exchanged for money. Cash eased tension as nothing else could.

Thomas thought it a shame that a husband and wife could not share this simple, splendid place. He doubted the locals had such inhibitions. For a moment he allowed himself to imagine the sight of bare, brown skin glowing against the pink. The natives were a comely race for the most part, until they grew aged and wizened and their tattoos melted into blurred crinkles.

The bathing regime for settlers was strictly controlled. He and the men had had to wait behind distant bushes while the ladies took their ease in private, and then they'd changed places, the women still flushed with heat as they tripped down the path. ''Tis heaven in there!' one pretty girl had cried as she approached the impatient men, damp curls clinging to her neck.

'Come join us then,' said Rupert with a grin, already unbuttoning his shirt. 'Heaven should be shared with angels.'

The girl's mother had glared at his impudence. 'That's quite enough of that,' she snapped.

* * *

THOMAS HAD one more day of business at Ohinemutu before setting out on the bumpy forty-mile ride back to Tauranga. He discussed a loan with an investor keen to build another hotel in Rotorua. They met on the site, eyed its size and the money required to fund the project. They joked too about whether they could dig down to lay foundations without setting off a new steam geyser.

The joshing had a serious edge. The entire place was like a thin pie crust, crisp on top but concealing a bubbling ferment below. It made Thomas a little uneasy to tread on some parts of the landscape, but the prospects for tourism were huge, especially if a railway line could be pushed through from the coast. And the wondrous Terraces! He was convinced that in time to come the whole world would clamour to see them. He would recommend the new hotel venture to his superiors. But for now, he was anxious to get home.

* * *

'RATHER THE WORSE FOR WEAR,' he reported to Anna when she met him at the coach stop and asked where Rupert was. 'When I tried to rouse him this morning, he merely groaned.'

'Was he ill?'

'In a way.' Thomas waited for the coachman to throw down his bag from the roof. It landed with a thud in his weary arms, setting off a small explosion of the dust gathered on the trip. He sneezed. 'The bars at that place stay open until all hours. So did Rupert's gullet.'

'Watch me, Pa!' shouted Jamie, running ahead as they turned away from the coach. Hoisting his bag on his shoulder, Thomas fell in beside his wife to begin the walk home. He watched his boy climb upon a seat outside a store, raise his arms high and jump dramatically to the ground, springing up with a grin to make sure his daring had been observed.

'Very good, lad,' he called as Jamie turned to do it again. 'It's a sad thing,' he said to Anna, 'that every man starts off his life with all of Jamie's bright spirit and grows to manhood to find himself insensible, unable to even raise his head from his pillow.'

'Should you have left him there in such a state?'

'I can't manage Rupert's life for him.' He looked down at her worried frown. 'He was coming to no harm where he was. And perhaps waking up late with an aching head might teach him to curb his appetites next time.'

'I thought your rowing together might have done him some good.'

'Yes, well, I hope next time we go out he'll be in better form. It's not long till the regatta. Mind you, yesterday his head might still have been addled by our hot bath.' Thomas told Anna about the pink, soporific pools. 'One day, we'll go together. Perhaps when your mother comes next she could be Jamie's keeper while we take a few days away. Would you like that?'

'Oh, yes!' Anna could not remember when she had last had a full day of leisure. 'Next time, let it be me. Rupert can amuse himself — he has friends enough. Though they seem only too eager to lead him astray. Fanny Bell tells me he recently placed many bets at the Katikati races and won handsomely.'

Ah. That would explain his free spending on the grog last night.'

Rupert had insisted they have a whisky when they arrived back at Ohinemutu's Lake House Hotel. 'Medicinal,' he'd said, with merry eyes. 'A peg or two will ease our aching bones.'

'So it might,' Thomas conceded. 'But just one.'

'Spoken like a parson's whelp,' Rupert teased him. He was always full of easy mockery but because there was no malice in him it held no sting. The whisky had been raw and strong. Rupert had been eager for a second round, waving a full coin purse. Thomas fended him off, feeling a twinge of unease at having helped spark his friend's thirst. 'I'm off for my dinner. You'll join me if you know what's good for you.'

'Now when have I ever known that?' Rupert laughed, raising his empty glass to his lips again. He all but sucked at it.

Thomas took a brief walk by the light of the moon after he had eaten, breathing in the sulphurous air along the lake shore before being driven inside by clouds of black midges — and the fear of inadvertently stepping in a dark pool of searing water or viscous mud. Peering into the bar, he caught a glimpse of wild red hair. Rupert was up on a chair, arms swinging wide in time with the bawdy song he was bellowing. A swell of guffaws went up as he reached the last line. Thomas went up to bed, the noise following him up the creaky stairs. He wondered how long the house's more abstemious guests would put up with the racket before complaining to the publican. Too tired to care, he quickly fell asleep and was barely aware of Rupert staggering in hours later.

* * *

RUPERT HAD the grace to look slightly awkward as he stood at the doorstep. 'I've come to apologise, Mrs Hamilton,' he said. 'I led your husband into sin and perdition at the Hot Lakes. Here.' With a bashful smile he held out an oddly shaped parcel. It was wrapped with brown paper and had a trailing yellow ribbon. 'For my penance, I bring you a rare and precious gift.'

'Oh, Rupert,' she said. He had that effect on her, making her warm to him even when half a day earlier she'd been regretting they were even acquainted. 'And you know my name is Anna. Please do use it.'

Thomas came curiously to the door. He had been trimming a wick and now held the lamp high as Rupert stepped inside. 'What do you have there? A brazen gift for my wife or a bribe to keep me quiet about your exploits?' 'A gift. And none like it in the colony.'

Anna led the way to her kitchen. Her mother would be appalled at how easily she now hosted guests wherever was convenient. Sitting stiffly in the parlour seemed very much an old-country habit to her now, for the kitchen was where she had to spend most of her time. And besides, if she wanted to offer tea (and tonight she'd certainly not be offering alcohol to Rupert) there was nobody else to make it but herself.

She fed wood into the oven's fire box, slid the kettle over the heat and wiped her hands. Rupert laid his package on the table. 'My apologies for my clumsy package. Round things are rather hard to wrap.'

Anna pulled at the ribbon, opened the paper and found a most curious fruit. Or was it a vegetable? Oval and green and as big as her fist, its skin gave off an exotic gleam in the glow cast by Tom's newly cleaned wick. 'What is it?' Anna asked.

'I had no idea until today. There are two trees behind my quarters bearing a few of these. I'm not much a man for nature myself, but I had a visitor today who's stopped in Central American ports. He said they contain a flesh known as midshipman's butter. It's too hot for cows to thrive there so they spread this on their bread instead.'

Thomas picked it up and pressed with his fingertips. 'But it feels hard as stone.'

'He said they don't begin to ripen until they're off the tree. I don't know how long it takes but it'll be amusing to see. I've put one on a windowsill. We can make it a contest — your butter fruit against mine.'

'Everything's a contest for you, my friend,' said Thomas, 'except the one that counts. We've missed a few days of rowing.'

'I know, I know. Five tomorrow evening?'

'I'll be there.' Anna reached for the fruit and put it to her nose. There was no fragrance. 'Thank you, Rupert. Should I put it in sunlight, do you think?' Its green surface reminded her of a vivid snake she'd once seen. Stuffed and mounted on an ebony tree branch, it belonged a gentleman who collected curiosities. The thought made her feel quite queasy. Ireland had no snakes. No one had ever seen one in New Zealand either, which was something to be grateful for in a land full of other perils. 'Are you sure it's not poisonous?'

'I asked the same thing, but my visitor assured me of its goodness. He said native women also use it to soothe their skin.' Rupert came to a stop, on uncertain ground now. Gentlemen did not speak to ladies about skin, but Anna seemed unoffended.

'Truly? If it ever ripens I'll try it on my hands after washday.' She fetched a stout bowl from a shelf and placed the fruit inside. 'I wonder who planted your trees.'

'I asked Bell at the newspaper. He said a woman living in Bermuda sent them potted up as a gift to her brother, who lived in a cottage where my place now stands. Some ship's passenger was prepared to cosset them all the way here. It's remarkable they survived at all. The fellow who received them must have done some nurturing too, for I've paid them no mind at all.' He grinned. 'A taste of the tropics, sent to tempt us.'

* * *

THE NEXT AFTERNOON, the bankers closed the doors on their respective offices, walked along the shore to where Rupert's dinghy lay and hauled it down the beach. They unlaced their boots, rolled up their trouser legs, pushed off, and headed out for a long row to build endurance. The regatta's one-hundred yard race would require stamina as well as pace. Their backs bent as the oars dipped and rose, stout timber squeaking in the rowlocks. Thomas was pleased to see that Rupert looked sound and sober, his Lake House binge leaving him apparently none the worse for wear. They said little and felt well satisfied as they pulled the keel into the shallows.

Once they had the craft secured above the tideline, oars stowed beneath, Thomas stretched to ease his aching back. He tipped his head and gazed at the rugged outline of the Kaimai Hills, now hunched black against the fading glow of the western sky. A few stars began to prick out high above the zone where eggshell blue deepened to indigo.

They walked along the near-deserted Strand and turned into Wharf Street with its scatter of shops and houses. Lamplight was beginning to glow in the windows, offering peepholes into domesticity. Rupert grunted. His own windows would be dark and empty. He would have to light his own light and put some sort of single man's meal together. As they passed the Star Hotel's open door he couldn't help but think of its billiard table. He could while away a few hours there tonight. The play would be easier with a drop or two inside him.

Thomas said, 'Did I see you out on the water this morning, early? I spied a craft uncommonly like yours, with two oarsmen aboard. But it was too far out to see properly.'

Rupert kept on walking, eyes down, his bright hair dulled to dark brown as night came on. 'It would hardly have been me. You know how I detest rising with the larks.'

'Ah, some rivals then — out for a secret morning session and unwilling to display their strength.' Thomas laughed. 'Or their ineptitude.'

Still, he wondered whose dinghy it was. For when he had gone out to the privy in his nightshirt at sunrise, the boat's distant silhouette had looked very similar to Rupert's.

CHAPTER FIVE

> *'If proper precaution be taken to borrow only for works that are reproduc-*
> *tive, good railways, irrigation, promising harbours, resumption of lands*
> *at fair prices, borrowing must add to the population of the country an*
> *appreciable number of taxpayers, well able to pay taxes, and glad of the*
> *opportunity to pay them in a grand country like this.'*
> — *Letter to the editor, Bay of Plenty Times.*

FEBRUARY 5, 1886

Henry Sutton's tame London banker, Arthur Bushnell Esq., did
not sit well upon a horse in rough country. Henry rather resented the
man's lack of interest. Any potential investor needed to see up close the
route along which railway tracks could be hammered down in shining
lines. The looming trees, tumultuous with birds and tangled with
supplejack and clematis, deserved to be surprised by human industry.
These endless miles of gloomy forest needed taming.

After all, he thought, God had laid down his instructions. It was
there in the Bible: 'Be fruitful and multiply and replenish the earth and
subdue it and have dominion over every living thing.' Henry was not a
churchgoing man but those words from Genesis sang to him lustily, as if
booming from the lungs of a Welsh coal miners' choir. They were

framed on the wall of his study, written with bold flourishes by the finest calligrapher he could find. God's bullish sentiment underpinned all of his business decisions. Wasn't it the same for everybody in this grand era of England's expansion? The entire world was there for the taking. If only cautious financiers like Bushnell would see the good sense of this project and invest properly, these tracks could be started within the year.

'I say, sir!' Henry called over his shoulder. Bushnell's nag, the most amiable Henry had been able to hire for his guest, was plodding some yards behind. Bushnell was whacking at the flies that bustled around his hat. 'Is that not one of the best vistas you've gazed upon in all the world?'

His guest pulled up his horse and looked back out to the Pacific. From this distance its blueness was as thin as a slice of custard tart.

The men swung down from their saddles. Shrill cicada noise pierced the heat. Bushnell walked off a few paces, opened his trousers and loosed a relieving stream into the undergrowth as he gazed out to the glittering strip of empty ocean to the east. Rebuttoning himself, he kicked at the ruts in the path. The roadway, hard and dusty in this season, lurched its way inland and disappeared into ink-green stands of tall forest.

'This must be a damned uncomfortable coach ride. Forty miles, you say?'

Henry nodded. 'Leaves Tauranga after early breakfast, stops halfway to meet the coach coming the other way. Picnic lunch, change of horses and then on again in time for six o'clock dinner at Lake House.'

'Muddy?'

'In winter, always. There are parts that would be impossible had they not been corduroyed. There've been thousands of logs laid together further on to keep the way open.'

'Murderous, those log roads. No better than the Romans built when they ruled England. Hard on hoofs. Ruinous on wheels.'

The horses ripped lazily at the grass. Bushnell would endure wild country like this when he had to, in order to lend substance to the reports he would send to his masters in London, but Rotten Row was more his style. He preferred a civilised amble in Hyde Park, where ladies would tip flirtatious glances from the backs of gleaming steeds, silken skirts gathered over their side-saddled knees, and where, after his ride, a man could take his ease in a well-victualled club.

Instead, he was spending far too much of his life bucking over giant oceans and lurching around empty stretches of raw land alongside desperate strivers like Sutton, who might make a fortune or might lose everything. Bushnell's betters detested the latter outcome.

It was always hard to tell which way it would go. Plans could go awry because of setbacks never imagined in dim Mayfair rooms. There the day's most alarming disturbance might be the sound of silver cutlery dropped by a careless butler onto an expanse of parquet floor. In untamed lands like New Zealand and Australia, anything, simply anything, could get in commerce's way. Uppity natives, mysterious ailments, raging rivers, dying crops, foundering vessels. Bad news, Bushnell knew, lurked just out of sight over every horizon, like a pirate ship too cunning to turn up just yet. There was little comfort in his life, mental or physical.

Tomorrow he would sail on the tide south to Wellington to get the measure of the men running the government of this rough estate. Tonight offered a lumpy bed in the town's best hotel, which was little better, in his opinion, than a Bournemouth boarding house. Draughtier too, and with a cursed rooster in the back yard. But at least he'd be dining tonight at Suttons' home, where the surprisingly elegant and charming Mrs Sutton might produce something more pleasing to his palate than the gristly mutton he'd chewed on the previous evening.

* * *

As Bushnell climbed into his saddle again and turned the mare's head towards the sea, the same Mrs Sutton was leaning forward to whisper a question to Anna. 'Can you keep a secret?' They were in the Suttons' drawing room.

'Of course.' Her wounded arm had been inspected and declared to be almost healed. Hester was keeping Jamie busy in the kitchen.

'Rupert Beckford took me out in his boat the other morning.' Violet's eyes were alight with mischief. 'Henry was away with his London bore and we went at dawn so no one would see. I took an oar and learnt how to row! It was so splendid, Anna. And not hard to do at all.'

'Goodness,' Anna said. 'But so many people are up and about early. Surely someone would have seen you.'

'We were completely out of sight of the town. We walked to the boat separately. You know where that pohutukawa tree bends low over the water? One branch is so low it offers a perfect promenade. At high tide you can trip along its top and be handed into a boat without so much as dipping one's hem in the briny.'

Anna was astonished. 'Weren't you taking an awful risk?'

Violet was pink-cheeked with merriment. 'No one saw us. When I'd had enough, Rupert took me ashore and then rowed back out onto the harbour while I walked home. The sun was well up by then but if anyone saw me they'd have thought I was simply taking my constitutional. If Rupert was noticed coming in, then of course he'd just been out boating alone.' 'What was it like to use the oars?

Oh, Anna, the satisfaction of taking part instead of being transported like some useless beast!'

'Do you really feel so useless?' Anna's tea went untasted as she took in the fact of her friend's risky excursion. And felt a little twist of envy.

Violet shrugged. 'Sometimes. Don't you? In this world where everything is available to men while we women have so many constraints. What is ladylike, what is not. All the rules we must obey, all the. . . demands a husband can place on a wife.' She tossed her head, her mouth pulled in a fleeting expression that Anna could not read. Anger? Disgust? 'Besides which, Rupert is kind company. We talk about things I never discuss with Henry.' She flashed Anna an impish glance. 'He makes me laugh. I can't tell you what a pleasure that is. I've been so longing to laugh for such a long time.'

She stopped for a moment, as if she'd said too much.

'Will you go again?'

'Probably not. Everything would have to be in place — my husband absent, the weather calm, the tide high. It was one perfect moment, hard to repeat.' She slid a cool glance across the table. 'I thought you'd be excited for me, Anna. You look disapproving.'

'I'm just concerned for your reputation. There are so many gossips.'

'Including some you meet with.'

'I know, but Thomas prefers me to keep in with Fanny. For business, you know. And with Louise Archer, the postmaster's wife. They mean well. And there's kindness in them too. Why don't you come along next Tuesday? They're both coming to tea. If you have a broader circle of acquaintances then I might not have to be your only friend. I do know they admire your gowns.'

Violet smiled. 'Let's dress up a little and really show them! Wear the cream ensemble, Anna. I've not seen you in it again.'

'It's too beautiful for the sort of life I lead.'

'Nonsense. It's essential. Then I can come looking as grand as possible. Without saying a word we can demonstrate utter elegance beyond reproach. And then they can gossip about us nicely for a change.'

* * *

'VIOLET SUTTON IS VISITING on the sixteenth,' Anna told Thomas that night with a certain trepidation.

'Ah.' Thomas looked up briefly from the papers he was studying. 'Very well, then.'

'She's perfectly respectable.'

'I'm sure she is if you say so, my dear.' He chewed the end of his pen. 'Her husband is certainly doing his best to advance things in the area. Sutton's been squiring a London banker around the district, trying to persuade him to put money into a railroad. Apparently he has the ear of men with mighty funds at their disposal.' 'That'll be Mr Bushnell. He's dining with the Suttons this evening.'

Thomas raised an amused eyebrow. 'You have insights I would not have suspected.'

'You make me sound over-inquisitive.'

'Not at all, my love. It's good for a man and his wife to be aware of each other's affairs. And the district is in sore need of investment.'

As his attention waned and his eyes slid back down back to his desktop, Anna noted the emergence of a thought that once would never have risen in her mind at all: 'But do you, actually, know of *my* affairs at all? Have you ever wondered what goes on in my head, over and above my care of our son and the running of our household? Isn't it your interests that are paramount?'

But despite this stray, rebellious thought — for what was good for Thomas was inevitably good for her and Jamie too — she could not countenance the idea of labelling herself with Violet's phrase, 'useless beast'.

She went into her kitchen where clean surfaces and neatly stacked shelves were testament to how very useful she knew herself to be. She ran her hand over Rupert's green butter fruit, picked it up and felt its weight. Was its surface giving yet, just a little?

But then the house creaked sharply and spoons rattled on the table. She heard the sudden scrape of Thomas's chair and his quick footsteps. 'Good Lord,' he said, standing in the doorway, hands pressed against its sides. 'Was that an earthquake?'

CHAPTER SIX

> *'Every shade of blue is in favour this year, even the bright hues, which is probably owing to the fact that blue is almost universally becoming, as it suits both blonde and brunette.'*
>   — *Ladies Column, Bay of Plenty Times.*

FEBRUARY 6, 1886

Anna opened her kitchen door to a firm knock to find a Maori woman on her doorstep. Her skirt and loose cotton jacket were clean, her hair pulled neatly back behind a beaming face. She was thinly built and held herself like a young person but her wrinkles told a different story.

Anna focused on the woman's eyes rather than the grey-blue tattoo on her chin. It seemed impolite to linger on it. Her mother had shrunk back from their sighting of a Maori man with fierce whorls cut into his face. Anna was not so disturbed but did wonder at how painful the tattooing process must be. The shapes were somehow reminiscent of old Celtic designs. She had seen similar patterns carved on Irish stone and etched on old jewellery. Here, on the world's far side, it seemed the human urge to draw spirals was simply expressed in a different way.

'Ma'am, I hear you are looking for someone to work in the house?'

the woman said. There was a liveliness to her and a keen light in her sharp brown eyes. She had to speak up to make herself heard over Jamie, who was tugging at Anna's sleeve and whining about being denied more honey on his breakfast bread.

'Look at you,' the visitor chuckled. 'Wa-wa, wa-wa!' Her eyes popped and she waggled her narrow hips and her grin spread. Jamie's racket stopped immediately. He crept behind his mother's skirt but peeped out again.

Anna stepped aside and opened her door wide. 'Please, do come in.'

Her name was Dinah. 'Up at the Mission, they taught us ev'rything,' she said. 'Clean floors, beat carpets, shine up silver things, cook on the range, trim lamps, do laundry — wash, starch, iron. I know how to keep a proper Pakeha house. Be-yootiful!'

Anna didn't even ask for references. 'Can you start soon? I can pay eleven shillings a week.'

'Eleven and sixpence,' her new helper shot back firmly. 'And I start tomorrow.' She reached out and patted Jamie's tummy. 'You want me to feed you up, make this little puku big and round? I know nice things to cook.'

'Yes, please,' he said.

And so it was settled. Dinah went home each night. It was a walk of almost two miles to and from the Judea settlement where she lived, but unless the weather was really foul she arrived most days, tugging off her muddy boots at the kitchen door to burst in with a cheerful 'Kia ora!' Sometimes she rode a dappled nag that she hitched to the fence at the back of the bank.

* * *

ON THE MORNING of Anna's afternoon tea Dinah took great care in ironing the cream skirt and braided jacket. 'Ooh,' she said, running her hands down the fabric and eyeing the stitching. 'This is *very* fine.' She spit-tested the flat iron with great care to ensure she could eradicate creases without a hint of scorching. 'They must be grand ladies coming today.'

Fanny and Louise made no comment on her garb at first. But eventually Fanny could not resist. 'You look elegant today, my dear. A new ensemble?'

'Somewhat,' said Anna airily. 'Pale colours aren't practical here, as you know. It's a little foolish having it in my wardrobe at all but I decided it was time for an airing.'

At which point they heard voices in the hall. Then Dinah entered the room. She wore a white apron today instead of her usual rough brown wraparound. Her mouth was compressed as if to keep giggles in. She gestured with a small flourish. 'Mrs Sutton,' she announced and then slipped from sight.

Violet allowed a five-second pause for drama and then stepped into the empty space, wearing a demure smile and a powder-blue silk gown. The buttoned bodice was smooth and taut, the skirt drawn back into a flounced bustle of proportions probably normal for London but extreme for a colonial town. She wore pearls and diamonds at her ears. Her parasol matched. So did the pert, tip-tilted hat.

'Violet,' said Anna, sailing in to fill the stunned silence. 'Welcome. Do let me introduce you. Mrs Bell, Mrs Archer, this is Mrs Henry Sutton, who is new to our town.'

Violet gave them a smile rendered quite bizarre by the fact that her eyes were hidden by thick blue goggles. 'Aren't they a caution?' she said, unhooking the wire supports from behind her ears. They were spectacles, but *such* spectacles, with round disks of azure glass suspended in the frames. 'Henry had them sent as a novelty from California. They're quite the latest thing there to shield the eyes from the sun.'

'Oh, my goodness,' breathed Fanny. Louise was gaping with delight.

'Try them,' urged Violet.

Thomas was at that moment berating a farmer for failing to pay interest on time. He hated having to chastise his clients but when deep in debt they easily backslid into debt and misery, a fate their children did not deserve. If he'd been able to hear the chortling coming now from his parlour next door, his resolve would have been completely undermined. Especially when Dinah was also persuaded to don the goggles.

'Oh, I wish you could have heard her laugh,' Anna said to Thomas later.

'I'm glad you had a cheerful time. I was closeted with a man whose children have boils and whose wife coughs constantly. I fear it may be consumption.'

Anna felt for his bleakness and put a sympathetic hand to his cheek. He caught it in his own, held it for a moment and kissed her knuckles. Dinah had gone home (her erratic work hours were her one failing) leaving Anna to prepare dinner. The lemon juice she'd used on her fingers had not quite erased the smell of chopped onions but she looked very elegant in Violet's gift gown.

Thomas had felt uneasy at first at its extravagance, but didn't have the heart to insist Anna return it. It was of a quality he could not afford. 'You are most beautifully gowned for kitchen duties,' he said.

She smiled. 'I must change before I stain it with something. Truth to tell, I suspect it might soon be too snug, if not completely unwearable.'

It took him a second or two to understand and then a grin creased his face. 'Anna, that's splendid!'

'I thought you could count as well as me. No, better. Aren't you the accountant?' Her hands were clasped over her middle, as if containing the kernel of hope expanding there.

'This is the seventh week I've gone without my monthly visitor.'

He grabbed her and twirled her around, overjoyed but also terrified. Her agonies in giving birth to Jamie had been extreme. And they'd already lost one daughter. He didn't think he could bear another tragedy. 'All going well, when will this baby arrive?'

'I imagine September or October. A spring child.' *Maybe even another little girl,* she was thinking, but it was a yearning she hardly dared voice. 'Our secret for now, Thomas.'

Later, as they sipped hot milk before bed, she told him more about her day. 'Violet had them all charmed. And Louise, oh, the longing in her. She clung to those goggles like a child unwilling to give up a favourite doll. "Ek-tually," Anna piped, mimicking Fanny's querulous voice, "Mrs Sutton is more of a lady of quality than I had imagined, although she is somewhat *gaudy*." This opinion, of course, only delivered after Violet had made a splendid exit with a snap of the parasol and a swish of her hem.'

'You're wasted managing a household,' said Thomas. 'Perhaps we should put you on the stage.'

Anna lit up. 'Indeed we might. We were speaking of it only today. We thought a concert would do us all good before winter arrives. You could bring out your violin. We can have glees and solos and recitations — wouldn't that be good?'

Thomas could think only of the time they'd need for rehearsal when he was so immersed in his work. But he could see the sense of it too. Once the regatta was over he might relish something to take his mind off money. Also, he reminded himself, a man must do his best for his community. 'Perhaps it's also time the bank hosted another dance,' he said. 'It's a year since the last time we cleared the decks and got our feet tapping.'

There was a short pause but Anna summoned a smile. It would mean, as always, the effort of shifting furniture, rolling up rugs, pushing the piano through from the house to the bank, preparing supper and having to dance with rowdies and drunks, despite her condition. They would serve no alcohol — it was against the bank's policies to have any grog on the premises — but many of the men would slip down the road to one bar or another for a drink. And some ladies weren't averse to taking a few nips from someone's flask.

'Perhaps a few weeks after the regatta?' she said. 'And then we can plan the concert for May.' He'd noted her slight hesitation. 'If you contribute to my dance, I'll do my best for your concert.'

His bank dances would hardly be appropriate in Auckland but they passed muster down the coast. Thomas always took care to ensure that his clerk locked all cash, valuables, ledgers and documents behind the vault's iron door. His customers always attended the annual shindig in large numbers. He was sure it helped keep them onside — and less likely to make use of Rupert's bank. After all, business was business.

* * *

VIOLET'S EYE-PIECES had the whole town talking for days. Fanny Bell was now an ardent supporter of Violet Sutton. 'She's so very amusing,' she trilled to Anna when they happened to meet at the butcher's. She leaned closer, nudging Anna's arm with her stout bosom. 'I say, did you hear of that scandal in Wellington when men arrived at a ball dressed as women? One of them was so convincing that one gentlemen was completely taken in. Imagine how he must have felt the next day when the truth came out.' Fanny whooped. 'Hiding behind drawn blinds, I should think!'

'Poor man,' said Anna. 'No one likes to be made to look foolish.'

'But he *was* foolish. How could anyone not realise? There'd be bristles on his chops and a distinct lack of. . .' Fanny's hand made a sketchy pass across her well-filled bodice. 'Bust,' she whispered.

Mr Rogers, the butcher, had good ears. 'Strange days we live in, Mrs Bell,' he said, whacking his cleaver through a rack of pink pork chops. They flopped damply onto the block, a line of fleshy dominos. 'If our betters go on so lewdly,' he growled, 'what'll come next? Women wearing trousers?'

'Perish the day, Mr Rogers,' said Fanny, hefting her basket of bacon and kidneys. She tottered a little as the change in weight threw her off-balance, but there was more to it than that. Empty meat hooks slung on a rail at the back of the shop swayed and chimed: once, then twice.

'Again,' said the butcher, eyeing the restless hooks. Their swinging slowed and stilled. 'I've been here seven years and never felt tremors before.' Then he grinned. 'It's all right, ladies, you can breathe again.'

'Ooh,' said Fanny, spare hand pressed to her throat. 'I do declare this jelly-like country utterly unnerves me at times.'

Anna set off quickly for home. A benign sun shone down through a layer of thin lacy clouds. There was the usual seafront bustle of men at work. A small, still thicket of bare masts and webbed rigging rose from the two ships berthed at Victoria Wharf. The wheels of wagons hauled by slow, placid horses crunched on the rutted road. A boy whistled idly as he whitewashed a fence. It was as if there'd been no disturbance at all. Everything looked normal. But that queasy sway of the ground beneath her feet — that was something she would never get used to.

CHAPTER SEVEN

> *'The English are said to write a better hand as a nation, than any other people, while the Americans are placed next. The French write poorly, as a rule, especially ladies; the Italians still worse, and Spaniards hardly legibly.'*
> *— Bay of Plenty Times.*

FEBRUARY 21, 1886

My dear mother

This must be a quick scribble as I'm expecting to hear the mail steamer's whistle at any moment. Please forgive my silence in recent weeks. Thomas and I have both been so occupied that our days are filled from morn through to night. I trust life in Auckland is as agreeable as ever. I can allay your fears about overworking myself, as we now employ a perfect gem of a woman in the house. Her name is Dinah. I doubt it is the name she was given at birth but is easier for us to pronounce than some of the native tongue-twisters.

Apart from keeping occasional erratic hours she does her job well and I enjoy how she sings as she works. She is also of inestimable help in taking care of Jamie. He waits for her at the gate each morning. I thank God every day for his sound limbs, bright spirit and sunny smile. Of course, I still think often of our sweet Rosa. She would be six years old now. Sometimes it is as if a grey cloud still hangs over me. And yet I know I must lock her away in my heart's sore spot and seal it with a kiss if I am to give Jamie the love he deserves.

I am hoping however, that towards year's end a sister (or brother) may arrive for Jamie. Is that not a wonderful prospect? 'Tis early days yet but I shall keep you apprised of my progress. Thomas and his friend Rupert Beckford have been much engaged in practising for the annual regatta. It arrives with a splash next Saturday. They seem to have built up a strong rhythm, their oars flashing in unison as they dip and pull. The whole town is looking forward to it. There will be a band, bunting and a picnic. The whistle blows! Ever your loving daughter,

Anna

* * *

HENRY SUTTON'S eye was caught by a quick flash of shiny hair outside the bank window. 'Ah!' he said to Thomas, highly amused. 'Is your wife, too, in training for some athletic event?'

Thomas strode to the window just in time to see Anna's retreating back as she sped to the wharf. The postmaster, Horace Archer, would wait only so long for Tauranga's letter writers to run to him, panting, with last-minute envelopes. 'Time and tide!' he would shout, mail bag still agape as the *Albion*'s smoke stack belched sooty clouds and the master prepared to cast off. 'Last call!'

Thomas said, 'I keep telling her one of my clerks will do that hundred-yard dash for her, but she never seems to get her correspondence done in time. But then our womenfolk are always so occupied, are they not?'

Sutton's bulbous neck shook as he made a hmmph sound that could have been a clearing of a throat or a expression of derision. 'Can't say,' he said. 'I'm away so much that I scarcely know what my lady gets up to at home all day. I'm satisfied as long as there's good food on the table when I return. It's hardly an arduous responsibility and she has ample help. It seems to me that life's a sweet breeze for women like her. Most wives seem best at spending the money we labour so hard to acquire.'

Thomas hoped his nod gave the appearance of agreement.

'It's different for Mrs Hamilton, of course,' Sutton went on, 'with your son to raise. My belief is that motherhood brings out a woman's best instincts, don't you think? Gives full reign to her domestic abilities and sharpens her sense of duty.' He thumped his silver-topped cane on the floor. 'It's just a pity that Mrs Sutton has as yet been unable to achieve that lucky state.' He leaned forward, stomach straining against his green waistcoat. 'But enough of such trivia. The railway. Is there any news from Wellington that might give us cause for optimism?'

Thomas was relieved to move on to business. A bank manager's office was hardly the place for idle talk about women. He would have a word with Anna later about her habit of running for the mail boat. A brindle puppy had scampered along behind her just now, its small teeth snapping at her flashing ankles. It wasn't seemly. He settled in his chair and said, 'I wish I could say so, but all I hear is the usual taradiddle. The politicians say, yes, they believe a railway would open up the interior and boost trade, but that's as far as it goes. There's not a sniff of government coin to back up the talk.'

He was pleased to have this visit today from Sutton. Frequently now, Thomas was receiving carping correspondence from his superiors about the slow growth of deposits and the lack of profitable new ventures in the Bay of Plenty. 'Frankly,' the last letter had said, 'the bank has been disappointed in the results you have furnished to date. It is our hope, nay our expectation, that matters will improve. We trust that you will lend your best endeavours to the task.'

'Best endeavours?' he had shouted at Anna that night. 'They have no idea how hard I am trying.' He'd screwed the letter into a rough ball, thrown it into the stove and slammed the door. Anna had said, calmly, 'Let me get you some tea.'

'Whisky might do the job better,' he had growled as he sat down to write a testy reply.

'How can I be of service?' he said now, leaning forward in what he hoped was an eager yet not obsequious manner.

Sutton considered the room. 'Nice little building, this. Smartly turned out. Even some slight attempt at elegance in its architecture.' He waved a hand at the tall windows with their arched frames. 'Too big for its own boots though, eh what? Banks always do this — erect a building grander than required to persuade customers their money is safe. Is it?' he asked abruptly.

'Why, of course,' said Thomas, slightly stung. His own loyalties to the bank might not run deep, but even so its soundness was beyond question. 'Our governance is first rate and we are well capitalised. As you know, having favoured me with your earlier deposit, our interest rates are fair. I think you'll find no better.'

'Not even at Mr Beckford's establishment across the way?' Sutton used his cane to indicate Rupert's National Bank premises. 'Not even,' Thomas briskly confirmed.

After Sutton departed Thomas tidied papers on his desk and mused on whether his whole approach to banking was too stolid and earnest. His father had trained him to be politely upright. And yet Rupert, with his debonair charm, could coax deposits out of customers. Maybe it was time to stop being so much the soul of propriety. And yet, banking was all about trust and probity, wasn't it? That was certainly what his father would say. Could a customer have faith in a man who was too fond of the bottle and betting at the racetrack? Thomas doubted it, and yet he saw, every day, from his own window, the steady flow of customers who came and went through the green door of Rupert's bank. He had a knack that Thomas lacked.

And yet, on the other hand, Sutton had delivered a vote of confidence with his £1500 deposit. Please Lord, Thomas thought, let there be more.

* * *

'I HAD A VISIT FROM HENRY SUTTON,' Rupert told Thomas later as they settled into the dinghy for their last training run before the race. Thomas took a grip of his oar, dipping it in short, chopping motions to swing the bow out to sea.

'Did you indeed? Strolled over from my office to yours, no doubt. He seemed to be sniffing about, angling to play us off against each other. Did he give you that impression too?'

They both knew Sutton had been hosting the man from England who was seeking colonial investment opportunities. The whole town knew about Bushnell. Rupert grinned. 'Of course, if he does get good news from London then he'll need local banks to handle his business. Can you imagine the supplies that will be needed? The wages, the expenses, the comestibles? Ships would be queuing up for berths. Even the petty cash requirements would be substantial. It would be good news for the likes of us.'

'But maybe for only one of us. He could easily choose one bank and leave the other out in the cold.'

They fell silent for a moment, neither wanting to admit how desperately they feared being the loser. Thomas did not care to ask Rupert if he was also beset by pressure from his superiors. If he was, he showed little sign of it.

'He offered very little,' Rupert said. 'As you say, it was more a case of making acquaintance. So I took him off down to the Strand for one of Jessie Brown's good pies. We talked of horses mainly. He's very knowledgeable — gave me some good tips.' He slid Thomas a wink. 'Come on, lad, time to row.'

And so they did, thighs braced and arms strong, fierce in their physical effort, forging easily over the glassy sea. Five minutes later, his arms and shoulders burning, Thomas gasped, 'Enough!' They bent over their oars, chests heaving. Rupert scooped up cool seawater to dash it against his face. 'By Jove, my friend, if we don't win on Saturday then I'll want to know why. You're the best friend a man could have, d'you know that? Always ready, always industrious, always giving your best.'

'Hardly, Rupe. Just pulling on my oar.'

'But pulling like a piston. We'll win! Our rivals won't give us a chance. What, two men who sit at their desks all day against the likes of fishermen, farmers and tree fellers? But we'll show 'em. Money men against the world!' And punching his fist up to the sky, Rupert let out a whooping yell.

* * *

'I HAVE A SUGGESTION,' Violet told Anna as they strolled along the shore that afternoon. 'Rupert is going away for a night or two the week after the regatta. If the weather looks settled he'll leave his boat ready to row. Henry will be in Wellington. And I do believe the tide will be right for another excursion. But I'll need another hand at the oars. Would you like to come too?' Violet peeked at Anna, awaiting her reaction.

'Just the two of us, alone?'

'Yes, why not? Truly, the boat is easy to handle. I've been out with him twice now and have every confidence in my skills. Wouldn't it be fun?'

'Oh Violet, I've never tried it. It would be scandalous if we were seen. Two ladies rowing along like common sailors? Apart from which, I don't know how.'

'But it will be Wednesday, market day. Everyone will be there. Doesn't Dinah sometimes take Jamie with her early? Your Thomas will be hard at work in the bank. We will just go out for a few minutes and stay close to the shore around the point. Nobody will see us. I would so love you to know how good it feels to be in charge of even one small craft. We will stay dry, I promise you, and it's perfectly safe.' She spun around and walked backwards in front of Anna, eyes gleaming with hope and mischief. 'Do say you'll come.'

The small bubble of yearning that rose inside Anna was such a physical sensation that her right hand went to her chest as if to keep the feeling contained, her quelling palm pushing down the temptation. 'Thomas would be so disapproving,' she said, but couldn't help smiling. She declined to give Violet a definite answer, but as they turned for home both of them knew what she wanted it to be.

They walked up Wharf Street and then parted. Once Anna was out of sight, Violet turned and went back down to the sea. There were no ships in port today. She walked some way along the rough boards of Victoria Wharf. There was no activity save for some Maori boys jumping with whooping yells into the tide and then climbing up to do it again. Across the harbour, low bush-clad hills encircled the whole estuary and prevented her from seeing the empty ocean beyond. She turned her face to the north and gazed at Mount Maunganui's rearing flank. To its left lay the channel through which all shipping came and went — the town's only link with the world save for the staccato messages carried by telegraph.

It was the way letters arrived, all sorted by Horace Archer or his two helpers. His wife Louise sometimes lent a hand too. Everyone's business was Archer's business. She often wondered how private one's mail really was. How safe was it to ask questions regarding a loved one far away, or receive anything that was other than mundane? Archer might be forbidden by law to spread gossip, but mightn't a man who wanted to share something of interest, strictly in confidence of course, might he not do that with his wife, Louise, and might she not be tempted to let something slip when she was making small talk with the likes of Fanny Bell?

Violet's own outgoing letters were firmly sealed with wax. It was a very long time — six months, two weeks and three days, in fact — since she had dropped her last letter to London through the slot inside the Post Office and been assured by Archer himself that he would personally deliver the mail to the ship due in the next morning. She had stood in The Strand on a wet and miserable day to witness that same ship's departure for Auckland. From there, the mail would head out on the eight- or nine-week voyage Home.

She should by now have had a reply. Its absence gnawed at her heart. The silence might mean that a door she ached to keep ajar had been shut for ever. She did not know if that was something she could bear. A blob of grey excreta splashed at her feet as a gull flew over her head. It squawked its way along the length of the wharf and then dug more deeply with its wings, climbing up and away, its breast shining.

Violet felt a kinship with birds and had marvelled, during the long voyage out, at the occasional sight of albatrosses. So far from land! Imagine being a creature that could spread mighty wings and fly from one continent to the next, buoyed by wind, heedless of uncertainty, driven simply by its need to arrive. What an unimaginable freedom. How utterly glorious to be able to leave on a whim — to be able to fly and fly and fly and never stop until England's green hills slowly rose out of the mist and all that was dear and familiar began to slide by beneath one's wings.

Slowly she turned and walked through the rickety, gimcrack town that never, ever would she want to call home. Henry did not know it, but like a storm-battered albatross resting briefly on the poop-deck of a heaving ship, she was merely stopping here for a while, gathering her strength. And finding as much happiness as she could in the meantime.

CHAPTER EIGHT

'As the day wore on it became apparent to everyone that no matter how alarming were the indications of moisture at least it was not going to rain. A strong easterly breeze blew steadily all day.'
— Report on Tauranga Regatta Day, Bay of Plenty Times.

FEBRUARY 27, 1886

'She'll be right stormy off the outer beach,' said Jim Spooner. The other men of the racing committee considered the sky. Dawn on the annual regatta day had come up warm and dull with a brisk breeze from the east. Waves heaved atop disturbed seas. Clouds humped and then shredded to let in spears of sunlight. Mount Maunganui loomed as a dark, brooding triangle to the north. It gave the harbour some shelter but conditions were hardly ideal.

'It's not so bad,' said Jack Ward. The baker was stout around his middle. Spider veins pushed plum tributaries through his cheeks. The shirt sleeves that sprouted from his waistcoat were packed with muscle, bulked up by years of mixing, slapping and rolling dough.

'As long as the wind gets no stronger,' said Thomas Hamilton. 'It's a grand breeze for the sailing boats but we oarsmen will make heavy weather of it.' He glanced around. His rowing partner, Rupert Beckford, should have been here by now. No sign. He said, 'What do you think, Jim?'

Spooner, a watchmaker, was the nearest thing they had to a weatherman, if only because his shop had more barometers than any other place in Tauranga. They had appointed him to be starter. He gazed at the clouds from under his wiry brows, pondered, and declared that he thought conditions were feasible. 'Tapped the glass on m' way out. It tipped neither one way nor t'other, so I reckon we're set fair — or fair enough to give us a good day's sport.'

'We're all prepared, besides,' urged Ward. He waved a hand at all the boats being readied along the shore. It was clear that the rest of the town was taking it for granted that the regatta was happening as advertised. 'The bairns are excited, the wives have made picnics, the band's been practising its oompahs. 'Twould be a crying shame to cancel just for the sake of a few piping squalls. I say we go. We need a majority vote but will have to do without Beckford's. And if we're all agreed then his voice is not needed anyhow.'

Thomas looked around the circle, squinting into a flurry of grit. 'So it's yes?' There were mutters and nods of assent, after which they wished each other good luck and hurried off to prepare for their events. His own race was set to go at half after nine. He yanked out his fob watch. It was less than forty-five minutes until the starting gun.

Ward turned back and said, 'Thomas, you'll be looking for your rowing mate?' Ward would also be rowing the course alongside his equally hulking son. He was grinning. 'You might find him a little the worse for wear. When I left the Star last night — nice and early, mind, so as to be in fine fettle for this morning — your Mr Beckford was calling out for another round.'

Thomas ran the short distance home. 'What is it? You've a face like thunder,' said Anna. She stood at the kitchen table, packing buttered bread, sliced ham, tomatoes, cakes and lemonade into a basket

Pa! Pa! Is it time to go?' Jamie called.

'Almost, lad. Be quiet now.' His son's face fell but Thomas was in no mood for placation. 'Have you seen Rupert? He's not turned up.'

They looked out across the street at the locked door of Rupert's premises. They could not see if there was any sign of life at the windows of his private rooms around the back. 'Perhaps he's gone to get his boat. Surely he won't miss the race when you've put in so much practice.'

Thomas let out a gusting sigh and stamped out, slamming the door behind him. 'Mama?' said Jamie. She drew him close to her hip as she stood in the doorway and watched. Thomas crossed the road and was gone for five minutes or more. The sound of trumpets drifted up from the shore, borne on salty gusts. And then, at last, he reappeared. Rupert was with him, still buttoning his shirt, his blaze of bright red hair uncombed. He stumbled as they rounded the corner, putting out a hand to steady himself on the fence. Thomas strode on stony-faced. Rupert had to trot to catch up with him. He glanced over and saw Anna on her doorstep, gave her a sheepish smile. She raised a hand. 'Good luck,' she called.

* * *

'Sorry,' Rupert panted as they jogged along the shore to where his dinghy lay upended on the sand. 'My alarm didn't ring.'

'Did you set it when you came home full of grog?'

'Yes, I did. I'm sure of it.'

They reached Rupert's craft, braced themselves and heaved, turning the boat upright and hauling it into the shallows.

Thomas pulled out the oars from under a bush. 'In, Rupert!' Thomas snapped, not trusting his partner to be steady enough to step aboard with one leg and push with the other. They threw off their shoes. Rupert clambered in. Without stopping to roll up his trouser legs, Thomas waded deeper, pushed, and swivelled over the side and onto the seat. They fumbled with oars and rowlocks. Their rivals in five other dinghies were already bobbing about on the start line, fifty yards away. Their mocking laughter carried over the waves. 'Put your back into it, Rupert,' Thomas said.

By the time they'd joined the flotilla at the start — an imaginary line running from the end of Victoria Wharf to an outcrop of trees on the harbour's far side — they were running tolerably well. 'Hope you're not this late paying interest!' someone shouted.

'Not as late as you'll be at the end of the race!' Rupert yelled back, raising a storm of cheerful derision. Between them, he and Thomas had all the other rowers as clients. The course ran parallel with the beach along a hundred yards of foreshore. An anchored buoy of white-painted cork floated alongside a pinnace containing three sharp-eyed townsmen, all set to judge whose bow would take the race.

An orange pennant flapped at the wharf's end, signalling ten minutes to go. A local lad was hauling up the yellow five-minute flag. 'Spread yourselves out!' bawled Jim Spooner through a tin loud-hailer. 'Mind your oars, men!'

The rowers had drawn their positions the day before. Thomas and Rupert were in the middle of the line-up. Thomas hoped those to windward would keep well out to sea. The wind on their beam was strong enough to push them too close.

The dinghies jostled as their crews tried to keep abreast, mostly making a hash of it. 'Come on, Spooner,' shouted Rupert. 'Let 'er rip!'

And so Spooner did, raising his pistol high. All eyes went to his hand, anticipating the puff of smoke. Crack! And they were off.

Bend, dip and haul; bend, dip and haul — Thomas and Rupert fell into the routine they'd practised so often, setting a solid pace at the outset but with enough energy in reserve to forge out in front close to the end.

'Pull. Pull. Pull. Pull.' Thomas grunted out the rhythm with every stroke. They had to be synchronised. On calm days they'd played at feathering the oars on the sweep back to reduce wind resistance, but it was too rough today for any fancy work. 'Pull. Pull!'

The din was huge. Waves slapped at hulls and curses rose from the boats and their straining occupants. From onshore they could hear yells, whistles and hollering. People waved kerchiefs and scarves. Rock-basking shags, shocked from their morning torpor, thrashed their black wings and flew away. 'Row, Sam, darlin'!' shrieked some woman on the shore.

'Sink, Sam darlin', sink!' yelled another voice. A great shout of laughter went up.

Thomas reckoned they'd got a good start, judging that they were at least even with the boats to the left and right of them. After twenty strokes the others were already drifting back. 'Pull. Pull!' Thomas began to step up the pace. If they eased off here they were as good as finished. Rupert stayed with him. *We're a steam engine,* Thomas thought. It was grand to feel the power of their arms working side by side, muscles corded and veins bulging beneath the skin, the fitful sun lighting the red fuzz on Rupert's forearms and the darker hairs on his own.

They were bucking through steep, short waves. It was a rougher ride than they had expected. Waves sloshed over the gunwale and it wasn't long before an inch or two of water was slopping around their feet. The crowd trotted along the beach, keeping pace as the boats passed the three-quarter mark.

'Row, Pa!' A child's treble voice stretched out over the sea. Thomas thought it was Jamie's, but then many of the rowers were fathers and they probably all took heart from the piping call. The burn was beginning now, in arms, back and shoulders. He could hear Rupert taking great gulps of air, grunting hard as he took each pull. Now there were just two boats in contention, theirs and the Wards'.

'Faster!' Thomas heard the elder Ward roar. The two dinghies were nudging together now, opposing oar tips dipping and flying perilously close. He looked over his shoulder to see the pinnace jerking at its anchor. Almost there! But the Wards, ah, damn it, they were slightly ahead.

And then two things happened. Rupert's stroke suddenly faltered. Somehow he fell into disarray, like a hand juddering on a clock face, just as Thomas gave a mighty pull. At the same time a dark heaving wedge of sea rose up and pushed the Wards' bow towards theirs.

They collided with a crack and a judder and the younger Ward was tipped, flailing, into the ocean. 'Peter!' shouted Jack Ward. His dinghy would have capsized had he not quickly shifted his weight. White-faced and anguished, he gripped his oar with one fist and hung on with the other. Peter's oar had snapped. *God in heaven,* Thomas thought. He realised their own craft had spun past the finish mark. They had won the goddamn race, for what it was worth. Still upright and with two good oars, they were able to turn and go back, somehow stroking in unison. The men on the pinnace were all shouting at once.

Ward cried out again, his head swivelling in a frantic search for a sign of his son. He could do nothing but turn his boat in useless circles.

'There!' yelled Rupert, pointing. Peter Ward had surfaced nearby, hands grabbing at air, eyes bulging, mouth gaping in a terror-filled grimace

'He can't swim,' cried his father. With frantic corkscrewing of his feet, Peter somehow spun around, his arms windmilling, facing every quarter of the horizon as he craned his neck, as if to take his last look at sky before sinking into the realm of liquid. And then he was gone.

Rupert yelled at the pinnace's crew. 'Give us a line!' Someone threw out a rope that lay snakelike on the sea, pushed up and down by the action of the waves, and then it too dropped out of sight.

Rupert shoved the end of his oar behind him back into the bow. 'Mind that,' he said. He tore off his shirt and stepped off the stern seat into the sea. Thomas grabbed Rupert's oar and swung into the wind so he could see what was going on. Suddenly all the shouting stopped. Ralph Ward stared, mute with anguish. The men on the pinnace were wide-eyed and grim, one of them wrapping his end of the rescue rope fast around a cleat. Rupert's head popped to the surface, his soaked hair dark and sleek. He raised a quick fist with the rope wrapped around it to show them that he had it, took a great gasp, upended himself and went below again.

Apart from the scudding, sucking, hissing, splashing, dreadful sounds of the sea — there was silence. The onshore crowd looked like figures carved on an Athenian frieze. Many stood with hands pressed to mouths and hearts, the women's skirts wind-pressed against their thighs. Men held on to hats. Even small children were quiet, caught up in the hush while they waited. And waited.

And then, like a bubble of air rising to the top of a boiling kettle, two heads broke the surface. Rupert, disorientated, looked wildly around for assistance. 'Pull us in!' he yelled. Peter Ward's big head lolled against his substantial shoulder.

Other dinghies had now joined them and another competitor leapt into the sea, helping to loop the rope around Ward's chest so the pinnace's crew could haul him out. With much heaving and grunting they managed to pull the young baker up and over the stern. He slid over it like a lardy rag doll, limbs all aflop. And then Thomas could see nothing but the curved backs of the race officials as they leaned over him. He assumed they would be pressing on his body to make him spew water and slapping his cheeks and shouting into his ear, for how else did you bring a drowned man back from the dead?

Rupert was still in the water by the pinnace. He turned his white, exhausted face to Thomas. 'I'm coming,' Thomas called. Rupert let go, dog-paddled over and wrapped his fingers over the upper edge of the stern. He made to pull himself up but could not do more than raise his chin a few inches.

'I'm done in,' he told Thomas. 'Don't have the strength.' He was shivering now, his lips pale, jaw juddering. Thomas said, 'Can you hang on? We're not far from shore.' Rupert nodded, closing his eyes. Thomas turned the bow, trying to avoid jerks that might dislodge him. At one stage all he could see was white knuckles and desperate fingertips. 'Are you with me?' Thomas shouted, heart thumping. 'Don't let go now.'

Rupert's face reappeared over the transom as a following wave boosted him up. His eyes were open again and he managed a grin. 'Not likely,' he called. 'I like living too much.' Soon his feet found firm sand. As Thomas beached the dinghy, Rupert stood in water to his waist and turned back out to sea, hitching up his sodden trousers. His ivory torso shone bright against the darkening sky.

The pinnace had up-anchored and was making its way to Victoria Wharf, its narrow smokestack emitting chuffs of steam that were swiftly shredded by the wind. The remaining dinghies were also making for home, one of them towing Ward's crippled boat. As half of Tauranga watched, an arm was raised on the deck of the pinnace and the little steamer let out a toot. 'He's alive!' someone yelled, and the crowd cheered.

Onlookers dashed to shake Rupert's hand as he waded out. They slapped his back and called him a hero. ''Twas nothing,' he kept saying. 'You'd all have done the same.'

Most of the well-wishers were men. The women held back, smiling, shy, clutching their babies. Except for Violet Sutton. She pushed her way through the throng. 'Mr Beckford,' she said. 'Please, wrap yourself up.' She handed him a wool blanket that she had ripped out from beneath a spread of Hester's picnic goodies, upturning cake stands and plates of sandwiches. Gratefully, Rupert slung it around his shoulders, hunching into its warmth. 'Thank you, Mrs Sutton.'

In front of all the men she reached forward to pull the edges together more securely, her fingers brushing his bare chest. 'You must go home now and tuck yourself up in bed or you'll catch a chill.'

'A glass of something strong inside him'll do him more good,' someone said. He was pulled away by admirers then, still wrapped in her rug. 'Mind you,' quipped one of his friends as they jostled him up the steps of the nearest pub, 'if Mrs Sutton herself was prepared to tuck you in nice and cosy, that'd be a different kettle of fish.'

And as they cheered Rupert gladly accepted a solid slug of brandy and downed it in one gratifying, life-affirming gulp.

CHAPTER NINE

> *'On the subject of courtship and marriage we can report some interesting sayings. A German writer says a young girl is like a fishing-rod, the eyes being the hook, the smile the bait, the lover the gudgeon, the marriage the butter in which he is fried.'*
> *— Bay of Plenty Times.*

FEBRUARY 28, 1886

'Your friend Mr Beckford came to the rescue at a thundering gallop,' said Henry Sutton as he drove a spoon into his soft-boiled breakfast egg.

Violet's face was impassive as she cut up an apple. 'He is not my friend. At least no more than any other tradesman in this town.'

'Tradesman, eh? I'm sure bankers have a more exalted view of themselves than that. Even if it's banknotes they're handling all day rather than rolls of tweed or fillets of fish. I rather think the banknotes have a nicer smell, don't you? It's a mystery why they call money filthy lucre when it has so many admirable qualities.'

Violet looked out the window at the steely Sunday. Yesterday's wind still blew, tossing the trees and ripping petals from her blowsy end-of-summer roses. She could hear shrieks from their neighbour's children.

Strong breezes often seemed to send small people mad. 'The word lucre comes from lucrum in Latin, meaning profit and also avarice,' she said.

'I was commenting,' he replied, 'not asking for your opinion.'

'I know. You rarely do. Ask my opinion, that is. Anyway, it was not an opinion, merely a statement.'

'How very schoolmarmish you are this morning.' Sutton picked up the two-week-old Sydney newspaper folded at his place. 'Rather different from the behaviour you exhibited yesterday on the foreshore. You all but embraced the man.'

'He was chilled. Offering a warm blanket was the least a thoughtful person could do.'

'Ha! There's been little thoughtfulness of late in your offers of warmth to me. A husband has needs, Mrs Sutton. It's what he has a wife for. Might there be a chance of you thawing out just a little one day soon?'

She looked down at the untasted wedges of apple on her plate. 'If you insist.' And then she flinched as he brought a fist down on the table with a thump, making the cutlery tremble. Milk slopped over the jug's rim. Cups rattled in saucers.

He lowered his voice to a harsh whisper lest Hester should hear from the kitchen. 'Insist? Insist? I shouldn't have to insist. My wants in all things should be anticipated and your willingness taken as read. Goddamn it, woman, you've given me no sons and not likely to at this rate.'

'I have tried—,' she began.

'Tried? What use is that? We both know you have the ability to bear a child.' Her face went white. 'So why are you incapable of bearing one for me?'

* * *

LOUISE HOSTED TEA AT THE ARCHERS' cottage the next day. She offered cucumber sandwiches and gingerbread and poured tea with a shaky, excited hand. "We must thank the good Lord for a man with presence of mind,' she declared.

'I believe it took him no more than two seconds to cast himself into that awful sea,' said Fanny.

'He must be uncommonly strong,' said Anna.

Louise's normally sallow cheeks were flushed with ardent pink. 'Did you see how he managed to heave young Ward up to the surface in his wet clothes? We know the weight of sodden cloth, do we not?' The ladies, wash-day veterans all, nodded solemnly.

'How is young Ward?' asked Mrs Bell. 'Does anyone know? I've heard he has a fearful cough.'

* * *

'I'M SORRY,' Rupert said to Thomas. It was the first time they'd met since the race. They were in Jessie Brown's shop on The Strand. Rupert took a big mouthful of one of her scones and then dashed crumbs from his lap. 'I have this great appetite today. It must come from being too close to Death's clammy grip.' He nodded thank you to a passing customer. Everyone passing their table wanted to pat his shoulder and wish him well. 'I left you to tidy up,' he went on when they were alone again. 'While I was being feted, you had to haul my boat in.'

'No matter. Someone else helped me take it along the shore and leave it shipshape. You'll find your oars in the usual place.'

'Was it damaged?'

'Not as far as I could see. Just a scrape or two of paint.'

'Bill Gregg says I can store it in his boatshed come winter, which is mighty kind of him. Better than leaving it out exposed to all weathers.' He took another mouthful of his brew. 'We were lucky.'

'Peter Ward was lucky. He'd have drowned but for you.'

Rupert shrugged. 'If not me, then someone else.'

'But it wasn't someone else. It was you. He was so close to being done for.'

'Can you swim, Thomas?'

'Not very well. Not enough to dive deep and haul up a dead weight like you did.'

'Actually, he wasn't very deep and he was still kicking. My shins are black and blue. I tend to forget that not many men can swim, let alone women who never enter the briny at all, poor creatures. Rather sad, that. Can you imagine never feeling the sensation of invigorating salt water on the skin? Imagine the chaos if ladies were to fall in with all their skirts and other clobber. There'd be no saving them at all.' He paused. 'Why weren't we named the winners?'

Thomas frowned. 'Given the emergency it was decided to it call the race null and void.'

'What? After so much effort?' Rupert grumpily wiped his buttery fingers. 'It's not as if anyone died. Is that fact not to be celebrated?'

'It was a close thing though, Rupe. We didn't think it was seemly, in the circumstances.'

'Seemly! I hate that word. My mother used it a dozen times a day.' He pushed his voice into a sniping falsetto. '*Don't do that, Rupert, it's not seemly.*' He pushed back his chair. 'Well, so much for that. Win the race, save a man's life and the trophy stays on the shelf. Sometimes this town is small-minded enough to drive a man to drink.' He strode out, leaving no coins to cover what he'd consumed.

Thomas went to the counter. Jessie saw him coming and waved him away with a grin. 'You and Mr Beckford? I'll not be charging you a penny.' She leaned forward against her counter, her braced arms squeezing double swells of freckled bosom over the top of her bodice. 'Even if the Wards are my competitors, I would hate that boy to have been swallowed up whole.'

* * *

ANNA CALLED on Rupert later that afternoon, delivering to his office a parcel wrapped with paper. 'Thomas brought your shirt up from the beach, so I laundered it,' she said. 'And Dinah has given it the most thorough pressing it is ever likely to get in its entire life. "Nothing but the best for Mr Beckford," she told me.'

Rupert smacked himself on the head as he got to his feet. 'I had forgotten it entirely. Thank you! Quite unnecessary, Anna, but very welcome.'

'It was the least we could do. Now, you're welcome to visit us for supper this evening if you'd like. I thought we could perhaps take a celebratory sip of Madeira and take a knife to your butter fruit.'

After she had gone Rupert used Anna's brown paper to make another string-tied parcel. Then he told his clerk he was off out for a short while and went away up the hill and along the rosebush-lined path to the Suttons' front door.

Hester answered his knock. She pressed her hands to the wide expanse of her apron as she beamed at him. 'Oh my, the rescuer,' she said. 'Pardon me for saying, sir, not my place, I know, but is there any other name today on our lips? We want to clasp you to our hearts, we do.' She chortled. 'Don't be afeared, I shan't be doin' it. But come in, come in. Mr Sutton's out, but m'lady's at home.'

He waited at the threshold as she bustled away and then returned to beckon him along the soft carpet runner. 'Mr Beckford,' she announced, and stood aside for him to enter the room, instantly aware (for hadn't her mam given her a touch of the gift?) that there was a peculiar surge of atmosphere as the young man stepped forward and Mrs Sutton rose to greet him.

He stood, full of life, in a shaft of sunlight from a tall window, his hair blazing. Coincidentally, Violet was wearing a silk gown of coppery hue, a rich shade reminiscent of autumn leaves. The two strong colours — his hair, her skirt — seemed to set off a shimmering vibration in the otherwise shadowed room.

'I've come to thank you for the loan of your blanket,' he said. 'It's been rinsed and hung upon my clothesline. It dried in no time at all.' Their fingertips brushed briefly as he stepped forward and handed her his clumsy parcel.

'How thoughtful,' she said. 'Mr Beckford, would you like tea and some of Hester's seed cake? My husband will be home at any moment and I'm sure he'll be parched.' 'If you have time.'

'I always have time, Mr Beckford, especially for the town hero.'

He flushed. 'I wish people would not say that. I must have heard it a dozen times since Saturday.'

'And so you should. You afforded us more excitement than we've had for an age.' Henry Sutton arrived home then. They heard the turn of the front-door handle, the clatter of his cane in the umbrella stand, the thump of his heels. Hester, waiting so as not to clutter the doorway just as he was coming in, noticed how Rupert took two deliberate steps back to put careful distance between himself and Mrs Sutton before Sutton entered. 'Ah!' Henry said. 'The man of the hour.'

'Mr Beckford is just returning our picnic rug,' said Violet, still clutching the parcel. 'I've invited him to stay for tea.'

'Tea? Far too delicate for this hour of the day. Hester, some dry sherry if you will.'

'And Hester, you might like to take this into the kitchen to ripen as well,' said Rupert. He dug into a jacket pocket and pulled out one of the mysterious fruits from his garden. Henry Sutton regarded it with some surprise.

'Ah, subaltern's butter,' he said. 'I did not know it grew here. Tried it in the Indies. Bland but palatable. Lemon juice gives it some welcome sharpness and fends off the scurvy too.'

'I thought it was midshipman's butter,' said Violet. 'Midshipmen, subalterns, no matter. A treat for junior ranks, but too rustic by half for the average captain's table. Still, no captains here, eh what? I shall enjoy tasting it again.'

Rupert felt pleasantly abuzz as he left the house an hour later. Good Spanish sherry, stimulating conversation — it made for a satisfactory ending to the day. Sutton had been ebullient, having had a telegraph from London indicating strong interest in the railway investment. 'There'll be good business in this, mark my words,' he said. Violet Sutton had been charming and scrupulously correct, as befitted a wife.

Rupert hoped it would not be too long, however, before he might meet her once more. There was not a single unmarried girl in this town to match her. Their walks and their early-morning boating excursion verged on foolishness, but she was so very entertaining and pretty. And, he suspected, so very unhappy.

* * *

THAT EVENING he sat at the Hamiltons' table and took up a sharp knife. 'Please,' said Anna. 'You do the honours.' A slice of crusty bread lay naked before him. He held the fruit in his left hand, inserted the knife's point into the skin until it met with resistance and drew it right round the fruit's circumference. Then, laying down the knife, he gently exerted pressure with his fingers to split the fruit in two.

It opened to reveal a weird sort of beauty. Two fleshy pale green ovals shone beneath the kerosene lamp's soft glow. An egg-shaped brown stone lay in the centre of one half. The other had a perfect concavity in the space vacated by the stone. Rupert bent to it and sniffed. There was a slight musky odour. 'Should it have those brown marks?' Anna asked. 'It looks to be spoiling.'

Rupert squeezed the stone-less half. The flesh was spotted with jelly-like, brownish patches. It did not look appetising at all.

None of them felt inclined to taste it. 'How disappointing,' said Thomas. 'We must have left it too late. But then how do you diagnose ripeness in something so strange?'

Rupert probed firmer areas of flesh around the fruit's fatter end. 'Perhaps it's still sound here. Does anyone want to give it a try?' He laughed. 'I've made enough brave moves for one week.'

Anna shifted back in her seat. 'Nothing ventured,' said Thomas. He picked up a teaspoon, scooped out a small chunk of green flesh, pressed it onto a piece of bread and gingerly took a bite. He made an indecisive quirky-mouth gesture, shaking his head. 'Odd. Neither savoury nor sweet.'

'Sutton says it's tasty on toasted bread with a dash of Worcestershire sauce,' reported Rupert. Thomas tried another nibble. 'Yes, I can see that.' He gave Anna an enquiring look.

'Don't ask,' she said. 'My stews are all the poorer for its lack. There's no sauce in the town until the next shipment arrives.'

Thomas asked, 'Have you already tried it chez Sutton?'

Rupert shook his head and explained that he'd left a fruit with Hester only that day.

Anna said, 'Next time I talk with Violet I shall warn her not to let good things linger on the shelf.'

Rupert said blandly, 'I was thinking the very same thought.'

CHAPTER TEN

'Cough [. . .] is originally a curative process, the means which nature uses to rid the body of that which offends, of that which is foreign to system and ought to be out of it.'— Hall's Journal of Health.

MARCH 1, 1886

In the morning, those who rose early were witness to a chilling sight — that of a good lady from the Presbyterian Church slipping into the Ward house. The news spread that Betty Lewis, known to be adept at the proper laying out of a body, had been seen at the bakery's back entrance with her basket full of soaps and cloths. There was no Mrs Ward to carry out that melancholy task and widower Jack couldn't bear to do it on his own. Not for his own darling boy.

Louise had the details. 'That coughing we heard about? Apparently it never ceased.' She had run into Anna by chance outside the baker's premises, which were still shuttered up. There was no wafting of good smells from the Ward oven. No sound from the adjoining house. Embarrassed to be lingering outside the stricken address, they moved away, speaking more normally once they were at a respectful distance.

'Oh my Lord, and him only eighteen years old,' said Anna. 'But I thought he was recovered. Didn't they say he was speaking to the men on board the pinnace.'

'Yes, but his breathing was ragged and there was froth.' Louise's face screwed up with alarm and distaste. 'And he stayed confused and weak. I suppose he still had seawater inside. Can you imagine the struggling for air?'

Her hand pressed up to her throat. 'I heard the doctor said he simply seemed to give up, worn out with the strain. He thinks maybe he had a weak heart.'

* * *

THOMAS AND ANNA were subdued over their lunch. 'Rupert feels badly about it,' he reported.

'There's no need. He did his best.'

Thomas crumbled a piece of cheese between thumb and forefinger. 'I've heard, however, that Ward senior is not exactly grateful.'

'What do you mean?'

'Questions are being raised about how our two craft came to collide. We were on parallel courses and then suddenly we swung close just as a big sea pushed against their bow.'

'But the water was so rough, pitching you this way and that. Surely there can be no fault in that?'

'I know. Even the judges in the pinnace say they saw nothing amiss. All those on shore were too far away.' Thomas fidgeted. 'But I felt it. . .'

'Felt what?'

'Rupert was flagging, losing his concentration. And I don't know what happened exactly, but he seemed to bungle a stroke. I gave a big heave and he did not match it. Our bow yawed towards Ward's. Then a surge of sea came up, and crack, it was all over.' He looked bleakly at his wife.

'You're not saying you feel somehow to blame?'

He frowned. 'I was so angry with him, Anna, for letting me down and I was determined to be out there. We'd prepared so diligently and I was furious at the thought of not even being there for the starting gun. I dragged him out when he was still affected from the night before.'

He got up and went to the window, unable to sit still. He could see Dinah coming up the street, Jamie skipping alongside her. They'd been down to the wharf to buy fresh fish. He wanted to say his piece now, and then never mention it again. 'Anna, when I went to his house on Saturday he was dead to the world. He'd been ill. His room was rank with it.'

She rose with a small snort and took their plates to the washing bowl. 'He needs a good woman to take care of him. It's a pity he seems little interested in courting anyone.'

'That would take too much good sense.' Even as he looked, Rupert came out the door of his bank and set off down the street. He'd told Thomas he had a midday appointment with his drinking friends to down an ale. The aim was to solemnly mark the passing of Peter Ward, God rest his soul.

Thomas watched his receding back. 'He is such good company, has so many good points, so much potential. He could really make something of himself. But there's that larrikin streak in him.'

'But if he was the worse for wear that day, how did he manage to make that rescue? Where did he find the strength?'

Thomas turned and leaned wearily against the sill. 'He barely did. You saw how I had to tow him back to shore. It was all he could do to hold on. There may be no clarity about what happened, but in his heart he knows he was at least partly to blame — which also makes me somewhat partly to blame.'

'Poppycock. It was not you who drank his fill the night before. And it's not your fault the wind came up. There is never any one thing or person to blame for events like this.'

Thomas folded his napkin and smacked it on the table's edge in frustration. 'I love him like a brother, you know, despite his excesses.'

She set her lips. 'But you cannot be responsible for him. He makes you so anxious. We have enough of our own worries without being concerned for him as well.'

* * *

IT WAS A HUGE FUNERAL. Because the Wards' bakery supplied the whole town, everyone knew them. 'Besides, it's always that way when a young man dies,' Fanny warbled to Anna. 'Gone in the full flower of his youth, with so many friends to mourn him.' She sighed extravagantly. 'Sometimes it pays to die young. When we're withered, my dear, with our peers already buried, the mourners shrink to a few reluctant and merely obligated souls.'

The town's bleak mood passed quickly, however, except that some did think their bread and buns had a slightly leaden texture for a while, as if grief seeped through the heels of Jack Ward's sorrowing, kneading hands and rendered his loaves bereft of air.

* * *

NEITHER RUPERT nor Violet noticed any shortcomings in the bread the next time they met a few days later. They shared sandwiches in her drawing room. Rupert had arrived at the door asking to see Henry Sutton on business, knowing full well he was not at home and putting on a show of reluctance over disturbing Mrs Sutton. But he was, of course, invited in, and, of course, he accepted and seated himself on the spindle-back sofa opposite her chair.

As each of them chewed a thin sandwich they observed each other slyly and minutely, she noticing the length of his thigh beneath his worsted trousers, he admiring the narrowness of her waist and the swell of her bosom beneath her bodice as she bent to pour tea and accomplish all the accursed fiddly stuff that was required. The milk jug clinked against her fine, flower-painted cups and her hand trembled very slightly as she offered him a plate of sweet cakes.

'Tea,' Violet said, with some exasperation. 'I'm not even very fond of it. It's merely the lubricant for conversation, don't you think?'

She knew that Rupert was leaving town. He had farming clients to see up at Katikati, and horse races to attend. She knew his adoration for swift steeds. He'd be gone for three days. She cleared her throat. 'May I still borrow your dinghy? I should so love to go rowing again.'

He looked worriedly into his cup. 'I know I said you could, but after what's happened, do you think it's wise? If anything went wrong I would never forgive myself.'

'What could go wrong on a calm day? I would go out only if the sea is like a mirror and there is no wind at all. Could you not leave it for me tied to the tree, as we agreed?'

'You have not rowed on your own.'

'I do not intend to be by myself.' 'So who—?'

She stopped him with a smile. 'A friend. I know already how much she'll enjoy it.'

'That sounds even more daunting. How would two ladies cope, with your skirts and suchlike?'

The look she gave him now was a mix of merriment and impudence. 'Who says we will wear skirts?' He spluttered, 'My god, Violet, you're a bold one.'

Two open doors stood between them and the kitchen and they could hear staccato thumps as Hester chopped at something on the scrubbed wooden table. 'Best call me Mrs Sutton,' Violet whispered. 'She's a dear but she might misconstrue.'

When they had rowed together in the calm cool of the morning, Rupert had been acutely aware of her slender arm next to his, keeping time with his strokes. He shortened them to make it easier for her to keep up. He had tried not to become fixated by the round knees bending rhythmically underneath the thin skirt she'd worn for their adventure. The shape of her legs was so clear, he thought, she must not be wearing a petticoat.

She turned her face to him as their keel slid across the sea, her eyes sparkling. 'I love this,' she said. 'You have no idea how wonderful it is to work at my own progress. We women, especially *ladylike* women,' and she curled her lip, 'are trained into a state of passivity.'

Rupert had to pick up his pace a little for she begun to row harder as her anger fed her energy. 'We are treated as if there's no strength in our bones at all. And yet if you men could see and feel the effort and endurance required in giving birth you would have an utterly different opinion.'

Rupert was puzzled. She did not have a child, did she? As if she had heard his thought, she said, 'I know of it, the pain and anguish.' Her voice faltered then and her rowing rate dropped off. Rupert feathered his oar for a stroke or two to straighten up their course but he did not detect exhaustion, at least not in her physical body.

As they slowed she sighed in a more contemplative way. 'This reminds me of playing with our gardener's son. He was close to my age.'

'No sisters?'

'Yes, but she was three years older and paid me little attention. When I was small I preferred boys' games. We grew up in the country in Kent. My mother was inattentive, my father very strict, but he was often away for long periods. My nursemaids came and went and because my mother paid little heed I often ran wild with the lad, especially in summer.' She laughed. 'It was excellent. But then, of course, we grew up. And my mother died and I grew up and went into prison.'

Rupert turned a puzzled face to hers. She laughed. 'I mean every woman's prison, our iron-maiden corsets and long skirts. A woman cannot run in such garments.' After a moment she added, 'Or run away.' Now, in the formal surrounds of her drawing room, she would not give up on the idea of taking out his boat. As they stared at each other, she whispered, 'Please?' And he was unable to resist.

* * *

'You are a true Freethinker,' Anna said to Violet as they strolled The Strand a week later. 'I do admire that in you.'

'It's not such a sin, is it? Doesn't every person have a right to their own thoughts?'

'I doubt that Reverend Larkin would agree, given how ardently he tries to press the contents of his brain into ours each Sunday. Oh, it's so tiresome!'

Larkin had made a visit to Anna's home that morning, eager to ensure that the May concert being planned for the Temperance Hall would be suitable. 'We'll not be wanting any of those bawdy music-hall turns they're so fond of in Auckland and Wellington,' he said. Anna felt a flare of annoyance. He was not part of the organising committee.

What was the concert to do with him? If he got involved it would all be sepulchral airs and dreary poetry.

He had knocked at the door and received a cool welcome from Dinah. Despite her Mission training she'd still not warmed to the idea of a god in pale human flesh come to save them all. Dour men in clerical collars never seemed joyful about the 'good word' they spread. She nodded, led him to the kitchen and resumed peeling potatoes. He followed to find Anna wrestling from a Jamie a sharp stick he was using as a play sword. 'Behave!' she scolded him as he slashed it perilously close to the parson's knee.'

Small boys, such a handful. Spare the rod,' Larkin said primly. 'Yes, Reverend, I'm sure you're right,' Anna replied.

Jamie reached for the stick and tripped over a bucket, sending a slosh of dirty water across Dinah's clean floor. 'Aue!' she yelled. 'Outside! Bad boy!' Jamie fled, wailing. Then a pot of soup on the stove boiled over with a hiss. A beefy stench filled the kitchen. Dinah darted to mop up the spill.

'Perhaps I should go,' said Larkin, but only tentatively, as if by his very presence his desire for tea and a tasty biscuit should be attended to.

'Yes,' said Anna brightly, 'that might be best. As you see, we have a degree of tumult here.'

'I'm sure you'll have wholesome fare at the concert, Mrs Hamilton,' he said as he left. 'If you have a paucity of performers, don't forget I'd be only too happy to recite Hamlet's soliloquy.'

'I was very quick,' Anna now assured Violet, 'to say our programme was already full.'

'Which it most certainly is not.'

'Indeed. But we can do better than that.'

But Violet had little interest in Larkin. 'Anna, tomorrow is the day for our excursion. Did you remember? It's Wednesday. Henry is still away in Auckland, it's market day and so our little escort there,' she indicated Jamie, who was skipping ahead of them, 'will be busy with Dinah.' She raised her hands to the blue and cloudless sky. 'The weather is holding fair, the tide will be lapping high at seven and I'm hoping you can't think of a single other excuse for not coming out to play.'

She spun round on her toe and walked backwards, almost dancing. 'Will you? Will you? Please say you will.' Anna sighed. 'You really are the most obstinate creature.' But Violet could see that despite Anna's diffidence, the small quirk of her mouth meant they would be rowing partners in the morning.

CHAPTER ELEVEN

'A woman who was arrested garbed in men's clothes in the public streets by the Inspector of Weights and Measures is not the only one in Auckland who wears the "breeches" by a long way, though her female coadjutors are not all so frank about it. The disguise of the fair heroine was tolerably complete, but the experienced eye of the Inspector of Weights and Measures soon detected that there was a "missing link" somewhere in the martial strut of the Amazon and he "run her in".'
— The Auckland Observer.

MARCH 10, 1886

Late summer had stretched on and it was hazy and still when Violet set out, carrying a shawl and a coarse linen bag. Wanting to look like a woman ready for domestic chores she wore no corset, just a camisole and pantaloons under her most sensible, workaday clothes — the drab skirt, overblouse and apron she sometimes put on for tending her garden. Henry thought planting and pruning demeaned her. Violet insisted fresh air was good for her health. Henry told her, scowling, that she looked like a common tramp in 'those appalling garments'. She wore them anyway.

'Out walking,' she said to Hester as she strode through the kitchen.

'Ma'am,' Hester muttered, stoking the fire, still half asleep. Violet felt oddly loose-fleshed without her usual underpinnings. She wrapped her plaid shawl tight around her and headed for the shore. The new day was smearing a long wash of pearly light behind the harbour's eastern hills. Though she'd risen early there were already other residents out and about. Market day was always the busiest morning of the week. As people cursed dogs and scolded their children, their voices floated over the town. Smoke drifted from kitchen chimneys, outhouse doors creaked on hinges and wagon wheels crunched on shell. Violet made her way in a wide circle to the fore-shore, walking around the backs of neighbouring gardens and sheltering hedges, leaving tracks in damp grass and avoiding commonly used paths.

She and Anna had agreed to meet beneath the huge tree. Rupert's dinghy floated beneath its sprawling branches. The pohutukawa hung over a tiny, semi-circular bay ringed with rocks and lined with fine, white sand. At Christmas this tree and its companions along the shore had blazed with fiery blooms. Violet loved them for that, for she badly missed the seasonal changes that made autumn so beautiful in England. This country was so relentlessly green. Her soul ached to see more scarlet, apricot and gold. Now the pohutukawa had only its greyish leaves and twisted limbs to please the eye. Still, its sinuous strength was pleasing, even without its paintbrush blooms.

There was a foot of clear water between the boat's keel and the creamy sand. Rupert had tied it fore and aft to the tree's low-dipping branches. Tiny wavelets lapped at its blue stern. Rupert had told her where the oars could be found and she pulled them out from behind some clumps of flax, laid them upon the narrow beach, sat down upon a rock and waited. Fifteen minutes later, in almost full daylight now, Anna finally arrived. 'I'm sorry! Dinah was tardy and Thomas was so late over his breakfast as well. I've told him we're taking morning exercise and he seemed to accept it well enough.'

'As he should, for it is true, is it not?' Violet stood and took off her apron.

'Only partly.'

'Nonsense. We do not have to tell our husbands every jot and tittle of our day's activities. They'd find it very tedious.' She took from her bag a bundle of brown cloth.

'What is that?'

'Trousers.' She laughed. 'Don't look so alarmed. I bought them at a jumble sale pretending they were for a charity case. Be our lookout now. Go down the path a few yards and tell me if anyone comes.'

'Why? Surely you're not going to wear them. Violet, you could be arrested!' Anna dashed back and forth in alarm, checking both directions, and was thankful to see nobody at all.

'Nobody's going to see me. The whole town is occupied elsewhere.'

'But why? It's enough of a risk for us to go out alone in the boat, but in trousers!'

'One of us needs to wade into the water to push the boat out. I'm not doing that in petticoats.' And with that Violet loosed her skirt, unlaced her boots, grabbed the trousers and shoved first one bare foot and then the other into them, stuffing her pantaloons down the legs. She giggled as she tied the waist cord. 'How do I look?'

'Oh, Violet,' Anna said. 'Are you sure about this? I really don't think—.'

A roil of frustration crossed Violet's face. 'Don't refuse me now. We cannot be faint-hearted. We promised ourselves! It's just for a few minutes, Anna. Don't you want to have even a small adventure?' 'You didn't tell me about the trousers.'

'Oh, for pity's sake,' said Violet. She bent and picked up her apron, thrust it over her head and knotted its tapes. 'Look, it covers most of me. Even if the entire town board were here they'd only see a couple of ankles. And when we're seated it will cover even those impudent appendages.'

Anna still hesitated. 'Well,' declared Violet. 'I am rowing regardless.' She pushed her discarded clothes into the bag and hid it behind a bush. Then, tucking up her apron to keep it dry, she splashed into the tide, put the oars into the dinghy and unloosed the bow line from the tree. Her trousers were now soaked well over her knees. Anna stood and watched, thinking how clownish and peculiar Violet looked, and yet, at the same time, how capable.

Violet pushed the boat around so that the stern nudged neatly beneath the tree. The broad trunk jutted almost horizontally from the bank. Once, when out walking, Anna had seen small Maori children jumping gleefully into the water from this natural wooden landing. It felt like a safe and friendly place.

Ripples spread out from Violet's legs as she waited. It was as if she were a pebble dropped into the calm of Anna's life, setting up unexpected disturbance.

'Are you coming?' Violet asked.

'What do I do?'

It didn't take long. She shuffled along the trunk and Violet reached up to help pass her into the dinghy where she perched on the central seat.

Violet turned the bow, slung one long leg over the side, pushed with her other leg and then was in, eyes gleaming. 'Shift over a little. Look, we're away.' She grinned. 'Aren't you pleased?'

'Oars,' quavered Anna. 'Else we'll drift off.' They took care to push them home into the rowlocks.

'Onwards,' said Violet, making a couple of strokes to turn them away from the town. 'Match what I'm doing so we can keep a straight course.' Anna took a first dip, choppy and overly deep. 'No, no. Just put the blade in a little, so that only the end is in the water. Make it long and slow. We're not in a race.'

'Thank heavens for that,' said Anna. They flubbed their strokes at first, but after a little while they found themselves cruising easily in unison. Anna hoped that with the low, bright sun behind them they'd appear as a mere silhouette to anyone who paused to look, but she felt safer when they rounded a sandy promontory and were out of sight of the last sprawl of settlers' cottages. She was thirsty suddenly, but a cautious contentment stole over her, despite the way her corset bit into her flesh with every forward bend.

'You know, I don't like using the oar on this side,' said Violet a few minutes later. 'It feels odd. I usually sit where you are. Do you mind if we switch places? And then we'll go back. People will be heading home from the market soon. Not many live out this way, but even so. . .'

Anna stopped stroking. 'How do we switch?' A note of uncertainty crept into her voice. 'I don't want the boat to wobble.'

'I'll crouch down, you slide over, and then I'll sit back up again where you are now. Look,' she said, putting the end of her oar in front of her feet. She slipped off the seat and squatted low, looking back over her shoulder at Anna. 'Now you move over.'

Anna took care to wedge her oar into the bow behind her before easing sideways. The boat turned broadside to a small wave as she shifted and her hand flew out to grasp the gunwale. The dinghy swayed. At the same moment, Violet pushed up to sit where Anna had been and momentarily lost her balance. Her toes hitched under the resting oar. With a dull rasping sound it lifted up out of the rowlock. Anna reached for it but it was smooth and round and slipped away. It reminded her of those times when Jamie's firm limbs eluded her fingers when she soaped him in the tub. The oar bobbed to the surface and floated six inches from her reaching fingers.

'Use the other oar, pull us around!' Anna snapped. Violet did, but her effort merely spun them in a circle. For a moment the oar drifted close but only the tip of Anna's longest finger brushed its surface before it bobbed further away. They sat, stunned, watching the pale streak of timber rocking on ripples that had not been apparent ten minutes before. A breeze was picking up.

Anna clenched her fists to stop them trembling. 'Oh, I knew this was foolish,' she burst out.

'Stop that. We must think!' Violet looked towards the land. They had stroked their way at least fifty yards out. The town was well behind them. 'At least we're not heading out to sea,' she observed. Abreast of them were mudflats and a mass of tangled mangroves. 'But if we drift ashore here the mud will be a challenge.' She laughed drily. 'Little chance of persuading people we've just been out for a ladylike stroll when we're coated in filth to our eyeballs.'

'Was it high tide when we started out?' asked Anna.

'Yes, I think so. Why?''The wind is from the south — can't you feel it? The tide will run northwards out of this estuary and we'll get caught in the wind and the current and then we will be pulled out to sea.' Her voice was thin. Every settler knew to beware of the harbour's muscular currents.

Violet screwed up her eyes, considering. 'But that's good. We'll drift past the town. Someone will come and help. There are always people on The Strand. You can take off your petticoat and wave it to draw attention.'

Anna winced. It was a plan that would have them gossiped about for weeks. Even Aucklanders might get to hear of it. Thomas's superiors would be appalled. It didn't bear thinking about. But it was preferable to the alternative. She fixed her eye on a distant tree to check its position against the hill behind it. 'We are already drifting,' she said, despair rising again. 'If we're too far out we'll never be seen. Can we use the oar as a paddle, like gondoliers in Venice?'

'Are you willing to stand up in this cockleshell? We'd risk falling in, like Peter Ward.'

Neither of them wanted to finish that thought. Violet said, 'Maybe I could get onto my knees and try it that way.' She swivelled around on the seat, shifted forward and knelt in the bobbing bow section.

Anna was very afraid they'd lose the second oar too. The shore looked miles away. She had a sudden vision of oblivious Thomas, brow furrowed, seated at his quiet desk in the bank at this very moment, scratching away at his columns of numbers. She was not about to leave him. She was not about to leave Jamie. Her face screwed up with tension, arm muscles trembling, she extracted their remaining oar from its rowlock and passed it to Violet's waiting hands. But it was hopeless. Gripping the oar close to the blade, Violet managed to take some swipes at the water, but the dinghy was too wide to be paddled easily. Holding up the oar's swaying weight took all of her strength. With a despairing grunt she let it fall. It cracked like a gunshot against the side of the boat and she held it there across the rocking gunwales, her head lowered over it like a woman clinging to an altar rail. But in the next second she turned. Someone was calling from across the water.

A Maori canoe had emerged from a mangrove-clad inlet, powered by six men. Their brown fists rose in unison on each upstroke. 'Help!' Violet shouted. 'Wave, Anna.'

The canoe headed towards them and as it approached so did its sound — a grunting chant from deep in the chests of its crew.

Digging their blades into the green water, the paddlers brought the canoe to a stop some eight feet away. Sunlight gleamed on coppery skin.

Two of the men were older, with charcoal whorls grooved upon cheek, jaw and forehead. Hair dark as shag wings stirred in the breeze, though some had cropped heads. Their craft lay low in the water, rocking gently, as the men sat in silence, paddles still across their knees.

Then one of them said something and began to laugh. He nudged his neighbour who giggled in his turn and soon the whole crew was rocking with mirth.

'Why are they laughing?' Anna whispered.

'They have the upper hand,' Violet said fiercely. 'And we look so feeble.' She was more angry than embarrassed. 'Please, can you help us?' she called. She lifted up their one useless oar an inch or two, and then thought how foolish it was to be indicating the obvious.

'Kia ora,' said Anna tentatively, uncomfortably aware how little she knew of the Maori language. What was the name for their canoe? Was it a waka? Thomas knew more than she; he'd grown up in this land, after all, while she had only six years' acquaintance with it. His missionary father was fluent. Anna knew that in his youth the old man had hobnobbed with chiefs. And now here she was, in dire need of assistance, able to speak no more than a simple greeting.

A young man stood, grinning. He tore off his shirt, dived neatly over the side and swam to the dinghy, sleek as an eel. He grasped the side of their craft and flashed white teeth at them. 'Where are you ladies going?' he asked in mock innocence, as if they were in total control and not drifting out to where the Pacific's waves crashed at the harbour's narrow mouth.

'We are just. . . out,' Violet replied. 'And, as you see, we are in trouble.'

He jutted his chin, but not unkindly. 'You are weak.' He shook his head like a schoolmaster remonstrating with slow pupils. 'You want to go home?'

'Yes, yes,' they chorused. 'Please, yes.'

'Mmm,' he mused, and thrust away from the boat. Anna and Violet let out a gasp, raising another gust of merriment from the canoe. The swimmer came back to them, smiling. 'We save you. Big money for saving ladies, eh?'

With a muscled brown arm he groped inside the boat, plucked up the bow line and swam away with it back to his own craft. He heaved himself back over the side and fastened the line. The men turned their backs to the dinghy and began to paddle, tugging the women along in their wake.

As Rupert's blue dinghy jostled along, jerking at its leash, the women talked in fierce whispers. 'What did he mean?' Anna asked. 'Does he want a reward?'

'I don't know. We should give them something — they are saving our lives.'

'But not our reputations.'

'Why should they give a fig for that? They know nothing of our lives. We are just silly white women to them.'

'I have no money with me. Do you?'

'No, not a penny.'

'They might hold us for ransom!'

'Don't be foolish, Anna. They live here, they trade with us. They're not pirates.'

'Where are they taking us?' Anna suddenly realised that the paddlers were not heading towards the town wharf. She felt a surge of hope that they would at least avoid ridicule at being abandoned there with Violet so scandalously clad. They were being towed back in towards the overhanging tree. 'How did they know the place we came from?'

Violet shrugged, thinking that the paddlers may well have watched them right from the start. Perhaps very little happened in these waters that they were unaware of.

Soon they were back in the shallows. Two of their rescuers clambered over the side to unhitch the dinghy. Anna began to stand. She wanted to climb out with as much grace as possible. But then she squealed as a giant of a man bodily lifted her out and placed her upon the beach, where she tripped over her hem and fell hard on her backside with legs spread wide. She rolled, pink-faced, and stumbled to her feet.

Violet leapt out unassisted and flailed out of the water in soaking trousers, holding the waist cord to stop them slipping down. Their rescuers chortled. Shaking their heads, they pulled the dinghy up onto the sand and waded back to their own craft. As the last man climbed in they called out a noisy farewell and paddled away.

'Help me, Anna,' Violet ordered. 'We must leave it as we found it.' Together, they heaved and grunted to refloat the boat and Violet re-tied it to the tree. 'Do not say a word,' she warned as she sploshed up onto the beach. 'I feel so foolish that nothing you say can possibly make me feel any worse.'

Anna just wanted to go home. 'What do you think the time is? Thomas will be wondering.'

Violet drew Anna back into the scrub to find her bag. 'Nine, perhaps. We've not been gone so long. He'll barely even notice, as long as you don't look panicked. We must stroll back. No running, no pink cheeks, no panting. Wait while I get rid of these trousers.' She fumbled with rope tie and buttons.

Her shoulders began to shake as she struggled to pull down the sodden cloth. For a moment Anna thought she was crying but then came a snort and soon they were both convulsed with laughter. 'Oh, God in heaven,' said Violet when she could finally speak. 'That was so excellent. Did you like it?'

'Before we came to grief, yes. After that, no.' Anna yanked at Violet's outstretched trouser legs and they finally came off. 'You want these?'

Violet shook her head, squashed them into a dripping lump and threw it further into the bushes. She used her shawl to dry her feet and put her boots back on, then her skirt. 'And now look at you, you've got sand down your back and leaves in your hair.'

Fifteen minutes later, relatively clean and tidy, they sauntered back into town. They saw nobody but the butcher's boy on his delivery round. He doffed his cap but otherwise looked merely bored.

'Do you think they'll talk about us?' Anna whispered.

'Who?'

'The paddlers. What if they tell everyone in town? What if they do want payment?' Anna's anxiety grew with every step closer to home. 'What if they come knocking at our doors with hands out, asking our husbands for money this very day?'

'Only the boy who swam to us seemed to have English. They may not even know who we are.'

'One is enough,' said Anna. 'They'll all know it is Rupert's dinghy. One whisper is all it would take for us to be a laughing stock.'

They had reached a fork in the path that would take them their separate ways. Violet gripped Anna's hands briefly. 'We are here, my dear. On dry land, alive and well. If we are found out, then we'll manage. Until then, we carry on as normal, yes?'

When Anna slipped into the house she had excuses all ready for her long absence. But there was only silence. Thomas was presumably in his office next door and Dinah and Jamie still out. Dinah much preferred shopping and talking to household chores. This morning it was a habit for which Anna was grateful.

She stood for a moment before the hall mirror to check her face. Remarkably, it revealed nothing but her customary calm. When she turned to find a hairbrush she heard the gritty twist of sand under her sole. Quickly, she pulled off her damp boots and scurried out the back door to brush them clean. By the time Jamie burst back inside she was sitting down darning a sock.

* * *

Unease returned the next day when Dinah arrived. There was a certain tension, a display of flashed glances. She said nothing out of the ordinary until well into the morning when, as they worked together to polish silver, she glanced sideways and asked, 'Did the fish bite?'

'I beg your pardon?' Anna could hear the quiver in her own voice.

'Did you go out for kai?' Anna put down a shiny spoon and picked up another.

'Tamure are tasty,' said Dinah. 'Snapper. Is that why you were there?'

'I don't know what you mean.' Anna rose from the table and bustled to the dresser to pick up a sugar bowl that she'd buffed up only the day before. When she turned, bowl in hand, Dinah was giving her a long and sceptical gaze. Anna could not meet her eyes.

'Aue, you were lucky,' said her housekeeper. 'Tangaroa was watching out for you. And my son was, too.'

That made Anna look at her at last, with widened eyes. 'Kehu and his friends,' said Dinah. 'Without them. . .' Her voice tailed off and she shook her head.

'Does anyone else know?'

'What? About you two white ladies playing games with the sea?' she scoffed. 'That water, it can take life like that.' And she smacked her palms together with a crack that made Anna blink. 'Peter Ward, if he had been ours, that place would be tapu. Before it was lifted, no one would go out there.'

'Tapu?'

'Ae tika! Do you know nothing?' Dinah swept the cleaning rags into a bucket. 'The sea took the baker boy. You must respect it.'

'I'm sorry,' said Anna in confusion. 'And grateful, believe me. So grateful.'

'If you do not respect nature it can bite you like a dog. Maybe it still will.'

'Please give my thanks to your son and the others. We did so already, on the beach, but I know it was not enough.'

Dinah was still seated with sinewy arms folded. Anna stood awkwardly before her as if she was the servant being humbled. Dinah said, 'What are you saying, that we want to be paid?' Eyes fierce, she thrust out her hand, rubbing her fingers. There was disgust in the gesture.

Anna sat down with as much grace as she could muster. 'I don't know what you want,' she said. 'Your son and his friends — they talked about money but they were laughing too. We did know not what to think.'

'I know what you want.' Dinah let out a smile then, a small and knowing one. 'You ladies. You want this story to be secret. Mrs Sutton in trousers! Ha!' She chuckled, slapping her knee. 'I wish I had seen that.'

'Yes, well. We were perhaps unwise.'

Dinah tossed her head. 'So many rules. So many things you cannot do or say. Your rules! Your corsets! How do you even move? How do you breathe? How do you sing?' She stood abruptly. 'Your lady friends, they would gossip if they knew about the trousers. You could be arrested if a constable saw you dressed like men.'

Anna nodded, cheeks scarlet at the thought of the talk that could stain their reputations. Thomas's reputation, too. What would his righteous father say if it ever leaked out? What would her own prim mother say? And yet she felt a surge of anger too. She hadn't worn the ugly trousers. Only Violet Sutton had — only shameless, daring Violet. But just having joined her in that adventure would be enough to drag down the Hamilton name.

'Twenty-two years ago we were at war in this town,' Dinah said. 'But on the sea now we look out for each other. Your people, my people, what does it matter? The water is bigger than all of us. But, dear lady, there may be a time when we ask you for help. And then you will help.' She nodded firmly, as if there was no doubt of this at all.

'Yes,' said Anna. 'Of course. It is a great debt that I owe.'

Dinah stood then to gather the polished pieces of silver onto a tray. Her mood turned conspiratorial. 'Women need their time away from husbands, eh? Good out in the boat, was it? At least while you had two oars.' She giggled, clicked her tongue, and then slapped Anna on the arm in a way that Anna found slightly impertinent but about which she could do nothing but offer back a grateful smile.

CHAPTER TWELVE

'A mother's health, both of body and mind, is worth more than additional acres of land, or finer livestock. The heart should not be allowed to grow old. Life should not have lost its charm, the heart its spirit, and the body its elasticity at forty years. And yet how many women are faded and wan, and shattered in mind and health, long before they are forty?'
— *Bay of Plenty Times.*

MARCH 12, 1886

Two days later, as Anna stood at her dressing table, about to fix pins into her plaited coil of hair, she felt a sharp internal pain. It was as if some creature inside her had pinched a pleat of hidden flesh. Warmth slid down her inner thigh. She snatched up a cloth, tucked it between her thighs and went out to the closet with tiny steps, legs pressed close.

She locked the door and tugged up her skirt. There was a blooming scarlet stain on her pantaloons. As she eased them off a viscous clot came away with the fabric. Dark dribbles traced tributaries down her legs. A deep, grinding ache settled low in her belly as she sat upon the oval hole in the sturdy timber seat and heard the dull splat of lifeblood falling upon the soil below.

She sat there for some time as the pain ground on. It was hot.

Buzzing flies wallowed in circuits under the ceiling. When one landed upon her bare knee she let it crawl for a moment before disgust gave her the energy to swat it away. Finally, she bundled up the soiled towel, wedged it again between her legs, adjusted her skirt and went to the washhouse. There was a bucket of water there for soaking stained things. She dropped in her pantaloons and pushed them down with a stick.

Dinah was pulling carrots from the vegetable patch. She stood straight when she saw Anna's stricken face.

"I am bleeding and should not be,' Anna said. She raised a hand to shield her eyes from the sun and could smell the stickiness on her palm. Dinah, no stranger to the loss of human life barely begun, led her inside, brought fresh water and soap and put her to bed with a supply of clean rags.

Anna lay with a stone in her heart, guilt curdling the grief. Was this her fault? Had she loosed those clots from her womb when she thudded backwards onto hard sand? Or was it — her soul cringed from the thought — that their lack of respect for the sea had somehow blighted the tiny life just as it began to bud?

Dinah kept coming into the room. Anna sent her away.

Thomas arrived, timorously, in the afternoon. Anna asked, 'Did Dinah tell you?'

'Yes, she said you'd taken to your bed.'

'There will be no baby, did she tell you that?'

'Oh, no, Anna, no, she did not. Oh, my dear. . .'

Anna rolled over, turning her back, too ashamed to witness his sorrow. 'Please. I need some peace,' she muttered into the fist clenched to her mouth. She felt his ineffectual pat on her shoulder, heard the creak of his shoes as he tiptoed out.

* * *

THE NEXT DAY Anna did light chores around the house but moved slowly, rested often and stayed close to home, making frequent trips to the washhouse with more rags to add to the bloody bucket. The doctor visited, but could only advise her to rest.

For several nights Thomas slept on the narrow cot they kept for visitors. One moonless night was so black and silent that, worrying about his wife and his job and its interminable demands, he felt as if he was the only man awake for miles around. Lonely, he inserted himself into the cold side of his bed.

They did not speak once he had turned down the lamp. He held her hand but even that light touch seemed intolerable to her and she slipped her fingers from his. Even when Jamie cried out in the midst of some turbulent dream she did not move. It was Thomas who padded to the boy and soothed him back to sleep.

Gradually, their normal daily round resumed.

* * *

When Violet came to visit Anna was pleased to have bright company. It was time, she knew, to pull away from her sadness. Women lost unborn babies all the time. Sometimes it happened very early, as with the life that had just slipped from her. Sometimes infants died when they had taken a mere few breaths of God's good air. Sometimes, Anna told herself, it was merely a woman's lot to endure sad times and then attend to the here and now. She had done this before when her daughter went.

That had been worse than this, so much worse, she told Violet. 'We'd had time to know her little ways. She was a whole person for us with her bright eyes and all her future intact. But the fever took her when she was nine months old.'

Violet fiddled distractedly with a ring on her finger. 'I know how you feel. I'll tell you why, too, though only if you promise not to share it with any others. Do you promise?'

'Of course. We already have a secret, you and I. One more is not likely to burden me.'

Violet frowned. 'A child of mine, not much older than your Jamie, lives in London.' Her lips compressed. 'I have not seen him since he was newborn. I think of him constantly, but he is utterly gone from my life.' A single tear spilled down her cheek and she dashed it away with the back of her hand.

Anna reached out. 'Oh, Violet. Here I am awash in my own gloom when you—.'

She took back her hand at the sound of footsteps and the squeak of an opening door. If Thomas noticed the silence when he ambled into the room, he gave no sign of it. 'Mrs Sutton, good morning, a pleasure to see you.' Violet bent to pick up her basket. Then she gave him her usual smile, apologising for being in his home so near to his midday break. She had to go, she said. Henry needed his lunch.

'Mustn't keep him waiting then.' Thomas was jovial, having done good business that morning. 'But do call again. It's capital for Anna to have a friend. Ladies have much to share that I'm sure it's best for mere husbands not to hear.'

An hour later, as Thomas finished his soup, he said idly that he'd heard a rumour at Jessie Brown's tea shop. Two white women had been rescued on the harbour by some Maori boys. Rowing on their own. So foolish. They had lost an oar. It was Rupert's dinghy, too — he was being well and truly joshed over it.

Anna's spoon froze mid-air as Thomas buttered more bread.

'Of course, the greatest noise surrounds the fact that one of the ladies was in trousers. Trousers! Who'd have thought we had such a mannish filly in our midst?'

Dinah brought milk to the table for their tea and set it down with care before returning to the kitchen, her footsteps loud on the floor. Anna did not dare look up.

'Still, to the town's great frustration, their identity is unknown. The story came from a woodcutter who was actually in the canoe but says he can't tell white women apart. One face is the same as the next for him, apparently. But by Jove, they were lucky. Had you heard of it?'

Anna shook her head and forced down a mouthful of soup. It felt slippery on her tongue.

'Rupert denies all knowledge, of course,' Thomas said. 'He came home to find his dinghy where he left it, all shipshape, if minus an oar. He's stowed it in the boat builder's shed now. Cursed thing. I'm sure Ralph Ward must prefer it out of sight. What, my dear? Are you quite well?'

He watched, a little perplexed, as Anna rose and left the room. She needed to see to Jamie, she said.

'Ask Fanny Bell,' Thomas called as he reached for an apple. 'She knows all that goes on in this town, does she not?'

* * *

THE NEXT DAY Anna took her son up the hill to the Sutton house in the afternoon. When Jamie went into the kitchen to see Hester, Violet drew Anna out to the veranda. They sat with embroidery on their laps, pretending to stitch ladylike flowers into white linen. But their backs were stiff, their fingers barely moving. 'They know!' said Anna. 'The whole town is talking.'

'But not about us, surely. Our names are not known?'

'No. But surely it's just a matter of time. Dinah knows. I can't stop her telling people.'

'But you said she gave you her word.'

'In a way she quite approved of us. She thinks we live such dull lives. I am thinking more darkly now. It's as if she has some power over me.'

'Perhaps she merely wants to keep her job. After all, you'll dismiss her straight away, will you not, if you hear she has gossiped?'

'But how would we know who has gossiped? There were six men in that canoe. Her son, with his good English. The other five. Any one of them might talk. If I dismissed her it would just show me up as vengeful.'

'Anna, you worry too much. Since when did our husbands pass the time of day with Maori fishermen? And what is the worst consequence we might face?' Violet let out a harsh little bark of mirth. 'My own husband already has a low opinion of me. We are hardly churchgoers except for show, so I'd care little if some dour clergyman scolded me. And who says it's true anyway? There are plenty of lively girls in this town who would dare to do as we did. And even in the worst case, would your Thomas disown you?'

'No, but scandal might ruin his prospects. You know what they'll say: if he can't control his wife, how can he command the respect of his clients?'

'I'm not talking about the cold-faced men at the bank, I mean Thomas himself. Would it really be so dreadful for him to hear you have a sense of adventure?'

Anna's mouth twisted. 'Maybe not. But it would break the trust between us. Even when he asked me directly if I'd heard the story, I said nothing. My silence stands between us now like a wall.'

Violet reached for Anna's hand. 'Oh my dear, you must not blame yourself for that loss of a life barely begun. It happens all the time to many women.' Jamie scampered round the corner, fresh from rolling dough at Hester's table. Anna sighed because she wanted to ask Violet more about the loss she'd mentioned the day before — of the boy not seen for years. It would have to wait. Jamie tucked himself against her warm side. She gave him a hug so fierce that he wriggled, struggling to escape.

'Calm will return,' said Violet. 'Trust me.'

CHAPTER THIRTEEN

> *'People who pooh-pooh all seemingly inexplicable phenomena simply because it is, or appears to be, inexplicable, do so as the result of ignorance and prejudice. There are but few educated people nowadays who are not prepared to admit the existence of certain agencies, mysterious because they are so little understood.'*
> — Auckland Observer.

MARCH 16, 1886

Another Tuesday rolled around. 'My dears,' crowed Fanny, 'here's Madame Francini, just arrived in town. I'm so delighted, Madame, to welcome you to my humble home. And, ladies, we are very fortunate because she says she'll hover over *all* our hands today and tell us what's in store. Tea, Madame? Do sit down, please.'

Fanny had heard from her husband, as she heard of most things before news spread to the rest of the town, of the impending visit of the famous palmist, Madame Francini of San Francisco. She was touring Australia and New Zealand to practise her ancient art. 'Your life is in your hands,' said the advertisements.

Wilfred had mentioned it to Fanny in withering terms, for he thought it was all folderol — not that it deterred him from accepting money for insertions in three issues of his newspaper. His wife had been secretly intrigued.

Violet had also been sceptical. 'I note that she does not mention the size of her fees,' she pointed out when they scanned the classifieds prior to Madame's arrival.

'Ten shillings,' said Anna. 'Or so I've heard. For a brief summary. Five pounds for a longer reading.'

Eyebrows had gone up. Five pounds! That was as much as a gold watch at Stewart Dawson's shop in Auckland.

'She'll only visit as a way of getting us to spread the word,' said Violet.

Fanny had sniffed. 'How very doubting you can be.'

'Well, why else would she spend time with us? We can hardly be as interesting as the ladies of San Francisco.' Fanny had been first to suggest that they invite the palm reader to one of their afternoons. She volunteered her home for the occasion and now the day had arrived she was full of nerves.

The corset beneath Madame Francini's plum silk bodice creaked as she sank onto a chaise longue. She was large, muskily perfumed, wore copious strings of pearls and had curiously short grey hair worn in a halo of curls. 'I can give you only a soupçon of insight today,' she said. 'For a full reading, we need much more time.' She let slip a confiding smile as she sipped from one of Fanny's best cups. 'Some things are best spoken en privé, you understand? From my lips to your ears.'

'Do you read tea leaves as well?' asked Fanny.

'Phht! Foolish nonsense. But the hand, it never lies.' She held up a palm. 'People have long consulted the masters on what lies in these lines. Mrs Bell, you are the hostess. Let us begin with you.'

Fanny looked pink and pleased. 'Oh, I need not be first.'

'But I would like that. Venez ici, s'il vous plait. Come, your right hand please.' Long seconds of inspection followed. 'Your hand is quite Venusian,' said Madame. 'I think it likely you can turn it to all manner of things.'

'Oh that's so true,' breathed Fanny. 'We have to be capable of so much here, living as we do so far from true civilisation.'

'But you also enjoy idleness.'

Fanny tried not to be affronted.

'I do not mean that you are lazy, Mrs Bell, just that you appreciate the rare times when you can do as you please.' Madame Francini shot Fanny a shrewd glance with her blackcurrant eyes. 'I understand, naturellement, that such time is precious. Also, I think you like to talk, yes? To know what is happening around this pretty town.

'Now your fate line, here at the wrist, starts deep and straight, which tells me you had a good start in life. And I see some prosperity showing up in your later years. That is good, because I see here,' she said, stroking the base of Fanny's longest finger, 'that you like your comforts. Your lifeline is deep and unbroken, with no crosses along it. You should have a long life. You are a fortunate woman.'

Fanny retreated with an air of satisfaction to the teapot. Then it was Louise's turn.

Madame Francini trapped her hand in both of hers for a moment with a small, kind smile. 'Such a young, smooth hand with curious fingers, untested in so many ways. Ah, don't take offence, ma cherie, we all are young at one time. Ladies with more maturity,' she said, darting a glance at Anna and Fanny, 'no doubt envy you.

'Now, let us see.' She considered Louise's narrow palm. 'This is a Mars hand. Not large, which would make you domineering, but dainty. I would say you can be somewhat excitable and sometimes, if you will excuse me, a little lacking in courage. Perhaps there are times when you need to hold firm a little more.' Louise kept her head down, with hooded eyes. 'Your heart line says you have capacity for much affection, but again there is timidity there.' Madame Francini patted Louise's hand as if it was the head of a scared lapdog and then pushed it away, looking up to see who was next. 'Mrs Sutton?'

'This will be intriguing,' said Violet as she took her place on the chaise longue. She thrust out her hand. 'Do your worst.'

Madame Francini chuckled. 'I like an unbeliever. So, let us see if I can alter your view.' She was silent for some time as she made her assessment. 'Intéressant.' She looked up sharply to meet Violet's eyes. 'Your hand is of the Solar type, your palm hollow and firm. You love reason and have no time for empty theory.' Madame's mouth twisted into a wry smile. 'That is why you doubt me.'

'You do not need my palm to tell you that.'

'C'est vrai. And these little lines at the base of your forefinger indicate pride.'

'Touché,' Violet replied.

'The pointed fingers suggest you are artistic.'

'Well, of course,' broke in Fanny. 'She has a beautiful home.'

'Thank you, but please do not interrupt.' Madame gazed again. 'As with Mrs Bell, I see you enjoy comfort, but you have these lines, see? Running from the Mount of Venus across your lifeline. This one shows some incident, perhaps a love affair, that has been very painful for you — perhaps not far in the past.' She did not look up as she went on in a low voice. 'And I must tell you that another dalliance still to come has the power to destroy a whole life.'

Violet snatched back her hand. 'Whose life?'

The palmist shook her head. 'I cannot know. The hand does not say. And it only points to a possibility. Our free will plays a big part, and you, cherie, you have such a deep heart line that there's no doubt you have a powerful will.'

Violet stood abruptly. 'I have courtesy too and Anna has been waiting very patiently. Here, my dear, it's your turn.'

'So, the last lady,' said Madame Francini. She looked tired suddenly and Anna wondered at her age — surely she was well into her sixties — and how she managed to endure the constant travelling, always calming the anxious, reassuring the weak, stroking the vain and duelling with the sceptical.

'I'm sure mine will be very ordinary,' she said as she proffered her palm.

'Ordinary hands do not exist,' said Madame Francini. 'Each is unique. And yours is Saturnine. The world needs people like you, Mrs Hamilton. You are a solver of problems.'

'My husband *will* be surprised to hear that. He's the banker in the family.'

'Your analysis is not about numbers, it is a deeper skill, more about emotions, n'est-ce pas? You see how people are feeling and can anticipate the perils in the paths they take. As for your own path, aah, this cross on your heart line — a great unhappiness, mmm? A few years ago?'

'A lost child,' Anna murmured.

'I cannot tell you how often I have seen this mark. Of course, to know that gives you no consolation.' Anna ventured a quick glance at Violet, who was sitting stony-faced.

Madame Francini went on. 'You are careful in your opinions and keep things to yourself. There's no harm, you know, in expressing your own needs sometimes, such as the one you have for more freedom in your life.'

She let Anna's hand go and sat up. 'Enough for now. I am a little tired. But ladies, you are welcome to make an appointment. There is much more I can tell you all.'

'Forgive us,' gushed Fanny. 'We sit here taking our ease while you have not even had a *morsel* to eat.'

They gossiped about her, of course, after she'd gone.

Fanny was pleased. 'How very fortunate I am.'

Louise was mortified. 'She made me sound like a frightened mouse.'

Violet was derisive. 'A destroyer of lives?'

And Anna was perplexed. 'I don't hide my worries. What could she have meant?'

None of them admitted to wanting a longer, expensive appointment. Not until they'd given it some thought. But as Anna and Violet walked home, they did agree that Madame Francini had mysteriously known of their separate losses.

Anna was still curious to know more of Violet's past and almost asked but her friend seemed subdued and the moment passed. Anna took to teasing to lift the mood. 'Oh, Violet, a dalliance! Should I be polishing up my fabled powers of perception?'

Violet snorted. 'Ha! How could such a thing happen in *this* town? After all, is there any man living here with whom any woman would want an affair?'

At the same time, at the Bell house, Fanny was asking Louise much the same question. 'Can it possibly be true? That comment was *scandalous*.'

'Can she really see people's lives in their hands?' Louise shivered. 'I don't think I'll go to her again. She is too. . . too odd. I could never trust such a gypsyish person. And how can I possibly ask Horace for so much money to spend on a mere diversion?'

'Thus proving,' said Fanny with barely suppressed triumph, 'that she was right. Timid, you see?'

Louise, hurrying home on her own a few minutes later, for Horace hated for his meal not to be on the table at exactly the same time each evening, thought about how dearly she would have liked to mention the palm reader's veiled barb about Fanny's ever-clacking tongue. But, she glumly admitted, her courage was indeed in short supply.

CHAPTER FOURTEEN

WINES. BEERS, SPIRITS, LIQUEURS, & BITTERS, Including, besides their well-known "Three Fort Brand", other first-class brands of Cognac, Geneva, Gin, Rum, and Whiskies, Champagnes — fine and sound but low-priced.

— advertisement by Mann and Co, Wine and Spirit Merchants, Bay of Plenty Times

APRIL 3, 1886

Then came dance night at the bank. Those who could bang out a tune on the piano went at it in relays, boosted by fiddlers, accordion players and an old banjo maestro who had learnt his skills on a Californian goldfield. Volunteers had cooked like fury. They always needed a hearty supper at two in the morning to get the toes tapping until four. The rugs were rolled up, ledgers and valuables locked away and extra oil lamps brought in.

Shyness made for a slow beginning but after a while the music began to have its way with everyone's souls. The floor shook with the stamping and twirling.

It seemed that most of the town was there, the invited and the uninvited, the eager and the curious. Rupert arrived too, business rivalry put aside for the night.

With no alcohol supplied, many of the men slipped out from time to time, returning with reeking breath. Some had bottles hidden behind nearby fences. Wives seeking a jolly-up also popped out 'for a little fresh air, you know,' to take a taste.

When bladders ached, the men could go along the street to find a handy shadowed garden in which to relieve themselves. The women arranged with each other to make use of closets behind nearby houses.

It was almost midnight when Rupert spotted Violet slipping out the bank's side door. Her husband was on the room's far side, apparently deep in conversation. Rupert observed this in a split-second gap between bobbing shoulders. Turning on his toe as if enslaved to the banjo's thrum, he spun himself out the door and looked to see where she'd gone. Her yellow hem was just disappearing around the side of a house fifty yards down the street.

A cheerful, roistering group spilled out of the bank and set off in the same direction. Rupert fell in behind and then let them go ahead. Slowly, it grew quieter. A jig came to an end and there was a burst of applause before the musicians struck up the next tune. Nobody else left the building. The street was quiet. Rupert followed Violet into the garden and stepped across the small lawn to the shadows cast by a tree's rustling canopy. A half moon shone through its shifting leaves. He waited until he heard a different kind of rustle — that of Violet's skirts as she made her way back.

He saw her profile and the gleam of pearls at her throat and softly called her name. She stopped, startled, turned and saw him. He smiled. She stood there, deciding, her golden gown turned silver by the moon. Then she came towards him across the grass. When he reached out and took her hand she did not resist. He saw a narrow path leading to the house's hidden side and coaxed her there to hide them both from the street.

'Mrs Sutton,' he said, mock serious. 'The intrepid mariner.'

'Mr Beckford. I'm sorry about losing your oar.'

He shook his head. 'No need. It washed up on shore the other day. A customer even delivered it to me. I propped it in the corner. Now, when I should be labouring over ledgers, I sit looking at it.' Rupert wound the ends of her filmy shawl around both hands until he had two fists full of chiffon, tugging her towards him. He whispered, 'I was appalled when I heard what happened. It could have been the end of you, and then I don't know what I would have done.'

She stepped back, forcing him to let go, but then was stopped by the thick ivy that covered the house's brick wall. Rupert bent closer but she turned her face away, eyes glittering. 'I am married, Rupert. This is very unsuitable.'

The sound of revelry and clomping feet drifted to them beneath the trees. Violet shifted against the dark curtain of leaves and a child let out a thin wail inside the house. She put her hand to her mouth to suppress her laughter.

'Suitability does not seem to concern you in most things,' he said. A silence rose and stretched out between them. 'I find myself seeking glimpses of you everywhere,' he whispered. 'I want to spend more time with you, like this, on our own, without fear of discovery.'

'Oh, Rupert, it's too small a town to take risks in. We both have so much to lose. Your position. My reputation. Believe me, I know what it is to lose that. You've reminded me of how it feels to have a light heart, and I'm so grateful for that. But as for more—.'

'Would you not like more?' He raised a hand to the side of her neck, felt the throb of her heartbeat beneath her warm skin. Felt her tremble.

Violet made a faint noise in her throat, a tiny exhalation that sounded like yearning. She glanced towards the street. 'I must go back before I am missed.'

'Then meet me. Can we meet somewhere soon?' His voice was low but playful in the dark. 'Perhaps we could deem it a class. Lessons in seamanship.' 'You've not told anyone I took your boat out, have you?' Rupert raised open moonlit hands. 'Soul of discretion.' Violet gathered her shawl around her. Women's voices, tipsy and garrulous, rose from beyond the hedge that shielded them from passers-by.

'We shall talk more,' Rupert whispered, and then pressed briefly against her, both hands on her shoulders, lingering for a long beat as their bodies touched.

'Wait!' she whispered. She reached up, brought his head to hers and kissed him swiftly, once, then twice, with feeling.

He groaned. 'My God, Violet, how can I leave now?'

She pushed lightly at his chest. 'Go.'

So he did, slipping along the wall so he could exit to the lane on the house's other side. Violet smoothed down her skirts and returned to the dance, giving the women a blithe hello on the way.

'Why, Violet,' said Fanny Bell as she stepped inside. 'You have a pretty ivy leaf in your hair.' She plucked it from the back of Violet's chignon. Its brilliant emerald was turning scarlet at the edges, glossy in the lamplight.

Violet took it in her palm. 'So I do. They are growing up the wall next door. See, a sign of the changing season.'

* * *

THERE WERE many weary heads attending to business as usual the next day, but not so weary that ladies could not meet to advance plans for the upcoming concert. And not too weary to discuss the dancing. 'I am astonished,' breathed Louise, 'by how very freely some women dance. I never know how to behave. My mother always said a maidenly expression is more flattering than a huge grin.'

'But my dear, you are young. You should be smiling fit to beat the band! Did you not see in the *Observer* that wide mouths are in fashion? Look!' Fanny plunged her hand into her purse and brought out a crumpled page of newsprint. 'No longer, it seems, should we be telling our daughters to say "prunes, prunes prunes". The pursed mouth has gone quite out of style.'

Violet sighed. 'May we move on to the concert?'

They drew up a list of settlers who might be persuaded to take the stage. Fanny declared herself talentless except in the field of spreading news and so was delegated the advertising role. Louise could play the piano and was willing to accompany a singing ensemble, if singers could be found.

'Anna, you must give us one of your recitations. You do that with such feeling,' Fanny said.

'If you like. And Thomas is willing to unearth his violin if he can find others to form a quartet.'

'And Violet, what about you?'

She looked up from her notepaper and shrugged. 'Possibly I could dance.'

Fanny sat up straight, eyes wide and avid. 'You dance? On the stage? My word, how very brave.'

'It's not so unusual in London these days. Mothers are thinking that exercise is good for the deportment of their daughters — as of course it is. But it might be seen as unbecoming here. Ignore me, it's a foolish thought.'

'No, we are so starved of fresh forms of culture,' Anna said. 'I can play the piano for you if the music's not too testing. I should love to see you dance. Wouldn't you both?' she pleaded.

Louise and Fanny did not demur and so it was settled, even though Violet walked home with the clear impression that when Fanny had said how brave she was, the word she had really wanted to utter was brazen.

* * *

THERE WAS a letter in the shallow silver dish on the hallstand. It was not for Henry, whose mail made up the bulk of their correspondence. Just this flimsy envelope of eggshell blue lay in wait. Violet slowly unpinned her hat, staring at the pale rectangle, no more than an ounce of paper but with the potential weight of a cannonball.

It looked fresh and new, giving no sign of having been crammed inside canvas mailbags for months. In the top right corner were two depictions of Queen Victoria. A tiara weighed down the queenly brow as she stared blankly from her Royal Mail postage stamps to a distant horizon. This letter from had come twelve thousand miles, as far across her empire as it was possible for a letter to go. Violet called Hester for some lemonade and went into the drawing room. While she waited for the tray to arrive she held the letter in her hands, turning it over, dreading to crack open the seal.

Hester came. 'Ma'am, is there anything else?'

'Thank you, no.'

Later, Hester would say to a friend, 'I've seen 'er look churned up before, but that look she gave me? Stretched tight as piano wire. She well nigh never gets a letter, y'know. Don't she have no family at home at all, is what I wonder.'

* * *

VIOLET, I am in receipt of your letter. You may complain that my reply is slow, but I have been poorly of late and your father's absences have made my responsibilities even more burdensome than before. There is little time left for chitchat, either in person or on paper. You may have native servants to do your bidding in the colonies, but these are straitened times in London. Even people of quality are having to mind their expenditures, which makes running a good house tiresome in the extreme.

Now, to the matter of your enquiry. I am dismayed that you still harbour desires to retrieve the child who was so unfortunately brought into the world as a result of your careless alliance with that utterly unsuitable man.

Given the shame that you brought upon this family you surely cannot think that you can play any part in John's upbringing. He is happily settled as an Underhill and does not have — and must not ever have in future — any inkling of how he came to be born. Do you wish him to grow to manhood knowing that he is a bastard? With all the world knowing it? Surely even you, with your foolish and impetuous ways, can understand that he is far better off where he is, with parents of good standing who care for him.

As their only son, he will never want for anything. He has the inestimable advantage of a good name and, in due course, an inheritance, which, believe me, would never have been possible had he remained the fatherless whelp of a scarlet woman. Your ungratefulness is astonishing. We rescued you from your situation at great expense. Given your disgrace, you had no possible future but that of being a lowly paid governess in some provincial village. You were not only relieved of your burden but were also found a husband who was prepared to take you on despite your tarnished past.

How fortunate you are! Mr Sutton has taken you to a place where your shame is unknown. You even have the chance to bear other children. You will forget the first. It is best if you forget now.

What you wish for will never come true. Please do not refer to this matter again. Any future correspondence asking for news of your abandoned child will be ignored. It shall in fact be burnt, just as has been the case with your recent letter.

There is no evidence in this house of what happened four years ago and I do not intend to carelessly leave any of your pleadings lying in places where they might be seen by prying eyes. Let me impress upon you, though of course you already know it, that your father is also not sympathetic to your cause. There is also no point in writing to your sister. Jane's own reputation suffered as a result of the gossip about you. For a time she was not received in many households, which wounded her to the quick.

Sufficient time has passed for that embarrassment to have faded, aided of course by your subsequent respectable marriage and removal from England. But you should believe me when I say that any revisiting of the scandal you caused would be extremely unwelcome.

You ask yet again for the Underhills' address, presumably so you can also approach them. That would be most unwise and also without point. Mayne and Lydia no longer reside in London and have moved to a post in the Far East which I shall not reveal to you. I take this course deliberately in the hope it will, once and for all, convince you to cease your obsessive quest.

* * *

'SHE WENT OUT AFTER THAT,' Hester later told a friend, shaking her head with such mystification that a corona of hair wisps she'd failed to lash down floated free from her bun. 'In her stout walking boots, with a cane, slashing at hedge tops as she went. Weren't back until nigh on dark. Went straight to her room. No supper. Not a word. If it weren't such an easy house, with no noisy young 'uns to dirty my floors, I'd be thinking to turn in my notice. When your lady's unhappy, there's a certain murk to the air.'

CHAPTER FIFTEEN

*'It is a fact that every man with close growing hair is the owner of a decid-
edly bad temper. Coarse hair denotes obstinacy.'*
— *Bay of Plenty Times*, 1886.

APRIL 5, 1886

'Good news,' said Henry at breakfast. He was bolting down his
food, leaving for Wellington on the high tide to plead the case to government for financial support for the Hot Lakes railway. 'A telegraph from
Bushnell in Sydney. He's had word from London. His bank is apparently well disposed towards investing. So it's at least something positive I
can take to those reluctant fools in the south. One can only wait of
course for Bushnell's full report. Wheels do grind so exceeding slow
when one does business out here. Still, if capital is forthcoming, then life
will fair spin in this small port of ours.'

He considered Violet's downcast face, his greying whiskers in
vigorous motion as he chewed on toast and marmalade. 'It might even
increase the quota of cheerfulness in this house.'

She nodded with little enthusiasm. 'Possibly.'

'Possibly? A man deserves to see an amiable face in the morning,
don't you think? Mmm? Mmm? A benign start to his day? Is it too

much to ask, Violet?' Henry snatched up his cup, spilling tea in the saucer.

'No. It's just that I've had correspondence too, from my stepmother. It was less than generous. Not even civil.'

'So what does she say?

'Very little. I shan't bore you with it.' The long-ago reality of Violet's offspring was never spoken of in the Sutton house. There was too much risk of his small presence becoming some wispy gossamer shape that might seep into the fabric of the building and turn every room sour.

'Overbearing snob, that woman. I don't know why you should care to hear from her at all.'

Violet maintained an effortful silence and sipped at a glass of milk. *I did not abandon him. And his name is George, not John.* When she had faith that she could keep her voice steady, she said, 'I shall be out quite often in the next week or two. We are planning a concert, some of the ladies and myself. Some music and entertainment. We shall be rehearsing.'

'And where will this eruption of culture take place?'

'The Temperance Hall. It has the best stage and there's room enough for those townspeople who might enjoy something other than billiards and grog.'

Henry groaned. 'So when husbands are dragged along we can't even rely on a bolstering sip of something to help us endure scraping violins and tremulous dirges?'

'It may not be so bad. I aim to dance.'

He shot her a sharp glance and raised a shaggy eyebrow. 'In public?'

'That is usually the nature of a concert.'

'I suppose you will do what you wish regardless of my opinion. But make it a demure exhibition. I'll not have my wife being the target of scuttlebutt. Even the most maidenly dance will have the town's hens clucking.'

'Let them. I care less and less. It was the clucking of London's hens that sent me here to the edge of the world.'

Henry pushed back his chair, thumping its legs on the floor. 'By God, Violet, your ingratitude tries me. You sit here, so cosseted, in a land full of promise. This place is made for men of vision. Do you really want to be back in London's foul noise and dirt with people who despise you?' He moved swiftly round the table and bent to whisper in her ear. 'You do not know, my dear, how close you come sometimes to pushing me to my own edge.'

* * *

ANNA WAS ALREADY at the piano when Violet arrived at the hall. The sound of the banging door set up an echo in the room's high corners. Dust motes eddied in the beams of light that slanted through narrow windows.

'What a gust of energy you bring!' said Anna.

'Of a sort,' said Violet. She dug into her bag and brought out sheet music and dancing slippers. 'Here, let's begin.'

They didn't do well at all at first. Unfamiliar with the music, Anna struggled with its flow. Still, in half an hour they'd made tolerable progress.

Afterwards, Violet went to the shore, where she could just see the receding shape of Henry's ship. He would not be looking back. She did not wave.

As she watched she heard the crunch of footsteps and a hesitant voice. 'Mrs Sutton?' It was the shy young clerk who worked at the National Bank. 'Mr Beckford asked if I'd give you his compliments, and this.' He had a small ivory envelope in his extended hand.

'Why, thank you,' she said. 'Please give him our regards.' A careful 'our', not 'my'.

She took a seat on the bench outside Jessie Brown's. Jessie had only one customer, who left, munching on a pastry, as Violet arrived.

It was quiet on the wharf after the departure of Henry's vessel. Gulls soared and squawked. She could hear the shush-shush of sandpaper on timber, the worker whistling tunelessly. A repetitive clanging sounded from the forge along the bay. It was the sort of empty day that sometimes made her want to scream. She would almost rather have gone to Wellington with Henry than stay here. It would at least have given her a change of scene. But he had not asked, being full of his schemes.

But now there was this. Rupert had written 'Mr and Mrs H. Sutton' in his large hand on the front of the envelope. He would have known, however, that Mr Sutton had just sailed away for at least two weeks. In a town this size, the whereabouts of every prominent citizen was common knowledge. There was, therefore, only Mrs Sutton available to receive this piece of correspondence. She tore it open.

Dear Mrs Sutton,

At our last meeting we spoke of the usefulness of instruction in the art of navigation. As it happens, an opportunity has arisen.

My humble craft is now stowed at Gregg's place. He is abed this week with a painful case of the gout and has requested I keep an eye on his stock, his tools of trade and so forth.

It seems to me that an inspection is warranted and so I plan to make a visit at noon tomorrow. You know it, I am sure — the chandlery and boat yard at the north end of the town. Gregg's men will be away home for their midday meal, leaving the way clear for me to mind the store, as it were, and acquaint you with some of the finer points of boat handling.

I write this merely to notify you of this possibility and shall not be offended by your absence, although of course I should be most gratified by your presence.

Yours truly, R. Beckford Esq.

You toy with me, she thought. But even so, she smiled as she tucked the paper back in the envelope. It would be consigned to the kitchen fire as soon she as she got home.

* * *

Later, Rupert would carry in his head a host of sensations arising from the time he spent in the boat shed waiting for Violet. The wafting smells of sawdust, turpentine, varnish and tar, and softness beneath his feet where drifts of wood shavings made a cushion between his boots and the floorboards. When a fantail swept in through the boat-ramp doors, perched on a ceiling beam and fluttered out again, he heard the tiny thrashing of its wings.

Gregg's workers had left for their noonday dinner. Rupert could see they were midway through building a sailboat. He ran his hand along a curved piece of planking, admiring the workmanship. He picked up a dry paintbrush and thrummed its feathery ends against his other hand. Tools hung on hooks on the wall, neatly arrayed. A chisel had been left on the workbench. He tested its gleaming tip with a finger, felt its keen edge.

His own dinghy, the little *Iris*, was stowed at the back of the shed, propped on its stern and leaned against the wall so that only its blue hull was showing. It was one of his few assets. He could see it needed scraping off, sanding and repainting. If only he had the spare cash he would get Gregg to do it. Instead, he'd have to roll up his own shirt-sleeves over the winter to get the job done. Or he might sell it.

He was constantly surprised at how his salary melted away each month. He spent it — guiltily, but with such ease — on things he should shun, the things his mother had always hounded him about: the brandy that took the edge off his empty evenings, and the bounding, beautiful horses. He rued the bet he'd made after hearing Tartan Davy would win the first race at Katikati the previous week. Instead, his purse had been lightened by five pounds.

As for Violet Sutton, now there was a beautiful mare. Slender flanks, shining hair. How he would love to see it springing loose like a mane, instead of bound up so tightly in plaits and knots. He took out his watch. Twenty-five minutes past the hour. She was not coming. How foolish to think she might.

But as he turned, there she was. The aromatic shavings on the floor had silenced her tread. She wore a demure dress of grey-blue lawn, a colour so drab that it seemed she might have worn it on purpose so as to cause little notice as she slipped through the dozing town. She had a covered basket that she placed on a tool-strewn table.

'Good afternoon,' she said.

'And here I was thinking you would disappoint me.'

She looked around the shed at the stacked timber, coiled ropes and rolls of canvas. 'Would I have, if I'd failed to be here?' She moved past him, away from the sunlit windows into the shadows at the back of the shed. 'Ah, there it is.' She spotted the upturned *Iris* and patted its keel. 'Scene of my crime. Were you very angry when you heard about it?'

'I'm not altogether sure what did happen. It was all just rumours, but then my missing oar was a kind of proof. I knew then that it had to be you. I was frightened for you rather than angry. And guilty too. I should never have let you persuade me. Is it true about the trousers?'

'Are you shocked?'

He grinned. 'More disappointed that it's a sight I missed.'

She laughed. 'Thank heavens you did. I looked a fright. But oh, Rupert, you'd not believe how a change of clothing could bestow such a sense of freedom.'

His hand went out to touch her dress but she moved away, back to the sunlight. The intensity of their last meeting, in moonlight, seemed to have melted in the raw brightness of day. She took the cloth from the top of her basket. 'As you mentioned lunchtime in your note I've brought some pound cake. I thought perhaps, as a single man, you don't get to eat cake very often.'

'You're very thoughtful. As well as beautiful.' He broke his gaze for only as long as it took to reach for the knapsack he'd left on a chair. 'I have only the last of my butter fruits. This one feels ever so slightly soft so perhaps it is ripe for the eating. Shall we see?' Unclasping his penknife, he inserted its tip deep into the fruit's skin and drew the blade round in a circle to cut it in half. Then, with a twist of his wrists, he coaxed the fruit apart. The green, oily inside of it was unblemished, one half centred with its single dense brown stone, the other with its flawless cavity.

'They're strangely handsome,' she said.

'Did you know this is said in some societies to be beneficial for the skin?'

'I had heard that, yes.'

'I've not tried it for that purpose, have you?' She shook her head. 'Well, shall we?' He scooped out a knob of the fruit with his finger and turned mock obsequious. 'If madam will allow?'

She proffered her right hand with an odd sense of déja vu. It reminded her of her experience with Madam Francini. But the two occasions were so very different.

Rupert had no interest in the lines that crossed her palm. Instead he applied a knob of green and smeared it over her skin, massaging it with both of his hands. The fruit's oily flesh melted under his touch. Their palms slipped and slid as he rubbed. Then, gazing at her face, he gently tugged at her thumb and each finger in turn before lifting her hand to his lips and slowly taking her forefinger in his mouth, sucking it clean.

She gasped a little.

He dropped her hand and stepped in and this time when their kiss began it did not stop. She moved back with the momentum of his push until her lower back thudded against a table spread with charts. Still kissing her, he reached down and plucked at her skirt, pleating it up with urgent fingers, diving into the layers of cloth until he could press his palm against her lawn pantaloons and the mound beneath. Wet, it was. *Good Christ*, Rupert thought, *she is ready for this*. They broke for air in the same instant, eyes wide, mouths open, panting.

And then both their heads whipped round at the sound of heavy boots trudging up the steps to the door. Rupert spun away and Violet frantically swished her skirt into place. By the time Gregg's apprentice carpenter stepped back into the shed to begin his afternoon's work, she was merely a pink-cheeked housewife with her basket, offering Rupert flyers about an upcoming concert. 'I know Mr Gregg's partial to music,' she was saying, 'so perhaps you could give him this? You might like to come along yourself. Oh, and my Hester heard he was very poorly with his gout so she sent along some cake for him.'

She took it from her basket and laid it down, fragrant in buttery brown paper, giving both Rupert and the carpenter a teasing caution. 'Be sure not to eat it all up yourselves before it gets to his door.'

'Mrs Sutton,' said Rupert, reproving. 'What do you take us for?'

She clicked her tongue as she departed. 'It's my observation that most men find a sweet slice of something very difficult to ignore.'

The carpenter's mouth twitched with a sly grin.

'Have some respect,' snapped Rupert. 'Get on with your work now so I can report to Mr Gregg that all is well.'

As Violet walked along The Strand the breeze got up, chilling her well-buttered right hand. She quickly wiped it with the cloth from her basket. It was foolish, of course. How could anyone know or even care that she had been trying out an exotic but harmless salve from a local garden. What harm was there in that?

She glanced down. The massaged skin looked unchanged, but still tingled from the sensations she'd felt as Rupert slowly rotated his firm thumb in the soft cup of her palm. He'd ignited her desire with that lingering, impudent suck. His bright hair, sunstruck, had dazzled her eyes as his hand slid between her thighs.

She kept her face formal and polite as she passed people in the street so that nobody could sense the heat she felt inside.

CHAPTER SIXTEEN

'DANCING, DEPORTMENT and CALISTHENICS — bonne tenue et maintien. Monsieur Paul Bibron, from Paris, has commenced tuition at Masonic Hall Princes-street as follows: Select Adult Class, Wednesday, 7.30 p.m. Select Juvenile Class, Saturday, 3 p.m.'
— Advertisement for dance classes, Auckland Observer.

APRIL 15, 1886

Violet and Anna disagreed about the recitation choice for the concert. Anna was fond of *The Courtship of Miles Standish*, Longfellow's epic tale of the love lives of three *Mayflower* pilgrims.

'There's only one scene that speaks to me,' argued Violet. 'It's when they're watching the *Mayflower* as she sails away, leaving them behind. Here, let me see.' She took the book from Anna as they walked to the hall for their next rehearsal, flipping through it to the lines she wanted. She read them aloud:

Sun-illumined and white, on the eastern verge of the ocean
Gleamed the departing sail, like a marble slab in a graveyard;
Buried beneath it lay forever all hope of escaping.

'That part is so bleak,' Anna said.

Violet snapped the pages shut. 'Well, what hope do *we* have of escaping? And they went merely across the Atlantic. It's a pond compared with the oceans we've crossed. When I watch ships depart it always makes me feel marooned.'

'But people go back and forth, despite the distance. Mr Sutton could surely—.'

'Henry will do only as he pleases. He travels, yes, but without his permission I do not. Well, *cannot* is more the truth of it as I have no money of my own.' She gestured with the book. 'And as for the ninnies in this poem, they are simply irksome.'

'But it's so popular.'

'I know, but I like my characters more decisive. Have you read William Kingdon Clifford?'

Anna shook her head.

'The Freethinker leader, and so brilliant! He died, poor man, from consumption, and only in his thirties. He wrote a line that I admire above all else: "It is wrong always, everywhere, and for anyone, to believe anything upon insufficient evidence".'

'How very sensible. It seems somehow heartless, though. Is there no room for faith?'

'No, Anna, that's the whole point! No dogma, no tales ladled out as unalterable truth, no mindless deference to men in pulpits laying down the law. We must think for ourselves. It's why the Freethinkers' flower, the pansy, is so perfect.'

'How so?'

'Because the name comes from the French word for thought, pensée. Pansies look like little faces nodding in the breeze as if they're thinking.'

Anna chuckled. 'No wonder we don't see you often in church. Mr Larkin would be thoroughly alarmed. Even Thomas might take issue, though he's not anywhere near so godly as his father. Still, when you grow up in a missionary's house it can't help but rub off.' Violet laughed. 'Will you tell him of my shameless thoughts?'

'Certainly not.' And even as Anna said it, she realised she'd snipped another tiny thread in the complex knot of trust that bound her to her husband.

* * *

WHEN FANNY HEARD that more rehearsing was planned she was eager
to observe. 'May I come?' she pleaded. 'It will so ease the ticket selling if
I can wax lyrical.'

The talent list was building. Thomas and some passably musical
friends would play the lively *Marche Romaine*. Fanny had talked a
euphonium player into tootling a velvety tune or two. A fisherman with
a clear tenor voice would sing a rollicking sea song. Susan Spooner, the
watchmaker's daughter, was roped in too. 'Uncommonly good at the
fiddle,' her father assured Anna. She needed no persuading. Any talent
was welcome.

Now, with less than three weeks to go, a few on the list had gathered
for a run-through. Anna had picked a part of Longfellow's saga about
how hard it was for a person to take back something already spilled from
their lips. In four minutes she was done, flushed and anxious. 'Well done!'
Violet cried. Louise found enough confidence to play a solo. Another
volunteer launched into a tremulous sentimental song called 'Far Away'.

'You see,' Violet whispered in Anna's ear. 'We are all obsessed with
distance.'

And then it was Violet's turn. She had slipped into a side room to
change into dancing clothes and then waited her turn in a long red cloak
that showed only her dancing slippers. But now she stood and put it
aside.

'Oh, my word,' said Fanny. Violet wore a sleeveless white silk bodice,
lightly boned, with a fichu of gauze wrapping her creamy shoulders. It
was tied in a soft knot between her breasts, leaving her arms exposed.
There was a wide gathered skirt, scandalously short, barely covering her
knees.

'It is as well, is it not,' said Violet into the silence, 'that my
pantaloons cover up my wicked shins?'

She ran up the short flight of steps to the stage, struck a pose and
said, 'Anna? Let us begin.'

Anna's fingers knew the tune now and Violet began on cue, her skirt
a diaphanous bell that cast spinning shadows against the rear wall. Her

audience had not seen such a sight before. Dancing was the jigs, polkas and awkward waltzes they'd all done at the bank a few short weeks earlier. This solitary expression of grace — with lofting arms, tilted chin and pointed toes — was a different sight altogether.

As they watched, the main door squeaked open, but so riveted were they that none of them heard it. If Violet noticed the entrance of a black-suited figure she did not falter. Even after the visitor roared, '*What is this*?', the swish of Violet's ribboned shoes continued for a few more seconds before she came to a stop.

'Reverend Larkin,' she said. 'How kind of you to call.' She stayed where she was, pink-cheeked with exertion.

'What is this?' he repeated and then strode to the steps and climbed onstage. Violet swiftly switched places. She tripped down the steps, retrieved her cloak, wrapped herself in its folds and turned to face him. He stood isolated on the bare boards. Anna pushed back the piano stool. 'We are rehearsing, Reverend,' she said. 'For our concert — I expect you've heard about it — to raise funds for schoolbooks.'

'Is there some difficulty?' asked Violet.

'We cannot have this exhibition!' He thumped back down to the main floor of the hall. 'Concerts are for uplifting music and poetry, not to display women in flimsy clothing.'

'Could you see my ankles, Mr Larkin? Oh my, I was sure I had them safely tucked away from public gaze.' Mocking a worried frown, Violet hitched her cloak and looked down at her feet. Her dance slippers revealed small half moons of skin on the tops of her feet.

Larkin averted his gaze. 'You are not one of my flock, of course. But the rest of you!' He scorched the group with his glare. 'I'm surprised you should be party to this unseemly display. In the Temperance Hall, of all places.'

The soprano picked up her bag and, muttering an apology, headed for the door. The euphonium player hitched his instrument over his shoulder and also left. Louise began to gather her things, too. 'This is all so unfortunate,' she whimpered.'

You must give us some credit for our public spirit,' said Anna. 'We wish only to help the school. Only last week you were saying how important it is for we townsfolk to pull together.'

'Not towards depravity.' Larkin shook his head with such disapproving vigour that specks of dandruff took flight.

'How dare you accuse me so,' said Violet. 'I was taught by a French master of dance in London. Look at the newspaper. You'll find such lessons being advertised in Auckland at the Masonic Hall.'

Larkin sniffed. 'Who knows what they get up to there. This is our *Temperance* Hall, Mrs Sutton, where we do not countenance anything but the most moderate behaviour. And moderation is not the word I'd use to describe the sight of your unclad limbs.'

Violet flung off her cloak and stood straight and furious before him. 'Oh, my arms.' She turned back and forth as if to taunt him with their nakedness. 'Useful things these, good for lifting and gardening and sewing, but never to be seen? What is wrong with them? Are they not just like yours?' She reached out and lightly slapped his right arm above the elbow.

There was a collective gasp from the other women. Larkin took a startled step backwards, clapping his left hand to his sleeve as if he'd been stung.

'Mrs Sutton!' hissed Fanny. 'How could you!'

Anna swept up the cloak and threw it over Violet's shoulders. 'Please stop. It's not wise.'

Violet turned away and stalked, cloak billowing, into the changing room, slamming the door.

'What extraordinary behaviour,' said the parson. He flicked at his assaulted sleeve with disdainful fingers.

'I'm sorry,' Anna said. 'She is not herself.'

'I most certainly am!' came a shout from behind the door. Fanny and Louise let out small distressed noises.

'Well, whatever self she is, I trust we will hear no more of this. The hall's management committee meets tomorrow and I was hoping to tell them of the wholesome evening you're planning. It seems we must decide if there'll be a concert at all.'

'But people have been practising for weeks,' said Anna. 'We've sold tickets! We cannot cancel and disappoint everyone.'

'Better disappointed than scandalised. I bid you good day.' He nodded stiffly. His boots cracked on the floorboards as he left.

'I am mortified, mortified,' moaned Fanny.

Anna slammed down the piano lid 'Grim old tartar.'

'What?' Fanny protested, jabbing her finger at the still-closed door. 'Always, she goes too far. We must do as he wants. I, for one, have no interest in being ostracised by people I've known for much longer than I've been acquainted with *her*.'

Louise nodded in vigorous agreement. 'She wheedled her way into our circle with her blue goggles and her fancy style. And now are we all to be laughing stocks?'

'Especially me,' said Fanny. 'I've been persuading the whole town to come along. Imagine the shame if I now have to spread word that it's cancelled, all because of that *scallyhoot*.' She snatched up her parasol. 'Come, Louise. We'll catch up with Mr Larkin and smooth things over.' She flung over her shoulder, 'Anna, you must make sure she withdraws.'

Anna sighed. 'Please don't be too hasty. I'll talk to her.'

Fanny and Louise hurried out. Silence fell. The sun was low now, its slanting rays making opaque screens of the dusty windows. Anna had to go home. Chores beckoned, as always, and Dinah would be anxious to get away. She knocked on the door of Violet's lair and went in. She was fully dressed in her street clothes now, sitting in the gloom on a low bench, shoulders slumped.

'They've all gone,' Anna said.

'With feathers all awry. My temper is so unpredictable. I keep it buckled down so hard, Anna, but then moments erupt that are so provoking it's as if someone has lit a wick in me.' Anna saw the shine of her teeth. 'It was fun, though, wasn't it? Do you think the Reverend has ever felt the measure of a woman's hand before?'

'You are incorrigible. Don't you realise I have to go and sit in front of him again next Sunday to hear another sermon? Which this week will no doubt be all about the modesty of women.'

'Why do you have to go?'

'Because Thomas expects it. It's where we see people and smile and converse and take part in the life of the town. He has to be seen as a good, upstanding man who can be trusted to handle people's money.'

'Mere social ritual, then? I'd have thought that for Larkin church-going is about avoiding hell and arriving in heaven. And how do we know they even exist?' Violet rummaged in her satchel and pulled out a printed journal. 'Here, this is for you. I've received some back copies from England.' Anna took it, aware of the minutes thudding by, barely glancing at the front page except to notice its title, *The Freethinker*. 'What about your dance? We have no choice but to go along with him.'

Violet shrugged. 'Cancel me, then. Strike me out. Tear my name from the bill. It's not important enough to fight for — just another small victory for narrow-mindedness. And another reason for me to leave this place somehow.'

'Are you really intent on that?'

'Oh yes.'

Anna felt a stab of sadness. Was it envy or the prospect of loss? She didn't know. 'I would miss you.'

Violet rose, put on her hat and stabbed it into place with a pin. 'I also, my dear. But in my heart and my mind I know what I need to do.'

* * *

'WHAT'S THIS?' said Thomas after Jamie had been put to bed. He flipped pages of *The Freethinker*. Violet had scrawled, 'For Anna' in a flurry of violet ink across the top of its front page. Anna had dropped it on the hallstand when she got home half an hour late, full of placatory noises for impatient Dinah, fractious Jamie and hungry Thomas.

Anna yawned as she stacked plates on a shelf. 'Oh, I haven't had time to even look at it. Violet lent it to me.'

'A radical sort of organ, isn't it? Take care, Anna, that she doesn't turn your head.' She heard him turn a page, grunting at something he read there. 'Does Henry Sutton share these views?'

'I don't know. We've not discussed it.' Anna felt a swell of irritation. 'Don't judge me, Thomas. It's just words on paper and I know very little about it. But I would like to be able to make up my own mind.'

She turned to look at him then and caught the lift of a dubious eyebrow. He said nothing, but put the journal down and pushed it from him. 'My father is visiting late next month. Better not have it on display then.'

'You did not say.'

'I knew only today when I received his note. And of course you've been out.'

'So he'll be here for the concert?' Anna tried to lighten the mood. 'Best produce a scintillating *Marche Romaine* then.'

Thomas sighed. 'If only that was all I had to worry about. Business is not good, Anna. I keep on receiving harsh letters from Auckland. Nothing is moving. There are so many investment openings here — the cheese factory up the coast and White Island with its sulphur just waiting to be harvested. Farmers are desperate for fertiliser. And yet do the locals have a vision for profits to be made? Do they dare to buy shares? Pumpkin heads, the lot of them.'

'Will your father stay with us?' Anna hoped not. The old man was much given to silent hours of study and writing. Presumably he had somehow tolerated noise when his own tribe of children were babies, but Jamie's shrieks seemed anathema to him now. His last stay had been a trial.

Thomas smiled. 'You can breathe easy. He'll be at the Clarendon. He has meetings with the local clergy and intimated they would need silence for their deliberations.'

'Ha! Noise from the drinkers will not disturb the good gentlemen then?'

'I imagine it's a clamour they're used to.'

Anna went to check that Jamie had not kicked off his blankets — the nights were getting chilly now. It was true, she thought, as she kissed his forehead and tucked his chubby fists under the bedclothes, that the Church was overly intrusive in directing everyone's lives. Everyone knew the weight of expectations from the pulpit. One usually did not kick against them, but the very thought of Larkin's interference made her swell with indignation.

On the other hand, Violet had certainly provoked him. Someone would have to smooth down everyone's feathers if the concert was to proceed. It seemed it would have to be her.

CHAPTER SEVENTEEN

'One of the pluckiest of colonial banking corporations is the National Bank of New Zealand. The National is a younger brother of the Bank of New Zealand and has, I am told, done the latter a great deal of harm. In Tauranga and other country towns, business men are divided into two cliques, viz., National men and New Zealand men.'
— *Auckland Observer*, 1886.

MAY 5, 1886

'Those fools in Wellington have to force themselves to dredge up even the slightest pinch of vision,' Henry Sutton grumbled to Thomas. They were in the Clarendon's noisy bar. Henry had returned on today's tide after five weeks of absence. At home he had exchanged a bare few words with his wife. Her welcome was cool, so he set out sourly back down the path to the shore, hauling Thomas out from behind his desk on the way so that he could complain to him about the perfidy of politicians.

'The last time I was there they regaled me with assurances that land valuation along the route would be expedited. It's all London is waiting on so they can order plant, secure ships, hire the right sort of navvies.

Advertisements are already being prepared to attract special settlers. We need the best rail layers we can find and there are such men wanting a fresh life in a new land.' Sutton banged down his glass, slopping whisky on the table. 'But here, we get no enthusiasm at all. *Nothing*. It's enough to make a man sell up and flit off to a place more ready for muscular endeavour. What d'you say, Thomas? Are you prepared to languish in a land that doesn't have the sense to pull its own boots up out of the bog of apathy? Eh? Eh?'

'Henry was rather the worse for wear,' Thomas told Anna when he finally arrived home. 'He insisted I should match his consumption but it was more than I could manage, even if he is my largest investor. And then in walked my father, cold sober after a day out at some Maori village, calling for broth. Broth! The other patrons were chortling into their beers. And there I was with a glass of ale at my right hand, just to keep Sutton company. Father was polite, of course, but I could feel his ire.'

'Was Mr Sutton polite to him?'

'Boisterous, more like. He looked up and yelled, "Zounds, another worshipful! Would you join us in a dram?" Rupert saved me, grinning away as if he found the situation achingly mirthful. But at least he saw my embarrassment and stepped in. Dragged Sutton off to the bar, giving me a wink on the way.'

'So you could explain the ale, then, to your father.'

'Oh yes, lamely. He mumbled darkly into his beard in the fashion I remember so well from when I was a lad. And of course, the Reverend Larkin was there too — only too happy to chip in about the den of iniquity that Tauranga is becoming with its bars and unseemly roistering. He mentioned Sutton's wife too.'

'Oh? How unkind was he?'

'The name of Jezebel was mentioned.' Thomas got up and groaned. 'Oh, ale and tea combined make too much liquid for a man to endure in one sitting.'

Anna waited as he went outside to the closet. She was sitting upright and still when he returned. He would have gone straight to bed had she not said firmly, 'I believe I shall not be attending service next Sunday.'

Thomas sighed. 'Please, my love, can we not discuss this at some other time?'

'Violet is my friend. She is a good woman who does her best to live with a tiresome bully. And she is no Jezebel. Mr Larkin makes completely unwarranted assumptions.'

'A bully? Who is making assumptions now? You will not make an issue of this, Anna, and we will carry on as normal. And I'm tired now. I bid you goodnight.'

Too annoyed to settle, Anna did not follow him immediately. She could see *The Freethinker* still lying where it had been tossed a few days earlier. She picked it up, took it to the kitchen table, turned up the lamp and sat down to read beneath the flame's buttery glow.

'*The Freethinker* is an anti-Christian organ,' she read, 'and must therefore be chiefly aggressive. It will wage relentless war against superstition in general, and against Christian superstition in particular; and it will not scruple to employ for the same purpose any weapons of ridicule or sarcasm that may be borrowed from the armoury of common sense.'

She made a small, muffled sound of surprise, slapped it shut and slipped it into a drawer, out of sight. How incendiary it was. How curious it made her. Best, she thought, to read it later, in private, when she was not so very tired.

She needed sleep. The concert was tomorrow night and they had much to do before opening the Temperance Hall's doors.

* * *

IT WAS plain by mid-morning that not merely one but two of their performers had fallen ill. Both the soprano and the euphonium player had some chesty ailment that was spreading through the town.

Fanny was in a lather of anxiety when she met Anna at the hall. 'This place will be full, but now we have only a scant half hour of items for the bill.'

Violet was there, too, having offered, by way of placation, to help put out chairs and arrange greenery. She was quiet, saying little as she pushed fern stems into vases.

'Maybe you can find the banjo player who had so many feet tapping at our dance?' suggested Anna. 'Might he be prevailed upon?'

'Perhaps, though he is rather a rough sort of fellow.'

'Better a dishevelled performer than a dissatisfied audience. And we have little choice.' But soon Louise dashed in with news that the banjo plucker had gone to work the gold mines at Waihi. 'Oh my heavens,' Fanny quavered. 'What are we to do?'

'There's always me,' ventured Violet. Silence fell among them. She ended it with a laugh. 'Don't look so alarmed. I'll not upset the Reverend again. I do have a voice, however. There's no time for me to learn a recitation, but I could do a reading.'

Fanny looked wary. Violet might have apologised for her temper but was still not in Fanny's good books. 'What would you read?'

'I don't know yet. I'd have to go home to find a suitable passage.'

'Something light and bright,' said Anna. 'A dry passage would not fit the bill, I think.' 'Of course. You know you can depend on me for drama.'

'Oh, not too much drama,' pleaded Louise.

Violet smiled. 'I'll keep it brief, no more than five minutes, so there'll be no time for anyone to expire from boredom.'

'But it still leaves us lacking a performer,' fretted Fanny. She hesitated. 'There is one possibility. Madame Francini is here again, on her way back from Napier. I hear she sometimes demonstrates hypnotism. Do you think it would appeal?'

'Of course,' said Violet. 'We'd have everything then from song to sensation.'

Louise winced. 'But would Mr Larkin approve? And would she expect payment? If she demands a fee we'll make no money at all.'

'We can but ask,' said Anna. 'And as for Mr Larkin, this is our concert to manage even if we are using his hall. Our cause is just, our need is pressing. I vote we make an urgent visit to Madame.'

'Bravo,' said Violet. 'That's settled then. Shall I go and ask her?' She thrust some leafy stems at Anna. 'Can you finish the flowers? I'll make her come, I promise!'

They watched her go. Louise wrung her hands. 'Are we mad to do this? Horace doesn't hold with hypnotism.'

'Oh, Louise, where's your backbone?' Anna snapped. But she felt anxious too. What did any of them know of hypnotism? There was a good chance the Reverend Larkin would see it as the devil's work. She remembered then, too, that Thomas's father would probably attend. The thought made her sigh.

CHAPTER EIGHTEEN

'A very successful concert took place in the Temperance Hall on Tuesday evening last. An attractive programme had been arranged, and was the means of drawing a very good house, the Hall being well filled, though not overcrowded.'
— *Concert review, Bay of Plenty Times.*

MAY 6, 1886

Madame Francini agreed. The news spread as Fanny made her rounds. Few had seen mesmerism in action and there was soon a rush on the last tickets.

By 8 p.m. there was standing room only. The early items went down well, Anna thought. Even her own recitation fetched pleasing applause.

Singers and musicians came and went. Then it was Violet's turn. She had chosen a dress of grey silk with a touch of white lace at the throat. Her hair was pulled into a neat knot. Behind Anna, Fanny declared to her husband that Mrs Sutton could join a nunnery looking like that. 'Shhhh,' someone hissed.

Violet stood for long, silent moments at centre-stage, her pale face illuminated by the row of oil lamps at her feet. And then she smiled, and began.

'I'd like to read a short passage by an author for whom I have great respect. She lives in Italy now but I did in fact meet her once in London when I was young. She took scant notice of me that day on the corner of Portland Place and Regent Street. My father introduced me. I learnt years later that he used to attend her salons in the Langham Hotel on that corner. Her name is Maria Louise de le Ramé, but some of you may know her as Ouida.'

There were mixed reactions in the hall —many of the townspeople could barely read and an author's name was of no more account than that of an obscure beetle. There was a whispered chorus of 'Who?' as neighbours consulted each other.

'I can see,' said Violet, 'that many of you are not familiar with her, but the power of her words may impress you nonetheless. She lived at the Langham for four years and held court in her bedroom there.' Small murmurs arose. 'The room was lit by candles day and night and filled with flowers. In this space she received statesmen, politicians, soldiers and literary lights.' There were a few jeers and whistles. Violet calmly added, 'And occasionally, my own father.'

'What game is she playing?' Thomas whispered to Anna. 'It seems most disloyal to her family.' He could see Henry Sutton further along the row, leaning forward with jutting chin. He looked as if he might spring off his chair.

Violet waited for the fuss to die down. 'While that may sound some-what decadent, she wrote many touching stories that show her concern for the children of the poor. You know, I'm sure, that tonight your generous purchase of tickets means that children in our own small town, so very far from Portland Place, will have a chance to read books and better themselves. The ladies who organised this evening's enter-tainment are most grateful to you.'

'However, Ouida's work also reminds us that many children have little to eat, are forced to work ferociously hard, with scarcely any rest, and are often cruelly treated.'

Henry Sutton suddenly stood, his back and shoulders rigid, but before he could speak, she smiled sweetly down at him. 'You are eager for me to begin, Henry, I know, but be calm, I am nearly there.' He glanced back, saw the whites of many goggling eyes fixed upon him, and subsided.

Violet continued. 'This story, called "Folle Farine", was written in 1871. It describes an episode in the life of a young girl employed by a miller. He decides she does not work hard enough and decides to teach her a lesson.' She began to read, her voice slipping into tones that were drenched with emotion.

He seized her by the shoulder with one hand, and with the other lifted the rope. It curled round her breast and back, again and again and again; she shuddered, but she did not utter a single cry. He struck her ten times with the same number of strokes as there remained sacks uncarried. He did not exert any great strength, for had he used his uttermost he would have killed her, and she was of value to him; but he scourged her with a merciless exactitude in the execution of his threat, and the rope was soon wet with drops of her bright young blood.

Wives and husbands shifted uncomfortably on their hard chairs and muttering began to rise, but Violet read on with a ringing voice.

And in the warmth the child shuddered under the scourge; against the light the black rope curled like a serpent darting to sting; among the sun-fed blossoms there fell a crimson stain.

Violet came to a stop at last, snapped the book shut, and curtseyed. 'Thank you,' she said, stepped down from the stage and went back to the seat alongside her husband's rigid shoulder. There was a thin scatter of applause. Some were startled, some puzzled, some moved, some shocked by the ghastly contrast of blood and sunlight that she'd poured into their minds.

Violet turned her head to Anna, her eyes seeking reassurance. Anna could only give her a strained nod. What she really wanted to do was stride over and shake her. Where were the bright words Violet promised to deliver? They'd wanted something light and frothy but instead she had brought brutality.

Anna did not dare turn around to check the expression on Fanny's face. She could see it without looking. Her mouth would be making a scandalised 'O'.

Thomas cleared his throat. 'Well, my dear, that was quite an act. I think I feel a little ill.'

'I don't know what she was thinking.'

'Such a lurid passage. Did you know she would read it?' Anna shook her head.

Then Thomas saw the bulky figure of Madame Francini as she climbed up the steps to the stage, steadied by her husband's supporting arm. 'And what's this? Yet another surprise?'

The Francinis were an odd couple. He seemed slight in his dark suit alongside her stout frame. Flung around her shoulders was a deep purple shawl embroidered with brilliant Oriental birds and flying dragons. Gleaming earrings swung from her fleshy lobes. Her eyes glittered, round as dark grapes in the golden lamp glow.

Mr Francini set a chair and a small table at centre stage. He placed a gong and a candelabra on the table and drew from his pocket a shiny pendant on a chain. After a flourish it too went on the table top.

His wife took up a mannish stance and surveyed her audience. There was a bold energy about her that had had been absent the day she came to tea. Then she had been a domesticated creature who simply read palms; now her persona had shifted to something altogether more wild. She was contained, however. Showmanship was all the more powerful when an audience wondered (and were a little afraid of) powers they suspected were being kept hidden.

'Bonsoir,' she announced. 'I believe that when you depart you will be impressed by the power of ze mind. C'est enormé, n'est-ce pas? *Very big.* What is in 'ere,' and she leaned forward to tap on her broad forehead, 'is the most wonderful part of your body. C'est merveilleux!'

'What's she saying?' muttered Fanny's Wilfred. 'Why can't she speak English?'

'Just listen!' Fanny ordered, jabbing his ribs with her elbow.

'Maintenant,' declared the hypnotist, sanding up straight. Her sharp eyes roamed over the crowd. 'I need a volunteer.' A silence lingered. 'You, m'sieur?'

All heads turned to the man at whom her finger pointed. 'Aye, Beckford, take the stage!' someone yelled. 'Show us what you're made of.' A chorus of encouragement rose to the rafters.

Rupert got up from his chair and — willingly enough, to judge from his grin — sprang up the steps and took a bow. Madame Francini asked for his name and he gave it. 'Well, my young buck,' she said. 'Let us see how well we do.'

A hush fell as she turned her back to the audience, apparently taking time to compose herself as her husband silently ushered Rupert to the chair, drew out some matches and lit the candles. Chair legs scraped as people nudged their seats sideways to obtain a better view.

Madame Francini turned to Rupert, stood over him, took up the pendant and swung it before his eyes, speaking in such low tones that no one could hear her words. Mr Francini was merely a dark, still shadow at the back of the stage. Her muttering went on for quite some time. The coin-shaped pendant gleamed in its gentle arc. Rupert's eyes were fixed upon it. Nobody coughed or passed a remark. Instead, a tension grew, waxing fat and expectant. Outside in the night an owl let out three plaintive calls and still the silence endured.

The smile faded from Rupert's face and his eyes closed. He looked to be asleep, though he still sat upright on the chair. Madame Francini laid the pendant down and addressed the crowd. 'Your friend, M'sieur Beckford, is now in my power.' Uneasiness rippled along the rows, but before it could increase she raised a hand. 'There is no danger. He will feel at ease all the time and on waking will remember nothing.'

Rupert would not wake at all until she sounded the gong, she said. Also, she would not ask him to do anything unseemly. In any case, his moral training would hold firm even in his trance. She turned to look at his impassive face. The audience gazed too, fascinated by being able to stare in a way that was so strangely intimate.

'My purpose is to show you that our minds are deeper than we know. It is, as you know, terra incognita.'

Louise Archer whimpered, making her Horace sigh. 'T-e-r-r-a,' he quietly spelled out. 'It's Latin for land, unknown land.'

'Some of you have heard — yes? — that hypnosis can ease pain,' Madame Francini said. 'Before the discovery of ether many people used it so they could go to the doctor or dentist without fear. That was good, hmm?'

There was, however, thought Anna, something slightly predatory in the way she now circled Rupert's chair as if deciding how to use him to best effect. 'This evening we see a mere soupçon, small evidence of the power of the mind.' And with that she took from under her sash a long hat pin. The wicked glint of lamplight on its shining shaft was visible to all. 'Mr Beckford,' she said quietly. 'Open your eyes. We are about to prove the depth of your trance. You will feel no pain when I penetrate your skin. And there will be no blood.'

She asked him to stand and remove his jacket. He did so, placed it on the table, and then took his seat again with an untroubled face. Madame Francini beckoned her husband. He came forward, unfastened the end of Rupert's shirt sleeve and rolled the linen up to his elbow, turning the arm out to reveal the smooth, pale skin. 'You would like to see more closely, yes?' Madame asked the audience. 'I know my needle is fine and this room is large. Three of you may come up on the stage to observe. Is anyone willing?'

An eager trio were soon out of their seats and up the steps, keen to see Rupert flinch.

'Voila!' cried the hypnotist and brought down the glittering point, pushing it three times into Rupert's arm between elbow and wrist. She pressed so firmly that a half inch of the needle's shaft disappeared into his flesh with each jab. Rupert did not move. One of the observers, a hulking young stevedore, fainted, hitting the floorboards with a thud. A woman whimpered at the back of the room.

'Leave him!' snapped Madame Francini when someone started forward. 'It is only a faint.' She kept her eyes on Rupert. 'Sir, do you feel well?'

'Of course,' he replied, looking without concern at the line of pink but bloodless puncture marks. Madame put her needle away and her husband rolled down and re-buttoned the sleeve.

'Now,' she said. 'It's time for you to enjoy yourself. We must clear a space. Vite, vite, Mr Beckford! Hurry! Pretty girls are coming and you must be ready to choose one for a dance.'

She ordered him to put the furniture back against the wall and then sweep the floor. He instantly got to work with an invisible broom. The swooner pushed himself upright, flushing with embarrassment as the audience applauded.

'Enough!' she cried. Rupert stopped. She went to him and cooed, 'Look, Mr Beckford. Such beautiful ladies are here at the ball. See? They love to dance.' And as the audience hooted, she pointed to the townsmen on the stage. One was Gregg the boat builder, recovered from his gout and wearing a none-too-clean shirt that barely contained the swell of his rotund belly.

Madame Francini whirled her arm. 'Music, maestro!' The notes of a sprightly waltz rang out. Mr Francini had slipped to the piano stool and was plunking out the melody. The entire hall rocked with mirth as Rupert gave Gregg a courtly bow, pulled him into his arms and held him close, twirling him around the stage and beaming fondly into Gregg's amazed and ruddy face.

* * *

AS PEOPLE CHATTERED AND LAUGHED, lingering outside the hall, Anna knew she should be satisfied with the evening's success. Rupert's unconscious antics had ended the programme on a high note. Madame Francini was handing out dozens of cards; more good business would be coming her way. Rupert's friends were smacking him on the back and Gregg was being thoroughly mocked. 'When will you two be plighting your troth?' one of the pie-shop cooks asked with sly good humour.

Thank God, thought Anna, they'd not had to end the programme with Violet's blood-soaked reading. She looked around the thinning crowd and could not see her. Did Violet have to conjure up a child's pain to explain the reason for the concert? Or prattle about an author most of them had never heard of and a London hotel so very grand that almost nobody in the room would have dared venture inside?

Not that she would frame her questions so hurtfully. Her biggest concern was the state of Violet's mind. The Suttons were nowhere to be seen. Anna's eye did happen to light on the Reverend Larkin at a precise moment when he was looking at her. Their gaze did not lock for more than a second, but in that brief moment she saw deep coldness.

CHAPTER NINETEEN

'A modern dispute: A. "Are you a thought-reader?" B. "No, not I." A.
"Lucky for you, else you might feel offended."
— Bay of Plenty Times, 1886.

MAY 7, 1886

'Thomas, a word!' Thomas turned on his way down to The Strand.
It was early morning. He saw Rupert loping after him, fox-bright hair
bouncing, a hopeful smile on his face.

'Ah, it's the town's most elegant dancer,' said Thomas. 'How
famous you are. First the gallant rescuer, next the gallant swain.'

'Oh, please. The rescue, if you'll recall, was in vain and my stage
romancing? I was quite oblivious, after all, to the hairy charms of my
dancing partner.'

Rupert fell in beside Thomas. 'I have something I want to ask. Can
we talk?'

Thomas consulted his pocket watch. 'Well, ten minutes — my
father's leaving on the coach at seven. I must say goodbye.'

'It's all I need. Come, quickly, this way.'

Thomas followed as Rupert led them along a narrow pathway
between two cottages to a quiet spot behind an unkempt honeysuckle

hedge. Bees were at work in the long throats of its trumpet-like orange flowers. Jamie had recently learnt to pluck the blooms and suck sweet juice from them. Rupert grabbed one now, distractedly, and mashed it in his fingers, hesitating over how to make his request. It came out in a mutter. 'I'm in a bit of bother, Thomas, you see.' Silence. And then, 'It's somewhat…embarrassing.'

* * *

'I THOUGHT I'd be leaving without a farewell from you,' said Thomas's father.

'My apologies, Pa. Unavoidably detained by a debtor.'

The Reverend's battered bag was already tied onto the roof. The horses' flanks twitched as flies rose from the piles of dung beneath their swishing tails.

'You'll have an uncomfortable day,' Thomas observed. 'It's a rough road you're taking.'

'Hardly as uncomfortable as that concert. Your own item, Thomas, that I enjoyed, and Anna's, too — she entered well into the spirit of the thing. But there's something troubling about Mrs Sutton and her grisly choice of entertainment. I trust she and Anna do not keep company on a regular basis.'

'Just occasionally. This is not a large town.'

'And that mesmerist woman and her dark and dubious arts? Toying with men's minds involves a dangerous sort of glamour.' The old man sniffed with disdain. 'And what about you, m'lad? I've hardly seen you on this visit. You're heeding my advice?'

'All aboard,' shouted the driver, hoisting himself up to his seat. 'All aboard for Paeroa and Thames! Nip up now, d'you hear? Them that's not aboard within a minute shan't be travellin' today.'

With a grunt, the Reverend Hamilton climbed up into the coach, settled himself by the window and peered down at his son, who was clearly fidgeting to get away back to his ledgers.

'What advice was that, Father?'

'A caution I gave you years ago when you told me you were launching into the money trade. Neither a borrower nor a lender be.'

'I'm a banker, Father. It's the nature of what we do. Lending to clients is every bank's duty.'

The Reverend's gaze was fierce. 'I know, boy, I'm not a fool. I have my own investments. However, you'll be keeping the Lord's word at the forefront of your dealings, I trust. Honesty and probity in all things.'

The door slammed, the driver's whip cracked, and the wheels began to roll, shells crackling beneath the battered rims.

'Of course, Father,' called Thomas. 'Till next time!' He strode alongside for a few moments amid the calls of farewell from others who'd come to wave kerchiefs and blow kisses. The Reverend raised his hand and then the creaking, squeaking, swaying vehicle merged into its own cloud of dust and was gone on its twelve-hour run to Thames.

* * *

AT THE SUTTONS' front door, Anna was refused entrance. 'Mrs Sutton is indisposed,' Hester told her.

'I'm sorry to hear that. Is there anything I can do to help?'

'She will be on her feet in a day or two, Mrs Hamilton. 'Tis nowt to worry about.' Hester stood implacably at the door, gripping the handle, her pale bulk filling the doorway. She glanced back over her shoulder, as if to be certain there was no listening ear nearby. 'Just ladies' troubles.' A confiding, gravelly whisper. 'I'm sure you know what I'm meaning.'

Anna was taken aback, thinking it rather remarkable that a housekeeper would share intimate information, even with her mistress's friend. She was not even sure what Hester meant. Violet had not complained to her of any of the aches that so many ladies had to suffer each month.

'I see. Please give her my best, will you? I may call back later with a note, and perhaps a book she might like to read to pass the time.'

'I'm not sure she's bonny enough today, ma'am, but by all means. As you wish.' She withdrew, firmly shutting the door.

* * *

'Rupert has asked if I'll lend him some money,' Thomas told Anna over the lunch table.

She frowned. 'How much?'

'Eighty pounds.'

Her hand went to her throat. 'How is it that he needs so much?'

'You know how the horses lure him.' Thomas shrugged. 'He placed a wager or two too many. His "sure things" turned out to be tentative at best. One came in second to last. The other fell and broke a leg.'

'Who is his creditor?' Her voice was sharp.

'Some crafty dodger in Auckland. One with ruffians at his beck and call who, according to Rupert, will not hesitate to demand payment with cudgels.'

Anna pushed back her chair and stood up, stiff with anxiety. 'But we. . . you. . . cannot lend him eighty pounds. Surely not. Do we even have so much savings? Or is it a bank loan he is wanting?'

Thomas took a bite of a scone, chewing without relish. Dinah made a damn fine scone but he could not taste this one. 'He knows I could not lend him the bank's money. My superiors would disapprove.'

'Do we have so much capital at our beck and call?'

'Approximately, yes.'

'Well, then, it is too much, is it not? Can he not borrow from his own bank?'

'Hardly, my dear. The National would ask how he has come to be in such need — and the answer would not be good for his reputation.'

'Don't tell me you feel obliged to lend him our own savings. How could you be sure he would repay you?'

'I haven't decided to oblige yet, you understand. But he promised he would do so. Monthly. And with interest a little better than I can achieve elsewhere. Not markedly so, but satisfactory enough to make it worth my while. He is more sober now. Recent events have shocked him somewhat.'

'As they should have done.'

'Anna, I know you have doubts but I do trust that Rupert will settle. He is a gentleman deep down and determined to mend his ways. And I know that if I was in trouble he would do his best for me. It would be a business arrangement, with terms understood by both parties.'

Anna began, noisily and abruptly, to gather crumbed plates and tea things on a tray. 'If you have regard for me—.'

'Anna, my sweet, you know I do.'

'Then you will not do this. That money is for when you leave the bank and we want to buy a house of our own. We have our future, and Jamie's, to consider. I do not want to endanger it.'

* * *

'SIXTY,' said Thomas at day's end as he strolled with Rupert to the end of the wharf. 'I can let you have sixty. My own account is not so fat that I can lend you more. And Anna must not know. I well nigh promised I would keep our savings under lock and key.' Thomas was determined to be stern but a dry laugh slipped out. 'She sees you as a bit of a bounder, you know.'

Rupert looked sheepish. 'I'm more grateful than you can know.' He pumped Thomas's hand. 'That's an uncommonly sensible lady you have there. I won't let you down. Those steeds can race without so much as a glance from me. You can expect my first repayment at month's end and every month after that until we're square.' He glanced at the dusky sky. 'Shall we drink on it?'

Thomas's smile faded. 'No, Rupe. That's something we shan't do. It's the other resolution you must make for me — to become a man of sober habits. That way you'll keep your salary intact and your head clear. It's hard to turn aside from temptation when your mind is befuddled.'

Rupert sighed. 'I know. I have let it get the better of me at times. But no longer. Abstemiousness shall now be my second name. The Reverend Larkin could not give better advice than you, Tom. Or your good father for that matter.'

'Oh, I *know* he wouldn't approve. He gave me a right dressing down about prudence yesterday. Made me feel like a callow youth again. I'm extending this loan only because I have faith in you, Rupert. But I hope you realise the risk I'm running on your behalf.'

'Of course. Truly, I do.'

'And can you gather sufficient funds to placate the bookmaker?'

Rupert grunted. 'I trust so. I'm going to Auckland on the steamer on Friday — summoned by my superiors, y'know, for my regular brow-beating and exhortations to do better. While I'm there I can at least take a respectable cheque to give him partial satisfaction. I've sold the *Iris* too, and some other assets. If I can see him face to face I'll be able to forestall his brutes. When I've finally paid him off, and you too of course, I shall be properly skint, but at least I'll be able to sleep at night.' When he looked at Thomas his light brown eyes revealed, for a moment, a mixture of shame and hope and relief. 'You'll let me know, Tom, if there's anything I can do for you.'

'Well, if you're off to Auckland perhaps I can prevail on you to take Anna under your arm on the voyage. She and Jamie are going to stay with her mother for a spell.'

Anna had asked that morning if Thomas would mind her absence for a fortnight. 'I've been so weary of late. Violet's not well either, apparently. She needs rest, Hester says.' Her face was a little downcast. 'I've not seen her since the concert.'

'Well, that's possibly not such a bad thing,' ventured Thomas. 'Her last outing did not exactly offer balm for the soul. You need a little cosseting, my dear. Your mama will be only too pleased to do that — and she's not laid eyes on her grandson for months. As for Violet, she'll do well enough here on her own without you to egg her on.'

Anna's face had coloured but she'd held her tongue. She had been uncommonly snippy lately, he thought. A sojourn up north might well restore her former contentment.

He had not confessed to removing her copy of *The Freethinker* from the house. Browsing through it out of curiosity, he'd been astonished at its radicalism. He did not like to think of his wife relishing the view of one writer that Christian belief was 'the most debasing and mischievous of sentiments'. And, further, that Christ must have been 'insane' to set out on his forty-day fast in the wilderness.

Thomas was far from ardent in his beliefs, but even so, he had been raised in a pious household and such stridency — Christ was 'insane'? — was unnerving. He had shoved the journal into a pile of old papers in his office. His clerk might have burnt it by now. He preferred not to know. That way, if Anna looked for it, he could profess ignorance without an overly disturbed conscience.

Of course, Rupert assured him now, it would be his honour to accompany Anna and the boy. In a piping late autumn wind — and lately there'd been plenty of breeze — it could be a rough voyage up the coast and around the tip of the Coromandel Peninsula, followed by the haul across the gulf to the wharf at the foot of Queen Street. Ladies liked to have a strong arm to hold onto on a wet and sloping deck.

'Thank you. I'd appreciate that.' Thomas paused. 'I'm a little relieved, I have to say, to hear about your upcoming browbeating. I thought perhaps it was only the Bank of New Zealand that behaved that way.'

He felt slightly disloyal to be discussing his employers' attitudes, but the longer he worked in this outpost at arm's length from head office, the more he yearned to share some of his frustrations with someone who understood.

'You too?' Rupert laughed. 'I shall count myself lucky not to be put in the stocks and pelted with rotten eggs until I promise them more profits. But we both know it's beastly hard trying to wring blood out of stones.'

CHAPTER TWENTY

'The Popular Scientific Monthly asks asks,"What are crowds?" The science of love says the third party is a large crowd.'
— Bay of Plenty Times, 1886.

MAY 12, 1886

It was always a pleasure for Anna to see her mother, whose excitement over every visit was invariably huge. Amy Vincent, widowed now for a long time, ached for the sight of family. She longed to see her one remaining son, Cedric, but he was prospering with the East India Company. She had not laid eyes on his dear face for eight long years. He was not very diligent about picking up pen and paper to write proper letters but he did his duty in the financial sense. Fortunately, the bank drafts providing her allowance arrived like clockwork.

She was down at the wharf in Auckland when the ship came in, pink-cheeked and eager, curls of greying hair whipping out from under her hat. She swooped to hug her grandson, who flinched a little. 'Her chin's prickly,' he complained to Anna later, compelling her to hush him.

Anna had not seen her mother for six months. As always, after a lengthy absence, she noticed signs of increasing age. A slight lack of nimbleness meant that Amy was forever tripping over steps and bruising her elbows. But her good cheer endured. There was much visiting, with endless cups of tea and morsels of cake and jugs of lemonade along the way.

Before long Anna's contentment began to slip into boredom. There was not enough to do in this neat Parnell house with its efficient cook. Even Amy could see that her daughter's spirits seemed low. 'The Misses Brookside, lovely girls, you know them, Anna. Mabel and Charity, from down the street? They're going rinking on Wednesday evening. I'm told it's quite the latest excitement. They asked if you'd care to join them.'

'But they are so much younger than I. And unattached, besides.'

'Oh, everyone goes, Anna. It's the talk of the town. Go. Let Jamie stay here with me while you have an evening out. It'll be something to tell them about down the coast.'

* * *

THE IMPOSING Choral Hall in Symonds Street stood like a beacon, its tall windows agleam with golden light. Eager groups of chattering skaters stood on the broad steps waiting to get in. Chaperones kept a keen watch on roving young bloods whose eyes were more for women than sport.

Once inside, Anna stood nervously in line to find skates that would fit her boots. A hundred or more skaters spun past on whirring wheels. Above, in the gallery, an orchestra played lively waltzes. Some people, Anna saw, were clever enough to dance, spinning and swooping to the music. Young men were the speediest. One hurtled past, wobbled and fell, grabbing his friends on the way down. Everyone around them lurched and shrieked.

'I'm not sure I can do this,' Anna said.

'Of course you can,' cried the Brookside girls. An attendant buckled wheels onto their boots with leather straps. They were heavy, and Anna's feet felt like lumps of stone as the three of them pushed out over the hall's gleaming floorboards, gripping hands and giggling like five-year-olds. Mabel broke away after a few circuits to skate alone. Anna was feeling a little steadier by then.

'Do you want to try by yourself?' Charity asked. 'It's better that way. You'll find your balance more speedily if you're not holding on.'

'Very well,' quavered Anna. Charity sped off with a smile, leaving Anna to push on alone.

It was quite jolting, she discovered, to slip and land on her rear. But in half an hour she was revelling in the laughter, the music and the slight breeze on her face. Bodies flew by, elbows nudging, hands touching. The room was hot and happy.

She heard a high squeal and a shout behind her as someone skidded and then a hand grabbed at her back and she was down in a tangle of skirts and skates. A man's hat bowled across the floor, and a voice, full of laughter, complained, 'You pushed me!' And then, 'Anna?'

Violet was sprawled alongside her, their skates entangled. Rupert helped them up — a laughing Rupert, repeating, 'My fault, it was all my fault. Are you hurt?'

'Not a bit,' Anna dusted down her skirt. 'Merely very surprised to see you both here.'

'Thomas would be wild to hear I've knocked you over. Come out of harm's way.' He pulled them over to the wall.

'This is so delicious, don't you think?' said Violet. 'I love it! Imagine what Mr Larkin would say if we launched such an evening in the Temperance Hall.'

'God forbid,' said Rupert, making to skate off again. 'You'll want to talk. I'm returning to the fray.'

'I didn't know you were coming to Auckland,' said Anna. She sat gratefully on an empty chair, legs aching from the strain of staying upright. She patted the seat beside her. 'It's so good to see you. I've been concerned. I tried to see you after the concert but Hester said you were ill.'

'Oh, I'm well enough now.' Violet perched on the edge of her chair. Some of her hair had pulled free to lift into flyaway tendrils. Her eyes were alight. But at her lower jaw, it seemed to Anna, there was puffiness and a bruise.

Anna raised her hand to the mark. 'Did you hurt yourself?'

'Oh, it's nothing. I went walking and didn't see an overhanging tree branch. Next thing, bang! Smashed my blue goggles too. You know me.

I go much too fast for my own good. I had a sore head for a day or two, that was all.'

'I'm relieved. Hester said. . . Oh, never mind.'

'What did she say?' Violet's eyes were sharp.

'Something about women's troubles. And how we all have plenty of those.'

Violet looked away. 'I was hoping we'd see each other here,' she said. 'Henry went up to the Hot Lakes about some business venture, and grudgingly — oh, so grudgingly! — he allowed that I could take this trip on my own.'

'Where are you staying?'

'A guesthouse in Ponsonby. Terribly dull and respectable. Henry always puts up there and insisted I should too. Mrs Hadley, the land-lady, patrols her corridors like a cat. I went to the kitchen for water at three in the morning and there she was slinking around the house, fully dressed. I swear she never sleeps. I won't be at all surprised if she's not noting my every move in the hope of reporting transgressions.'

'And are you giving her cause?'

Violet laughed. 'Anna, such a suspicious look! I'm shopping, my dear, seeing my dressmaker and the milliner. And the dentist, as it happens. I have an ache. If I need to lose a tooth I'm not inclined to put myself in the hands of that old man in Tauranga.'

'You never told me.'

She waved a dismissive hand. 'A little laudanum keeps it at bay. But still, I need to get it seen to.'

Anna's eyes wandered around the hall. Bobbing heads and flying feet were filling the floor. 'And Rupert?' She had to raise her voice over the clatter and whir of skates and the sawing of the orchestra.

'Such a sweet man, don't you think? We happened to see each other in Queen Street and he kindly invited me tonight. I thought, what's the harm?'

With a clash of cymbals, the music came to a stop. Applause rang out. The skaters scattered. Anna spotted Rupert's red hair as he spoke with a tight group of young men.

'You can be sure, however,' Violet added in a lower tone of voice, 'that the evil landlady will not catch sight of us together. An uncharitable mind might make something of it.' She considered for a moment as she looked at Rupert. 'He's a little lonely, don't you think? He needs a wee wifey. Perhaps you and I should contrive to find him one.'

'It would do him good. But perhaps he has more urgent priorities.'

Violet frowned. 'Such as?'

Anna shrugged, hesitating to mention his financial troubles. It was none of her business. 'Oh, pay me no attention. I am merely conjecturing.' She patted Violet's arm. 'Take to your skates, my dear. I've had my fill.'

Before they parted Anna suggested another meeting. She and Jamie had only one more day in Parnell before boarding the steamer for the trip home. Once again, Rupert would accompany them on the overnight voyage.

'Lucky you,' said Violet lightly. 'Yes, why not. Let's meet somewhere where we can talk. The tea shop in Victoria Arcade, ten o'clock?'

She stood, kissed Anna's cheek and turned to scoot across the floor. Rupert, alone now, extended his hand to catch hers and slow her down. He pulled her in towards him to grip her at the waist and they turned in a single tight circle on their wheeled feet, smiling into each other's eyes, before they finally drew apart.

It was slightly discomforting, Anna thought, that both of their faces swung towards her then at exactly the same moment. They stood erect, with a slight hint of defiance, as if checking to see if she was watching. Anna smiled and they both waved back, their expressions somehow overly bland.

'When they looked at me,' she would say to Thomas much later, 'they wore the oddest of looks. No one else would have noticed in the middle of the crowd, but I had the distinct feeling that they were wondering how suspicious I was.'

There was no reason why Anna should feel out of sorts, but even so, a feeling of unease stole over her as she turned away to join the Brookside sisters at the table where punch was being served.

* * *

TEN MINUTES after Anna and her companions left for home, Rupert and Violet also slipped away, walking towards the rear of the building beneath the windows that gleamed amber in the night. The rowdy noise faded as they walked beneath shedding oaks. Drifts of yellow leaves softened the stony path beneath their feet so that they trod silently and unseen to the private quarters at the rear of a nearby shop on Princes Street.

There was the narrowest of gaps between buildings and Rupert led Violet down a damp alley, feeling his way in almost total darkness, shushing Violet's small shriek and subsequent giggles as a skinny stray cat shot between them.

'You're certain the owner will not mind?' she whispered as Rupert pulled from his pocket the key he'd wheedled from a friend the day before.

'Of course not. He's a gentleman and a very generous. Also, marvellously absent. He'll not be back tonight.' Rupert felt for the keyhole, inserted the key, struggled with the stiff lock, and then they were inside. He already knew the layout so he guided her from the hall into the parlour. Then he struck a match and put its flame to the wick of a candle on the mantelpiece. The room's one leather armchair, a small table, a ticking clock on a bookshelf and a square of Persian carpet were dully illuminated.

'There,' he said. 'What more could we want for?' It was a small room, musty and unaired — a bachelor's room, smelling of pipe smoke, book leather and last week's newspapers. The heavy curtains did not quite cover the windows. The first thing Violet did was tug them together so that not the smallest chink of glass showed.

She turned to Rupert. 'So, now, Magenta Man. . . Do you know they call you that?' He shrugged and pulled a silver flask from his pocket, looked around for glasses, found none. He held it out to her. 'For courage?'

'Put it down,' she said. 'We don't need that. Too much is not good for you. And I know how partial you are.'

He took one cheeky swig, put it on the mantelpiece, reached for her hands and gave her a lazy smile. 'You're more of a school marm that I imagined.'

'Hah! Not so much school marm as scarlet woman. We are a red pair, you and I. Your magenta label suits you. It is so bold a shade. Already courageous. It carries with it not a shadow of doubt.'

He stepped closer. 'And you? You have no shadow of doubt about being here?'

Her eyes glittered. 'Of course. It is insanely foolish. But you offer. . . liberation. I feel free and light in a way I can never be in that house in Tauranga.'

'What else do you feel?'

'Fortunate. It's an endless time since I felt young.'

'You *are* young.'

'It does not feel that way.'

He loosed her hands and began to unbutton her jacket. 'What else do you feel?'

'Anticipation,' she breathed as he pushed it off her shoulders to imprison her arms. He kissed her then, bending her backwards. Then he slowly wedged his hand sideways down into the top of her corset until the hard nub of her nipple was wedged between his thumb and forefinger.

She came close to buckling and he pulled her jacket right off then, laid his own cloak on the carpet and pulled her down on its silky lining, her skirt discarded and her pantaloons soon drawn down and pushed aside by their urgent feet while her fingers worked the buttons of his shirt and trousers, and his hands pushed her chemise up to her waist and pulled on its ribbons and unhooked the top of her corset to expose her rounded, dark-tipped breasts.

As he pushed into her they both gasped and strained and cried out and her hands pulled at his hair. And finally they were spent, on their backs, looking at the dim, smoke-stained ceiling in the candle's sooty light as the clock faintly chimed.

'You forgot the midshipman's butter,' she said.

He laughed and draped an arm over her stomach to dabble with proprietary fingers at the wet, salty junction of her thighs. Frustration welled in him then. 'How can we ever repeat this? Tauranga is so small. There is nowhere we can go.' He rolled over and took her face between his hands. 'I shall be driven mad every time I see you. And driven out of my mind with jealousy when I see you with that boorish husband of yours.' He fell back again. 'I shall even have to be properly proper whenever he comes to the bank.'

She put her hand over his. 'We are not the first people to have loved outside society's rules, Rupert. We shall find ways. Don't let's think about the difficulties now. Tonight is delightful. Tonight is enough.'

The clock chimed on the mantelpiece. She groaned. 'It is also enough to remind me of Cinderella.'

* * *

'You're late,' said the landlady. 'Lucky I didn't lock the door.' She'd heard the sounds of huffing horse and jingling harness and emerged from her private room to watch with narrow eyes as Violet came in, rummaging for her room key.

'My apologies for the hour,' said Violet, pausing on the treads. 'I'm hardly used to city ways. La! That rinking requires a great deal of stamina. I shall be sore in the morning, Mrs Hadley. The company was good, however — a lady friend from home was there and the time just slipped away.'

'Can't say rinking looks pleasurable to me. Not very ladylike, neither. Did your friend take to it?'

'Oh, yes, very much. Though I must say I found myself on the floor rather more often than she did. Staying upright is devilishly hard to do. You should try it.' And with a smile Violet continued up the stairs.

CHAPTER TWENTY-ONE

> 'Much ridicule has been heaped upon women because they can't keep a
> secret. A gentleman sat down to write a deed, and began with, "know all
> women by these presents". "You are wrong, said a bystander; it ought to be
> know all men." "Very well," answered the other, "if all women knew it,
> all men will of course."'
>
> — *Bay of Plenty Times.*

MAY 23, 1886

Violet's eyes were bright as she and Anna buttered scones and
dabbed them with strawberry jam. The shop was busy. There was so
much noise that no single conversation could be heard. As a twosome,
they were as private as they would have been on an empty road. But here
it was so much more pleasant. It was warm and smelled of fresh baking
and sugar.

'This is so much more fun than Jessie Brown's, don't you think?'
said Violet. In green silk and a feathered hat she looked chic and sleek.
'There are *strangers* here, Anna. Faces we don't know! It's such a relief.'

Anna was wearing the yellow dress Anna had mended many weeks
earlier, though she had purchased, with Thomas's permission, a good

new wool cape to go over it. It gave her only a modicum of confidence. 'We are bumpkins come to town, you and I,' she said.

'We are not! I wager our conversation will be the most civilised in the room.' Violet glanced around. 'They'll all be discussing recipes for tongue in aspic. And how to take stains from their husbands' moustaches.'

'How would that be possible?' Anna scoffed.

'I don't know but there are some truly dingy moustaches in the world.'

It was good, Anna decided, to be sitting with an amusing friend in an unfamiliar place, with no chores to run home to, no dinner to cook, no steaming grey laundry water to be stirring with a heavy paddle. It was a blessing that Jamie was with his grandmother, who didn't want to miss a day of his company. 'You look happier than I've seen you for a long time,' she remarked.

'I am. Yes, I am. For now, at least.' In Violet's sideways glance Anna saw the signs of a secret suppressed.

'Dare I ask why?'

'Of course. The real question is, dare I answer?' Violet stirred her tea and sucked thoughtfully at the spoon before laying it in the saucer. Then she sat up straight and looked at her friend. Her face was resolute but a tic beneath her left eye signalled nervousness, too. 'I have so missed the love of a good man,' she said.

'But you are married. And Henry seems to hold you in great regard.'

'Does he?' Violet's mouth rolled in a bleak twist. 'I exasperate him, Anna. He is an impatient man. He wants a son because he's getting older. He. . . tries. I'm sure you know what I mean. But success does not often attend his efforts. And the more he tries and the longer it takes, the angrier he becomes. And then because he is angry I no longer want to be in his bed.'

She touched the place where the bruise she'd dismissed earlier still showed, pale yellow now but still visible. 'I did not walk into a branch, Anna. I did not break my goggles that way. They were stamped under-foot. And I have a loose tooth.'

Anna gazed at her.

Violet nodded, her earlier merriment gone. 'It was the night of the concert. He was enraged by my reading — he thought I was signalling to the whole town that he likes to punish me.'

'But if you are mistreated, then you have every right to feel badly.' There was a silence between them then. 'My God, Violet, how do you bear it?'

Violet took a cake, broke it apart, ate a piece without relish. 'It is rare for him to mark me where a bruise can be seen. Hester helps me. She is the queen of kindness and liniment. I fight him sometimes, that's the trouble. But he is stronger. In a perverse sort of way it helps to arouse him. If he can spend his energy naturally then he is less inclined to use his fists. It is very tiring, Anna. I sometimes dread the nights he is at home.' She offered a shaky smile. 'And so it is a joy for me to be away from there, away from him. To do light-hearted things such as rinking. And to spend time with Rupert, too, if you must know.'

'Oh, Violet. Do you realise what peril you are in?'

'What, from my husband? Oh yes, truly I do.'

'No, dear, from all the other possible outcomes, the scandal, the gossip, if you and Rupert. . . Surely you're not involved with each other?'

Violet gazed into her cup. 'Well, yes. Yes I am.' She bit her lip. 'I'm sorry, Anna, only last night I was jesting about finding him a wife. You remember?'

'Of course!'

'It's the last thing I would want. He is lighting up my life. I would hate that to change, despite the risks. There's no point in me denying it. We should say these things loud and clear, I believe, if we are to follow the Freethinker philosophy. Tenderness is a lovely thing. Why should we not speak of it out loud?'

'Because you have a husband! For good or ill. And while you live under his roof, surely you must be careful to avoid any other entanglement.'

Violet leaned back in her chair. 'Aye, well, there's the rub. I would so like to leave. But how can I? Where would I go? In a divorce I'd be left with nothing. Do you know what I am, Anna? A remittance woman. Some of the food on our table comes from money sent every quarter by my father. But it goes to Henry, not to me. My family wanted me sold off, got rid of, sent to the ends of the earth under the thumb of someone who could control me, and Henry was the man who obliged.'

'I don't understand.'

Violet pushed away from the table. 'It's stuffy in here now. Let us walk.' And so they left the noisy tea house and picked their way around boggy patches in Queen Street before climbing Shortland Street. There was a halfway seat where they could look out over the harbour. As they made their way up the hill, Violet began to talk. 'Remember me telling you about my lost child?'

Anna nodded.

'George,' Violet said, and let out a dry, painful sound. 'I almost never even utter his name. And I've learnt lately that it is not his name now. They changed it to John. Now I cannot even bring him to life by saying it out loud. I've had no one to confide in until now and it eats away at me.'

'But why is he not with you?'

'Henry is not his father.'

'Then who?'

'A sweet man I knew. Also gone from my life, aboard a ship that has disappeared. "Never heard of" is the phrase they use in the maritime listings. He was a trader in chinaware and silks, travelling often between England and the East. I lost my head when we met during one of his sojourns in London. He was impetuous and had an air about him that was so infectious that I had no doubts. Rupert reminds of him, in so many ways.

'We both longed to wed but my father and stepmother were opposed. His background was not of sufficient *quality*, they said. Still, we kept on contriving to meet — and then he sailed away, promising to return in four months. We were still determined to marry. When half of that time had gone by I realised my monthly flow had not come. And there were other changes.' She swept her hand up her bodice to indicate how her breasts had begun to prickle and swell.

'Four months, I thought. When he's back, if we marry swiftly, all will be well. I stayed slender for a long time. My maid knew. They always know. But I kept giving her little things — gloves, silk shawls, little jewels, even money — to ensure she'd not betray me. I even threatened

her, which was unkind of me, told her she'd be banished without references if she let anything slip. My stepmother was in such a hectic whirl
with my elder sister's wedding that she barely noticed how quiet I was.'

Violet took a deep, shuddering breath. 'My father was inviting
Henry home for dinner around that time. They met at their club. And
Henry was clearly intrigued by me. "What prospects he has!" my father
kept on declaring. "A man with ambitious plans. You could do worse,
my girl." But I answered that he was too old for me and I kept fending
him off. I was waiting for my love.'

She snapped a tall grass stalk and twirled it in her fingers as she
remembered. 'Then one day I picked up the *Times* and saw that his ship
was missing, presumed lost. Do you know how many ships sink out
there on the sea every year? Hundreds, Anna. Hundreds.'

Anna said nothing. Could think of nothing to say.

'I remember that morning,' Violet went on, 'sitting with my stepmother and sister, everyone prattling on about flowers and lace, while I
just wanted to scream. Eventually of course I could hide it no longer. I
couldn't sleep. I was desperate. Then I fainted one day, short of breath,
for I'd tried to keep my corset tight despite my expanding waist. When
my stepmother put me to bed she saw immediately the state I was in.'

'What did she say?'

'Oh, the wailing! If anyone had looked at our house that afternoon
they would have seen it rocking on its very foundations. She was
outraged at the prospect of my sin spoiling my sister's wedding. She kept
on moaning, "How could you, how could you!" Of course, nothing was
spoiled at all. By the time Jane was wed a month later — with much
jollity and laughter, I imagine — I was far away. They told people I was
poorly with a weak chest and needed a rest cure and they sent me to stay
in Ireland with my stepmother's brother, and Harriet, his wife. Cold
people, Anna, so cold. So stiff. So correct. He's a clergyman, always
trumpeting his Christian values in public but he showed me no kindness in private.' She let out a barking laugh. 'That's partly why I cannot
abide Mr Larkin. I detest all clergymen now.'

'And then?'

Violet shrugged. 'My baby came, as babies will. Painfully, with much
struggle.' She gave Anna the haunted sort of look that friends can share

when they have both been through similar trials. 'You know how it is. And not long afterwards I was back in London, ostensibly the same and recovered from my *unfortunate* indisposition — but of course, no matter how much pretence was put up, I could never be the same.

'After I was sent away, the maid I had trusted was dismissed. My parents were enraged that her loyalty had been to me, not to them. Poor girl, I had placed her in such a difficult position. She was flung out without a reference. And of course she was so furious that she spilled her secret to the cook, and soon it was out in other kitchens and then spread upstairs into drawing rooms and then rumours about Miss Violet Foster's absence were being whispered everywhere.'

'But the baby, Violet, what became of him?'

'They took him away the night he was born and gave him to a local wet nurse. They said they would find a family for him to go to — a proper, God-fearing family. I knew I could not keep him. How, they kept on saying, could that ever be possible? I had no husband, no money. I felt like a great bruise that could only ache and leak.'

'Did you see him again?'

'Just once, a week later, the day I was leaving. They could not wait to see the back of me, but I'd had a fever and my departure was delayed. I was standing in the hall, my bags at my feet, and I heard a baby's cry. I found him in the kitchen on the gardener's knee, him and the housekeeper chuckling over what a sweet scrap of humanity he was.'

A gust of wind from the sea made Violet's hat feathers swivel and shake. 'They were kind, those two. They were sorrowful for me. The gardener said nothing but simply stood up and brought George to me. I'd already decided that should be his name. He stopped crying straight away and grabbed my finger and looked intently at me. It was just for a minute. And then Harriet stormed in and that was that. I was in the coach and on my way back home.'

By then, said Violet, rumours of her pregnancy were racing through her parents' circles. The Fosters denied the tales, of course, but their social life shuddered to a halt. Backs were turned. Notes were not replied to. Invitations did not come. At the few occasions they did attend, there was much whispering behind hands.

'I had to be made an honest woman. A husband had to be found, and there was Henry, still willing. They worked out an agreement, he and my father. Father would pay him, and keep on paying him, to take me off their hands and put a ring on my finger. And Henry would take me far off around the world where I would no longer be an embarrassment to them. That suited Henry very well. He detests London. Well, except for its seamier streets. He's a gentleman only on the surface, when it suits him. He likes back alleys where he can break rules and get away with it.'

'Did he know you'd borne a baby?'

'Oh, yes, all cards were on the table. But it didn't deter him. He told my father I was good enough a woman for him, despite my folly. He was doing me a kindness by rescuing me from my plight.' Violet rolled her eyes. 'But I suspect he drove a hard bargain. My father probably winces every time he sends a bank draft.

'Of course, Henry did have other motives. His first wife was barren. She died at thirty-two. They found her in the sea on a Cornish beach. Unsound mind, according to Henry. I believe it was probably despair. That I had proven fertility was important to him.' Violet rolled her eyes. 'It made me feel like a breeding sow.'

Anna began to lift a comforting arm but Violet moved away slightly, steely in her story-telling. 'Why did you agree to marry him?'

'I was low and needy. And Henry can put on a show of charm when he needs to. I knew I'd never feel for him the same passion I'd had before, but he offered an escape from my angry family and my terrible sadness. Fresh fields.' She extended an arm out over the ramshackle town and laughed dryly. 'Fields rarely come fresher than this.'

'What is it that drives Henry?' 'Restlessness. Ambition. He wants above all to put his stamp on the world and create wealth that he can pass on to a son. He's obsessed with the idea of dynasty, is always droning on about other men who are lucky enough to have a quiver full of sons. He's quite put out, on a monthly basis, that I am failing him.' A dry smile. 'My fault, always, of course.'

'Is he succeeding as he hopes to, in business, I mean?'

'I don't know. He shares so little with me. He has such wild ideas that they rarely succeed. There was a good tin mine in Cornwall — closed down now, but I think he got out of that with a healthy pile of

capital. There've been failures that I do know about — a cotton plantation in Jamaica where the soil was quite worn out, a fertiliser venture in
Spain that collapsed just after he invested in it.'

'I understand he's consumed by the railway idea now, the new track
to the Hot Lakes.'

'Well, yes, that's why he's there again now. But Anna, can you see it
happening? Such an expensive undertaking, to reach what? A
ramshackle little town full of boiling mud and stinking steam.'

'There are the Terraces.'

'Oh, the fabled Terraces, which neither you nor I are likely to enjoy.
But is that enough? You need industry and farms and townships to feed
a railway and there's precious little of any of that in the land around the
lakes.'

Anna stopped her. She'd heard enough of business. 'Violet, what
happened to your son? Do you know?'

Violet folded her arms and watched a ship steam east down the
harbour, a banner of oily smoke unfurling from its stack. 'I found out a
week after our wedding — our modest wedding, I should add. No
festive champagne toasts for us. We were about to leave London, never
to return as far as I knew, and so I bailed up my stepmother and insisted
she tell me.' Violet's eyes were dark and furious. 'I heard that he'd gone
to Harriet's own nephew, Mayne. He and his wife had been childless for
years and so were easily persuaded to take on my "unwanted" mite.
'Unwanted! You can't believe the pain I felt. This step-cousin, whom
I've never met, now lives somewhere in Asia — India or Burma or
Ceylon, God only knows! — filling some managerial post. He has an
address that nobody will tell me and is raising my child as his own.'

Violet's hands were curled into fists now, thumping on her thighs.
'A child who probably has no idea that he is not theirs, but mine, and
does not even have the name I gave him.'

* * *

IT WAS a calm voyage back to Tauranga, the sea uncommonly flat for
late autumn. Rupert sang sea shanties to Jamie and taught him how to
tie knots with a length of cord. Anna sat wrapped in her new cape and

watched them as they squatted together on the deck in the sun, their heads close together.

She looked at Rupert's shining red hair and Jamie's flyaway blond locks, listened to Rupert's deep, patient murmur and the high answering giggle, and thought a great deal about the nature of love, pain, friendship, secrets and parenthood, and what a perfectly awful mess humans could make of all of it.

She would say nothing to Thomas, she decided, about Violet's revelations. Violet's troubles were private. And if she felt drawn to Rupert, that was something she would need to work out on her own. Violet was starved for affection, that much was obvious. And very unhappy in her marriage. But, oh, the dangers in it!

Marriage. Probably most women put up a good front in public as year churned after year. But what other option was there? You got married and you got on. Anything else was far too fraught with risk.

Rupert looked up. 'Penny for them,' he said. She liked that at least he seemed cheerful now. He'd been quiet and morose when they boarded.

For a second she hesitated, as words flew through her mind. She wanted to talk to him but Jamie was there. His ears heard everything. And what could she say? Be careful with my friend's affections? Do you know what a wounded soul she is? Do you want to hurt her all over again? Do you realise the risk to your own career? For God's sake, stop?

'Nothing,' she said. *Coward.* 'Just thinking it will be good to get home.'

CHAPTER TWENTY-TWO

> *'Some people carry their hearts in their heads; very many carry their heads in their hearts. The difficulty is, to keep them apart and yet both actively working together.'*
> — *Bay of Plenty Times.*

JUNE 1, 1886

Tauranga was having a taste of winter and it was unusually cold. Soon after the still, sunny period during which Rupert, Anna and Jamie had steamed home a southerly blow brought icy gusts that whipped heavy rain across the town. Parlour fires were lit, chimneys billowed smoke and cats curled on hearthrugs when not nudged aside by chilled feet just eased from muddy boots.

Violet Sutton had also returned, her pale face wrapped in scarves, handed down the gangplank and bundled home by her impatient husband.

Thomas and Rupert met one afternoon at the Hamiltons' quarters after their respective banks' doors had closed. Thomas closed the parlour door so that Anna and Dinah could not hear from the kitchen.

Rupert handed him an envelope. 'I have to let you know that it's not quite what it should be. This month, I'm sorry, I cannot pay you interest.'

Thomas ripped it open, took out five pounds and sighed. 'Rupert. You promised.'

Rupert slumped into a chair. 'I know, I know. Auckland fair took it out of me. My meeting with the bookmaker was testy to say the least. He's an utter weasel. My superiors were little better.' His voice rose to ape their carping tones. 'When will business improve? Why is there no growth at your branch? Where are your new customers? How will you improve your results?' Rupert raised doleful eyes. 'I tell you, Thomas, they were like tigers cornering a sheep.'

'A sheep? You?'

'A timid bleater, Tom. Business is so slow. And as for my personal finances, realising assets has been harder than I thought. I sold a fine old clock to an antique shop. It was my father's once. Quite a wrench to see it go and it fetched nowhere near as much as I'd hoped for.'

Thomas let out an exasperated sigh. 'Did you get a good price for the *Iris*?'

'Tolerable.'

'Perhaps if you'd scrubbed her down and applied a new coat of paint you might have done better.'

'I know, but that would have taken me weeks to achieve and I needed cash faster than that. The bookmaker took nearly everything I'd scraped together and I still owe him twenty.' Rupert sat up and leaned forward intently. 'Your interest will be forthcoming, Thomas, and the rest of your principal. There's still some acreage up north I can sell. Believe me, I'll live like a church mouse until it's done.'

'And who will receive your first spare twenty? Me or the book-maker? Or the barman at the nearest pub?'

Rupert ran a hand through his hair. It needed cutting, Thomas noticed. 'Not the latter, believe me. As for the two of you. . .' His look turned impish. 'Ten pounds each.' Noticing Thomas's stern look, he added, 'And then another ten, quick as a whistle.' He slapped his knees, stood up and announced his departure. 'Confession done, I shall not keep you. I'm off to my lonely bachelor cave.'

But, as he'd hoped might be the case, because he really was lonely much of the time and because they were still friends, he was invited to join the Hamiltons for a plate of lamb stew.

* * *

IT WAS late in the day and dark. As Anna, Thomas and Rupert sat at the table, a dog howled near the door and another of those small, unsettling earthquakes made the surface of each serving of stew tremble before them. A window creaked. China rattled. Anna let out a small sound of distress. Jamie, in his bed but only half asleep, cried out. And then all was quiet again.

'That's the second one this week,' Anna said in a low voice. 'I was talking with Dinah. She says one of the elders at the pa, their tohunga — is that the word? — is very disturbed, talking of omens and of how the earth is stirring beneath our feet. He's a very old man and he's not ever felt such a succession of tremors here.'

'Yes, tohunga,' said Thomas. 'My father used to speak of them. In the old days there were cunning seers in every village whose word held sway over whole communities. Tyrants, many of them, obsessed with their chants and rituals. He had many a battle with them. Pagans, of course.' He ripped up a piece of bread to dip into his gravy. 'They see spirits in everything, omens in every blade of grass. Only when their influence has gone will the tribes make much progress towards civilisation.'

'Thomas,' chided Anna, 'how can you say that? Dinah is entirely civilised. She makes the best raisin pudding in the land, as you shall soon discover, and she's been teaching Jamie his letters when she's not stitching your shirts.'

'Oh, I don't mean her. She had the benefit of all that training at the Mission. I mean out in dark corners of the hinterland, where settlers and natives barely know each other yet. In some places there's a long way to go.'

'But their skills on the water. . . We can learn from them there,' said Rupert. 'They know the vagaries of this harbour like the backs of their hands. The currents, the shellfish beds, the fishing spots. They fish by the moon, did you know that? And their boats never come home empty.'

'Perhaps you could get one of their canoes to replace the *Iris* and get a few fishing lessons at the same time.'

'You no longer have your dinghy?' asked Anna.

'Sold,' said Rupert shortly.

'But you loved that boat.'

Rupert looked down, toyed with his knife. 'Yes, well, I'd had my pleasure. It was time to move on.'

* * *

IT WAS STILL blustery the next morning but Violet went walking nonetheless out along the path past the leaning pohutukawa which had formerly served as Rupert's marine hitching post. The tree's great twisting roots were entangled on one side to form a niche that was sheltered from the elements. It was only large enough for a hand to slip into but deep enough to make it an ideal place to hide an envelope. Violet checked the path both ways to ensure she was unseen, bent down, swiftly pushed a message into the gap and continued on her way.

She ran into Rupert by accident later that day at the Post Office, he departing its door, she on the point of entering.

'Mrs Sutton,' he greeted her, doffing his hat.

'Mr Beckford.' Formal tones of voice. Mannered inclinations of the head. Appropriate smiles. Then, 'Oh, silly me,' she said as she dropped her basket, spilling groceries on the steps.

'Allow me,' he said. A swift gathering of items, crouching together, an excuse for lingering for a couple of seconds as he reached for the scattered items from her basket and handed them to her. 'I found your note,' he whispered.

'That's most kind,' she said as he helped her to her feet. The Post Office was a busy place, with others stepping around them in the doorway. 'Thank you. Good day to you, Mr Beckford.'

She went into the building and Rupert turned and walked away, beginning to hum and then catching himself at it. He fell silent and composed his face so as to look as if it was a normal, serious day of business with not much to look forward to at all.

* * *

HENRY SUTTON LEFT town the next morning on horseback, intent on visiting farms he owned near Waihi. His tenants were turning in miserable results. This land had looked as if it should be good for dairying. He had felt secure in buying substantial holdings. But the herds, for some unfathomable reason, failed to thrive. Henry intended to find out why. He suspected farmer laziness or indifference. 'Good for nothings, the lot of them,' he'd complained to Violet as he hauled on his boots.

'Perhaps something here doesn't suit the cows. Too much rain or sun, or not enough. Perhaps the soil is not as rich as it looks.'

'Nonsense. The grass grows green. Nothing wrong with it. Mind you, some fertiliser would not go amiss.' Henry was having little luck in raising either interest or capital for the formation of a fertiliser company. It was yet another reason for his foul mood today, Violet thought.

She spoke to him meekly in the interests of keeping his mood as calm as possible. He would be away for several nights. She touched his shoulder and allowed him a kiss as he left, not that he seemed much interested in receiving any sign of affection.

As the crunch of his departing steps faded, she quietly closed the door and leaned against it with a sigh. Hester was also away, staying the night with a friend. Violet would have the house to herself. Rupert would come at nine, she hoped. At least that's what she'd suggested in her note.

The narrow crust of the waning moon would emit little light. She hoped the gloomy clouds that had hung over the town all day would add to the darkness. Most citizens would be yawning by the fire. There would be little likelihood of anyone seeing Rupert as he heading up the hill towards the Sutton home. Even so, his quiet knock at the appointed time surprised her.

'Damn shells,' he said. His trousers were damp to the knee. 'I've been wading through grass to avoid being heard.' He reached for her. 'But I'm here. By God, how good it is to see you.'

They kissed, deep and long. Violet pulled free and said, 'Come.' She pulled him past the cold parlour, its fire and lamps unlit. The kitchen, at the back of the house, was the warmest room and had small windows with shutters she had already closed. She took him there.

Three candles flickered on the table. She'd put out a decanter of Henry's fine port and two crystal glasses. She poured out a good measure for them both and handed one to Rupert. They clinked the glasses. A clear, sweet chime rang out.

'A toast to us,' he said. They drank. His eyes were alight. 'Let me look at you. But slowly this time. I could look at you forever and never grow tired. It was so hard yesterday at the Post Office not to take hold of you there and then. To have to be so devilishly polite.'

She put down her glass. 'Let us then be not polite at all.'

Violet's silk blouse had many small buttons. Rupert's hands trembled as he went down the line, eager to get into the next layer, closer to her skin. Impatiently he tore at the final button and its thread broke. It bounced on the floor. He slipped the silk from her shoulders, ran his hands down her bare arms.

A bow of narrow tape closed the top of her chemise. With a quick pull, that too was undone and she wriggled until it hung loose over the waistband of her skirt. Now there was only her corset with its sturdy hooks and eyes. He made short work of them and flung the skin-warmed bony shell to the floor. It landed at their feet with a smack. Her breasts were free now, the nipples swollen hard. Rupert groaned and pulled her to him, his mouth first seeking hers and then ducking down to nip and suck, making her cry out, and then he was kissing her even more fully, tasting port upon her eager tongue.

Grappling, panting, he pushed her back against the table's edge and reached a hand down to pull up her damn skirt, to grip a handful of pantaloon and wrench it down her thighs. But then, as he struggled with her clothes, he pulled back for a moment and saw her face. Felt her freeze. Saw her horror as she looked over his shoulder. Felt her fists up against his shoulders as she shoved him away.

CHAPTER TWENTY-THREE

'It is manifestly absurd that two people who hate each other cordially, should be bound together, with only two loopholes of escape — death, and the divorce court, the latter "loophole", most unjustly favouring the male partner in the matrimonial firm.'
— Auckland Observer.

JUNE 3, 1886

Henry Sutton would never forget the sight of his wife bent back against the table. Her nakedness. The candlelight on her skin. The lurch of her breasts as she wriggled her hips to give easy access to that impudent searching hand among her underthings. Her blazing eyes, the fierceness he saw there, the passion he had never seen when he had her in his own bed. What he also saw in a flash, when their eyes locked, was shock but also defiance.

And then there was Beckford, only turning when he saw Violet's face change, still fully dressed but bulging in his trousers, at least in that first second or two before he saw Henry's rage. As he sprang back from the table his hands went up to rummage at his ridiculous hair as if desperate to find words in his cranium to explain himself.

'By all that's sacred, you'll pay for this!' Henry roared.

Violet saw the gleam of his eye as he turned towards the door of his study. She knew at once what he was looking for. Hanging on the wall there was his father's sword. How Henry loved it. He kept the blade oiled and frequently boasted to visitors of how it had gutted enemy soldiers, that when he had first seen it as a boy it had dark stains on its lethal edge that he'd thought of as blood.

'He'll kill you,' she gasped to Rupert. Then Henry tripped and fell flat in the dark hallway, bellowing as he tried to rise. Violet grabbed a cloak that was draped over a chair and gave Henry one more frantic glance before she fled. She could see only his legs. His pale wool socks were just visible in the candlelight as he struggled for a toehold on Hester's shiny floor. He must have taken off his boots before creeping along the hall towards them.

Rupert hovered in the doorway, the blackness of night behind him. 'Quick!' she snapped And so they ran, disappearing into the trees behind the house. Rupert hauled her over a fence, hearing her skirt rip on tangled wire, then pulled her along through thick bush. A drizzling, drenching rain came down. Wet branches whipped leaves in their faces. Her thin house shoes were quickly sodden.

As they stumbled on Rupert could hardly speak for fear and exertion, the words jerking out. 'You said he'd be gone for days!'

'It's what he told me. Something must have happened to turn him back. God, Rupert.' She plucked at his sleeve. 'Stop, think. We'll get lost. Where are we going?'

The night was silent except for the drip and splatter of water. There were no sounds of pursuit. No angry shouts. Just a single, plaintive morepork call. Rupert put his arms around her. She was shivering beneath her inadequate cloak. 'You need somewhere warm and dry,' he said.

'But where?' Her voice was shrill with panic. 'I can't stay in your quarters. I'd be seen. You'd be ruined.'

'I know, I know. Damn and blast!' He took a few heaving breaths, came to a decision. 'Stay close, there's a path ahead. I've got only one idea. God knows if it's a good one.'

* * *

ANNA, slow to find sleep that night, heard the tapping first. Thomas was on his back, snoring gently, when she poked him in the ribs. 'Thomas, there's someone here. Someone's knocking.'

Grumbling, he rolled out of bed, wrapped a robe around himself and padded into the hall. Damn it, it was dark. He felt for matches on the hallstand, struck a match and lit a candle. The knock came again. 'I hear you!' he called irritably but not too loud, reluctant to wake his son. Then he picked up a stout walking stick and opened the door.

Violet Sutton stood there, huge-eyed, solemn, with hair rain-plastered to her face, wearing a cloak tightly wrapped about her body. She looked up at him with pinched lips. 'Mr Hamilton, may I take shelter here?'

He blinked in surprise, stepped aside and silently ushered her in. She stood, dripping onto a rug as Anna bustled out of the bedroom, a woollen shawl over her nightgown. Her mouth opened in alarm. 'Why are you here? Whatever's the matter? Quick, let's warm you up.' She took Violet by the shoulders and turned her towards the kitchen. 'Thomas, could you stoke up the stove? She is chilled to the bone.'

He threw in kindling, stirred the embers into life, put a pot of water over the fire. Violet was slumped in a chair, her eyes closed, as Anna rubbed her cold hands. It was only then that he noticed Mrs Sutton's cloak had fallen open a little. He had clear sight of a narrow strip of pale skin from throat to waist, could see the swell and crease of one of her breasts. The woman had come to their home well-nigh naked.

He was so shocked he made a sound deep in his throat that he turned into a cough. 'I shall leave you,' he said, backing away. 'This is, perhaps, women's business.'

Anna nodded. 'Best you return to bed. I'll see to her. But first, could you put up the spare cot in the parlour?'

'Can she not return home?'

A roll of the eyes. 'Can't you see the state she's in?'

He did as requested, found sheets, blankets and an extra quilt, went back to his own now-cold bed and lay there awake, hearing the murmur of voices from the kitchen. After several minutes Anna tiptoed into the bedroom and gathered an armful of garments from a chest. 'Is everything all right?' he said.

'Hush, go to sleep,' she said, as if he was a child.

'But is it?'

'Yes. Well, no, not really. I'll tell you tomorrow.' And off she scurried with night attire for the waif who'd come to their door.

* * *

'Hello,' said Jamie, hair mussed from sleep. His small feet were bare and tender on the cold morning floor. 'Are you having breakfast here?'

'Don't be impertinent,' said Thomas.

'And it's not "hello",' said Anna, bringing a pot of honey to the table. 'It's "Good morning, Mrs Sutton".'

Jamie parroted the greeting. Violet took a spoonful of porridge. 'Yes, Jamie, as you see, breakfast it is.' She smiled at him. 'I'm very fortunate to be here.'

'Will Hester be coming too? She likes porridge. She told me.'

'No, dear. It's just me for now, having a little holiday. Hester's still up the hill.'

'With Mr Sutton?'

'Yes, Jamie, I imagine so.'

'Why?'

'Jamie!' said Thomas.

'Obey your father,' Anna said. 'Enough! Come and get dressed. You can go out and play. It's stopped raining, see? It's a lovely day.'

* * *

On that sunny day, life went on as usual in Tauranga. Fishermen unloaded their nets. The engineer got up steam on the mail boat, ready for sailing. Ralph Ward pulled hot loaves from his ovens. The grocer put out boxes of rosy apples, keeping a sharp eye out for children who might be tempted to filch one on the way to school. Jessie Brown swept her floor and called out a cheerful greeting to early customers.

Dinah arrived at the Hamiltons', put on her apron, and began her day's work. As she went into the parlour to sweep ashes from the grate she was surprised to find Mrs Sutton there. 'Oh, ma'am,' said Dinah. 'I'm sorry. I didn't know—.'

The visitor nodded, her face impassive. 'Of course not. Take no notice of me.' She was reading a newspaper, wearing clothes that Dinah knew well — the cream nun's-cloth skirt and jacket. There was a cot with folded blankets in the corner of the room.

Dinah said no more, quickly swept and dusted and left the room.

Anna came to find her. 'Did you see that Mrs Sutton is here?'

'Hard to miss her.'

Anna smoothed her hands down her skirt. 'It's. . . awkward. She is here for, well, I don't know how long. Things are difficult, you see, for her at home. Do you understand?'

'I do, I do. Very hard for men and women to rub along together all the time, eh?'

'Yes. But the problem is she has no clothes, none of her things, not even a hairbrush.'

'Nothing?'

'No. So could you go to her house later, very quietly, to the kitchen door, when Mr Sutton is likely to be out, and ask Hester if she could put a few things in a bag for her? You know Hester, don't you?'

'Yes, ma'am, of course I do. But I don't need to go there. Look.' Anna peered through the window and saw Hester hurrying along the rutted road towards them with a bag in hand, sidestepping mud patches, mouth grimly set.

In a few minutes she was at the back door. 'Is she here? Is she well?'

'Yes, she's in the parlour, but—' Anna began, but Hester had already swept through and closed the door behind her with a sharp snick of the lock.

'Well, don't mind me,' said Anna, taken aback.

Thomas came through the connecting door from the bank, grim and displeased. 'Is anyone minding our son while all this flurry is going on?'

'Yes, sir, saw him just now in the garden,' reported Dinah. She looked from Thomas to Anna, felt their tension. 'He can help me collect eggs.' She grabbed a basket and escaped.

Thomas sat heavily at the table. 'Her housekeeper's here?'

'Yes. Hester.' Anna sat opposite him. In front of her was the bowl in which Rupert's strange fruit had ripened. She pushed it away.

'She must return home,' said Thomas. 'She is a wife. It's her duty.'

Anna looked bleakly at him.

'What did she tell you?' Thomas asked. 'She must have had some reason for running here in the middle of the night with barely a stitch on her back.'

'Henry, Mr Sutton, was threatening her, she said. She was afraid. She had nowhere else to go.'

'What, so afraid that she would run half-naked through the town? I find it hard to believe. There was not a bruise on her that I could see. And you must admit, Anna, that one could see quite a lot.'

Anna sighed. 'Oh Thomas, not all men are as reasonable as you. Some are exceeding rough with their wives. Even gentlemen can be rough. Henry is rough. He hit her in the face only a few weeks ago. I saw the mark on her cheek when we were in Auckland. We talked then, Violet and I. She says he's one of those men who seems equable in company but is different at home. She said there are times when she can hardly stand to be in the same house. Something must have happened last night to make her flee.'

'But what?'

'She talked about a sword. She was frightened of his sword. He came home late, as I understand it. She wasn't expecting him, the house was cold and dark, and he flew into a rage. Or so she says.'

Thomas folded his arms. 'If true, then I grant her a modicum of sympathy. But is it true or a touch of hysteria?'

'I have no reason to doubt her,' said Anna. *Although I do, actually.*

'Well, she can't stay here, can she, lodging in our parlour, taking up our small space. It's a domestic affair, Anna, and none of our business.'

Anna rose from the table. 'Except it *is* about business, isn't it. Sutton is a client. What you mean is you can't upset him by giving refuge to his wife, even if she's desperate.'

Thomas got up too. 'Indeed. I need every client I have. What goes on between a man and his wife may be deplorable but it should never spill into anyone else's domain.'

There came a firm knock on the door then — the one that led to the bank, the door that had the word 'Private' painted on the other side. Thomas strode to it and wrenched it open, ready to scold. The nervous clerk spoke first. 'Excuse me, sir, but Mr Sutton is here. He demands to see you. Somewhat forcefully. I put him in your office.'

Thomas managed a calm smile. 'Thank you. Please give him my compliments and tell him I'll be with him in a moment.' He closed the door and turned to his wife with cold eyes. 'You see. Here's what your foolish friend has brought us to — a situation which I dare say I'll be lucky to emerge from unscathed. If he wants to know if she is here I shall not lie to him. And you should warn her that she must emerge sometime soon and that what she does then is her affair. But it cannot be ours.' He swung through the door and closed it in her face.

CHAPTER TWENTY-FOUR

'The colonies offer openings even now for men of small capital, and even men of no capital, vastly superior to any to be found at Home, for those of the right kind.'
— Auckland Observer.

JUNE 4, 1886

Henry Sutton was standing at the window. As Thomas entered he swung around, bulldog chin jutting, eyes narrow and mouth set, his walking cane tapping sharply on the heels of his boots. 'No need for greetings,' he snapped. 'I know she's here.'

'Please.' Thomas extended a hand to usher him to a chair as he slipped behind his own desk.

'I'll not be sitting.' But Sutton did then abruptly take a seat, bristling. His mouth worked, his beetling eyebrows churned. He thudded his cane upon the floor, fists wrapped around its head. 'Why, in God's name, did they run here? What's the whore told you?'

'Mr Sutton!' Thomas wrestled for a second with the shock of hearing a man so describe his own wife and with perplexity over the possibility of there being more than one runaway.

'She came alone. And as for what she said, I left her with Anna to talk in private. It seemed like women's talk and she was quite distressed. It was late and she was cold and wet besides. We could hardly eject her into the rain.'

Sutton sprang back to his feet with a snort. 'Distressed? She has no right to that emotion or to any finer feeling whatsoever. Cold, conniving, deceitful *pinchcock*!' He pushed his face at Thomas, glowering. 'You must have asked Mrs Hamilton what story she spun, hmm?'

Thomas could feel his own face heating with embarrassment. 'Just that you had come home unexpectedly and found the house unwelcoming. And that you had your temper up and that she was afraid. We could hardly shut the door on her. But believe me, I told Mrs Hamilton not five minutes ago that your wife cannot keep sleeping in a cot in our drawing room.

'Mr Sutton, I believe that what happens in a man's home should best stay within those four walls. I have no wish to interfere or to harbour a woman who is likely merely suffering from some form of hysteria.'

'Some form of harlotry, more like it. She's not revealed her perfidy then? This woman who I took on from the foolish kindness of my heart, a shamed woman what is more, who had no place in London society before I rescued her and made her *respectable*.'

Mutely, Thomas shook his head. Sutton pointed a forefinger at the window, through which they could see the neat premises of the National Bank on the opposite corner.

'Within those walls he cowers: the mealy-mouthed Mr Magenta, sporting that foolish brush upon his skull. I should have seen it for what it was — a brazen flag of piracy. D'you know what I saw last night, Mr Hamilton, when I entered my own abode, tired and sore from a day on the road and tip-toeing in my socks so as not to disturb my wee wifey? He had her stretched upon our kitchen table, sucking at her dugs, dabbling at her madge, straining to get inside her. Then they saw me. By God, they saw me in the doorway. She said I was angry? Indeed I was, Mr Hamilton!'

Sutton's eyes were bulging, his meaty hands closed into fists. 'Ran for my sword. Would have run him right through, given the chance. But

I wasn't swift enough.' He was trembling now, his face flooding with fury and humiliation, quickly suppressed.

'Please, sit and calm yourself. A dram might help,' said Thomas.

He strode to the sideboard where he kept whisky for the rare occasions when clients needed a bulwark against shock. He poured a solid dose of for Sutton, and a smaller one for himself.

Sutton threw back his head, swallowed it in a gulp and held out his glass for more. Silently, Thomas poured another tot and sat down. Sutton did too, slumping now. It seemed to Thomas, sipping his own medicine, that some of the man's stuffing had been knocked out of him.

'I must go to Jessie Brown's,' muttered Sutton. 'Breakfast calls. Absent wife, absconding cook, cold kitchen, empty table. None of it makes for a good start to a man's day.' His lips stretched in a brief, self-pitying smile.

'I'll join you,' said Thomas, whose own breakfast had been scanty. He was acutely aware that his clerk would be carrying out normal business outside his door. Sutton would not, he was certain, want the details of his drama to be overheard. 'We can discuss what's to be done as we walk, yes?'

Moments later, anyone who bothered to look would have seen Messrs Sutton and Hamilton, two gentlemen of the township, walking down Wharf Street with an air of intent. Neither of them glanced at the National Bank as they departed the crossroads on which the two banks sat. Soon they were stepping along the quiet lane down which Rupert had taken Thomas for his own quiet word eight weeks earlier.

Thomas stood with Sutton beside the honeysuckle hedge that in late summer had still been festooned with orange flowers. Someone had trimmed it; the flowers were long gone. All that remained was a mesh of naked, sharp-tipped stalks. 'What do you want of me?' Thomas asked.

'Discretion, first. I'll not have scandal spread about. Not that I have fears for my own reputation but people, and women especially, are ready to listen to any sort of scuttlebutt and believe every word.'

Thomas wondered how kindly Anna might receive that judgement, but merely nodded. 'I will have a meeting with that man,' Sutton went on. 'And with her. It will take place in my home, at six tomorrow evening. It is my intention to demand a substantial solatium to compen-

sate for the injury that man has caused me. I want you there as a witness
to proceedings so that no false accusations can later be made against me.'

Thomas was appalled. 'I have no qualifications in such matters, sir.
Surely a lawyer is the sort of man you need.'

'Not at this point. I simply need someone of good standing and
sharp mind. You shall do.'

'I hardly see—.'

'Only three men know about this. You, myself and that impudent
masher up the road. That is the way I want it to stay.'

'But there's my wife, too, and our domestics.'

Sutton raised a critical eyebrow. 'Surely you can prevail upon your
wife's good sense? And the drudges? I imagine a little coin in the hand,
and promise of more, might ensure their silence.'

'Very well,' Thomas said, uneasy at the thought of engaging in
bribery. On the other hand, domestics earned only a scanty living and
if Sutton was handing out money neither would be likely to spurn it.
'What of Mrs Sutton? Do you want her returned home this
morning?'

'Certainly not. Let the vixen stew. Can you keep her for now? I
don't want her flitting off to a hotel where she'll be gossiped about from
here till doomsday. But I need the cook. Tell Hester to keep her lips shut
and go back to the kitchen so at least I can eat.' He pulled out a purse
and passed over a handful of notes. 'This will keep her quiet, and your
Maori woman too. Split it between them. If Hester refuses, let her know
she can pack her box today and leave with no references — and none of
last week's pay to boot.' He turned to head for the tea shop, then
paused. 'And tell her I want that kitchen table hard-scrubbed with salt
and vinegar. You coming?'

Rupert Beckford often went to Jessie Brown's of a morning but
there was no sign of him that day, just Hamilton and Sutton sharing a
table as they munched and supped with set faces, saying little.

Thomas had no appetite despite his hollow stomach. The prospect
of next evening's meeting filled him with anxiety. He knew he would do
little banking this day. A house full of women awaited him. And if there
was any sphere in which he felt uncomfortable it was one filled with the
fluttering of anxious peahens.

* * *

BECKFORD'S CLERK was surprised to see Thomas Hamilton walk in. It wasn't customary for a bank manager to stroll into a rival bank unannounced.

'Sorry to intrude. Just wanted a quick word with your master. Is he in?'

'Thomas,' said Rupert, emerging from his office.

Quiet, pale, composed. You'd never know he'd been running through the rain last night with a wild, half-naked woman, thought Thomas.

'Good to see you,' Rupert went on. 'I imagine you've come for the book that I've had for an age. Would you care to come through?' He blandly ushered his friend in and closed the door.

Thomas swung on him. 'Missing book, indeed. It's the missing woman we must talk about. I've had Sutton in my office, ranting and livid. My household's been turned upside down. What were you thinking? Have you gone mad?'

Rupert flung himself into an armchair beside his ash-filled fireplace and rubbed at his face. 'I know,' he said through his fingers. 'I am a bit mad. Mad for Violet. Mad for the whole idea of her.' He dropped his hands, stood up and paced around his parlour. It was untidy, the air stale. Through the door that opened to the bedroom, Thomas could see twisted sheets on the narrow mattress.

'She's been so miserable, Thomas. I started out just trying to cheer her up but she was so willing. And so beautiful. And I realised I was hardly happy either. Everything was a tangle, and it was as if, oh I don't know, we were a form of nectar to each other's bee. She has so much hidden vitality, utterly suppressed by that vile toad to whom she's wed. We couldn't see the harm. And was there any harm, actually, in seeking just a crumb of happiness? Life's too short, Thomas, to deny ourselves a little stolen joy.'

He stopped to gaze at his friend, eyes sharp and intense. 'And even if it's over now, with my tower of hope all tumbling down, I still believe that. To the end of my days I'll believe it.'

'God in heaven, Rupert. You have no idea the trouble you're in.'

'I don't care about me. I care only for her.'

'You speak like a child,' snapped Thomas. 'And you've behaved like one. There are consequences, Rupert. For pity's sake, stop pacing.' He grabbed Rupert's arm, forced him back into the chair and drew up another so they were almost knee to knee. Thomas observed the golden sheen of whiskers on Rupert's unshaven cheeks, noted his bloodshot eyes.

'How is Violet?' Rupert wanted to know. 'Is she recovered?'

'She's dry and warm and fed, thanks to Anna. As to her mental state, I have no idea. She is closeted in our parlour and I've not seen her since you abandoned her at our door.'

Rupert shook his head. 'She insisted. She thought to protect us both from gossip by keeping me apart from her story. We had so little time to think. I couldn't bring her back here.' He waved distracted hands at his surroundings. 'My cleaning woman is due. There was nowhere to hide her.'

Thomas's lip curled. 'What makes you think Sutton won't tell the town what you were up to? He *saw* you.'

'What, Sutton talk about being cuckolded? He's too proud. No man wants to be sniggered about. And he'd not want a soul to know he's not good enough for a woman as beautiful as Violet.'

'Will you cease your gushing! Wake up, Rupert. She's a vain hussy. A woman with morals so loose the moon could shine through her. Do you expect to take her away? What would you live on? No bank would employ you with such scandal attached to your name. She'd have nothing. A divorce would leave her penniless and you can wager Sutton would toss her out without a bauble. Is that what you want, a scarlet woman whose sole estate is her wretched reputation and the clothing on her back? And, Rupert, while I hate to remind you in the midst of your woes, don't forget you're in debt. Not least to me.' Rupert flushed and looked away.

Thomas sighed. 'Her story is that she ran away because she was frightened of him. Is that true?'

'Yes. He was roaring like a bull. If he'd managed to reach his sword he would certainly have used it. He punishes her all the time. He's a monster.'

'If it's so then I'm sorry for it, but her marital condition is not for others to judge. He is still her husband. Well, at least until he decides to be rid of her, which may happen swiftly given his temper this morning. His justifiable temper, I should add. What were you thinking to tup her in her own house?'

Rupert lifted a sulky shoulder. 'There was nowhere else to go. And we thought he was away.'

Thomas let his hands loft upwards in resignation. 'Perhaps she will refuse to go back. There is, I suppose, some faint chance that she could be yours, but the prospects are gloomy. Where would you go, given your lack of funds? And even if you had the wherewithal, what would your plan be? You have much thinking to do. Mrs Sutton will stay with us for now.' And then Thomas told Rupert of the meeting they must attend the next night. 'I shall escort her there when the time comes. You may join us then.'

'May I see her?'

'Tomorrow night at six, but not before.'

'I can't face Sutton with no inkling of the state of her mind. Can't I cross the street and see her? It drives me mad to know she's a mere few yards across the road.'

'He specifically asked me to ensure I keep her incommunicado.'

'And you're complying?'

Thomas shifted in his seat. 'He's an important client, Rupe, one of the few men of means on my books. He has plans that can help this coast thrive. I have no wish to make an enemy of him.'

'You mean your bank needs his capital. And you need him to keep your career on course.' Rupert pushed his chair back with his feet, putting distance between them. His face was wan. 'Are his deposits and your post more important than our friendship?'

'Rupert, this mess is none of my making. I find myself the man in the middle and detest every moment of it. Sutton has asked me to be present as a witness. At least you'll have me in the room to ensure some sort of fairness. I'm not turning my back on you, but can't you understand how difficult this is for me? You are my friend, and yet you've put me in an impossible position.'

Rupert stood up abruptly, lurched slightly and steadied himself with a hand on the mantelpiece. He pushed a lank, fox-shaded strand of hair from his eyes. 'You had better leave,' he said. 'As you say, I need to think.'

'Have you been foolish with alcohol again?' Thomas asked.

Rupert shrugged. 'I've had some consolation.'

Thomas sighed, conscious that he had just dosed Sutton and himself to steady their nerves. 'Consolation or oblivion? You promised me you'd stop. It's the damn drink that's caused most of your problems.' He strode into Rupert's sleeping space and stooped to look under the bed. A bottle of schnapps stood there, open and empty. Thomas kicked it into a corner and hauled up a window sash to let in some air. The leaves of the butter-fruit trees just outside were aquiver in the breeze. 'You need to clean this place up, and yourself, if you're to have a clear head tomorrow. Not another drop, man, or you'll be sorry.'

Rupert made no comment, but took a book of verse from his mantelpiece without looking at it. 'Here. You'd better give the impression that you have what you came for.'

They re-entered the bank and enacted a cordial farewell. Thomas nodded to the clerk behind the counter and departed, sore at heart, the book in his hand. It felt greasy against the skin of his palm, this symbol of deceit.

CHAPTER TWENTY-FIVE

'Here is a purely ironical description of the fair sex: "A woman is a mighty handy thing to have about the house. She doesn't cost any more to keep than you'll give her, and she'll take a great interest in you. If you go out at night, she'll be awake when you get home, and then she'll tell you all about yourself, and more, too."
— Bay of Plenty Times.

JUNE 5, 1886

It was cold but calm with low clouds threatening more rain as a small procession wove its way up the path in June's winter gloom. Thomas inserted himself between Violet and Rupert to ensure they could not touch.

Hester came promptly when Thomas knocked. She peered anxiously at her mistress. A clock along the hallway chimed six times. 'The drawing room,' she said and watched as they filed inside. Thomas Hamilton. Anna Hamilton. Violet Sutton. Rupert Beckford. Hester reached in behind Beckford to pull the door shut and in that brief second took in the grim tableau. Sutton stood with his back to the fire, steely-eyed, chin jutting, hands clasped behind him. The Hamiltons stood close together, Violet at Anna's elbow, Rupert next to Thomas.

Violet stood with burning face, head up, eyes fixed on her husband. Rupert's head was turned towards her, eyes searching her face.

Sutton's fierce gaze leapt to Hester to order her out. She obeyed, but leaned her forehead against the door's cool wood for a moment, aching pointlessly to hear what would ensue.

* * *

'Mrs Hamilton, I do not recall inviting you here,' said Sutton.

'I took it upon myself to bring her,' said Thomas.

'It was at my request,' added Violet. 'You have Mr Hamilton here as a witness. I require her to be mine.'

'You *require*? Oh, that's rich. You are in no position to require anything of me at all. Do you really wish your friend to be privy to your depravity, to hear all the unseemly details?'

'I know them already,' Anna said.

'Oh, you do? And how long have you known? Does the whole town know? Am I the last person to discover what a *harlot* she is?' Sutton roared the word, spit spraying upon the Persian rug beneath his feet.

'Do not call her that,' Rupert snapped. 'She is too fine for your gutter language.'

Sutton took two swift steps towards him. 'But not too fine for gutter behaviour! I should have known when I married her that this would be the outcome. She'd been loose and foolish well before then. Did she learn nothing? Why did I think it would be different once I'd rescued her? Once I'd given her all of this?' And he swung an arm around the room to encompass the glowing silks, the paintings, the polished wood. 'She is a vain and grasping trollop, never satisfied, never grateful, slow to do her duty as every wife should. Until, of course, some shambling, wolfish, gambling, careless good-for-nothing like you comes along and offers her. . . what? What exactly what do you offer her, Beckford?'

Beckford squared his shoulders. 'My devotion. My honour—.'

'Honour? You don't know the meaning of the word.'

'You make her life utterly miserable. You're a bully, Sutton.'

Thomas interjected. 'Please, both of you, this is pointless. There is no point in hurling insults at each other.'

'It is only I who deserves to be angry, Hamilton,' spluttered Sutton. 'My wife has broken every rule of civilised behaviour and this lout has entered my home with every intent of entering her body as well. Do you expect me to remain calm? Look at his face!' He spun towards his wife. 'Look at hers! Not a skerrick of remorse to be seen in either of them.' He swiftly slapped Violet's cheek and she reeled away.

Rupert reached out to her, but Anna pushed him off. 'Leave her be!'

Thomas grabbed Rupert's arm. 'Enough. Can we not behave like adults? I will not stay here to supervise a brawl.'

A log shifted in the grate, spitting a small fiery coal onto the hearth rug. Sutton stepped on the spark and ground it in. The scent of scorched wool wafted to their nostrils. They were all breathing heavily.

Anna spoke. 'I suggest we all sit down. Shall I ask Hester to make tea?'

'No,' snarled Sutton. 'Goddamn tea. Last thing we need.' He abruptly took a chair and waved an uncaring hand. 'Sit then. Anywhere.' Rupert and Violet made to sit together on a sofa. 'Except you two! Can't abide to see you within two yards of each other.'

The Hamiltons lowered themselves onto the seat instead while Rupert and Violet took chairs opposite each other, Rupert with defensive eyes, she with her flaming cheek. Neither wanted to be close to Sutton so the circle was wide and yet the room still not large enough to accommodate so much churning emotion.

Thomas began. 'Mr Sutton, you asked for this meeting. I think it behoves us all to establish that you are the aggrieved party here.' He heard Anna begin to make a sound of dissent, but forged on. 'You told me you have certain demands. Perhaps you would like to outline them so that we can put this matter to rest.'

'How can you decide on my behalf what I will agree to?' said Anna.

He turned to his wife, astonished. 'We will discuss this later, if you must. Please do not interrupt me.'

'But—.'

'Anna!' She subsided but Thomas did not miss the glance that flickered between his spouse and the troublesome woman who had brought all of this upon them.

'First,' Sutton ground out, leaning forward, his paws gripping his broad knees, 'an apology from the pair of you.' He glared at the lovers, his heavy head swinging to and fro.

'What a lot you do ask,' said Violet shakily.

Sutton went on as if she'd not spoken. 'When this meeting is over you will go with Hester and retire for the night. She has prepared separate accommodation. I'll not have it said, or even thought, by anyone in this room, that I forced you unwillingly back to my bed tonight. But married we are and married we will remain, tomorrow, next week, next year. You will remain my wife.'

'For as long as it suits you,' she spat.

'Which is every man's prerogative!' he roared. He turned to Rupert. 'You've hardly piped up at all.' His lip curled. 'What a puppy dog you are, all eager tongue and tail until a bigger hound comes along and shows you who's master.' Rupert remained stiff but began to quiver as Sutton bored on. 'It baffles me how a cur like you had the brazen hide to manhandle my wife so. And what makes you think you can keep your wretched position at your tinpot bank?' Sutton drummed the arm of his chair with impatient fingers. 'So, the apology. Forthcoming, is it?'

Rupert's jaw was set. 'I shall never be sorry for trying to bring Violet some happiness.'

'No contrition at all?'

'No, sir.'

'Oh, "sir" now, is it? I suppose that indicates some slight awareness of your inferior position. Let's improve on that, shall we? You can begin by withdrawing my deposits from your bank, with the promised five per cent interest, and delivering it to me in cash no later than five next Thursday afternoon.'

Rupert went white. 'In *five days*? It's impossible. I don't have access to that kind of cash at short notice.'

'But I deposited it only a few short weeks ago. Whether possible or not, there is no other avenue for satisfying me. If you cannot rake up fifteen hundred pounds from your safe you must beg, borrow or steal it. I'm giving you two days, after all. Count yourself fortunate that I'm not demanding it by five tomorrow. Pay up and we will call this business closed. But if you fail I shall telegraph your superiors forthwith, not just in Auckland but in Wellington, Sydney and Melbourne. Your career in this benighted corner of the globe will be over. I have friends in the East and in London, too. My tentacles are long and strong, Beckford.'

Into the strained silence Thomas said, 'Are you done, Mr Sutton?'

'Hardly. You don't expect me to let him off scot-free, do you? I must have compensation for the hurt he's done me. I'm sure any judge would advise that two hundred and fifty pounds is a suitable solatium.'

'That's outrageous,' protested Violet.

'You dare to call *me* outrageous? A woman whom I found splayed on her own kitchen table, eager as a sow?'

Anna shot from her seat. 'Stop that at once. You will not insult her so.'

'Madam, you will not argue with me in my own house.'

Thomas got to his feet, hands outspread, palms pressing down in a bid to calm the room's tempers. 'Anna, you will take Mrs Sutton to the dining room, summon Hester to tend to her and then wait for me. We have business to do here.'

His wife gave him angry eyes. 'God forbid that ladies should have anything to do with *business*,' she said in acid tones. 'I will comply on one condition.' The men stared at her. 'They have not spoken since two nights ago. There are words they need to say to each other if this affair is to be ended. Forbid them and you can be assured they will find a way to talk elsewhere.' She looked at Rupert and Violet. 'Is that not true?'

'Absolutely,' he said.

'Yes,' she whispered.

'Chaperoned,' growled Sutton.

Anna sighed. 'If you insist.'

'Very well. When we're done here they can have five minutes. And no more.'

* * *

Violet and Anna faced each other across the gleaming table in the chilly dining room. A single candle flame cast a wavering pool of amber light. 'They will not be long,' said Violet. 'For what else is there to say?' Her eyes were bleak and hollow.

'You know Rupert is ruined either way,' Anna said. 'Such a large and sudden withdrawal of funds, so soon after they've been deposited, will prompt a sharp enquiry from his betters. I know how worried Thomas would be if he were in the same place. Rupert told me weeks ago, in Auckland, that he was already being hard-pressed. Bankers are ruthless. They will see him as somehow derelict in his duty even if they don't know the whole truth.'

'You are trying to tell me he is a hopeless cause.'

'Oh, we've been through this today already, Violet.' And so they had. After Thomas had come in, grim and stiff after his conversation in the bank with Sutton, he had bailed up the two women in the parlour and told them how things stood. But not until he had stunned Anna with the real reason for Violet's fetching up on their doorstep.

Anna had turned on Violet, stung by her silence, her fabrications, feeling the sting of betrayal. 'You could have told me! How did you think to keep this quiet? It's not as if I didn't know what was happening between you.'

'Did you?' Thomas had asked, stunned in his turn. 'And you didn't think to share your knowledge with me?'

'Violet told me in confidence.' When Thomas snorted at that she added hotly, 'Women have confidences they sometimes do not share, even with husbands.'

'We shall discuss this later,' Thomas had said, but there'd been no time, the day full of whispers and silences and careful curtain pullings and an unbearable tension that had descended on their formerly serene domestic life. All of it had led to their uncomfortable communal trudge up the hill to the Sutton residence. Dinah had stayed to settle behind Jamie who whined in protest, puzzled by the uneasy currents swirling over his head.

It was still not over, this evening of accountability and retribution, and soon three of them would be walking downhill again in the dark — weary Thomas, sad Anna and wretched Rupert.

Anna sighed. Violet — bold, *scarlet* Violet — had blown a keen draught into her ordered life, one that ruffled pages and raised the dust.

Everyone knew what sort of behaviour the world demanded of a respectable lady. But oh, *respectability*. Anna did know how stifling it could be. Sometimes a shawl woven out of rules feels more like a shroud than a comfort.

She eyed Violet now across the five feet of English oak that lay between them.

'Will you do as Henry demands and stay here, under his roof, despite everything?'

'I have little choice. No money. No plans. No escape.'

'Are you afraid?'

'Yes, a little. But at least I don't have to be with him tonight.'

'Where will you sleep?'

'Hester will show me. Though I doubt I shall sleep at all.' Violet stood and walked aimlessly around the table, pulling open the velvet drapes to let in the night. She let the fabric fall, turned and leaned against the sill. 'It is ironic, this turn of events. A few days ago Henry was, for once, being thoughtful and solicitous. Just last week I told him I think I am expecting a child, which is what he has been requiring of me all along — a son to call his own. He was full of good cheer as he set out in the morning, saying he hoped this could be the start of a better time for us. Which made it much worse when he found me with Rupert.'

Anna's mouth dropped open. 'How could you do that, knowing you. . .?' She waved her hands as if to enfold a roundness in her own belly. 'Is it Henry's?'

'Yes. I must have fallen some weeks back, well before Rupert and I became close.' Her mouth twisted into a rueful quirk. 'Henry will keep interrogating me, probing the when and where of it. If he thought I was carrying Rupert's child — oh, another bastard, Anna, I cannot bear the thought of it — he would cast me out. Though this time, at least, I would leave with my child and not have it torn from me.

'I suppose it's possible he may just accept it, for there are the financials too. Discard me and he loses the flow of money from my father as well.' She rolled her eyes. 'How he would detest that prospect. And to be honest, it terrifies me too as I have no idea how I would make my way in the world without any funds to call on.' She went back to her seat, put her head in her hands and let out a barking sob before controlling herself. 'Oh Anna, I have made such a mess of my life.'

'You took such risks, Violet.'

'I know, I know.'

'When are you going to tell Rupert about the child?'

Violet's hands flopped into her lap. 'Now. In the next few minutes, though next week was what I'd planned. In Auckland I wanted just that brief time alone with him. He was so deliciously incorrigible in loving me. Knowing the peril but daring to anyway. So alive. He made every part of me sing. It was to be one last happy time before I had to call an end to it. I dread telling him for I know it will plunge him into misery.

'I can see he is already miserable, as am I. But we must make the best of it. He has his livelihood to see to, his own life to get on with, some naive girl to find and settle down with, putting me out of his head. And I must at least put on the appearance of the dutiful and contented wife.'

The door opened. Sutton entered with head held high, somehow expanded in his chest, flushed with righteousness. The women stood.

'Where is Hester? Hester!' he shouted. She came padding along the corridor. 'Mrs Hamilton, return to the drawing room if you will. Hester, bring in a lamp, we need more light in here. Then return to the kitchen. You'll be called again shortly.' Hester did as she was told. Anna left, giving Violet a brief kiss on the cheek as she departed.

Sutton pulled the drapes wide open and stepped to the door. 'Come,' he called, and Rupert and Thomas shuffled in. 'Beckford, you have five minutes to take your leave of my wife, even though, by God, it's the last thing you deserve. You will sit at opposite sides of the table.

'Hamilton, you'll oblige me by stepping out on the veranda and observing them through the glass. When five minutes have passed you will rap upon the window, thus terminating their meeting. Understood?' He glowered at them all and without waiting for assent declared he was retiring to his study.

Thomas took up his post, fob watch in hand, in the keen evening breeze. He hated to look but carried out his chaperone duty as requested and watched Rupert on the edge of his chair. He could see only the back of his head. Violet leaned towards him and talked. Rupert interrupted her a few times, shaking his head at one stage and pounding his fist once on the table top, but she seemed steadfast, her eyes never leaving his face. Her voice was too soft for any of her words to penetrate the glass. It was like watching a play with cotton-plugged ears, a silent tragedy unfolding in the lamplight.

Then when the time had almost ticked away, Violet Sutton rose and came to the window looking at him with imploring eyes. Rupert got up and stood with her. She held up her hands to Thomas, palms pressed in prayer position, then put one hushing finger to her lips as she reached out for Rupert's hand and pulled him away from the window into the room's corner, out of sight.

Thomas raised his own hand to make a stern and bony fist, ready to knuckle-knock at the glass, but the look in Rupert's stricken eyes and the way his mouth shaped a silent 'please' stayed his hand.

They stepped behind the curtain away from his gaze. Thomas waited for endless seconds, seeing the hand creep swiftly up his watch face and knowing all too well that in his study along the corridor, Sutton would be watching his own timepiece.

He shut his eyes and rapped upon the glass. Rupert and Violet stepped back into view, faces strained, and by the time Sutton strode back through the door they were back in their chairs. Violet rose and left with her head down, glancing at neither her husband nor her former lover, heading for the kitchen and calling Hester's name.

CHAPTER TWENTY-SIX

'Sometime between 1 and 2 o'clock on Thursday morning the inhabitants of Tauranga, or those amongst them who were up, were startled by repeated and vivid flashes of lightning shooting at intervals of a few seconds, from a dense mass of black cloud extending along the southern sky. The electrical display continued during the night, and about four o'clock in the morning a series of severe earthquake shocks were distinctly felt.'
— Mt Tarawera eruption reported by the Bay of Plenty Times.

JUNE 9TH, 1886

My dear Anna

Thank you for your kindness in standing by me, even when you learnt I had let you down with my sins of commission and omission. I apologise for telling you foolish half-truths about that moment when Henry discovered us. This, it could be said, is simply another way of saying I fed you falsehoods. I did so only because I could not bear that you might think ill of me. Despite that, you have been gracious enough to remain my friend. At least I hope you still think of yourself in that way.

Four days have passed since I last saw you. I sit here in silence, cut off from the world. While most of my thoughts are of how Rupert is faring (for tomorrow is when he must settle with Henry or take the consequences) I am often also thinking of you and your welfare.

I hate to think I may have been the cause of unhappiness between you and Thomas, for before I entered your life I have no doubt that any upheavals you endured were ones that you faced jointly. But then along I came and provoked you into various new ways of thinking, I fear, and it sometimes does not serve a marriage well when two minds are not working in concert.

However, what right have I to speak of marital contentment, I who seems not to have the knack of finding it at all?

It is my hope that all is well in your home. If you feel discomfort, please forgive me for it. They tell me that time heals all wounds. I have not found that to be true as my own wounds still feel raw even after the passage of years.

I can tell you that I have, meanwhile, been taken down a peg or two, as I sleep on a cot in the corner of Hester's own small room, there being no other chamber in the house which Henry deems suitable for me in my sullied state. Mostly I am confined to the kitchen or out on the veranda where we used to do our embroidery.

Henry says this is my punishment but in fact I find my exiled state quite companionable, given Hester's kind forbearance. She is not exactly stimulating company but her steady presence is a comfort and she is also kind enough to deliver this note to you today. I am forbidden to leave the house at all.

I miss my solitary walks to the shore. Twice now Henry has ordered me to the dining room where I must sit like a child before the headmaster while he badgers me for assurances that the child is his. What else can I say but yes? I am almost sure it is so as the timing favours that conclusion. He is torn between triumph and anxiety.

But, oh, Anna, what would my fate be if this baby emerged with a head of flaming hair? Of course, a girl will hardly fit his expectations either. So much lies in the hand of Fate.

I would be grateful for any news you feel free to impart and assure you I remain your affectionate friend,
Violet

* * *

THOMAS WAS shocked awake early on the tenth of June by a combination of assaults. Jamie was screaming and Anna's panic was loud in his ear even as his head shot up off the pillow. The very earth itself was in an uproar. Deep rumblings jangled his nerves and brilliant vertical flashes of light seared into the room through gaps around the curtains. The house was groaning. Chair legs jittered on the floorboards. 'God Almighty, get up Anna, out of bed!'

She needed no urging, was already staggering in her flannel nightgown through the creaking doorway to get to her son. 'Mamma, Papa!' he called over and again. When Anna lurched into his room with Thomas close behind, Jamie was huddled in his bed, curled tight, fists over his ears, eyes screwed shut. She gathered him up and they huddled on his narrow mattress with heads tucked down, arms tight around each other.

Thomas ripped the curtains open. The sky to the southwest glowed with a weird and ruddy light, curdled with leaden clouds. 'Stay here,' he ordered.

'Don't leave us,' wailed Anna, but he couldn't stay still, couldn't sit, had to see. And as he fumbled for his boots, wrenched open their front door and went out into the street it seemed half the town's people were out there in night clothes or blankets. He'd grabbed his overcoat from the hallstand and shrugged it on but it felt flimsy as a cobweb as he gazed up at the roiling blackness that blotted out the stars.

'Dear Lord, we shall die!' a woman screamed.

'It's the end!' wailed another.

'It's an eruption,' said Rupert at his shoulder. 'The Hot Lakes. Something's gone up. Where d'you think — Rotorua? Taupo? By Jove, can you imagine what they're going through?'

Thomas turned to him. A lightning flash revealed Rupert's pale face and burnished his tangled mane. For a second or two his hair seemed to be aflame. They were both breathing hard. Another thunderous boom rolled over the town. 'Come in with me,' he said. 'We can't stay out here.'

Rupert shook his head. 'Can't leave my premises. Look at the panic.'

And he pointed at the huddles of swearing, weeping townsfolk around them. 'Tomorrow — if we survive until morning — will be bedlam. We should be at our posts, right?'

'It is morning, isn't it? Despite the dark?'

'Not yet. Only just past two, I think, though it's exceeding hard to tell.' His mouth stretched in a wild grin, teeth agleam in the dull flickering glare. 'At least my financial day of reckoning is postponed, don't you think?'

Dark, shouting shapes pushed between them, and Thomas turned to go back to his family. At least Rupert had the good sense to see where his responsibility lay tonight. And who cared about his indulgences now? What did it matter if a man had another's wife when the world was ending?

He could see Anna bent over in the doorway, her arms around Jamie as they peered out at the nightmare. 'Inside!' he yelled. 'Stay inside!' He stepped into the hall and slammed the door. Jamie grabbed him around the legs and hung on.

They went into the kitchen then and waited, debating what might be happening inland. Jamie refused to be put back to bed and so they sat at the table as the booms kept coming. Sleep was impossible. And then there came loud knocking at the door.

Anna opened to find a crowd. Dinah stood closest, wrapped in a thick rug, eyes wide and beseeching, and at her shoulder was one, three, five, no, at least a dozen more. 'Please, can we come in? You have a strong home, the strongest here. Our roof is cracked from the shaking and my mokopuna is ill. See?' And she uncovered a bundle in her arms to reveal the small grey face of a tiny child who had dry, open lips and a heaving chest.

Thomas pushed past Anna out onto the step to help them in. They were followed by what seemed like an entire village, young men and old, ancient crones and mothers, trailing a horde of children. 'My people,' she said. They followed Dinah into the kitchen, seemed at once at ease, sinking to the floor, huddling close to the warm stove. They were singing a little, or humming. It was hard to name a word for their ancient, mournful noise.

Anna raised the wick in a lamp to provide more light. She frowned and brushed at Thomas's shoulders. "Look! It's snowing."

He swiped at his coat in disbelief, saw minute, pale, lamp-lit specks drift to the floor. 'Not snow,' he said grimly. 'Ash.'

Their visitors had brought in smells of sulphur and clay, muddy earth and salt. Never had the kitchen been so full of brown faces. Furrowed brows and rolling, fear-filled eyes had taken over his domestic domain, yet Thomas had no desire to take to the privacy of the cold drawing room. Company was preferable on this turbulent night. Outside the rumbling went on.

Dinah worked at the stove to heat some water, dropped some herbs into a pot, veiled the baby's head in a cloth and held its small face over the steam. The baby's breathing eased after a time and she was able to place the tiny boy in his mother's arms.

Unable to stay still, Thomas paced the house for hours, stepping over stretched-out legs to peer out at the gloom. He lit the fire in the parlour after some time, for more people had streamed in, just as needy as the first group. Now bodies were huddled on his rugs and in his chairs. When he periodically went out with a lamp held high, its glow could barely penetrate the dusty blizzard. A stinking gust of ash billowed into the hall every time he cracked open the door, provoking whimpers and shrieks.

'Thomas, no!' Anna called. 'We'll choke on it.'

He could see only far enough to judge that the ash was inches deep. He was suddenly bone-tired. He worried about farmers and their stock. He worried about his own roof. He worried about the windows. He worried about the building that sheltered them, even though Dinah was right; the building was sturdily constructed and their quarters were part of the main structure. Only a catastrophe could destroy it.

Even so, he unlocked the internal door to the bank, shut himself in for safety's sake and prowled around, shining his light behind the counter and into every dark recess. All seemed normal, if normal was a word one could apply to anything on this interminable night. He turned and became aware that the unrelenting black of the window-panes was giving way to murky grey. Feeling weak with relief, he went back to the kitchen.

'I see daylight,' he announced.

Bleary faces turned to him. Jamie had been curled, quilt-wrapped, in a corner, but now he blinked and looked up. His eyes were hollow. 'Papa? Is it morning? Where is the sun?'

'Rising, my boy, as it always does. It's just hard to see it now.'

'Can I go outside?'

'No dear, not yet,' said Anna, smoothing his dusty hair. 'It's not safe. And too dirty besides. There's ash everywhere.'

'In the garden?'

'Yes.'

'And on the road?'

'Yes, everywhere.'

'Even on the sea?'

'I suppose so.'

'Why?'

'It's a volcano,' said Thomas. 'Fire has come up from under the ground and made all that noise and pushed ash up into the sky.'

'Will the fire come here too?'

'No, Jamie,' said Anna, though the tremor in her voice hinted she wasn't at all sure. 'It's happening a long way from here.'

'I'll go to the telegraph office,' said Thomas. 'See if there's news. Surely Archer will be there.'

'Take care,' Anna called. He was already wrapping a scarf around his face and stepping into the half-dark. A hazy horizontal slit of light seared the eastern sky, casting eerie slanting shadows.

All colour was expunged. The town was grey and black. Ash lay like dirty snow, heaped against fences and walls and making a powdery blanket on every level surface. A chill breeze shifted and stirred it all the time so that it never lay still and Thomas had to stop often to conquer a sense of dizziness — it was as if the ground itself was sliding beneath his feet.

Every move made the ash rise, blinding him as he walked. It was like wading through stinking fog. A black dog raced up the road leaving a tumult of dust in its wake, panicked but silent, its golden eyes on fire as it ran. Other people were stirring too, calling anxiously to each other through carefully opened windows, but their voices were strangely muffled.

Thomas turned down Wharf Street, constantly touching walls and fences to keep his orientation. People had lights burning and the flickering glow was a comfort. A few shopkeepers were even opening their doors. It had not even occurred to Thomas that he might open the bank on this day. He pulled out his watch and squinted to make out its face. It was past eight o'clock and yet the daylight was failing to increase. If anything, the sullen light to the east seemed dimmer than before.

At the telegraph office a crowd had gathered. The small room looked to be packed and others pressed around the door, everyone gabbling, many coughing in the fetid air, desperate for news of missing family or friends, their voices tight with tension. Thomas could see little point in trying to push his way through to Archer's desk.

'Any details yet?' he asked the men in front of him. 'Do we know what's happened?' The stories came flooding back at him. Mount Tarawera had exploded. Many lives were lost. Lake Rotorua had risen. There were boiling springs flooding up everywhere. Panicked residents were fleeing.

His heart sank. 'Good God,' he blurted. 'It's the end of everything.' And then regretted it instantly because those around him looked shocked by how undone he sounded. If he, who held the keys to the bank in which so many of them placed their trust, gave an impression of despair, then what hope did the rest of them have?

He stood tall, with an effort. 'We don't know how much of it is true. It's easy for rumours to spread like wildlife, hmm? It may be days before we hear the right story. Let's just go home and sit it out, what do you say? Comfort your ladies, reassure the little ones. The skies will clear tomorrow.'

'But look around you,' said Jack Ward, whose ovens would clearly turn out no loaves today. 'The land will be ruined. There'll be no feed for animals, the crops will wither.'

'Not at all, man, it's too early to tell. A volcano does not erupt forever and the next rain will wash everything clean. Things will return to normal.' But the ash was so thick now that Thomas's voice dried in his throat. A gust of wind blew in their faces and they all hunched away from it, pulling collars and scarves up around their mouths.

Thomas turned and churned a gritty track back up the road towards home. Anna was alone there, after all, with a throng of natives who seemed thoroughly settled in for however long this emergency would take to unfold.

* * *

ANNA WAS in her parlour where Dinah was pacing with a baby over her shoulder, trying to soothe its fretful whimpering.

'Is this all of your family?' Anna asked . 'Is everybody safe?'

Dinah nodded. 'This is the whanau, yes. And look, you know this one.' With her toe she prodded the sleeping form of a young man who was curled up in a corner, wrapped in what looked like a sheet from Anna's linen press.

He muttered but did not wake. 'Young men, they sleep like the dead. Kehu!' she snapped, louder now. 'Get up. Meet your hostess. On dry land this time.'

He struggled to his feet, squinted at Anna and nodded blearily. He seemed not to know her, but in the half-dark that was not surprising.

'Sit down again,' Anna said. 'Please rest. After what you did for me, this floor is yours as long as you want it.'

* * *

WHEN THOMAS PLODDED inside she met him at the door and leaned against him. 'I've put Jamie to bed. He complained but he's asleep at last,' she said.

He pushed her away, aware of his own filth, leaving powdery blooms on her shoulders where his palms touched her, and told her what little intelligence he'd managed to gather.

He was exhausted now and envied his son. A short nap was called for. The damn chanting was still coming from the crowded kitchen. He eased his feet from his boots, padded to his bedroom and stopped short. It was just light enough for him to make out a thin old man lying there under the blankets, snoring. His tattooed cheek lay on Thomas's pillow and two small children nestled against his back and thighs.

Something snapped in him then. He spun and stamped back to Anna, who still stood at the front door. 'There are strangers in our bed! Can a man not get some rest in his own home? How long are these people going to eat our food and make their infernal noise?'

Anna raised her hands helplessly. 'I don't know, Thomas, but we cannot expel them into the storm.'

A shadow slipped through the kitchen doorway to stand behind Anna. It was Dinah. 'We will leave when it is safe,' she said. 'Mrs Hamilton owes us this debt. She promised that if I asked for help she would give it.' She waved a hand at the small crowd in the kitchen. 'This is that time.'

A child began to bawl and Anna slipped past Thomas, her face drawn and anxious. 'Not now, Thomas. They're hungry. We all are. There's too much to do.'

* * *

ONLY AT ABOUT ELEVEN in the morning did the gloom begin to lift again. Thomas opened his front door. The brass plate on its step had gone black. The air was marginally clearer but still had a sulphurous whiff. The dreadful rumbling had ceased. The earth seemed quiet now.

As he took a step out onto his path he heard an oddly sharp sound, the cracking thump of a sharp axe on wood. It was quite close. He crossed the road to the corner. Standing in the small garden outside Rupert's windows was a man braced on outspread legs. He was chopping ferociously at the butter-fruit trees. One was already down in the dust.

With every stroke of the axe the second tree shuddered, ash flung out from its outspread branches so that it, and the axeman, were lost in a billowing haze. Every swing of the blade caught a gleam of baleful sunlight. Then the second tree was down, falling with a rustling thud. Henry Sutton turned from the naked stumps, his chest heaving, and saw Thomas standing there. He dropped the axe. It disappeared into the grey cloud that swirled around his knees.

He managed a brief rasp of mocking laughter as he came out to the street. 'Not likely to get any other sort of satisfaction from him today. D'you think that'll do as a reminder?' He jerked his head at the tangled mess of branches.

They stared at Rupert's windows. There was no sign of lamplight or candle. 'I think,' said Thomas, 'that we have much more to do today than indulge in vengeful pruning.'

Sutton turned away and began to walk back towards his home. 'Is all well at your house?' Thomas called after him. 'Do you need any assistance?' Sutton merely made a dismissive backwards swatting motion with his hand as he disappeared into the dust cloud.

June 12, 1886

My dear Violet

Hester has only just brought your note of the 9th to me today. We are all of course so very occupied with cleaning up the smothering ash. So many people are dead and missing at the Hot Lakes. It breaks my heart to think what a terrible time the survivors have endured. They say that Rotorua is not as much affected as we heard earlier but that the landscape is much altered elsewhere and that the Pink and White Terraces have probably been wiped away. We were going to visit, remember? Now we never shall.

Our distance from the devastation has kept us safe but it has been bad enough with so much foul dust still lying over all. We clean and clean and yet it still clings in nooks and crannies.

I took all of our clothes outside yesterday and beat them on the clothes-line and clouds of matter came flying out of every pleat and pocket. The Strand has been packed with herds of mournful, hungry animals waiting for ships to take them away, for with the land so blighted there is nothing for them to eat. I find their distress hard to listen to.

There is little milk to be had and it seems the hens have been too frightened to lay more than a few token eggs.

You do not need me to tell you this, of course. Your own household will also be plagued. I miss, however, being able to sit opposite you to share stories, for this event will be surely one to tell grandchildren about in years to come. Hester tells me that it is wise for me to stay away for now. She also tells me you are well, however, and I am thankful for that. Please, dear, do write again when you can and assure me of your good health.

For all that the eruption has shocked me, it can never come close to how shaken I felt after the meeting in your drawing room. It's almost as if the weight of everyone's emotion soaked into the ground and caused the whole earth to explode. That is fanciful, I know. But I worry now about how difficult your situation is.

Thomas has been busy with desperate clients whose farms are struggling. I have not seen Rupert but I note a similar flood of people going in and out of his doors. Thomas says the ash will, in time, be a boon for the land, making it more fertile than before, but few are inclined to listen.

Our home has been full of people, including Dinah and her entire family who sought shelter at the height of the eruption, and then slipped away yesterday once the worst was over'

Is there any news of Rupert? The deadline for his payment to Henry has come and gone. Thomas tells me the telegraph office has been in huge demand with only emergency messages being transmitted, and so I have wondered if Rupert has had time or opportunity to muster the funds he needs to satisfy Henry.

Has H given him more time? Forgive me, it is not my business, and I cannot ask Thomas if he has heard anything. He certainly cannot interfere in R's affairs, especially as they work for rival banks. Thomas would in fact be very disapproving if he knew I was even venturing to ask you!

I hope that all will soon be settled and that the arrival of a baby will bring the balm needed to heal what has gone before. Perhaps the time will come when we can sit upon your veranda again with needle and thread and laugh about the adventures of our young and foolish years.

In answer to your query, yes, I am still your friend, Anna.

CHAPTER TWENTY-SEVEN

'Mankind descended from a pair. Mankind's troubles from an apple.'
— Bay of Plenty Times, 1886

JUNE 13, 1886

Thomas rose very early and went out with a bucket and shovel. In the middle of the night he'd thought of a way to assure people that all would be well, that the cursed ash would turn out to be a blessing for the Bay of Plenty.

The town's colours had returned. Leaves and grass were mostly green again. Ash was hard to find now, dispersed by wind or washed away by showers, but there were still corners where it lay. He went down the street, found gritty piles between tree roots and in the corners of adjoining walls and scooped it all into his bucket. The morning was quiet except for a distant croaking rooster. It was as if people were unwilling to climb out from beneath the covers to make themselves pick up their old routines.

With his bucket full, Thomas went back to his gate and glanced over to Rupert's rooms. They'd not laid eyes on each other since the night of the eruption. Now, there he was in his garden, looking at his ruined trees. His shoulders were slumped, his hands dangling loose. 'Rupert?' Thomas called. His voice sounded cracked. It was tired; all of him felt tired. He crossed the street and called again, more softly this time,

'Rupert, how have you been?' Rupert turned slowly, shocking Thomas with the bleakness in his eyes. He indicated the mangled branches and raw stumps. His lips twitched in a dry smile. 'When he has his revenge he thinks of every detail.'

'I saw him do it and told him much the same thing.'

The handle of Sutton's axe poked out from under curling leaves. Rupert bent and picked it up. It was small and beautifully tooled. He turned it in his hands and then suddenly bent back, raised it high and with a single hoarse, explosive yell flung it at his house. It turned once in the air with lethal grace before the blade cracked into the wood close to the open door. It stayed there, wedged at a slanting angle like a knife thrust up under ribs into the heart. There was silence between them.

Thomas switched hands with his bucket. Damp ash was surprisingly weighty. 'Did you manage to repay him?'

Rupert's face was empty of emotion as he pushed back a hank of tangled hair. 'I told him that with the eruption, the rush of work, clients desperate for cash for food and repairs and animal feed and transport, it was impossible to meet his deadline. Much to my surprise, he gave me more time.' Rupert's bark of laughter was mirthless. 'Tomorrow, my friend.' He surveyed the ruined garden once more. 'Tomorrow is the day.'

He hasn't shaved, thought Thomas. Mind you, neither had he. This day was still very new.

'I trust he will be kind to her,' Rupert said. 'I hope everyone will show her kindness.' He lifted his hand to Thomas for an awkward moment as if set for a handshake, but turned and went unsteadily inside past the embedded axe. He quietly closed his door.

Thomas lugged bucket and spade to his back door, set it down, went into the kitchen and washed his hands. He sagged into a chair and reached for the teapot. 'Saw Rupert just now,' he told Anna, 'giving off waves of misery.'

'Foolish, stupid man,' she said, clucking her tongue. 'Would you help him if you could?'

'Of course. But it's impossible. Only he can mend his situation.' Thomas sighed. 'Though I cannot see how.'

He did not dare tell his wife that he had already tried to help and their savings were sadly depleted as a result. Perhaps his father had been right all those years ago. The borrowing and lending of money could indeed lead a man to trouble. He found he could eat little of the porridge in his bowl. Jamie's prattling, which usually added charm to the day, bored into his skull like a hot wire. In an hour, he would be at his desk again, faced with an endless stream of worried men in shabby clothes, and not a few women, pleading for loans so they could pay their bills and feed their families.

Rupert, Rupert, feckless friend. Thomas felt a rush of rage. So many wild wagers on the horses, so many drinks ordered over sticky bar tops and poured down his throat, so much lusting after that restless, vain, foolish woman up the hill! It was hard on this morning to dredge up much kindness for either of them.

* * *

HE WAS WALKING the next morning for some exercise, just before opening his doors, when he heard a shout behind him. It was Ward on the street outside his bakery, flour-coated as always, his face pale. 'Hamilton, go to Beckford's place. There's been an accident!'

Thomas ran back along Willow Street with pounding heart and turned the corner onto the steps in front of the National Bank. The door was closed but when he rattled at the handle it gave way instantly. Rupert's clerk was inside, white-faced, while Jim Spooner, whose watchmaking shop was nearby, stood taut and anxious, guarding the way to Rupert's private rooms. 'Thomas,' he said. 'Best not to go in. Dear Christ, such a sight. We've sent for the doctor and the constable so there's nothing you can do.'

'But what's happened? For pity's sake, Jim.'

Spooner stepped aside. 'Brace yourself,' he said.

Rupert was sprawled on the floor. A ghastly pond was spreading out from under his head, some of his bright hair soaked with it. There was a small dark hole between his right ear and sightless eye. His face was blank. If there was any expression at all it seemed to be one of slight surprise.

Thomas staggered, groaned and went to one knee, steadying himself against a chair as he pressed a hand to his mouth to stop himself from howling. He wanted to vomit too but some clear portion of his mind told him the room's mess and odour were already vile enough. A fly landed on Rupert's forehead and Thomas flailed at it. 'God in heaven!' he shouted. 'Can we not at least find a cloth to cover him?'Spooner filled the doorway, looking everywhere but at the body. 'I thought perhaps we should not touch anything yet.'

Thomas pushed himself up, went into Rupert's bedroom, tossed a blanket aside and ripped the top sheet off the bed. He noticed small things in the second it took to do this. He saw the indentation Rupert's head had left in his pillow. He saw two brandy bottles on their sides beneath the bedstead. He saw a small book on the dusty bedside table. Leaning against it was a clean white envelope. Scrawled on it, in Rupert's looping script, was his own name and underneath that was the line, 'Private and personal, for his eyes only'.

Thomas picked it up, pushed it into a trouser pocket and took the sheet into the parlour. Tiptoeing to avoid stepping in gore, he draped it over the body. A corner of the sheet fell into the blood. It instantly oozed through the weave. He looked away, feeling a new wave of nausea.

Voices began to build in the bank's main chamber and in moments the room was full. Here was the doctor, removing the sheet and exposing Rupert's corpse all over again. Here was a constable, telling Thomas to go, please, and that the inspector would be in to see him later. Curious neighbours were beginning to peer in the windows. There were small shrieks and sobs and a hum of questions and gossip.

Thomas slipped out, spoke to no one, went back to his house and suffered the sight of Anna's face blanching and then crumpling as he told her the news.

Wails went up in the Sutton house an hour later. 'Oh mercy, oh God, no,' Violet moaned. And then, 'Who killed him?' Eyes blazing, wild with anguish and rage, shrieking, 'Do they know who killed him?'

'Nobody, Violet,' said Anna. She had run up to the Sutton house as soon as she could, ignoring Thomas when he implored her to stay away. She had gone to Hester's kitchen door, determined to avoid Henry Sutton, and found the women there. Their faces had swung to her, blank with surprise, when she burst in. 'They found the gun beneath him, Violet. It was an old one of Spooner's. Rupert bought it just a week ago.'

A terrible silence fell, filled only by Violet's heaving gasps as she struggled for control.

'You mean he took his own. . .?' She could not finish the question.

Anna reached for her then and held her for a long time, rocking her friend in the same way that she would comfort a desperate child. Hester collapsed onto a chair and reached into her apron for a kerchief, shaking her head in sorrow. 'Dearie, dearie me,' she muttered. 'God bless his foolish heart.'

CHAPTER TWENTY-EIGHT

'GUNS. GUNS. GUNS. To Sportsmen. D. Evitt, Gunmaker, 251 Queen-street, Auckland, offers for sale, at unusually low prices: Double breech-loading guns, double muzzle-loading guns, single muzzle-loading guns, Curtis and Harvey's Diamond Gunpowder. Gun work of every kind done on the premises.'
— Auckland Star.

JUNE 14, 1886

'A six-chamber, breech-loaded revolver,' said Thomas to his awed clerk. 'The constable said five of the chambers were still loaded.'

'And it required only one bullet.'

'Indeed it did.'

He had a string of visitors. The first was the town's inspector of police to tell him the inquest would be held that afternoon at the Commercial Hotel, there being no other suitable large room available, and asking him to attend. Next was one of Rupert's habitual bar companions, Rogers the butcher, who was full of anxiety. He'd been asked to give evidence and wondered what he should say. 'Rupert talked about it, you see. I feel so guilty now. We all do.'

'What do you mean?'

'In the Clarendon last week, nigh on closin' time. We'd sat there too long, had grown loose-lipped on the ale. And we 'ad one of those wanderin' talks where you go on about things that go bump in the dark. And we got ter chaffin' about how a man might do away with 'imself if he was of a mind ter. But we never reckoned we'd soon be at his inquest, and in the same four walls n'all.'

'What did he say?'

'That he thought it'd be fast and easy.'

'Did you not take him seriously?'

'No, we were all a bit maudlin by then, makin' jokes about how to tie a perfick hangman's knot or how many gobfuls of Rough on Rats powder it'd take to kill a man of Ralph Ward's girth.' Scott chewed on his lower lip in an awkward, shamed way. 'We were all a bit mad that night, stupid as roosters. Rupert even play-acted, holdin' up his hand with a finger to his noggin. "Boom!" he hollered. And he laughed. We all did.'

'Good lord,' said Thomas.

Rogers' chin quivered and he stood up. 'Not sure when I'll crack a smile again.' He turned to go.

'Wait,' said Thomas. 'Tomorrow I have to plan his funeral.'

'*You* do?'

'His employers have telegraphed me and my superiors concur — it seems to be down to me as the only other banker in town. He has no kin here and we used to be close before drink got the better of him. We can't let him go without a Christian burial.'

'But he were never much of church-goin' man. Not as I could tell.'

'The thing is, he can only be buried properly if it's thought he was of unsound mind. If he's considered to have done it deliberately we'll not get any churchman to preside.'

Rogers frowned. 'Why is this of any moment to me?'

'Well, at the inquest, can you say he seemed unbalanced, not in his right mind?'

The butcher scratched his head. 'I suppose so. Though, to tell the truth, he were no more addled than any of us that night.'

'But as a friend of his, can you do that much for him?'

Rogers hesitated, nodded. 'That I will. He were well-liked, young Rupert. We'll all miss him. In truth, we already do.'

* * *

IT WAS UNSEASONABLY warm for the inquest. The hotel was packed. 'Inquests always draw a throng,' Thomas told Anna later. 'There's a drear fascination for scandal.'

'And the verdict?' she asked.

'Died by his own hand whilst in a state of insanity.'

'Due to his drinking?'

'Oh yes, there was no end of evidence about his love of the bottle. The jury was well ready to believe he was severely troubled.'

'No mention of any other possibilities?'

'No. The coroner said he thought there was little point in further investigation. Not that he knows anything, of course. He seemed anxious to put a lid on proceedings as fast as he could.'

'Was Sutton there?'

'No. Her neither, of course. Not a seemly place for a woman, even one as foolish as her.'

They were sitting at the kitchen table. Thomas felt as tired as he'd ever been. He picked up a fork and poked pensively at the soil around a potted geranium. 'Rupert wrote to me the night before, telling me he'd soon be far away. I wasn't the only recipient apparently. Half the witnesses got one of his notes saying it was better for him to be gone. And that he'd been, apparently, a "reckless fellow".'

'Is that what he wrote to you?'

'Partly. But he added more for me. Finally, he was feeling some guilt. His anguish was mostly about her. He begged me to not to tell anyone else of their entanglement. Protecting her reputation to the end.'

Anna took the fork from him and used her apron to wipe crumbs of earth from its tines. She'd polished it only that morning. Her mouth was set. 'I'm so *angry* with him,' she declared as she smacked it down. 'How dare he make us all so miserable!'

'He was reckless. It always breeds bad consequences. She was reckless too. I can't feel any sympathy for her. Silly, empty-headed strumpet.'.

Anna looked at her folded hands, her mouth crimping. 'Hardly that.'

'Hardly what?'

'Empty-headed. She is one of the most thoughtful women I know.'

'Anna, will you please drop this attachment to her? She's a scarlet woman, a blight upon this town and upon our peace of mind. I do not want her in this house again, do you hear me? I don't want her even mentioned! I've had enough of her attitudes and her subversive literature. Look where freethinking and loose behaviour have sent poor Rupert. Straight to his grave.'

Anna stared at him. She said nothing but her eyes were mutinous.

He sagged. 'It wasn't just her who did for Rupert, though. It was the drink and the money as well.'

'What money?' Thomas got up with a groan to ease his aching back. He had to go and see the Reverend Larkin about the funeral service. It needed to be held speedily. Mrs Lewis would have done her best with her herbs and bandages but the bullet had apparently made a fearful mess at the back of Rupert's head. Thomas was relieved that the neat dark circle of the entry wound was all that he'd seen.

'He had many debts.' Thomas was wishing now he'd not raised it. 'He couldn't pay Sutton, he couldn't pay anyone. It was gnawing at him. He told me so himself.'

'In the letter?'

'No, weeks ago. He'd been in trouble for some time.'

'Where is the letter?'

Thomas indicated the stove. 'Burnt. I didn't want to have to produce it in court. Thought it best to just say nothing about it all.'

He left to plod his way to the parson's cottage. Churning inside him was the knowledge that not only had he again avoided honesty with his wife, but also that the packed room had heard him testify that to the best of his knowledge, the deceased had no financial worries.

* * *

LARKIN OPENED his door even before Thomas knocked. 'Here you are. I heard you're to organise the service.'

'This town hears everything before a man has time to even eat his breakfast.'

'Come and sit down. The sooner we can expedite this sad matter the better.' Larkin shook his head, wearing a mournful look that seemed genuine enough. 'It's no fit way for a young man's life to end. Ah, the evils of alcohol.'

He ushered Thomas into his study and showed him to a seat. His eyes glinted a little as he asked if Thomas knew of any just cause why Beckford should not be lowered into his grave with the blessing of God.

'That is a question you need not ask, Reverend. You were at the inquest. You heard the coroner. Rupert Beckford, being of unsound mind, was blameless in his demise.'

'Ah, but the legal mind stands apart from the mind of a moral man. I must be assured, for the good of my conscience, that Mr Beckford had no pressing issues in his life other than too much enthusiasm for spirits and that what happened was brought about by liquor's evil effects and nothing more.'

Thomas tried not to sigh or fidget. 'Yes, Reverend. In my experience, Rupert was the best of men. We were close in the past and, at least when he was well, I counted him as a good friend. As you may recall, he was even a hero in the matter of the Ward boy's rescue. He was well liked. People are distressed. I think therefore that we need not waste any more energy in trying to guess his state of mind this morning. Our only duty now is to see him laid to rest with dignity.'

Larkin opened a record book, picked up his pen and dipped it in ink. 'Indeed, Mr Hamilton. With dignity and prayer. Our undertaker, Mr Dobie, is taking care of the body. We can only hope the Father is taking care of his soul — and be thankful that nobody who was truly close to him has to bear seeing him in his coffin. Now, what hymns shall we select?'

* * *

As Thomas wearily agreed to *Abide With Me*, Dobie was opening his door to a veiled woman who asked in a low voice if it was possible to pay her respects to the deceased. He reluctantly stepped back to allow her to come in. A few townspeople had already annoyed him with that melancholy request and he had shown them into the cool back room where the pine coffin lay on trestles, ready to be carried to the graveyard the next day. One small window let in just enough light to see by. Someone had left a posy of meagre flowers at the foot of the box.

As the visitor lifted the veil from her hat, he saw it was Mrs Sutton. He thought it odd and slightly unseemly that such a lady should creep in unaccompanied to visit the freshly dead, but then he was used to the peculiar behaviour people exhibited in the case of a sudden passing.

Her bleak gaze took in the coffin. She swallowed. 'May I see him?'

Dobie shuffled his feet. 'I hardly think so, ma'am. You must understand the circumstances. His head. . .'

She reached out and touched the lid. 'I know. But please?'

He coughed, irritated now. 'No, ma'am. It is not a suitable sight for a lady. I should hate my missus to have to view such a thing.'

'But I am not your missus. I am my own woman. And I should like to farewell a friend, no matter what state he is in.'

The impertinence of her, he thought. 'Very well, but do not blame me if you find yourself disconcerted.' He removed the posy and raised up the lid. It did not fit the box closely and it took him but a moment to reveal the corpse. Actually, the body did not, he thought, look too dreadful. Mrs Lewis had wrapped a bandage around most of the head and the visible portion of Beckford's slack face, framed by white linen, was unmarked, if now a drear shade of grey.

Mrs Sutton stepped forward and though she swayed for a second and pressed crossed hands to her heart, she made no sound. 'You may stay a short time,' Dobie told her. He leaned the lid against the wall and went back to his parlour where he'd left a cup of tea now doubtless gone cold.

When he returned a few minutes later she was gone. He looked in the coffin and saw scarlet and gold ivy leaves had been sprinkled down the length of the body. She must have gathered the last winter leaves from some vine. They glowed against the white linen like orange stars, some of them very similar to the colour of Beckford's hair. A few strands protruding from the bandage still shone bright even in the gloom.

He snorted, plucked up the leaves and cracked open the window to toss them out, offended by the garish embellishment of the shroud he'd arranged so neatly.

Dobie fetched his screwdriver. The lid should be fastened for good now. There were no local grieving parents or siblings to come cry over this body and he wasn't going to put up with half the town's sentimental womenfolk coming to mourn the Magenta Man. Too cocky by half, thought Dobie. Over-familiar with the ladies. And far too fond of the drink. Look where it had got him, all that carousing.

CHAPTER TWENTY-NINE

> *'Ah! It's woman's mission to make fools of men,' sighed a languid fop.*
> *'And how vexed we are,' said a bright-eyed woman present, 'to find that*
> *nature has so often forestalled us.'*
> —*Bay of Plenty Times.*

JUNE 15, 1886

The day of the funeral was calm and crisp. It seemed far too fine a morning upon which to lower into cold earth a man who'd been so full of life.

Violet was under orders to stay away despite her claim that her absence would seem out of character. 'I always go to the funerals of people I know. My absence may seem peculiar.'

'I do not trust you,' said Henry. 'You might give way to hysteria, make a spectacle of yourself.'

'Me? Hysterical?' Which had led to a loud and sorry argument about the character of Violet and of women in general. Henry had shouted. Violet had taken refuge in the kitchen. 'That's the way,' he'd jeered at her retreating back. 'Go back where you belong.'

After he'd stalked out she stood behind a lace curtain to watch him go. She knew he would be some time, for he would put on a show of farewelling Rupert as if they'd been the best of friends. Hester had gone to the funeral too. Violet was now as alone as it was possible to be.

Clumps of townspeople walked past her gate to the cemetery in their best black. There were couples and lone mourners and clumps of friends, walking with bowed heads.

They'd be more talkative on the way back. Funerals worked that way. It was as if the lowering of the coffin caused a commensurate rise in the spirits of those still standing. As soon as it was over, there would be a strange sort of relief in people's hearts. Because no one here was kin to poor Rupert there was no need to endure any widowish sobs and wails. There was much regret, of course, but moist eyes would dry miraculously after the first sods had landed with dull thuds upon the narrow lid.

'A grand but tragic lad,' said Hester to Dinah as they stood by the cemetery fence afterwards. 'Always 'ad a smile for me, 'e did. I still remember his swagger on that first day 'e came to call.'

'But there was something in him,' said Dinah. 'He was careless. You could see it in his eyes.'

The two housekeepers dawdled, enjoying the winter sunshine and watching the stream of men heading for one pub or another to raise a glass in honour of Rupert Beckford one more time. Or possibly three or four more times.

They knew more of the facts of the tragedy than anyone else in Tauranga save their employers. Sworn to silence, their purses were heavier as a result, but so too was the weight upon their hearts for they could not speak of the secret to anyone else.

'How is your lady?' asked Dinah.

'I wish I knew. She's gone into 'erself. She used to tell me things, little confidences, but now she's still as a mouse, just starin' out windows and reading old letters over and over again. She's deep, that one. I'll never know the 'alf of what's going on in 'er mind.' Hester sighed. 'If I weren't so fond of 'er I'd be packing m'bags. And I may still do. Plenty of work for the likes of us up Auckland way, m'dear. I hear the agency's got more posts than they can fill. I reckon I've had my time 'ere, just about.'

'I will never leave,' said Dinah. 'This is my turangawaewae. It is where I was born and where I will die.' She nodded her head back to the grave they'd just left. Workmen's backs were already bent over it, shovels swooping rhythmically as they filled in the gaping slot. 'But I won't be lonely like him. In twenty years, even ten, who will remember the name of that wretched red-haired boy? My mokopuna will know my name. But you British people, you come and you go and your people are scattered over the world. You are like stones skipping on water, never belonging. We are here forever.'

'Get away with ye,' said Hester, who had been widowed as a girl and was childless, too. She shuffled her feet in their worn boots, discomfited for a moment, for there were nights when she lay in her narrow bed and felt uncommonly lost being so far from the town of her birth. Not that she minded being away from the lazy, drunken father who was all that was left of her own family. If he died, and he probably had by now, there was no one who would bother to send her word across the heaving ocean.

'Ah well,' she sighed. 'At least I've got no ties and can go where the wind blows me.'

They stood and contemplated their different futures before Dinah said she had to go. Mrs Hamilton would be wanting refreshments and no doubt a humming circle of other ladies would be there too, all with something to say about Mr Beckford and the service.

'Spose I'd better shift m'bones too,' said Hester. 'Mr Grumpy will be back in a while, complainin' about something I should've done an hour before now.'

But after she plodded up the hill and around the path to the kitchen door and went inside she was struck by the silence of the place. She went into the hallway, stood under the archway halfway along its length and listened. Violet was not a noisy woman but there was usually some betrayal of her presence, the shuffle of her shoes, the rustle of a page turning over (for she was always writing furiously, that one), or the sound of the piano if she felt like playing some tune or other — not that she'd touched it lately. 'Ma'am?' Hester called. 'Mrs Sutton?' Silence.

Hester looked out on the veranda where her mistress often sat. The chair there was empty, the customary journal and pens absent from the small table.

She checked Mr Sutton's bedroom, the drawing room and dining room. The only hint that anything was amiss was that the doors of Violet's big wardrobe stood ajar. Hester knew well the clothes it contained, for their care was her responsibility. She'd handled every hem and sleeve. She'd laundered and pressed and brushed everything Mrs Sutton wore.

She pulled the doors open wider. It did not take her long to see that several garments were missing. Serviceable clothing for the most part — a dark grey skirt, jacket and a travelling cloak. Two blouses. A shawl. A hat. One silk gown. Hester went to the drawers that held undergarments. They were muddled. A hand had gone hurriedly through the mounds of fabric. Without counting garments Hester could not tell what was gone, but she did note the absence of a favourite nightgown and robe. And there was no sign of the silk pouch that held jewellery.

She heaved a long, ragged breath and went back to the kitchen. She felt stronger there in her own domain, but her heart thudded as she peeled potatoes and contemplated how hard it was going to be to tell her employer that while he (and she) had been out at the funeral, his wife had fled.

* * *

THOMAS OPENED the bank for the last hour of the working day but had seen few customers. Over the road, the National Bank's door had remained firmly shut, awaiting the arrival of Rupert's replacement or, probably, an inspector who would come to balance the books, check the records and ascertain that all was well.

They would have to be quick, Thomas thought, as he surveyed the locked windows and entrance. Rupert's customers would get anxious if they couldn't withdraw cash and make deposits.

Thomas had only just locked his own premises when someone rapped upon the door of his domestic quarters. Henry Sutton stood grim-faced on the step, periodically smacking a cane against his boot heels. He made no civil greeting, merely said, 'I would appreciate a few minutes of Mrs Hamilton's time.'

'Afternoon, Mr Sutton. I'm sure she'd be happy to oblige but she is somewhat occupied with lady friends,' said Thomas. He could hear the high clucking of women's voices in the parlour. Dinah's heels sounded on the timber floor as she swished through the hall behind his back with a tray of fresh sandwiches. 'Is there a way I can be of service?' he asked.

Sutton shuffled his feet. Across the street the dusty remains of the two trees he had axed still lay on the ground. 'I doubt it. She has gone, you see. Done a flit. With not a note, not a farewell, not an excuse of any sort.' His voice cracked and he coughed.

'Who has gone?'

'My *wife*, of course.' His cheeks flamed red but he clamped his jaws. His cheek muscles worked.

Thomas stepped back. 'Come in.' He took out his keys once more, unlocked the door leading through to his office, and ushered Sutton in. The air smelt of furniture wax, paper and coins. Sutton sat at Thomas's urging but in a moment was up again, too agitated to stay still.

'She had the gall to argue with me over attending the funeral. I forbade her to go and she acted outraged, while all the time she must have been planning this new betrayal. Must have had her bag packed the entire time, just waiting for her chance to abscond.'

'Do you have an inkling of where she might be?'

'Would I be here if that was the case? No. As far as I know, Violet counts your wife as her closest friend. I thought perhaps she might be here — even though I don't imagine you'd approve.'

'Indeed I would not. She has been a most unsettling influence on my household.'

'And Mrs Hamilton has said nothing to you of any plans she has detected?'

'No.' Thomas slumped into his chair. 'Though truth to tell, I suspect that she fails to share much of what has gone on between the two of them. I asked Anna not to see Violet, but within days she was scurrying up the hill to your door.'

'That damned Freethinking movement has much to answer for. Women imagining they are able to do as they wish. What utter folly.

Look what almost happened when the pair of them took themselves out in Beckford's boat. They could have drowned that morning.'

'What?' Thomas looked up at him, stunned.

'You didn't know? I found out myself only a few days ago. She was taunting me, triumphant that I'd been so unaware of what she'd been up to when my back was turned.' He raised an eyebrow and grunted. 'You'll be having words with Mrs Hamilton about *that*, no doubt.'

Thomas felt a rush of outrage that Anna had lied to him. He was also hit with a wave of dread over the thought of nearly losing her to the sea. The image of heaving waves and Peter Ward's blank, drowned face lolling over Rupert's shoulder filled his mind for a sickening moment and he pushed it away. He could not bear to stay seated while Sutton stood over him and so pushed back his chair. Its legs made a raw, scraping sound as he lurched to his feet.

Sutton scratched at his raspy chin. 'I'd not care about her going, you understand, if she weren't carrying my child. She can take herself off to perdition as far as I'm concerned, but I'm damned if I'll let her deprive me of my own flesh and blood.'

He shot a defiant look at Thomas. 'I suppose you find that hard to understand. But you have a son under your roof. I do not, and it's time. I'm not getting any younger while all this folderol is going on. And she owes me, dammit. I made her respectable when she deserved no respect at all. Nobody else would have had such a minx for a wife.'

'Do you think she may have sailed for Auckland during the funeral.' The *Maketu* had left as the assembled throng was singing 'Abide with Me'. Thomas remembered thinking how the whistle punctuated the gap between ragged verses. He'd been struggling not to weep at the time.

'She'd have had to buy a ticket to do that and I've been making sure there was no cash in the house,' said Sutton. 'If she's somehow laid hands on some paper then it's another way in which she's disobeyed me. But it can't be much. What does she think she can live on without my support? Auckland's a small place. She cannot hide for long.' Sutton smiled with grim derision. 'There is nowhere for her to go. Not until I'm ready, anyway, to send her on her way.'

'What will you do?'

'I'll wait. I'll telegraph people. If she's on that ship she'll be watched from the moment she arrives. I'll let her stew. She'll be pleased enough to come home when her money runs out. But first, may I see your wife?'

'What, now, when she has visitors?'

'Yes, now. It'll not take but a minute to quiz her. Then she can tell her friends. Women like to gossip. And if the ladies in your parlour hear the news, then in half an hour every house in Tauranga will know that poor Mrs Sutton, who is not quite right in her mind due to her condition, has seen fit to go wandering. They'll all be on the lookout for her.'

There was something about turning Violet Sutton into a fugitive that didn't sit easily with Thomas, no matter how reprehensible her behaviour.

On the other hand, the fact that Rupert was now beneath six feet of cold soil was partly her fault. She had also turned his Anna from loyal wife to secretive adventuress *and* risked her life in the process. He asked Sutton to wait, flung open the entry to his private quarters, went to the parlour and asked, no, demanded, that Anna follow him forthwith. 'She'll not be long,' he snapped to the astonished Mrs Archer and Mrs Bell, before closing the door on Anna's departing heels.

'My, he looks quite unlike his usual self,' said Fanny, nibbling on a last piece of cake. They had been at the Hamilton home for two hours and she'd been thinking she really should be departing. Not now though, not with this delicious interruption.

'A definite air of discombobulation,' Louise agreed. 'He's usually so composed.'

Anna was indeed not absent for long. She looked stricken upon her return. 'Mr Sutton is here,' she said. 'Looking for Violet. He says she's been acting strangely. And now she's missing.'

* * *

'GONE?' said Horace Archer, twenty minutes later. 'How very odd.'

'Yes,' said Louise, breathing hard from her scurry to the Post Office. 'It's shocking! She has disappeared into the night. Well, into the afternoon, while we were all at the graveside.'

Wilfred Bell shook his head at Fanny's avid story. 'Probably slipped aboard ship during the service. She'll not find a better provider than

Henry Sutton, silly hen. I always did think she reckoned she were too good for this place. No loss, if you ask me.'

'But according to Anna she's expecting a child. How can a woman go off on her own when she's got a baby 'neath her ribs?'

'More fool her.'

'But she might not've.'

'What?'

'Sailed away. We're all to be on the look-out, Anna says. Just in case she's not well and has gone to ground somewhere close by. Mr Hamilton came in and asked us to leave and so we did, of course. Poor Anna was limp with anxiety. She's probably taken to her bed.'

But Anna was not on her bed. She was facing her aggrieved husband. 'When were you going to tell me it was you and her out in Rupert's boat that morning?' He threw up his hands. 'The two *notorious* women who had to be rescued as they drifted out to sea.'

'How do you know? Was it Dinah?'

'What does she have to do with this? No, it was Sutton. His wife — if we can still call her that — recently apprised him of your adventure.'

Anna closed her eyes, compressed her lips. 'She shouldn't have!' she burst out and then said, 'Oh, Violet!' as if she was in the room and Anna could smack her cheek. 'It was our secret. She had no right.'

'She had no right to do all manner of things but went ahead anyway *and* persuaded you into supporting her. I cannot tell you how disappointed I am. You are usually so sensible. What possessed you to take up with such an unsuitable companion?'

Anna whirled to face him. 'Because she was lively, because she made me laugh, because she was a breath of fresh air in this town with its small minds and mean hearts. She simply gave me, a few times, a glimpse of moments when I could feel more unconfined.'

'What, have I ruled you with an iron fist? Have I said no to voyages to Auckland on your own? Have I forbidden you to organise concerts and show off your skills to a roomful of watching eyes?'

'No,' she said, drawing out the vowel in a long, despairing exhalation. 'You have done none of those things. It is just the prevailing *atmosphere* to which Violet has opened my eyes. It is all of society's tiresome rules. It is not about you, Thomas. I have not been deliberately slighting you.'

'It feels that way to me. Do you realise how much your secrecy pains me? We are man and wife. We are supposed to share our minds!' They heard a wail go up outside. 'See to Jamie,' Thomas said. 'You may not need society, or me, but your son needs his mother.' He stalked to the door and turned. 'You might like to think of that next time you consider taking some foolhardy risk.' He slammed the door behind him.

They spoke little at their evening meal, except for when Thomas asked Anna why she'd mentioned Dinah's name in connection with her boating mishap. She put down her soup spoon and told him it was Dinah's son and his friends who had pulled them into shore. 'She did not mention it to you because it was hardly her place to do so.'

Thomas nodded. Dinah worked in his home in daylight hours when he was in the bank. She took her orders from Anna. As the head of the house he was absent from that equation.

She glanced up at him. 'Remember when they all came here for shelter during the eruption?'

And then he did recall. He had quite forgotten Dinah's comment, driven from his memory by the chaos. 'You mean when she said we owed her some debt? That was it? Her son had saved your life?'

Anna nodded.

Thomas pushed away his plate. 'Again you disappoint me. You make me seem the most ungrateful of men. Had I known I'd have done more, and sooner, than merely giving her family shelter in a crisis. You have thought of nothing but your own comfort.' He snatched up a newspaper and buried himself behind its broad pages.

Later, ostentatiously, he fetched blankets and made himself a separate bed on the cot. He would have put it on the veranda but a chill wind from the south was lashing at the trees outside. There was no need for him to be more miserable than he already was. They lay in their bedroom on separate mattresses, a short but painful distance yawning between them.

After he blew out his candle he spoke to her again in the dark. 'Can I be assured that you have told me everything? Are there other secrets you have kept to yourself?'

She stared up to the dim ceiling. 'Am I to be allowed no secrets at all?'

'You are my wife,' he said, and the edge of surprise in his voice revealed that his ownership of her implied a right to know her thoughts.

'And you are my husband. But I do not insist that you tell me everything that crosses your mind or churns inside your heart.'

The only answer that came back was the arid squeak of the cot as Thomas turned his back to her.

CHAPTER THIRTY

*'All exciting topics of conversation should be avoided even at the family
table. Warm discussions and heated tempers interfere sadly with the
digestion and are in very bad taste. It should be made the study of every
lady how to turn the tide of a dangerous topic into some other channel.'*
— *Auckland Observer.*

JUNE 17, 1886

Several subdued days later Anna said quietly over lunch, 'You asked
me if there's anything else I know about Violet. There is something. She
left me a message.'

He looked up sharply. 'What? When? Why didn't you tell me?'

'I am telling you.'

'But only now.'

'I found it only yesterday. It was not posted. She had left it in a place
she mentioned to me once on one of our walks out along the shore.'

'What do you mean?'

'There's a huge pohutukawa tree where Rupert often kept his boat.
Its trunk is all twisting limbs and crevices. She once put her hand in one
as we walked past and it was very deep. "What a wonderful post box this
would make," she said. She was laughing. She said, "If we were children

we could leave secret messages for each other." So yesterday, on an impulse, I went there.'

Thomas stared at her. 'She left a note? Where is it now?'

'I destroyed it, just as you destroyed Rupert's. I knew you wouldn't want me to keep it. And before you ask, no, she did not say what her plans were, merely that her life with Henry was intolerable and that she was leaving. She thanked me for being her friend. There were messages for Dinah and Hester too, for both of them showed her kindness and she wished to pass on her gratitude.'

Thomas made a scoffing noise. 'Typical of her to be so dramatic. Why not use the Post Office?'

'She would not have wished to alert Henry. He kept a beady eye on all correspondence in and out of the house. Even if she'd given it to Hester to post he'd have been just as likely to rummage in her shopping basket. The Post Office is no sure route either. Louise sorts the mail sometimes and might have noticed that distinctive hand of hers.'

'How did she get out of the house? Wasn't she under curfew?'

'Yes, but hardly under lock and key. Violet loved the hour before dawn. She was often up early while Henry snored on. It must have been even easier for her to slip out once she was banished to Hester's quarters. And Hester would never have betrayed her.'

'But you might never have looked for it. It might have stayed in that tree until it rotted away.'

Anna shrugged. 'That is how Violet lives, by taking risks.'

Thomas shook his head. 'Sutton has my grudging sympathy then. A flighty woman like that — a man would never know where he stood with such a restless wife.'

Anna bit back the urge to retort that a woman would never know where she stood with a husband who couldn't conquer his tendency to rage.

'There is nothing more to say,' she said. 'I simply thought I should mention it in case you are intending to brood further.'

Thomas had by now moved back into the marital bed. The cot was, after all, supremely uncomfortable. But he looked up now with an expression that told her he was still displeased.

He was working harder than ever to encourage local enterprise, going so far as to plant three maize seedlings in pots to assure farmers that the volcanic ash would in time prove to be a boon. He'd planted one in ordinary soil, one in ash, and one in a mixture of the two. He was keeping them watered and awaiting green shoots, hoping the ash-boosted mix would prove to be the most fertile.

His desk was piled that afternoon with requests for overdrafts and so it was a relief to be interrupted by an unexpected caller. William Stewart was an inspector from Rupert's head office. His narrow shoulders were encased in dark tweed and his sharp eyes peered out from beneath beetling brows.

'Pardon my intrusion,' he said as he sat down. At the same time he took a sweeping look around as if keen to find fault in this bank as well as his own. 'I wish first to express our appreciation for your part in seeing to the funeral arrangements.'

'I was glad to be of service,' said Thomas. 'He was a lively lad until recently.' He was surprised to realise that he still could not speak of Rupert without a tremor in his voice. He cleared his throat. 'He was first-rate, you understand, and a good friend until he became. . . troubled.' He gathered himself. 'Did you know him?'

'Only by reputation. His troubles must have weighed mightily upon him to prompt action as drastic as plugging his skull with lead.' Stewart extracted an envelope from inside his waistcoat. 'I heard Beckford was busy with his pen before he went to meet his maker. Final notes like this were sent to all and sundry, I understand.'

'Yes, so it was said at the inquest.'

Stewart held his folded piece of paper as if it held some unhealthy taint. 'This one was left for me, as I had the miserable task of cleaning up after him. Did you receive one of his missives?'

'No sir,' Thomas felt only a slightly twinge over his deceit. He was not about to alter anything he'd said at the inquest.

'As one banking man to another I'd be grateful if you could assist me with a certain matter.'

Thomas shifted in his seat. 'Perhaps. But I knew nothing, naturally, of his business affairs. Our superiors demand discretion. We were both obliged to set banking matters aside in any conversation.'

'Discretion? Ha!' barked Stewart. 'Hardly discreet in his habits, was he? The drinking. The gambling. Had he not ended it all it's most likely he would soon have lost his position. Did you meet an Arthur Bushnell last summer? He was here seeking investment opportunities.'

Thomas nodded.

'Bushnell was unimpressed by Beckford,' said Stewart. 'It's hard to trust a man who seems so wayward.'

'I know. I did urge him, as a friend, to control his appetite for drink. It would work for a week or two but then I'd become aware he was imbibing again.'

'It seems he was no better at handling his finances. We've learnt he was never ashamed to ask friends for loans. I've spent all day fending off demands from his creditors. I trust you were not one of that number.'

Thomas felt a surge of embarrassment. Anger, too, both at Rupert and himself. 'Even if that were the case,' he said stiffly, 'I would regard it as a private matter, to be addressed in the settling of his affairs.'

Stewart grunted. 'I would wish you good fortune. It seems he made no will. The state of his own account indicates he left precious little behind to repay those from whom he borrowed. As a single man he had no heirs, but you were apparently a man he relied upon for good sense and acumen.' Stewart handed over the note. 'As you see, he requests that you handle his personal effects.'

Thomas took the paper, saw the familiar scrawl of Rupert's hand, could not bear to read the words. He let it fall to his desk.

'When you read it you will see he had a mother in Australia. Her address is there. He asks that after expenses have been defrayed you send her what remains of his possessions.'

'Why me?' asked Thomas, a little desperately. 'We'd hardly spoken in recent times.'

Stewart shrugged. 'Despite that, he still chose you. Tomorrow I'll send over a box of his things. Some books, a signet ring, a pipe, and the blessed gun. It's hardly a treasure trove, more's the pity.'

'For God's sake don't give me the gun.'

Stewart shrugged. 'We'll sell it then. It won't realise a fraction of what he owes but every penny may help. Do you know of any other assets?'

'He mentioned a half-share of a breeding mare, though he may have sold it. And I believe there was a small property at Katikati that a dairy man leases.'

'If it's so that would be a relief to us. There must be documents somewhere, but we've found nothing.' Stewart tilted his head at the National Bank building visible through the window. 'Perhaps his words were as empty as his pockets.' His eyes bored into Thomas's. 'There is a more serious matter. It must be kept confidential. I'm sure you'll agree that some things happen behind bank walls that are best not shared with the common man. No matter what the coat of arms above our doors, it is incumbent on all of us to ensure that no one doubts the institution of banking. Is this not so?'

'Yes, though surely it's also inadvisable to hide unpalatable truths.'

'Debatable, Mr Hamilton. Sometimes a little obfuscation is preferable to suffering unnecessary scandal.' He leaned his elbows on his knees, studying the floor between his feet.

Thomas said impatiently, 'Enlighten me.'

Stewart raised his head. 'A thousand pounds is missing from the safe.'

Thomas felt his jaw sag.

'We've been through the ledgers twice,' said Stewart. 'There is no accounting for it. Only two people had access to the cash — Beckford and his clerk. The latter strikes me as a sensible young man, who would hardly commit such a crime and then stay on, knowing that suspicion would fall squarely upon him. I have quizzed him thoroughly and believe him to be honest. His shock was considerable.'

'When did you know it was gone?'

'Yesterday. Beckford had the only key to the safe. The police found it in his trouser pocket and locked it away until after I arrived.'

'But how can I possibly assist?' Thomas said. He coughed, trying to rid his voice of its indignant squeak. 'How can a sum of that size disappear?'

'As you say, a thousand pounds is a substantial amount. Suspicion can only fall on our late colleague. I have to ask if you have any inkling as to what Beckford might have wanted it for.'

'Presumably to pay his creditors.'

'Quite so, and yet none of the anxious people who've called on me today have seen even a sniff of a shilling.'

'Some weeks ago,' ventured Thomas, 'he did volunteer he was being pressed by bookmakers in Auckland. He was forced to sell some personal assets.'

'Do you know who they were?'

'He did not say. And I preferred not to know.'

Thomas had been on the verge of mentioning his own unpaid loan but now that he saw the outrageous depth of the crater Rupert had dug for himself, it struck him that his own sixty pounds would never be recovered. Besides, he was damned if he was going to reveal his foolishness to this man. He stood abruptly. 'If you'll excuse me, I have matters to attend to.'

'Of course,' said Stewart. 'And this conversation will remain between ourselves, yes? No need for clients to lose faith in the entire banking profession.'

'As you say. But what of your clerk? Can you rely on his discretion?'

'Of course. The promise of a promotion and quite possibly a bonus is a capital way of sealing lips, don't you find?'

After Stewart had gone, Thomas opened his top desk drawer. He pulled out the envelope in which Rupert had placed his last plea that Thomas protect Violet Sutton's reputation by keeping their adultery quiet. He had obeyed. Now Rupert was gone and so, too, it seemed, was Violet. She had ploughed into their lives, churned up their serenity, turned Anna against him, broken Rupert's needy heart and left blood in her wake.

He had burnt the note but had kept the envelope — this final memento, marked by a fine spray of ink dots sent flying by the scrawl of Rupert's desperate pen. Thomas bent the stiff paper now in a knife-edge crease and tore it apart with a painful sob. He choked it down but continued to sit there, ripping paper into ever-smaller pieces, silent tears spilling down his cheeks.

* * *

THROUGH THE WALL, Anna was having her own conversation about correspondence. She too had a visitor. Hester had asked, via Dinah, to see her. 'It's about Mrs Sutton,' Dinah said.

'Of course, of course, bring her in.'

They sat on Anna's best parlour chairs. Hester perched awkwardly, unused to being served, especially when it was Dinah delivering a tray with a sly grin.

'Dinah, do stop hovering and sit down,' said Anna. 'Hester, has there been any word from her?'

'No, ma'am, nor likely to be, I reckon. Mr Sutton's well aggravated, as you can imagine. I've not seen 'im much, mind, as he's all over the town asking after 'er and scuttling off to the telegraph office every tick o' the clock.' She heaved a sigh and fiddled with a spoon in her thick fingers. 'She's left a great empty space, that's for sure. It's too big a place for 'im to rattle around in on 'is own.'

Hester frowned. 'I wasn't sure if I should come. And I'll not be sayin' nowt about it to 'im either. He keeps on at me with "You must know where she is!" But truly I don't. It's like livin' in a thundercloud bein' in that place. I've told 'im I'm orf soon. All I know is that she told me if there's one person in this place she could trust, it was you. And besides, she said just last week that if she ever left town sudden-like, then you'd likely 'ave somethin' for me.'

'Indeed I do. I have something for both of you.' Anna stretched over to her writing desk and took from its drawer took two crumpled envelopes. She handed them over. Each was marked a brisk capital letter to signify their names, penned in Violet's favourite purple ink.

'I came upon these only yesterday. Open them in private. She went to some trouble to ensure they could get to you without attracting attention at the Post Office.'

They heard the thump of the heavy door that closed the bank off from the house, and a scolding shout out a window from Thomas to Jamie. The two cooks sprang out of their chairs. Hester's envelope went into her bodice; Dinah's was slipped under the cloth on the tea tray.

'She's a good woman,' said Hester, 'despite 'er sins, and if I could 'elp her start a new life I'd surely do it. But I'm frettin' about 'er, for how will she get on without any means of support, especially with a baby comin' along?' She turned in the doorway. 'Besides, that Mr Sutton. I'd not utter it outside these four walls but oh, what a bully.'

'What was *she* doing here?' said Thomas when he came in, glowering, for he'd spotted Hester slipping out the back way and hurrying up the street.

'She's fond of Violet. She merely wondered if I'd heard anything of her whereabouts.'

Thomas grunted. 'The whole town's wondering that, but she seems to have gone without leaving a whiff of a trail at all. No matter. She'll not be missed.'

'I miss her,' said Anna, unrepentant.

'I miss Rupert too and because of her he's gone forever.'

'She didn't pull the trigger!'

'But she might as well have done,' Thomas flung back at her. Then he stalked out of the house and down the street, ignoring Jamie on his way out the gate.

'Papa, can I come too?' he called. When his father shook his head and strode on he wandered inside to find his mother, disconsolate. 'Is Papa angry with me?'

Anna smoothed his unruly hair. 'No dearest, he's sad about his friend who died.'

'Mr Beckford?'

'Yes, darling.'

'Why did he die?'

'Because he was sad too.'

'Why? Can being sad make you die?' His eyes filled with alarm. 'Will Papa die?'

'Hush now. No, Jamie. It was an accident — something that's hard for all of us to understand.'

Everything was hard to understand, Anna thought. Matters relating to caution and risk. Rules and rebellion. Love and loss. Fixed ways of thinking and the surety to be found there, versus the intoxicating freedom of entertaining fresh ideas. She and Thomas had been taught to obey the word of God and his representatives here on Earth, honour the same long-established conventions, do what was expected of them —

and yet where in all of that dutiful adherence to society's rules was there room for joy?

Violet had sought joy and look where it had led her.

* * *

IN THE KITCHEN, Dinah used a knife to slit open the envelope and gaped at the sight of twenty-five pounds in crisp notes. 'Dear Dinah,' said Violet Sutton's note, 'I cannot depart without saying a proper thank you to you for your help to me when I took refuge in the Hamilton household and for your discretion with regard to the same. I wish also to thank your son for his skill in rescuing me and Mrs Hamilton on the harbour last summer. I trust this small amount of money will be of help to you and your family. Please accept my gratitude and best wishes for your future.'

In the house on the hill, Hester gripped a similar amount of cash and whipped away a tear from her cheek with the back of her hand as she read how very much her mistress had appreciated her industry and kindness. 'Without your calm presence and practical wisdom, these last few weeks — indeed, months — would have been much harder to bear.' Also included on a separate sheet was a glowing testimonial 'to assist in your search for a happier placement than the one which you have had under our roof'.

* * *

THOMAS CAME HOME LOOKING WRETCHED that night. After they'd gone to bed he turned to his wife with a sort of desperation, running his hand up her thigh to her breast, kneading and gripping, pulling her towards him.

Afterwards, she lay beside him, her arm pressed against the damp beef of his bicep as he slipped into an exhausted sleep. Although she too was tired her mind churned behind her closed eyes as she thought of her own note from Violet, still white and crisp, wrapped in a square of lawn and hidden in the linen press.

She knew she should feel guilty over keeping a letter she'd vowed she had destroyed, but didn't she have a right to hold on to a private keep-sake? Did she have to share everything?

Some day, when she'd had time to put the pain of this time behind her, then she might consign Violet's note to oblivion. But not yet.

CHAPTER THIRTY-ONE

*'MENDER OF SOLES, UNITER OF THE DISUNITED, Restorer of
Union and Harmony, though of ever so long and wide a separation.'*
*— Advertisement by Tauranga shoe maker Thomas Buckland, Bay
of Plenty Times.*

IT SEEMED TO ANNA, LOOKING BACK MUCH LATER, AS IF THE
crack of Rupert's gun had been a turning point, bringing an end to one
chapter and at the same time acting like a race pistol, setting in motion a
new cascade of events.

She lost all patience with Fanny and Louise, who continued to
gossip pointlessly and poisonously over possible reasons for Violet's
disappearance. 'Fancy abandoning that good man!' trilled Fanny in
Anna's parlour one day.

'And those beautiful clothes,' marvelled Louise.

Anna turned on them. 'You know nothing about her or her situation. Either of you. Speak kindly of her in my home or do not speak at
all.'

Fanny gasped. 'What sympathy does she deserve, pray? I shall *not* be
spoken to in such a manner. Come, Louise!' And she stalked out of the

house, stiff with outrage. Louise, too timid to resist, gave Anna a confused and imploring glance as she departed too.

After that, they would nod to each other in the street, for appearance's sake, but the Tuesday afternoon teas did not resume.

Four months after Rupert's death and Violet's disappearance, Henry Sutton also packed up and left. Hester was long gone. His home stood empty, awaiting a new owner. The tips of the rose bushes lining the front path were fuzzy with tiny budding leaves, but neither of the Suttons would see summer's roses burst into bloom.

'Going so soon?' Thomas said when Henry came in to close his account. 'I must say I'll miss your custom.' He tried not to sound despondent but watched in some dismay as Sutton signed the authority to transfer all of his considerable funds to a bank in Sydney.

'Can't abide being here now,' said Sutton. 'When I arrived I thought the place had possibilities. But it's backing up like a reluctant nag, full of whinnies of complaint while it refuses to see the path that lies ahead. The cursed eruption killed the railway scheme — who wants to travel to the Hot Lakes now the Terraces are gone? The cheese factory has merely staggered along. It's clear to see that cows don't thrive on this soil, despite all of your touting the benefits of ash.'

Thomas wanted to point to the pots on his windowsill, where his container filled with a mixture of ash and soil hosted a vigorous green maize plant sprouting much higher than its companions, but he knew there was little point.

It wasn't as if Sutton had his eyes closed to the benefits of volcanic detritus. One of his interests had been trying to establish a company to make chemical manure. The close-at-hand White Island constantly emitted sulky puffs of pungent steam and its slopes were piled with sulphur, the necessary raw ingredient. 'It will make capital fertiliser and is there for the taking!' Sutton had shouted to an audience of local businessmen. But they had sat on their hands and wallets and declined to get rich by the simple expedient of digging up stuff that would improve yields and also turn a handsome profit if shipped to eager markets abroad.

'A more apathetic crowd I have yet to encounter,' grumbled Sutton. 'This town has gnawed at my soul. Good riddance to it, I say. Besides, these hard times we're beginning to feel. . . You've seen the *Times*. Business is suffering on every continent. A go-ahead man needs to be in a port with more appetite for enterprise than this place will ever exhibit. One needs to invest at times like this, not shrink back into a cowardly stupor.'

'Indeed,' said Thomas. He knew the realities of business all too well. Battered by the conflicting demands of his clients and his superiors, he often wished he could sail away to an easier life. He rather envied the angry man who sat across from him. 'I presume you've heard nothing of Mrs Sutton?' he asked as he blotted wet signatures.

'Not a whisper.' Sutton stood and grabbed his cane. 'But if I had news I'd not be sharing it. God forbid that any tender letters or kind words from here should ever reach that thieving whore.'

Thomas blinked. 'Thieving?'

'What else? In removing herself from my sphere she has also removed my child. I've not given up the search, mind. And when I find her I'll be claiming what is mine.'

Thomas did already know, as the whole town knew, that no woman answering Violet's description had walked down the gangway when the *Maketu* docked in Auckland. No one had seen her since the day of Rupert's funeral. It was as if she had vanished from the Earth. Her name was now not mentioned in the Hamilton house. Thomas had made it clear he did not wish for Anna to speak it at all.

A stiff amity had grown back between husband and wife but the trust they'd once had was stretched a little thin.

Their marriage went on, for the most part satisfactorily, but sometimes, when she knew Thomas was away and would not return for hours, Anna would slip her hand into the linen press, reach into the folds of a seldom-used tablecloth and feel for the folded paper hidden there. Then she would pull it out, unfold it, and read it again.

My dear Anna,

I write this the night before Rupert's funeral, not knowing if you will ever receive it. I shall slip out in the early hours to 'post' it. You will think to go there, I'm sure, for we both know of that ideal mail slot so cunningly wrought by Nature. When you hear of my departure you will wonder why I left no farewell, but I am confident you will remember the tree. It has also hosted other correspondence — notes passing between Rupert and me that enabled us to plan our meetings.

I am about to leave this town. My one regret is that it means I shall not see you again. But depart I must, for the sake of my own sanity.

That tree is precious to me as it bore witness to our seagoing adventure. I still remember it with joy, for before we came to grief it was the best of mornings, was it not? I prefer to cast aside our fright and dwell instead on recalling the sunshine on our faces, the jewel-like green of the water, the great upturned bowl of the sky over our heads, the inestimable freedom of setting out on our own. Of course we also ran into trouble, owing our lives to that passing Maori crew. I am therefore also including for you an envelope for Dinah, containing a token of thanks. There is also one for Hester to acknowledge her kindness and loyalty.

I cannot leave these letters in the house lest Henry should find them. I have no privacy here at all.

You'll doubtless be wondering how I can contemplate seeking a new life for myself, for such a move requires capital. The fact is, Rupert has left me a substantial sum. I am in such pain — swinging between extremities of heartbreak and rage — for I simply cannot understand why he took his own life when he had the means for both of us to run away together.

We did dream of it at one time but he was thrown into despair by my news. When he realised the depth of Henry's obsessive desire for an heir, I think he simply gave up. He argued desperately that the child could be his but I know it's not possible for that to be true.

After that, it was obvious there was no question of a future together. Even if he'd been willing I would have been torn between security with Henry (despite his boorish nature) and insecurity with Rupert (who was so charming and yet so reckless).

You cannot begin to understand the depth of my guilt over this. Rupert was so soft in his nature. It was an aspect of him that I loved, but that softness seeped into other parts of his soul too. I so wish now that his character had contained more steel.

He must have sunk into total despair that night, doubtless with the help of strong drink. Why did I not do more to persuade him to desist? Perhaps I might have if we had gone on together.

Anna, he left money in the tree for me, wrapped around with leaves so that anyone who peered into the crack would not notice it. I almost missed it myself. Such a risk.

Imagine leaving a thousand pounds in a tree! I went to the undertaker's to see him one last time. I was quite undone by his blank, dark face. I felt like dying, too. It is astonishing how very absent the dead are. He could tell me nothing but I knew he'd written farewell notes to others and surely he'd not have deprived me of that small comfort.

When I found the money I ached with frustration because he put nothing in his note but a declaration of love and I wanted — I still want — to know, why, why, why!

We could have gone away together with that cash. Instead I am bereft and caring not one jot for my 'good fortune', save for the fact that with Rupert's last act of generosity I am able to flee to some place where no one knows me. With a change of name and a widow's persona, I shall find some business to sustain me. I wish I could take Hester. Her presence would remind me of the good times in Tauranga. I would be able to think of how you and I once sat on the sunny veranda while your Jamie wheedled spoon-licks from her mixing bowl.

Please do not share this letter with anybody, dear Anna, for I do not wish to leave behind even the slightest clue as to my intentions. When it is safe for me to write to you, I shall certainly do so. Tender thoughts of you will remain with me until the end of my days.

With deepest affection, Violet.

Anna would finish it, sigh, refold the paper (for she could not bring herself to rip it up) and go back to her unremitting load of household tasks.

* * *

IN SPRING A TELEGRAPH came from her mother. Anna rarely disturbed Thomas in his office but she did now.

He looked up with tired eyes. Only minutes earlier he had told a pig farmer that if he failed to make good on his overdue mortgage payments in the coming week, the bank would have no choice but to possess his property. The man had actually sunk to his knees in his worn trousers to plead for another month's grace and Thomas had had to refuse and then watch the farmer's mouth screw tight with the effort of suppressing tears.

He sat back now in his squeaky swivel chair and looked so weary that Anna could hardly bring herself to speak. Then he noticed her grave face. 'What is it?'

'There's been a fire at my mother's house. She's not hurt, thank God, but it needs repair. She may need clothes, furniture, who knows what else. What is worse, her usual remittance has not arrived from Cedric. It's odd as he never forgets. It's a month overdue. She asks if we can make her a short-term loan. This is so unlike her. You know how proud she is. We can help, can't we? We have savings. It can only be a matter of time before the draft comes through.'

Thomas's heart sank. He ran a hand through his hair. Cleared his throat. Indicated the paper piles in front of him. 'Can we speak of this later? I have so much work to do today.' He consulted his pocket watch. 'A client appointment soon, too.'

'This is my mother, Thomas! She'll be awaiting a reply. We can't disappoint her. It's bad enough for her to have endured such a fright. Do you think something might have happened to Cedric?'

He gave her a placating smile. 'It'll be merely a shipping delay of some kind. We'll discuss it this evening, hmm?'

'No, Thomas, now. I must go to her. She needs me.'

'Where is she staying?'

'She doesn't even say. With a friend or neighbour, I suppose. I have to know she is well. She's so elderly now. A strain like this could be the end of her.'

'I can't travel with you, my dear.' He indicated his paper-laden desk.

She waved a dismissive hand. 'I'm perfectly capable of travelling alone.'

'Leave Jamie with me then. He'll be more of an irritation for your mother than a comfort.'

She nodded. 'And money — can you arrange a loan?'

He let silence spin out too long.

'Thomas? What is it?'

His glance gave little away, but she knew him too well to miss his discomfort.

'The fact is we do not have a great deal of capital to spare,' he said.

Anna sat down, ignoring the whiff of pigs left by the unhappy farmer. 'Why ever not? We talked of our savings not long ago, when Rupert. . .' She paused, and then her voice sagged low. 'Oh, Thomas, do not tell me that even after our conversation you went ahead and handed our savings over to him?'

'Some.' He heaved himself upright and went to the window. 'I trusted him,' he said to the glass. 'He told me he had assets he was about to realise — that he could pay me back and with interest.' He turned to her, his face pained. 'He was my friend, Anna. You knew his persuasiveness, the way he could turn people to his point of view.'

She leapt up and grabbed his arm, forcing her to face him. 'And when his troubles arose, did you ask him when he would repay you?'

'Of course.'

'And what did he say?'

'Soon, he kept saying. Soon he would be able to. He had already paid me a portion. But then—.'

'But then he was dead,' snapped Anna. 'Then he was *gone*. It was easy for him, wasn't it!'

Thomas's eyes flared. 'It most certainly was not. Can you not imagine how distressed he must have been?'

'Forgive me if I have exhausted my well of sympathy. How much was it?'

'The loan?'

'Yes, of course, the loan!'

He forced it out. 'Sixty.'

Her eyes went wide. She rubbed her face. 'So much? And to think how you scolded me for taking a risk. How you *lectured* me about being cavalier with safety out in his boat when all the time you had this secret agreement over money meant to provide for our future.'

'I know,' he said. 'I need no reminding.'

Anna expelled an explosive snort. 'Who is handling his affairs? Is the money retrievable?'

'It was a gentlemen's agreement. We shook on it. There is no paper to prove our transaction. He left no will and an impoverished estate to boot. It's likely none of his creditors will see a penny and it seems there were many.'

Ignoring his leaden heart, he said all of this quickly and airily as if such treatment would render his news light as a feather.

'That's what gentlemen do, is it?' she said. 'Grip each other's palms and swear to be upright, even when all the evidence as to a man's character is to the contrary?'

Thomas said nothing. They glared at each other, each burdened by secrets — the bank's missing thousand pounds over which Stewart had sworn Thomas to silence, and Rupert's gift to Violet of a thousand pounds which Anna also felt forbidden to mention.

She said, 'I am going this minute down to the shipping office to see if I can get a ticket for tomorrow's sailing. I'll instruct them to send you the bill.' And she stalked out of the room.

'Anna,' he called after her, 'I will make it right.' But then he saw his clerk stepping in the door, glancing curiously at her stiff, angry stride, and so there was no time to say more.

CHAPTER THIRTY-TWO

'Hundreds of subtle maladies are floating around us ready to attack wherever there is a weak point. We may escape many a fatal shaft by keeping ourselves well fortified with pure food and a properly nourished frame.'
— *Civil Service Gazette, quoted in the Bay of Plenty Times.*

DINAH DROPPED THE MAIL ONTO THE TABLE AS THOMAS AND Jamie were finishing their porridge. Thomas saw Anna's writing, snatched the letter up and tore it open.

October 20, 1886

My dear Thomas,

The news is better than might be expected. It seems Mother's initial agitation was such that she rather overstated the crisis. Fortunately, the fire was quickly doused by a gardener and his lad who happened to be there. The damage was confined to the kitchen and hallway and a carpenter estimates that repairs should not cost more than £50.

I had planned to ask that you deposit sufficient funds with her bank to cover said repairs. But yesterday, to our great relief, Cedric's bank draft arrived. It seems the mails were delayed when a ship went aground in

Fremantle. All its cargo languished for weeks until it could be transferred and sent on.

However, while he may be generously supplying the bulk of Mother's income we cannot be aloof from her current troubles. We must offer an equal share of the cost of repairs, and therefore I ask that you arrange for £25 to be credited to her.

I had hoped insurance would cover the damage, but she is becoming forgetful and had unfortunately neglected to pay her last premium. The time is approaching when we shall need to live closer at hand, for with no other family in Auckland, who else is there to take care of her? The other alternative is to take her under our own roof.

Thomas winced at the last point.

'Is it from Mama?' Jamie asked, tugging on his sleeve. 'Is it? When will she be home?'

'Yes it is, but let me finish. Be good and we'll go down to the shore in a minute or two and see if we can find some driftwood.'

In Anna's absence it was becoming hard to find ways to entertain the boy. Jamie stomped away and sat on the doorstep with jiggling knees while his father skimmed the rest of the letter. It seemed Anna and her mother were settled in a boarding house. 'She'll be back in a week or two, Jamie,' he told his son. 'That's not long to wait.'

But as they set off down the street he felt it *was* a long time. He missed Anna. It was not just her physical absence. He was also nostalgic for the contented and sensible wife she'd been before so much turmoil had pushed them apart. Now she seemed to have a crisp impatience with him and the world. She'd signed her letter 'with affection, as always'. Affection? It seemed a pale substitute for love.

Once on the shore he squatted on his heels while Jamie darted about the beach looking for treasures. The boy had an artistic streak; he loved collecting smooth driftwood and using a penknife to carve curious shapes upon it.

Later that day, when time allowed, Thomas would write back to tell her the money was on its way. He was reluctant to borrow from the bank at its current six per cent interest rate and so would dip into their own depleted savings account. They would then have to economise, put pennies and shillings aside and begin the long haul of replacing what he had so foolishly squandered.

Correction: it was Rupert who'd done the squandering. He had spent their money, and so much more besides, on God alone knew what idiocies. Thomas had simply helped make his carelessness possible. It was a lapse he hoped he'd never have to reveal to his father.

* * *

ANNA COULD HAVE TOLD him more. She could have said that when she settled her mother into the guesthouse the lugubrious landlady perked up at the sight of Anna's home address in the register. 'Ah, from the Bay of Plenty I see. I have a few regular guests from your town.'

'Really, Mrs. . . Pardon me, I don't know your name.'

'Hadley,' she replied as she closed the register. She tuned her narrow face to Anna, sharp eyes framed by wings of dark hair. 'We see Mr Bell, the newspaper editor, when he's up on business.'

'Oh, I'm well acquainted with Fanny, his wife.'

'In a town so small I imagine you're acquainted with everyone. Henry Sutton used to stay as well before he upped and left for Australia. And Mrs Sutton too, earlier this year. Is she also a friend?'

'Why, yes,' said Anna, surprised and then wary. Now she remembered the woman's name and Violet's dislike of her.

As she bent to pick up her bag Mrs Hadley carried on. 'It's my understanding that Mrs Sutton abruptly left the matrimonial home, causing him much anguish.'

'I don't believe it's my business to say. I also think we can assume all of us have private lives we'd wish to keep private.'

'In this case it's hardly private,' said Mrs Hadley with a shrug. 'Mr Sutton has many friends here. His wife's desertion has been the talk of the town.'

Anna backed away, anxious to put a closed door between them. 'I've not seen either of them for months.' She turned to go.

'Ah, but I think I have,' said Mrs Hadley. Anna knew she should keep climbing the stairs but the temptation was too great. As she swung around, she caught the flash of triumph on the landlady's face.

Mrs Hadley made a show of inspecting her book, flicking away imaginary specks of dried ink. 'There may be someone else with exactly her posture and profile and I did only see her pass by a shop doorway. I could have sworn our eyes met in the mirror above the counter, but by the time I made my way outside she was nowhere to be seen.' Mrs Hadley rocked on her stool. 'She must have fled down that street like a fox with hounds at her heels.'

'When was this?'

The landlady's lips pursed. 'I cannot really say. Perhaps late in June. I did tell Mr Sutton of my suspicions when he put up here on his way to Sydney. He was rather painfully excited for a week or two but there were no further sightings. He departed an unhappy man.'

Rage flooded Anna's cheeks. 'Well,' she snapped. 'No doubt his new ventures abroad will help him forget having treated his wife so badly that she felt compelled to depart.'

For the remainder of her stay, she and Mrs Hadley spoke no more often than was necessary. Once or twice she went into the tea shop where she and Violet had met. She also climbed the Shortland Street hill to the seat from which they'd looked out over the port. But there was never a sign of her.

* * *

In February the sun sailed high in cloudless skies. The citizens of Tauranga had long since crossed from their calendars the dates marking the final few weeks of 1886. Few had been sorry to farewell that year. But all the same this summer was uncommonly hot, especially for people accustomed to the cool and fickle climate of the British Isles.

Anna awoke, sweating into her sheets. Thomas was already up and gone from the bed. She could hear him talking with Jamie over the clatter of cutlery, smell the faint aroma of ham frying. It was nauseating.

As she rolled on the mattress the room seemed to spin. She pulled up her knees to ease a sudden grinding pain deep in her belly and then was appalled to realise she'd loosed her bowels. And in another moment, before she could reach for any sort of receptacle, she was vomiting into her pillow.

Thomas, humming to himself and more contented on this balmy morning than he had been for some time, took a moment or two to hear Anna cry out to him. 'Stay here,' he said to Jamie and went to the bedroom. She lay curled and small, white-faced, the top sheet pulled high up under her chin with her fists. The room reeked. 'I need clean cloth,' she said. 'Out of the linen press. Go to the bottom where the old things are.'

He stood rooted to the spot. 'Quickly!' she said. 'A bowl!'

He lunged for the water jug on the dresser and passed it her, just in time for her next spasm. She rolled over, bent over the jug and heaved. He darted to the linen press, threw out a blizzard of white linen, saw an envelope, tossed it aside, grabbed up handfuls of worn cotton and took the bundle to her. She reached down to wedge wadded cloth beneath her as Thomas stood beside the bed, horrified by the brown stains he glimpsed under her thighs. She lay back, covered herself and looked up at him with miserable eyes.

Jamie hovered in the doorway, puzzled and anxious. 'Is Mama ill?'

'Yes, so she needs peace and quiet. Go back to the kitchen and finish your milk.'

'I have.'

'Well, try to be useful then. Get wood for the stove and be quick about it,' Thomas snapped and then regretted his impatience for this new domestic crisis was not the boy's fault. Jamie did as he was told, his small shoulders slumped.

Thomas turned back to the stinking bed. He hoped Dinah would soon arrive to take care of the soiled bedding. As usual, she was late. They might need new linen, Thomas thought. And a new mattress. His heart sank. More expense.

Anna lay with her back to him. The things he'd flung from the linen press lay in disorder on the floor. He picked up embroidered pillowslips and kerchiefs, lace collars and flimsy shawls and laid them back in the press. The envelope he'd thrown aside lay half obscured beneath a curtain hem. He retrieved it, wondering why it been in among the sheets at all, and was about to put it back when he saw his wife's name scribbled upon its front in a flourish of violet ink.

He'd seen that hand before. That ink.

Its seal was broken. He turned it over. Curiosity made him raise it to his nose. He caught a slight waft of flowery scent, though he could not tell whether it came from the paper itself or the dried lavender sprigs usually scattered in the linen press. And then he heard a door opening and Jamie's self-important announcement of Mama's illness and the sound of Dinah's urgent heels thudding along the hall. He slipped the envelope inside his waistcoat. He planned to inspect it more closely in the privacy of his office.

* * *

'It's as if we're cursed,' she whimpered to Dr McPherson later in the morning. She fell back on her pillow after another bout of retching as he soaped his fingers in the washbowl. 'My little girl died of this.'

'There, there, Mrs Hamilton,' he chuckled. 'Tis all a matter of chance, not of curses. This is likely just a summer illness, a disagreement with some food that has spoiled in the heat. You can only rest and wait to recover. Take nothing but clean water for now. Later on, possibly some broth. Not a fatty one, mind.'

The very thought of fat made her groan.

Thomas waylaid the doctor as he left, anxious for reassurance. 'She's looking wan, to be sure, Mr Hamilton. Let her rest afterwards, if it's possible. It'll take a little time for her to feel chipper again.'

McPherson slapped on his hat. 'I'll see her again tomorrow, but call me if it seems necessary. She's been look a little peaky anyway lately. This country is hard on the ladies.' He took a step outside and winced. 'Devilish warm out. If only one could sit in the shade of an apple tree and muse the day away.' He hoisted his bag and left, soles crunching on the blazing road.

* * *

Anna took some time to regain her normal colour and vitality. Even then, Thomas thought, her emotional state was fragile. They'd been hoping for another child to come along but there'd been no sign of one. He hesitated to raise any subjects that might upset her — least of all the fact that he'd read her hidden (and shocking) correspondence. Still, as they navigated the humid funk of late summer, he thought they were moving somewhat closer to their former equanimity.

Jamie was five now and more demanding, sometimes petulant and inclined to answer back, despite sometimes having his backside smacked and being sent to bed without his dinner.

Thomas worried for his only child. Such boys had to cope with weighty fatherly expectations as well as the suffocating sweetness of maternal love. That syrup was best diluted by being spooned into a host of small mouths. Well, at least three or four.

Anna spoiled Jamie, he thought

So he, in turn, was harder on the boy. Jamie would be attending school soon. That would knock him into shape. And in time, God willing, another child would come along. Though given the number of times Anna shrank away from him in their bed it might indeed take holy intervention for another Hamilton baby to arrive.

Also, business was dire. Shopkeepers could sometimes go hours without a customer, but they did not dare shut their doors for a nap and cup of tea lest they missed the chance of taking even a small amount of coin. The newspapers were full of news about the Depression affecting trade all around the world. Thomas scolded dilatory clients, refused a painful number of loan requests and provided a weary listening ear for creditors moaning about the lack of diligence and honesty in the colony.

Then the bank increased the rent on their living quarters. It was a struggle to put even a small portion of his salary away in savings. At this rate it would take years to replace the cache he'd handed over to Rupert.

He began to lie awake at night worrying over how he'd cope if some new emergency or illness befell them. He had taken over the running of his mother-in-law's affairs and was receiving a tiresome stream of letters from her.

There had also been ongoing painful correspondence with Rupert's mother. She had written to plead for detail about her son's behaviour in the weeks before his death. After he sent her Rupert's small bundle of belongings he'd hoped that would be the end of it, but her letters kept coming.

At first, feeling sorry for her, he had answered at length. He assured her that her son had held her in tender esteem (though in truth he'd barely mentioned her) while at the same time glossing over Rupert's worst excesses. But her beseeching wore away at his patience, especially when she revealed she'd had a letter from Violet begging forgiveness for having become involved with her son.

'It is beyond my comprehension that she should intrude on your grief in this manner,' he wrote back in sharp scrawls. 'She is a vain woman with uncommon self-regard. You say you gave her a strong reply. I trust it was fiercely worded and I would advise you to spurn any further overtures from her.' And then, thoroughly angry, especially when he thought of the illicit cash that Violet had carried off, he wrote curtly that Rupert had drunk too much and too often, had ruined his life as a result, and that there really was no one else to blame for the tragedy but himself.

To his relief she did not write again.

He did not share any of this with anyone. He was still too ashamed to tell Anna he had read and burnt her hidden letter. At the same time he was sorely disappointed that his wife had never shared with him her knowledge of Rupert's 'gift' to Violet. He was disinclined to reveal to her that Violet had approached Rupert's mother. He did not want to see any unhealthy excitement flare in Anna's eyes.

His letters to Mrs Beckford had not mentioned that Violet might possibly have a Beckford grandchild in her womb. It could perhaps already have been born. Thomas could not be bothered making the calculation and instead loosed a weary gust of breath. Why should Violet succeed at that simple, elemental thing when there was still no sibling for Jamie? He was tempted to think of it as Violet's bastard, though of course if it was Henry's then it would have legitimacy. Whatever the circumstance, he fervently hoped that Violet Sutton would not ever cross their paths again.

Anna, however, hoped for it very much. It was a desire she kept to herself. She could not understand how she had somehow mislaid her precious last note from Violet. She had searched the linen press twice without success, peering between layers and unfolding the stacks of fabric. Dinah looked blank when asked if she'd seen it.

Now she had nothing to remember Violet by, not even the old

copies of *The Freethinker*. Thomas had admitted, when pressed, that he'd disposed of them, declaring them unsuitable reading for a Christian home. Surely if he had found the letter he would have mentioned it. Had he destroyed that too? She did not want to ask, for she had little energy for more blazing dissent. Even asking him about it would alert him to the fact that she'd been hiding something, which would drive another wedge between them.

Whether it still existed or not, the letter remained incendiary. And their household remained heavy with secrets.

CHAPTER THIRTY-THREE

*'May I suggest to the kind consideration of our obliging Postal authorities
what a boon they would confer on the public by giving timely notice in the
local papers when to post, in Tauranga, mails intended for despatch by
steamer. At present the public are debarred from this advantage, not
knowing when to post in time for the direct homeward mails.'*
— Letter to the editor, Bay of Plenty Times, 1886.

MADAME FRANCINI AND HER HUSBAND KNOCKED ON THE
Hamiltons' door one afternoon late in the following year.

'Good gracious, come in!' said Anna. Delighted, she drew them in
and settled them in the parlour, eager for news from the outside world.

The Francinis had much to tell for their restless touring life had not
ceased. They had been at sea sailing north out from Whakatane when
Tarawera's top exploded. Madame Francini exclaimed over how they
had all been roused from their bunks to witness the lurid, pulsing glow
to the southwest. She shuddered. 'It's something I never hope to see
again as long as I live.'

They'd arrived in Tauranga a day later but had had to leave almost
immediately. The town had been adrift with ash, panic and rumours. 'I
wanted to visit you all, but we had to take a coach up to Katikati that

very day to find anywhere to sleep. It was not so pleasant there either, squashed into an inn full of bébés, all wailing.'

They decided to move on to Thames to find berths on a steamer to Auckland, but for days there were more people desperate for a coach seat than there were places available. Added Mr Francini: 'It was while we were waiting to buy tickets one morning that we saw her.' He looked at Anna expectantly, as if she must know what was in his mind.

'Saw who?'

'Mrs Sutton.'

Anna's hand swept up to her mouth.

He leaned forward. 'Tis hard to believe, I know, but the poor lass walked that hard road alone, all twenty miles of it, with a weighty bag over her shoulder. She told us she hid in a woodshed and then trudged all night, laid low again during the next day and set out again.'

'Was she well?'

'Yes, but very tired.' Madame Francini gave Anna a piercing glance. 'You know she was running from her husband?'

'But of course, and she disappeared. The whole town was looking for her. Mr Sutton had word out everywhere, but he's gone too now.'

'Un cochon!' Madame Francini tossed her head. 'A pig of a man.'

'What happened to her after that? Where did she go? I've had not a word from her and I thought that surely she would have written by now.'

'Well, we could not leave her alone, and so all three of us hired a tinker with his cart and off we went. Of course, we are theatre people. We disguised her so well that her own mother would not have known her. "Pauvre chérie,"' said Madame, re-telling the story she had given to the tinker. '"She 'as lost her husband in the eruption and now barely speaks a word."'

The Francinis grinned at each other, looking as ordinary as any domestic pair. Anna noticed that off-stage and out of earshot of customers, the French airs and accents largely disappeared.

'And then?'

'We had tickets for a Melbourne steamship and she decided to throw her lot in with us,' said Mr Francini. 'It was odd because we could see she had money but she was desperate to keep a distance from her husband, so off we went for a run around Victorian towns. They love a good hypnotist in Bendigo and Ballarat. Gold mining's not what it was, y'know. It makes for a level of anxiety that's ideal for our line of work.'

'You *worked* together?' Anna couldn't imagine how Violet would fit in.

'Oh, yes,' said Madame. 'She said she had some means but needed more for the life she wanted to live. Besides, she could not bear to be idle. Such a free spirit! I was happy to take her on for I saw her dance here in Tauranga. She came to me for a private reading one day. When she learnt how I love a good dancer she did a turn for me in lieu of payment.'

Madame made a swooning action, flinging the back of one hand to her forehead. 'She was *extraordinaire*, like a nature sprite. So we added her to the bill. Miners love to see a comely woman on the stage. All she had to do was flash her legs and give them pretty smiles to make them sigh.'

'But it didn't last,' chimed in her husband. 'We grew so fond of her but—.'

Anna leapt into the gap. 'She would have had to stop, yes, because of her condition.'

Madame Francini frowned. 'When she left here we all knew,' said Anna, cupping her hands out in front of her bodice.

'You mean she was *enceinte*? No, no, my dear. There was no sign of *that*.'

Anna stared as Madame went on. 'She was with us for five months using a stage name she concocted. But then she said she had to keep travelling, to sail even further away.' Madame shook her head. 'Her dream was to claim something that was hers.'

'Where was she going?'

'She would not say.' Madame Francini dipped a beringed hand into her reticule. 'I believe she was still afraid and did not want to deliver any clue to the Post Office here. But when she heard we'd be returning sometime she asked me to bring you this.' She held out a crumpled letter. Anna took it, turned it over and felt a pang. On the back of the envelope, Violet had drawn a picture of a pansy.

The couple lingered expectantly but Anna wanted to read it alone. 'I promise that if there is news I can share with you, I shall. I so admire you. Most people would have been quite unable to resist the temptation to look inside.'

Madame Francini sighed. 'Well, I hardly needed to, ma cherie. The first time I looked at her hand I saw the heartbreak from past years, with still more to come.'

'You can truly see such things?'

'The hand does not lie. She also told me of the fate of that young man with the flaming hair — the one who also danced when we were last here, up there on the stage before you all. That colour often hints at a sensitive soul. Such a tragedy. I should like to have seen his palm.'

'We still struggle to accept what happened. My husband, especially, took it hard. He and Rupert had been such good companions.'

'So were you all,' said Mr Francini. 'Or so it seemed to us. Because we jig around so much we envy the friendships we see in towns such as this. But then we're also spared the grief of getting too close and then losing those we're fond of.' They nodded together like dolls whose necks shared the same spring. And then they departed.

As soon as Anna had closed the door behind them she tore open the envelope and pulled out Violet's letter. It was four months old and its first line made her suck in a sharp breath.

MELBOURNE, *July 20, 1887*

My dear Anna

By the time you read this I shall be on my way to India. My last note to you, which I trust does not still lie in that tree on your distant shore, contained hopes and dreams which have not come to fruition.

You will know now of my good fortune in encountering Bella Francini and of how she let me share her life for a season. My naive plans of taking on a small business came to naught, for Australian towns are hardly larger than those in New Zealand and I would have felt too conspicuous as a woman on her own. Henry has contacts in Melbourne and I would always have felt there were spies on every street corner. I felt safer constantly moving on.

And I have to leave again now. I feel vulnerable. Only yesterday I saw Arthur Bushnell on Collins Street. Do you remember him? He once came to dinner in Tauranga when Henry was desperate for him to invest in some mad scheme or other. I was so frightened he would recognise me but his eye went elsewhere. He is the sort of man, I think, for whom women are usually invisible. But the moment made me more wary than ever, for if Bushnell is doing business here, can Henry be far away?

More than that, I have decided I cannot remain here knowing that my only flesh and blood — my George — still exists across the sea. He is my only living child, Anna.

I truly did think during that terrible time in Tauranga that I had begun another, but it was not to be. That fact became plain the week after I left Tauranga. Perhaps it was the shock and misery of all that had unfolded or perhaps I merely muddled the dates on my calendar. Whatever the facts, my condition turned out to be a mirage.

I suppose I must see it as fortuitous, for while Henry believed I was carrying his child I had breathing space for a time under his roof. But my agony is that in also instilling that belief in Rupert I added to my poor love's pain.

Oh, if only I had known what he was considering.

After the tempest of his passing I knew I could not bear to stay another day and with his monetary gift in hand, I could make a fresh start.

Now I intend to find my son. I cannot endure the thought of never laying eyes on him again.

My destination is Bombay, a place in which I hope I can gain entry to society and look for Mr and Mrs Mayne Underhill. The English tribe there surely cannot be so huge that I will be unable to find them. I do know that is where they are. Remember me telling you of the kind housekeeper in the house where George came into the world? For an endless time I had no news from her. And then, just after our trip to Auckland — remember the fun we had rinking! — she wrote to tell me where the Underhills could be found. I sail tomorrow.

Dear, doomed Rupert. I carry only one memento of him, a curl of his bright hair in a locket. You will probably shrink to know that I snipped it from his poor head when I saw him in his coffin.

I can see you tut-tutting as you read this, despairing yet again over my behaviour. I try not to think of the future, having no idea how to proceed once I arrive in Bombay.

I hope you will forgive me if I seek out your brother Cedric Vincent, whose name you once mentioned to me. I am prepared to use all the contacts I can think of to work the miracle of seeing George. If necessary I may try to secure a position there. I hear governesses are sought after, for though every child has an amah they also need someone to teach them their letters. I shall need employment, for my money will not last forever.

Anna could not bear any longer to stop herself from mentioning Violet's name. But when she told Thomas her news she wished she had kept silent.

'India? On her own? Now we really know how deluded she is. What makes her think she can suddenly demand to see a child she abandoned years ago?'

'He was taken from her.'

'And rightly so. An illegitimate child is fortunate to be taken on by a well-founded family. Surely she did not think it better to raise it on her own, without a penny to her name.'

'I believe she did. Or would have done if her family had shown her even a modicum of tenderness.'

'Oh, Anna. Where is your good sense? Tell me when such an arrangement has ever been known to succeed.'

'I only know that if anyone could manage it, Violet could.'

A frosty pause fell between them. 'A woman cannot hope to rear a bastard child and expect him to do well in the world,' said Thomas in a voice that was steady, cold and sure. 'It is against all reason and every requirement laid down by the law and by God.'

'Oh, God and his rules,' scoffed Anna. 'How can the Almighty possibly notice the lives of every single one of the millions of people alive in this world?'

'Possible because he's almighty.'

'How can he possibly be troubled by the thought of a child being raised by a woman whose body has painfully borne that very child? Is he not of her very flesh and blood?'

Thomas shook his head with exasperation as she bustled away and slammed the door.

CHAPTER THIRTY-FOUR

'Indian chutney, pickles and curry for sale.'
— New Zealand Herald, 1888.

Bombay, January 1888

'There is a lady come to call, ma'am.'

'What, in this heat?' Edith Vincent turned a languid, exhausted head to her houseboy, Rashid, her hand holding a fan with which she continued to create inadequate puffs of breeze against her cheeks.

Rashid offered her a tray with a rectangle of card placed in its centre. She picked it up. Humidity had rendered it soft and pliable. She inspected the name that was printed upon it in a discreet font. 'Cedric?' she said. 'Do we know a Miss Violet Foster?'

He looked at her over his teacup. It was dim on their veranda in the late afternoon, the canvas blinds pulled down to shield them from the glare, but Harriet could see the irritated gleam in his eye. 'I don't believe we do. Surely she is not calling without an introduction.'

The houseboy hovered. 'Oh well,' said Edith. A visitor might at least break the boredom of this endless, torrid Sunday afternoon. The shuffle of Rashid's sandals and the neat clip of a woman's heels sounded on the teak floorboards. The boy ushered in a slim, dark-haired woman in an apple-green lawn dress and straw hat. She was not maidenly, being perhaps thirty years old, and held herself straight and tall. She offered a tentative smile.

'Mr Vincent, Mrs Vincent, thank you so much. It's most kind of you to allow me to disrupt your quiet afternoon without any warning at all.'

Cedric stood with alacrity. Edith had often seen how readily a pretty woman had that effect. 'It is our pleasure, Miss. . . Foster, is it?' he said.

'Yes indeed. I am newly arrived from Australia and staying at The Ambassador. Someone there kindly told me your address. Finding myself with time to spare I thought I might simply come to your gate and ask if you were at home.' She spread her hands, clearly delighted. 'And here you are.' Only then did she flag a little, taking a kerchief from her purse to mop her brow. 'My word, this is a very hot corner of the empire.'

'Oh, we are all desperate for coolness. Sit down, please do.'

Violet complimented Edith on her lush potted palms and embroidered screens. 'Tis all so vivid here,' she said. 'Enormously noisy and afflicted with very strange smells. But I am half in love with this place after only a few days.'

'What has brought you here?' asked Cedric. 'I take it from your comments that we have acquaintance of some sort?'

'I travel alone, ever since a death in my circle of friends. Sudden loss affects us in different ways. Some take to gardening but I have taken to roaming. It's interesting how many families have members dotted all around the world these days. It has been such a rewarding odyssey. Somewhat risky, to be sure — I truly thought I might perish in a storm off Australia five weeks ago. But there's great comfort too in facing adversity and surviving.'

'Good gracious,' said Edith.

'You have our sympathies,' said Cedric, 'with regard to your loss. Not too recent, I trust.' He assumed not, given that she was not in mourning dress.

Violet waved her hand. 'Time eases the pangs. At the beginning that's a saying that drives one a little mad but it is, fortunately, true.' She smiled. 'But yes, Mr Vincent, we do have a mutual acquaintance. I have been in New Zealand and can bring you the love and affection of your sister Anna, who was my dearest friend there.'

Edith gasped. Cedric stood up, grinning broadly. 'Well, bless my soul,' he cried. 'This is a surprise. My, my, what a small world this is.' He bent over Violet took her hand in both of his and pressed it warmly. 'When one lives in a foreign place any word of a family member is so appreciated.'

'And so is the sight of kith and kin. I have a distant cousin here whom I've not seen for many a long year and am anxious to find him.'

'And who would that be?' Edith asked.

'Mayne Underhill and his wife Lydia. He's with the East India Company.'

Cedric shrugged. 'Almost everyone is.'

'Do you know him, dear?' Edith asked her husband.

'Can't say I do. Can you tell me what type of post he has?'

'I'm afraid not. We were little more than children when we last met. My news of his whereabouts is only third-hand and is old news at that.'

'Well, I trust your long journey will not have been in vain. I shall ask at the club. Everyone sets foot in there at some stage. If he's here doing business we shall find him. Now, I do believe a small celebration is in order. Rashid!'

Lemonade arrived. Niceties were observed. And Violet sat and smiled and talked about life in the tiny town of Tauranga half a world away, about the Hamiltons and their son, and Anna's indomitable spirit in coping with the hard domestic life of every settler. 'How she would love to have a Rashid in the house!' she laughed. 'Good servants are so hard to find.'

'Do not be under any illusion that it's any different here, my dear,' said Edith.

Then there was the volcano to expound on and the dances and regattas and concerts. She said little about her own life there at all, except to say she'd stayed in the home of a local landowner.

Later, Cedric would not hear of Miss Foster walking alone back to the hotel in the fast-dying light and escorted her himself past the cows and carts, crying children, cooking fires and shouting traders, pushing a clear path for her beneath the violent shrilling of insects clouding the trees.

As they parted at the hotel's front steps she raised a finger. 'Please, Mr Vincent, a request. If you do meet my cousin, can I rely on you not to reveal my presence here to him? I should delight in surprising him.'

'Of course,' he assured her, charmed by her sense of play. 'You can rely on me to be the soul of discretion. And Edith, too.'

He bowed, extracted from her a promise to join them for dinner two nights hence, walked away and was instantly swallowed by the smoky darkness. She watched him go, elated with having met with success so soon in this strange and teeming city. As she lay cocooned beneath a mosquito net that night, she was confident he would keep his word. It was a comfort to meet a man with his sister's eyes. She hoped he also had Anna's steadfast soul.

'But who is she really?' Edith mused on that same sultry evening. 'How extraordinary for a woman on her own to sail around the world like that. A pretty thing, too. One would have thought her wed a long time since. She must have some means to be able to fund her journeying.'

* * *

It did not take long to find someone who knew Mayne Underhill. He and his wife had left six months earlier for Pondicherry to take up a new administrative post.

Violet sighed a little when Edith delivered that information at a tea party a week later.

Then she put down her cup and leaned forward. Female chatter was filling the room and it was difficult for Edith to make out Violet's whisper. 'And what about their boy? I think they have a son, perhaps seven years old.'

Edith did not notice her intensity. 'Oh, undoubtedly, he'll be at Home. All the children go Home for schooling at seven or thereabouts. I took back the second of our two darling boys three years ago. It is the hardest wrench a mother can bear to know her children are growing up out of sight, so far away.

'My parents take them in at Christmas and at end of term. Without that, I don't think I could bear it. Boys, especially, drift away from you. Their letters start out frequent and homesick and then the tone changes to sports and then they hardly write at all. If you ever have a child, my dear, try to ensure it's a girl. They will love you for much longer.'

'Nonsense,' said another wife, overhearing. 'Look at that flibberti-gibbet Fleming girl. Goes Home for a holiday and runs off with some man who turns out to be a scoundrel and leaves her carrying a bastard child. No modesty, no grace, no future. The family were utterly appalled.'

'Miss Foster left the party then,' Edith reported to Cedric later. 'Stood up, pleaded a headache and departed at a trot. She looked quite pale.'

* * *

CEDRIC WROTE to Thomas about three weeks later about business matters and to assure him that regular bank drafts would continue to arrive for the care and upkeep of his mother.

He added a postscript:

Before I close I should add we recently had an unexpected but welcome visit from a charming friend of yours, a Miss Violet Foster. She had only the kindest things to say about your good selves and gave us a capital account of life on your fresh and sunny shores. That she has since departed for England has vexed Edith somewhat for she enjoyed her bright company. Miss Foster asked to be remembered to you both.

When the letter arrived in Tauranga in April, Thomas opened it at the kitchen table. It was a Monday lunchtime. Anna was outside on a windy autumn day, helping Dinah wrestle with flapping linen as they struggled to unpin half-dry sheets from the line before the clouds opened and rain soaked everything anew.

He read the letter and frowned. Miss Violet *Foster*? What fresh mischief was this? He wanted no part of it.

In the two years since Rupert's death, an easier kind of peace had returned to the Hamilton household. But Anna was still not the woman she had been before. Men did not discuss their marriages with other men but had Thomas had anyone to talk to — in the same easy way he'd once talked with Rupert — he might have vented his frustration with a string of adjectives describing how Anna sometimes acted now. If they had cause to disagree about any small thing she would turn argumentative, restless, unaccommodating, snippy, bold. Always telling him it was her right to have her own opinions. And to voice them.

She'd always had a mind of her own, of course. It was one of the qualities that attracted him to her in the first place. But her former manner had been mild compared with what he had to listen to now. It was all because of that scheming, faithless, foolish woman from the house up the hill. Thomas was not about to give Anna any further news of Violet Sutton or Foster or whatever she was calling herself. Let her write her own notes to India seeking clues of Violet's whereabouts. The woman had, at any rate, already sailed into oblivion.

He tucked the letter into his waistcoat pocket as Anna and Dinah burst in pink-cheeked, laughing over some joke, their arms piled with damp wadded linen.

'This weather!' Anna cried as she dumped sheets into a basket. 'Ah, the post has come. Anything interesting today?'

'No,' he replied. 'No news at all.'

CHAPTER THIRTY-FIVE

*'The Prana Sparklet siphons — almost indispensable in summer for
made soda-water at home — and very economical in two sizes.'*
— David Jones Ltd advertisement, Sydney Morning Herald.

SYDNEY, JANUARY 12, 1911

Twenty-three years later, Anna stood at her front door hoping she
might yet receive an extra farewell wave or nod from Jamie before he
turned left between her gateposts and made his way to the station. He
did not look back.

She well knew the eagerness of young men to leave the company of
their mothers after making a duty visit. At thirty years of age Jamie was a
bachelor with a busy life as an art dealer and auctioneer. She had only
her quiet house with its ticking mantelpiece clock, her books and her
embroidery. And a dwindling flow of reluctant afternoon children sent
to her by parents seeking help with their reading. She liked to keep busy.

Thomas was two years dead. At fifty-seven he'd had a dizzy turn
behind the desk in his Sydney office. It made him drop his pen with a
clatter and raise one hand to his brow. 'Mr Hamilton?' his secretary said.

'I don't feel very well,' he replied and slumped in his chair.

Anna had grieved for him. Despite their differences they'd been companionable, especially as the novelty of moving to a new country had softened the edges of old hurts. When she was over the shock of his passing she sold their large house and bought a small cottage in Mosman more in keeping with her widow's pension.

Her brother Cedric, long since worn out by India's challenges, had returned Home with his wife. 'Why don't you join us here?' he sometimes wrote. 'Are you not lonely out there in that blazing land?'

But Anna felt no yearning for England. What was there for her now after so long away? She had Jamie here and her friends. They included Madame Francini who lived a short ferry-ride away and was still earning a living from reading palms despite her advanced years. She'd ended her travels a decade earlier, tired of lurching from town to town and of wedging herself into the humid berths of heaving ships.

Mr Francini had abruptly absconded shortly afterwards to take up with a theatre wardrobe mistress. 'Oh my dear!" Anna had gasped when she heard of it. Madame Francini had waved away her concern.

'It was always going to happen — I knew it all along.' She snorted with a knowing grin. 'He had his uses. He kept me warm for a while. But his major skill was always latching on to talented women.'

Tauranga was far in Anna's past. The Hamiltons had been forced to leave it after the town's early promise faded in the Depression of the 1890s. Anna had been glad to set up home in the infinitely larger city of Sydney.

She still swapped Christmas cards with a few remaining Tauranga identities. It was mere politeness, but also a faint, lingering curiosity about people who had figured in that brief but vivid part of her life. It now seemed so distant. Violet. Rupert. Scandal. Blood. Anguish. Rage. Revenge. Grief.

Now, as she stood at her door, the scent of frangipani blooms wafted to her. A pair of rosellas arrowed, shrieking, across her small garden from left to right. She loved Australia's raucous birds and had written to Cedric that she could not stand the thought of settling in some chilly English village cheered only by meek sparrows and squawking rooks. This was unfair, she knew, as a fine midsummer day in Britain was beautiful. She was, however, content where she was.

Jamie seemed to have come to a stop. She saw his pointing hand as he indicated her gateway. Then he was gone and another young man took his place, filling the space between the white-painted gateposts, looking straight at her.

He was dark-haired, had a thin moustache, and wore a suit that was better tailored than was common in Sydney. He was about the same age as Jamie. He took a few steps, his expression enquiring but also oddly intense. 'Pardon me if I intrude,' he said. 'I'm looking for Mrs Hamilton.'

'I am she,' she replied, wishing Jamie had had the courtesy to linger rather than making her confront this stranger alone. She blocked the entrance with a grip on the door's edge. What might a young man want with a widow of her years?. Sydney was full of cunning spivs and conmen.

'I have come a long way to meet you,' he said, doffing his hat. His voice was English, quite cultured. 'I'm told you once knew my mother and that if I want to know more of her story then I should find you.' A long silence spooled out between them. 'My name,' he said, 'is John Underhill.'

The hand Anna had clamped on the door went to her heart and the other rose to her mouth. 'Oh my dear Lord,' she said.

Soon Violet's son was in her parlour perched on the edge of her settee. He sat erect and stiff. The poised tension in his frame and something in the shape of his eyes and cheekbones were faintly familiar, but if they'd passed on the street she would have paid him no attention at all.

'I should get tea,' Anna said, desperate for something to hold onto, even if it was only the fragile handle of a china cup.

'No need. I detest tea,' he said. 'Although water would be welcome.'

Anna could not take her eyes off him. 'Your mother was not so fond of it either. But how. . .? Wait until I fetch a drink. Then you must tell me everything.'

By the time she returned with water jug and glasses rattling on a tray he was looking only slightly more at ease.

'When did you see her last?' asked Anna. 'Is she well?'

'She passed away about a year ago.' Anna heard that in the act of putting down the tray and it smacked heavily on the table. She put out a shaking hand to steady the jug's sloshing contents.

'Aah,' she breathed. The sound caught in her throat and she felt for a chair and sat down, shaking her head. 'Oh, I am so sad to hear that. I always believed she'd last forever. I could never believe she would be ageing like me. She was so beautiful.'

John Underhill stood, poured water for them both and handed a glass to Anna before seating himself again. He dashed it back. 'It's impossible for me to imagine her at all, for I learnt of her existence only after she died. She remembered me in her will. A lawyer's agent found me in London, a pompous little man. He came straight out with it. "Your mother's dead," he said.

'I told him I knew that, that she'd died years ago. "Not that one," he said. "Your real mother." It was a shock. Turned my life upside down.'

'Where did she die? Where was she living?'

'Here, apparently. She ran a boarding house in Paddington. I've been told by some that it is a house of ill repute.' He swallowed, looked down at the glass gripped in his fist. 'I must tell you that it's rather appalling hearing that about the woman who apparently brought you into the world.'

Anna's mouth dropped. '*Here*? In Sydney? Oh dear Lord, I never knew. The last I heard, oh, some twenty years ago, she was sailing from India to England.'

He shrugged. 'Why should you know? I imagine she was ignorant of your presence too.'

Anna sagged with disappointment, but then felt anger boil. 'What was the word you just used? Appalling? When appalling things happen in your life, Mr Underhill, then it's hardly surprising if the outcome is not exactly stellar.'

'You're not surprised?'

'By what you say about her profession?' She gave him a taut smile. 'At my age, one tends not to be surprised by anything. Violet may have been brought low but I can tell you one thing, she would have run that business — if in fact the story is even true — with honour and discretion, would have protected her employees and been respectful of her clients. Violet rarely gave a fig for public opinion but she did have faith in her own worth, no matter what — and the fact that you are here demonstrates that she had faith in you too.'

He shrugged. 'She said as much in a letter she left me. She also apologised for the fact that I grew up without her influence. I suppose I must give her credit for that, though I'm not at all sure how her influence would have helped me.'

'Credit! Might you consider expressing gratitude that you are alive at all? You came into this world when she was so young that she had no power at all. She was spurned by her parents and married off to an utterly unsuitable man who took her far away and used her cruelly. You were ripped from her arms.

'I used to see her on the wharf waiting for mail bags to be carried ashore from every ship that came in, desperate to hear news of you. And she never did because most of her family never wrote to her at all. The loss of you ate away at her soul.'

She regarded him stonily. 'For her, you were a baby she named George. A baby she never forgot. It was hard for her to know that not even the name she'd chosen for you remained.'

He swung away from her as if she had struck him. It softened her a little and she raised her hands, palms up. 'I'm sorry for my tone, Mr Underhill. It's just that I knew her trials so well, but of course you knew nothing at all.'

He turned back with narrow eyes. 'You say she was unhappy? Can you begin to apprehend how I've been feeling? One day I'm an everyday sort of fellow and the next I discover that my real mother was in fact a step-relation of some hideously complicated sort. And all the time I was becoming a man there was a woman alive in the world who knew who I was and where I was and kept me in total ignorance.'

Anna kept her mouth clamped shut, took a deep breath and let a seconds-long pause fall into place. 'Tell me how it is that you are here.'

'She knew she was dying. She wrote to her lawyer, told him of my existence and gave him an approximate address. I'm with Lloyds, the insurers. An agent found me there.

'Finding you was not so simple, Mrs Hamilton, as I had only your husband's last New Zealand position as a clue and he left that post years ago. But eventually I received advice that your husband had moved to the Bank of New South Wales. And a clerk there led me to you. Where was it you used to live in New Zealand, some godforsaken place called Ta-Ooh-Rangah? Quite impossible to spell, let alone to pronounce.'

'In point of fact,' Anna said quietly, 'God rather favoured that town. There are few prettier harbours in the world. The name means landing place.' She was astonished she could remember that small fact once bestowed upon her by Dinah, who had left one day and been replaced by a train of more forgettable cooks and maids. Dinah had been a treasure who had slipped from Anna's life.

He shrugged and pulled from a pocket a small gold locket on a chain. He leaned forward to pass it to her. It did not look familiar. Anna held it in her palm. The chain, warmed by his body heat, slipped between her fingers like water. She had no inkling of what it might contain. A picture, perhaps. A poem? She pushed her thumbnail into the concavity at its edge and pressed. There was a tiny click as the case sprang open. Inside a coil of bright red hair lay under an oval of glass.

She could not speak.

'Her letter to me intimated that if you were doubtful of my identity, this locket would prove it.'

Anna gazed at the hair, as shiny now as the day upon which Violet had cut it in Mr Dobie's back room. 'It was Rupert's,' she said quietly. 'Poor boy. His hair was so red that when he stood in the sun it glowed like a bright copper penny. Someone called him Mr Magenta and it stuck.'

Underhill cleared his throat with an almost painful hacking sound. 'Rupert who? Was he my real father?'

Anna smiled. 'Oh my dear, no. Just a very good friend of mine, and of my late husband's, and your mother's. Though, for Violet, he was more than that.' She assessed him and decided upon frankness. 'They were lovers,' she said. 'She was so miserable then and Rupert gave her joy, at least for a season, when we were all young.'

He sniffed. For a hopeful moment she thought he was upset but then realised it was an expression of disdain.

She rose, went to her sideboard, pulled out the bottle of good malt whisky usually broached only when Madame Francini called, took two crystal glasses and poured each of them a stiff tot. 'Violet was rather fond of cider but this will do,' she said as she held a glass out to him. 'Soda?'

He shook his head, downed a mouthful but stayed stiff and watchful. She plumped up a pillow beneath her elbow to brace her drinking arm. 'The last time I had a letter from your mother,' she told him, 'she was about to leave Australia for Bombay. She had heard that your parents had taken you there and she was determined to find you.'

'She wrote that she'd seen me once, not in India but in England. She'd managed an invitation to a country house where I was spending summer. I'd not seen India for years at that point. I was apparently playing some rough-and-tumble game in the garden. She wrote that when she saw how settled I was she thought she had no right to upset my existence. Never said a word.'

Anna cocked her head. 'You must at least grant her the sound sense she used then — though it must have broken her heart.'

He shrugged. 'If you say so.'

'I do say so! No one ever gave her credit for her powers of reasoning. It was something she yearned for. Women rarely receive that, even today.'

He shifted uncomfortably. She saw his eyes flick to the sideboard. 'By all means pour another,' she said. 'We're not done yet.' He filled only his own glass, neglecting to ask if she would also like more.

'Did you say your other mother is deceased?'

He nodded. 'I heard she'd died when I was fourteen. My school excused me from classes that afternoon. It was the done thing to look mournful but I struggled by then to remember what she even looked like.'

Anna felt her heart twist. He was so bleak and angry. 'You must be wanting to know how you came to be,' she said. 'Violet told me of it one morning in Auckland a long time ago.'

Anna looked out to the fading daylight outside her window, recalling their perch on the Shortland Street hill and the secrets spilled while the shipping noise from the shore below drifted up to them. She told him of Violet's exile and his adoption, followed by the marriage to Henry Sutton. John interrupted. 'What happened to him?' Anna told him what little she knew. Underhill's intensity was starting to feel oppressive. She wanted to be alone now to absorb the reality that Violet had spent years of her life just a few miles away across the harbour, and never once had their paths crossed.

'She left a letter for you too,' said Underhill. And he reached out and put a cream envelope on the table at her elbow. As she picked it up she saw how her hand shook. She turned it over, saw again the sharp incising strokes of that long unseen, unmistakable hand. On its back where the closing flap was glued and wax-sealed was a sketch of Violet's favourite symbol, the pansy.

'An interesting touch,' George said loftily, draining his glass. 'Did she like flowers?'

'This flower, most definitely.' Anna smoothed it over with a fingertip. 'I suppose you see it as just a pretty affectation — the sort of thing a woman does to adorn something plain.' She noted his blank look and did not explain. 'So many letters in my life. I think I've leant more from Violet's pen than I ever heard from her lips. I'm rather weary now. Do you mind leaving? I need to read and think and remember. Come back tomorrow. We can talk more then.'

Annoyance flashed across his face but he stood slowly. 'You can trust me,' she said. 'Your mother did.'

He smacked his hands against his thighs and blew a breath out hard. '*My mother*. Once I thought I knew what that word meant. I still don't know. I never quite managed to measure up for the mother I knew in my early life. She always used to growl, "Blood will out," when she was angry with me. I didn't know what it meant. I had dreams for years of waking up and finding myself lying in a bloody bed, the sheets red and wet.'

'I'm sorry for that,' Anna said in a voice that shook a little. 'And I know it would have disturbed Violet immensely.'

He lifted a doubting shoulder. 'It's immaterial now, isn't it, what she would have thought. Too little, too late, too pointless. I'll see myself out.'

She listened to his footsteps fading as he crunched down her gravel path. She stayed where she was. Underhill had left the locket behind.

The sun's low brassy light — it would soon be dusk — made Rupert's hair glow bright in its oval bed of gold. She snapped the case shut, rose with a grunt (her hips grew stiff if she sat for too long), took sharp scissors from her sewing basket and with great care, cut open the envelope.

CHAPTER THIRTY-SIX

'Now that the telephone is to be regarded as a purely business convenience, and its old delightful ease of communication guarded by the facet that each call costs a half-penny, it remains for debarred lovers of a yarn to devise other means of talking across the distance.'
— Page for Women, Sydney Morning Herald.

My dear Anna,

How long it is since I last wrote those three words! I sit here with my pen in Sydney in 1910 not knowing when or if you will read them. I don't allow myself to think the answer will be 'never' for that would be too sad to bear.

I imagine you are still living in New Zealand for it seemed to suit both Hamiltons well. Your Jamie will be grown by now. Possibly you will have expanded your family even more. But then, I have lived in India and England and Australia and you, too, might have packed up your worldly goods and travelled elsewhere.

My frustration is that I wrote so many letters to you and never received a reply. For a long time that made me perplexed and sad. Perhaps I have myself to blame because my address changed so often, as well as my name. I have, however, come to think you probably never received them, for I cannot believe you would so thoroughly ignore me.

After a few years it seemed sensible to stop trying because I knew your life would have marched on. My own was also unfolding in ways we'd have scarce believed in the days when we tried our hand at rowing.

If you are reading this it will have come via my son George, who I still cannot think of as John, for I plan to have this sent to him after my passing. The housekeeper who helped me at his birth has been constant over the years in sending me news of him. I even saw him in the flesh once and watched his eyes skitter over me. For him, I was merely a stranger on a crowded terrace.

I knew in that moment I had no right to descend upon him and change everything. I thought perhaps when he was grown I might confront him, but the time never did seem right. I did not seek to see him again in boyhood for it offered more pain than consolation. Besides, soon after that I went back to India with a new husband to make a fresh start.

Anna gaped at that and read on.

Now it is too late. My boy lives half a world away and I am too ill to travel. So I am going to direct him to the best friend I ever had, if he can find you. You can explain his existence to him. I would hate to think he might never know the truth.

Of course I had to offer some incentive for him to find you. For why should he blindly obey the whim of an unknown, possibly mad woman who claims to be his true mother? I assume he will be confused, even furious, for temper runs in the men of his adopted family and he will have been raised to be loud and assertive. But I also know that meeting you will help him understand his life.

I added an alluring phrase to the letter I wrote for him. It was that he may "learn something to his advantage". Money is a magnet for us all. My feeling is that it will not take him long to book a berth to discover what treasure may lie at voyage's end.

And treasure there is. I am putting you in command of it, my dear. Not the banker in your family, but you. It is a sum of one thousand pounds. Not a vast sum nowadays but neat enough, is it not? — and not stowed inside a tree this time but in a Sydney law firm's safe. I never did know if the thousand given to me by Rupert was his or if he raided the bank: I suspected the latter but I was in such need that I used it to spirit myself away.

If it was theft, no doubt Thomas heard of it. In that case he would surely have suspected me of collusion and thought even less of me. I was, after all, the town's scarlet woman.

Now, the same sum of money can be handed on to George/John to make up in some small measure for what happened to him — but only if you see fit.

You see, I wish to put him through hoops. I would like to think he deserves my gift.

Here Violet had drawn an emphatic underline beneath the word 'deserves'.

I apologise for imposing on you — for I am relying on your assessment of him. I want him to receive the money only if he seems likely to use it well.

If he appears irresponsible or vain or feckless then please do not allow him to have it. Instead, it will in that case go to you. It would be entirely up to you whether to use it for your own needs or to benefit some noble cause.

Are you smiling at this point? How ironic that I, who so blithely glossed over Rupert's reckless ways, should now insist that my son be above reproach.

As a Freethinker I should let him make his own decisions. And yet, when it comes to parental expectations, I find myself as bourgeois as any other over-protective hen.

I wish for my son not to be obsessed with the making of money, as was Henry, or the wagering of it, as was Rupert.

I sensed you were sometimes exasperated by sensible Thomas, who was so moderate in all things. However, I know now how admirable his attitude was. He told me once, at one of those merry dances in the bank, how in his youth his father had once enraged him by trotting out that old saw about being neither a borrower nor a lender. "The whole world depends on money's wise use and sound investment," Thomas declared. And then added sternly, "However, I must emphasise the importance of the two adjectives in that sentence."

Anna smiled at that. She could almost hear him being so pedantic. But Violet's next sentence pulled her up short.

Might Thomas have prevented my letters from reaching you? In my house Henry was the one who commandeered the post, and I have wondered if it was the same for you. If so, your husband might have quietly withheld any envelopes he thought were from me. I know he believed I was a terrible influence on you. However, it matters little now. Thomas would only have been trying to protect you from the toxin of my wild ways. I did behave badly — but I must say I regret none of it.

You will want to know about India. Colourful chaos, my dear. When I landed there and met your brother I learned John had already been packed off to England. Of course, nothing would satisfy me but following after.

On the ship I met a kind man on furlough. He was visiting Home for only three months before going back to his post. Once we were in England he begged me to join him. I said yes to him as he was a gentle soul and I had by then already decided against trying to reclaim my boy. So back we went to live on an indigo plantation, miles from civilisation.

The only person in England to whom I wrote in the next fifteen years was my faithful contact in Ireland, still apprising me of young John's progress. I retreated into colonial life until one day my husband slipped while crossing a river not far from our home. It was not deep but it was swift. His knapsack was heavy, he could not rise and was drowned. In time, I returned to Sydney. I had liked it there many years earlier. I was left with sufficient funds to set up a lodging house. Remember the awful Mrs Hadley? I was determined to make up for her and all the awful landladies in the world. I also ran dance classes there for young girls. I always did love the dance, despite the best efforts of the Rev. Larkin to dissuade me.

I am Mrs Millhouse now. No one in Sydney knows I was ever a Mrs Sutton. I know not whether Henry ever divorced me, so it is entirely possible I am a bigamist. Note, my dear, how my sins compound. It is up to you to decide whether to tell my son of this further perfidy.

Now the writing style became sharper and more emphatic.

Be a Freethinker, Anna! Feel free to grant him my legacy if he deserves it. There is also an alternative. He will have come a long way to see you and I cannot send him away empty-handed, even if he turns out to be a scoundrel. As you know, I have always been partial to scoundrels.

There is another item lodged with my lawyer. It was the only thing I took from the Tauranga house apart from some clothes and jewellery. I felt no guilt in taking it for I left so much else behind. Henry must have been furious when he saw it was gone.

I cannot remember if you liked it, or even noticed it, but I have carried it all over the world. It is a small oil sketch of a dancing girl that hung in the hall just inside our front door. If John Underhill seems like a man who might benefit from a touch of artistry in his life, then you may decide to make that his legacy instead. Henry always insisted it would grow in value.

It glows with colour and it witnessed, my dear, so many of our agile conversations. Those days spent with you were precious.

However, my days are short now. Consumption is a vile disease. It is as if some dark creature is steadily gnawing at me from the inside out.

Please, my good friend Anna, make your assessment of my son. And then write to my lawyer, Mr Fitzroy, with your instructions. Your choice is between Mammon and Beauty. Fitzroy will render to George whichever gift you feel is appropriate.

Whatever remains is for you to use as you please.

I send you my enduring love,

Violet

* * *

IT WAS DUSK NOW. Anna was straining to read the letter in the fading light. She got up briefly to pour herself another drink and sat on with the letter on her lap until the house was cloaked in velvet dark.

The sudden jangle of the telephone made her start. 'Mama,' said Jamie. 'It's only me. I'm curious about your visitor. I'd not seen him before.'

Anna smiled, realising suddenly that Madame Francini was not the only one in Sydney who could remember Tauranga days. 'It's a long story. Take me out to tea soon and I'll tell you.' She would share some of it at least. She knew Jamie had a few memories of the Bay of Plenty. The night Tarawera erupted was definitely embedded there — the roar, the blackness, the choking dust. They'd talked about it only recently after a fire started by lightning razed twelve houses on Sydney's western flank.

'It's a bit like the volcano,' Anna had said, 'dangerous but distant.'

The Violet-and-Rupert eruption had been like that too. The lovers had been at the molten core. The rest of them — herself, Thomas and Henry Sutton — had scrambled around in the emotional ash-fall, dodging the airborne white-hot rocks of rage and shame.

Sutton had unexpectedly turned up in their lives not long before Thomas died — looking much older and stouter but still bombastic, now a resident of Hong Kong. Just visiting Sydney, looking for a chinwag with Thomas. They had talked in Thomas's study so she heard only the deep rumble of their voices.

'Did he ask about or offer any news of Violet?' she had asked afterwards.

Thomas shrugged. 'Good Lord, no.' He snapped out his newspaper.

'Did he ever have the son he wanted?'

'Mmm, apparently so. Recently, too. Still just a lad.' Thomas peeked out from behind the folded broadsheet. 'He has a Eurasian wife now,' he said. 'A great deal younger than himself, I deduce.'

Now Anna said goodnight to her son and hung the phone back on its hook. She would not have bothered with the thing, but Jamie liked to be able to call her. It did not escape her that it meant he could avoid visiting in person so often. It was interesting how the chief benefit of some newfangled inventions was not bringing people together but keeping them apart.

CHAPTER THIRTY-SEVEN

'The woman whose mind is not alive to the great causes and effects that
are now making history, cannot bring to her children and her intimates
all the God-given possibilities implanted within her, nor can she herself
experience, except in half measure. the joyful facts of her existence.'
— Page for Women, Sydney Morning Herald.

18 Jan, 1911

John Underhill arrived promptly in the morning. He tolerated being
told the rest of what Anna knew, wincing with apparent distaste as he
heard the tale of Rupert's end. 'But what is that man to me?'

Anna put her hands firmly on her knees. 'I merely wish you to know
the fullness of it all, to try to help you understand her painful past, and
why she was reluctant to draw you into her life before you were ready to
understand.'

'I doubt that I do, even now,' he said stiffly. 'She sounds, actually,
quite degenerate. She conceived me out of wedlock, was fortunate to
marry someone — anyone! — and then attached herself to a man who
was so disturbed that he shot himself. She seems to have had multiple
husbands. Am I supposed to be proud of her? Frankly, I would hate any
of my friends to be appraised of my background.'

You really are a prig, Anna thought. She rose and steadied herself on the back of her chair. 'I understand you were told that if you came here you would hear something of advantage to you.'

'Indeed.' He waited.

Anna stayed silent.

'What part do you play in this?' he asked.

'First, I would like to ask a question. What do you want from life?'

'Well, my berth at Lloyd's awaits my return.' His confidence was supreme. 'I am doing, and will do, well there. Ships, cargoes, factories, railroads — all the wheels of industry need to be insured. My father hangs on in India but life there holds little appeal for me. The noise, the smells, the crowds. Ugh.'

Anna raised a hand towards the window. 'How about this land? A fresh new country. A keen man can make a name for himself here.'

'Here?' His voice high with disbelief. 'But Australia is so raw, Mrs Hamilton. I'm surprised you can stand this heat and glare — good Lord, the shrieking birds! Commerce is slight, industry little developed. Living here, surely you must long for some sophistication.'

She gave him a cool smile. 'As you already know, Violet left something for you. It was her wish that I meet you and tell you about her before it came into your possession. To gain access to it, I need to see her lawyer. Do you think you can withstand the discomforts of Sydney for a few more days?'

'I can contact him.'

She waved a hand. 'No, this is my task. I shall arrange an appointment. We will both attend. Violet would have wanted that.'

* * *

TWO DAYS later they were ushered into a dim, stuffy chamber that lay behind doors emblazoned with the words, Fairleigh & Fitzroy, Barristers and Solicitors.

They took seats on the far side of Mr Maurice Fitzroy's large, gleaming desk. There were squeaks from the friction of his posterior upon the buttoned leather of his chair. He had a sparse sheaf of papers before him. along with a rectangular package wrapped with linen and bound with string.

He favoured Anna with a professional smile. 'Mrs Hamilton, how excellent that all this time you've been living in our city. We thought you were in New Zealand until young Mr Underhill here traced your whereabouts. I thank you, madam, for your note. On your instruction there's nothing left to do but to hand this item over.'

He pushed the package diagonally over the desk. Underhill was swift to uplift it and examine the packaging that held it secure. It was about eighteen inches square.

Fitzroy passed him scissors so he could snip and clip. The outer wrapping dropped to the floor. Underneath it were layers of thin waxy card. Under that — multiple sheets of tissue paper.

Foster ripped them all off to expose a wooden box with a hinged lid. It was bound with stout fabric tapes. He swore a little as he struggled to cut them. With gleaming eyes, he lifted the lid, then turned to Anna, puzzled.

'A painting? This is it? She has left me a little daub of some dancing girl?' He extracted it with some difficulty for the box had been made to fit the picture's slim frame. He turned it upside down to check if anything was written beneath. A card fell to the floor. His hand swooped to retrieve it.

He read. He frowned, let out a stuttering laugh and let the painting drop back onto the table.

'This is what I've come round the world for? Should I be grateful?'

'I believe it is by Degas,' said Anna.

He frowned. Maurice Fitzroy looked none the wiser. 'Some French chap, wasn't he?'

'Still living, as I understand it,' murmured Anna.

'Not even dead yet?' said Underhill. 'But that's what counts in the art world. You have to wait till they turn up their toes before they're worth anything.'

'What does the card say?' asked Anna.

He flicked it to her. She squinted at the words written in Violet's hand:

Observe how the dancers reach up in mid-leap. See them as me, frozen in mid-movement. I stretch up my arms, always striving for the next moment of perfection, knowing that once attained it will immediately evaporate. You were a moment of perfection on the day of your birth, my son, but then you too were gone. All through my life you were the light on my horizon, always out of reach, but my life was richer for knowing you were there. May this painting remind you of the need to keep reaching for your own truths.

Anna looked up. Violet's son was waiting, one well-shod foot tossed over his other knee, fingers drumming on the heel of the shoe. 'Quite the scribe, wasn't she. The trouble is, literature never did draw me. Nor art.'

Anna fought to keep anger contained. 'Perhaps she sensed that given your father's position you would likely work in commerce. That can be a life bereft of passion and she was above all a passionate woman. Maybe she hoped you would enjoy this gift. You did tell me the other day that you thrive on elegance.'

'I rather meant the elegance of a healthy balance sheet.' He turned to the lawyer. 'Does it have any value?'

Fitzroy spread his hands wide on his desktop. 'You would need to have it appraised by an expert. However, I must say it is a small piece. I've observed the large prices tend to be paid for larger works.'

Underhill cleared his throat, slapped his knee and stood up. 'Mrs Hamilton, Mr Fitzroy, our meeting is over. If my benefactor imagined I would be crowing over the possession of a splash of French frippery then she was sadly mistaken.' He picked it up nonetheless and jammed it back into the box, slapped down its lid and reached for his hat.

Anna stood then with pounding heart. 'You're taking it despite your distaste for it?'

He shrugged. 'It may be worth something.'

'And does her message mean nothing to you?'

He gave her a steely glare. 'Quite frankly, Mrs Hamilton, everything about her makes me angry. I understand finally why my parents loved me so little. They couldn't forget I was a bastard. My respectable background is a sham.'

'You could have ignored the approach from Mr Fitzroy's agent.'

'What, when there was a chance there was something here' — and he rolled his eyes — 'that would be to my *advantage*? I assumed there'd be a legacy worth collecting.' He waved the box at her with short jabs. 'Instead, there's just this and some sentimental blather from someone I never knew. I shall return to London as soon as I can.' And with that he jammed the box under one arm and strode from the room.

'Mr Underhill, wait!' Anna snatched up her bag and dashed after him. He did not stop until she clutched at his sleeve. They were now out on the footpath, a few passers-by glancing curiously at the harried young man and the matronly woman. 'How much do you want for it?'

'You want to *buy* it?' His eyes narrowed. 'Is there something you know about it that you're not revealing?'

'No! It may be a Degas or a copy. I have no clue. I merely remember it hanging in your mother's house. I would like it to light my remaining years.'

His gaze swept her up and down as if evaluating the quality of her dress, her hat, her shoes. She felt a subtle shift in his manner, a slight swagger that told her he felt in control. 'What is it worth to you?'

A vein thudded in her neck. 'I imagine at a jumble sale its pretty colours might fetch twenty pounds. To demonstrate my intent I will offer you fifty.'

He laughed in her face. 'So paltry a sum for something that means so much?'

'I am not a wealthy woman.'

'What, with a husband in banking? You cannot tell me he didn't leave you well provided for.'

She ignored his derision. 'His provision was adequate but not handsome.'

'Well then, how much inadequacy are you willing to put up with to buy this?' He shot for the sky. 'A thousand pounds' worth?'

She took a step back and raised a hand to her eyes as if shielding them from the sun that baked Sydney that day. Be strong now, she thought. Don't give in. Stand up for yourself. Do it for Violet's sake. How relieved Anna was that Violet had not survived to see the man her son had become — how nurture, or lack of it, had made him so hard and cold.

She drew herself up, trying not to tremble. 'A thousand pounds? No one on Earth would give you so much. Henry Sutton might have said it was by Degas but it has no signature.'

Anna could tell from the way he blinked that he had missed that detail. She bored on. 'Proving it may take years and may prove impossible and then what are you left with? A desultory auction in a back room of some second-rate antique store.'

He flushed.

'I am willing to stretch to one hundred.'

He turned away, tossing his chin.

'Two hundred then,' she said. 'I can go no higher. I imagine it will pay for your travels here and back with plenty left over.'

She could tell from the split-second widening of his eyes that it was more than he'd hoped for. He dithered for one, two seconds, before pushing the box at her. Then distrust flickered on his face.

'My bank is along the road,' she said. 'Let us go there now, together, so you can be paid right now.'

In ten minutes they were sitting before her manager, who occupied the very desk once presided over by Thomas, arranging for Mr Underhill to receive two hundred pounds in cash. 'It is a substantial sum, Mrs Hamilton,' said the manager with a worried frown. 'You are quite satisfied with the soundness of this transaction?'

'My funds are mine to dispose of as I wish, are they not?' she said serenely. 'I thank you for your concern, but it really is unwarranted.'

As Anna Hamilton and John Underhill went to the bank's door, they joined a small cluster of customers reluctant to step outside. A storm had descended in the way that Sydney storms do. Rain was hammering down. A crackling blaze of lightning was followed almost at once by a vast boom of thunder.

Many years earlier Anna and Violet had met in a different doorway, sheltering from another storm, fifteen hundred miles away. Anna hugged the box closer. 'Why don't you go home via India,' she said. 'You should visit your father. It's never too late to mend fences.'

He shot her a derisive look, turned up his collar and dashed out into the rain.

* * *

WHAT WITH THE banking transaction and the storm, it took some time for Anna to return to Mr Fitzroy.

In his smooth-faced, lawyer-ish way he said little when Anna told him that having considered Violet's wishes, she was of the opinion that her old friend would not have wished for young Mr Underhill to receive the larger part of her legacy. As for the picture to which he was entitled, he had agreed to a fair price for it and washed his hands of the whole affair. Fitzroy allowed himself just a small smirk as he wrote out a cheque in her favour from the firm's trust account. 'An arrogant young chap, that. Best he doesn't know, perhaps, that he failed to pass muster. He came a long way for very little.'

'Ah well, he's fancy free. He's at least had an interesting adventure. Something to tell his chums about. Can you tell me what your instructions were if you'd been unable to find him, or myself for that matter?'

Fitzroy blotted his signature. 'If we had found him but not you he'd have received two hundred pounds and the rest would have gone to charity.'

Anna smiled. 'How very suitable that would have been.'

'She put a time limit on it. If neither of you had come to light by this time next year then it would all have gone to charity.' He pushed the cheque over the desk. 'If you'll pardon me, a jaundiced person might say you took the obvious — and self-serving — option in making your choice. I'm curious, however, for you seem fair-minded. Did you know what was in the box, or what value it had?'

'No, only that someone once paid a good price for it. It may not be valuable at all. Still, he received some recompense and I now have the pleasure of the painting.'

Fitzroy allowed himself a small smile. 'I know little about him, of course. Only that he was her son and they'd been long estranged.' He shrugged. 'There are many such stories.'

'Indeed,' said Anna. 'This world is full of secrets. I've come to think that sometimes it's best if they stay that way.'

She put the cheque in her purse, then ventured, 'If I may ask, what happened to the remainder of Violet's estate? I believe there was a lodging house.'

He nodded. 'Indeed yes. Of a sort. She took in fallen women, somehow persuading a range of benevolent societies to support the running of the place. She bequeathed it to the Freethought Society. Someone there is running the place now. Who would have thought Freethinkers would still cling on in the twentieth century?'

* * *

'MY WORD,' said Jamie an hour later. They were meeting over a tea table, as arranged on the phone two evenings earlier. The storm had evaporated. The sun shone on the small painting as Jamie held its frame in both hands to inspect the brushwork. He had an auction to organise later in the day and could not stay long. 'This is very fine. Such luminosity and splendid colours. One might almost pick it as a Degas. Or a very decent copy.'

'It's been left to me by a friend,' Anna said. 'You might remember her. Violet Sutton, back in Tauranga? You used to play in the kitchen when I took you along on visits.'

Jamie frowned, still distracted by the picture of dancers in filmy skirts. 'That I remember. And the cook, who let me lick her spoon. But the lady of the house? Don't recall her.'

'That was her son you saw the other day, arriving just as you departed.'

'Oh, right. Bit of a toff, I thought. Or trying to be. What did he want?'

'Just to talk about his mother. He'd not seen her for a long time. Neither had I. She died right here in Sydney a couple of years ago. She spent ages here and neither of us knew.'

Jamie heard her sadness. He put the painting back in its box. 'A wheel turns full circle, then.'

'In a way.' Anna nibbled on a piece of shortbread. She watched her son drain his cup. He was gathering himself to go. 'Jamie, Violet's husband said it was a Degas. He met him once in Paris. If it really is, would it be worth very much?'

'My word, yes. Hundreds, even though it's so small. But it's not signed, is it. Do you want me to make enquiries?'

'It's not important. Memories are worth more than money.'

CHAPTER THIRTY-EIGHT

'From careful observation comes knowledge and from knowledge of the beautiful must come love; and as love inspires the imagination, there we have the complete chain.'
— Article urging better teaching to children of the true nature of flowers, Sydney Morning Herald.

SOME WEEKS LATER, ANNA SET OUT ON A VISIT. SHE straightened the small picture of dancers that hung next to her bed, checked her purse, locked her door and set out to catch the ferry. She crossed the harbour and hired a horse cab to take her up the hill to Paddington. When they reached the address she wanted she paid the driver, stood at the gate and looked at the house.

The iron fretwork adorning the veranda needed a fresh touch of white paint. There was a brass plate over the door bearing a name that made her smile. Planter boxes at the windowsills were filled with flowers.

Anna stepped up and rang the bell. After a minute a woman in her middle years opened the door with a friendly hello. Anna could hear female chatter drifting along the tiled hallway from the kitchen.

Anna gave her name. 'You don't know me but I'm an old friend of Mrs Millhouse, who I believe used to own this place. May I come in?'

The woman smiled with surprise. 'Of course. If you were a friend of Violet's you're one of ours too.'

'Are you in charge here?'

The woman extended an open palm towards the parlour. 'Yes, I'm Nancy Greenall. Been managing here since dear Violet passed. Please, make yourself comfortable.'

A gale of laughter came along the corridor then, and an unmistakable voice. 'Get away with you, girl.'

'Pardon the noise,' said Nancy Greenall. 'People can be a little loud here.'

But Anna brushed past her, hurrying towards the noise. She came to a stop in a sunlit kitchen where three young women sat at the table. They were giggling at the flow of banter pouring from the stout, white-haired cook who gripped a china bowl in one arm as she fiercely beat butter and sugar with a wooden spoon. She looked up and dropped the spoon with a clatter as her hands flew to her broad cheeks. 'Oh my gawd!' she gasped.

Anna, speechless, could only smile until it hurt as Hester lumbered round the table, wrapped her arms around her and squeezed her until she was breathless.

* * *

TALK AND LAUGHTER ROLLED ON. Hester's apron was discarded. Her oven began to cool and her cake mixture stood untouched until one of the big-bellied girls took over and Nancy Greenall shooed Anna and Hester into the parlour and joined them there.

Anna learnt how Hester had been employed at a nearby hotel. She was hurrying along the road one day to catch the greengrocer's cart when she noticed her own name engraved on brass over a doorway. Hester's House, it said. She'd grunted with amusement and eyed it with some envy because it had some charm, but it was two months before she went past another time and saw Violet stepping out onto the street. They'd spied each other at the same moment and gaped in unison. 'Violet said it always made her feel safe to go through that door with my name over it. Of course I moved in 'ere the very next week.'

Anna nodded with a full heart as she heard how hard Violet had worked to help women and girls in the trouble she'd experienced so long before. 'There is never any shortage of residents,' said Nancy. 'We could be twice the size and still not cope.'

'What happens to the babies?'

'Adoption, of course. The girls have no husbands, no money, their families have often cast them out. At least until they can go back home with an excuse for their absence. We find new parents and watch the girls grieve. It's a bitter pain. And while they're here we try to teach them skills so they can earn their own money in the future.'

Anna looked around, saw worn furniture and patched holes in the curtains. 'Is it hard to find the funds to keep going?'

Nancy's mouth compressed. 'Always. The Society owns it outright because of Violet's generosity, but the outgoings. . .' She shook her head in despair. 'Sometimes, but only rarely, the girls' families will contribute. We have a few benefactors drawn in by Violet but they've been falling away. We take in work for the girls to do. Sewing, ironing, even some typing these days. But many of them can barely read and write. It's a struggle.'

'I like to help young ones with literacy. Perhaps I can assist there.' Anna opened her purse then and laid an envelope on the table between them. 'And perhaps this will help too. Think of it as another gift from Violet, come in a roundabout way.'

Nancy gingerly picked it up, peeked inside. She gasped. 'A thousand pounds? Are you certain? This is so. . .' She fluttered her hands, speechless. 'Can you afford it? Have you taken advice?'

'Heavens, no. My husband might have thought I've lost my mind but he is not here now. The world cares little for what ageing widows may decide, but as I told a doubting banker last week, I am in no need of counsel.'

'You're sure then?' Nancy asked.

Anna folded her hands in her lap. She felt immensely calm. Outside, a row of pansies in pots was just visible above the window sash, petals flying in the warm breeze. 'Of course. I am a free woman now.'

NOTES

This book is a fictional story spun from a real-life drama that happened in Tauranga in the late 1800s. My great-grandfather, Joe Buddle, was then the young manager of the local branch of the Bank of New Zealand. His good friend George Gair, from Melbourne, managed the National Bank across the road.

Joe wrote many letters and one of his sons later held on to a book of them — a volume of hard-to-read carbon copies on flimsy paper bound between stout brown covers.

It fell into my grandfather's hands, then my father's and then came to me, but it took me years to get around to transcribing Joe's handwriting.

Mostly he wrote about everyday commerce, but a few riveting pages are devoted to the tragic death of George, who 'formed an unfortunate attachment to a married woman' and, eventually, solved his many problems by shooting himself in the head.

Joe was called to the awful scene. Never before, he later wrote to a friend, had he been 'so unmanned' as he was by the sight of his friend lying dead.

In a suicide note George pleaded with Joe to keep the affair secret. Joe obeyed and made sure he had a Christian burial. His letters to the dead man's mother in Australia show how he also tried to shield her from the truth about her son's descent into ruinous debt and bad behaviour.

That much of this novel is true but all else is fiction, built on my curiosity. Who was the 'scarlet woman' who had attracted George's roving eye? Joe described her in one letter as a 'silly, empty-headed and useless woman', though did concede her husband 'never treated her well'.

But what, I thought, if she was actually miserable and desperate, and her husband a bully? Was that why she sought affection elsewhere and risked having an affair in a small town full of wagging tongues?

Only once in his letters did Joe use her name, which was Simpson. She is a mystery. I could find no Tauranga records from that time mentioning residents of that name.

That Mr Simpson discovered his wife's infidelity is not in doubt, as Joe wrote about a meeting of everyone involved, at which it was agreed that the relationship must end. It was common for 19th-century adulterers to be called to account by wounded spouses so that grievances could be aired — the colonial equivalent of today's 'family group conference'.

Financial compensation was sometimes demanded. When guilty parties had reputations to protect they could be forced to pay handsomely to ensure that no news of their wrongdoing could leak out.

I have changed people's names because it gave me freedom to play with characters of my own invention — and to conjecture on what might have led to the affair and how lives might have been affected. I have also altered time frames. The real suicide occurred in 1879 but I've placed it in 1886 so I could include the Mount Tarawera eruption, another event that rocked settlers' lives.

Some of the action of the novel is based on fact. Aucklanders had a very good time 'rinking' at the Symonds Street Choral Hall, which still stands on the corner of Alfred Street and is part of Auckland University, though the original open space has been divided into smaller rooms. A Monsieur Bibron did teach dance to young Auckland ladies. Roaming palm readers and mesmerists plied their trade in every town.

Tauranga settlers perked up their lives with annual boat races, picnics, concerts and dances at the bank. The 'servant problem' was rife, with good help hard to find. Early Tauranga settlers enjoyed their annual regatta days, with races sailed and rowed by European and Maori crews. In the year in which this book begins, 1886, the real regatta went off without a hitch.

Early sunglasses, or 'blue goggles', were being worn by fashion-forward ladies in the 1880s.

The writer Ouida did hold court at the Langham Hotel in London. Even today visitors occasionally ask to see her room, but after many refurbishments it no longer exists. The excerpt Violet reads is from Ouida's 1871 book, *Folle- Farine*.

Freethought, a movement advocating reason as opposed to blind faith, was growing in popularity in late Victorian times, promoted in England by the charismatic William Kingdon [sic] Clifford. *The Free-thinker* magazine's first issue came out in 1881.

I plucked my character Rupert's nickname from a lively little book, *My Simple Life in New Zealand* by Adela Stewart. She wrote about her homesteading life in Athenree, close to Katikati, from 1878 to the century's end, and included a reference to an unnamed bachelor with red hair so bright it earned him the Magenta Man nickname.

It so amused me that I just had to use it. (*My Simple Life In New Zealand* is still in print and can be bought from Athenree Homestead, which was rescued from ruin and restored over the last 20 years by community volunteers. It is open to the public. For hours and info see www.athenreehomestead.org.nz.)

I have entirely invented Rupert's two stray avocado trees. I read one tale of an attempt to grow plants imported from Bermuda in 1887, but it wasn't until the 1920s that one Charles Grey struck success with avocados in Gisborne and it took about 60 more years for them to become popular. Still, early settlers eagerly imported many exotic plants as they tried to establish what would grow. I like to think someone may have had a brief moment of glory with midshipman's butter.

Business people did their best in the 1870s and 1880s to build Tauranga as a thriving centre and plans for a railway to link Tauranga and Rotorua were much debated but came to nothing.

Many travellers passed through on their way to the Pink and White

Terraces, so tourism looked like a sure thing at the time. But the Mount Tarawera eruption, followed by a severe worldwide Depression in the 1890s, made business slow going.

Thomas and Anna are only loosely based on my great-grandparents. In real life Joe got fed up with the banking business and resigned, fell on hard times, and went to Australia looking for better luck.

He got a job in a country town, but his wife Minnie couldn't stand the heat and they returned to New Zealand to settle in Auckland. They had six sons, one of whom died in infancy. If they're out there somewhere, I hope they don't mind me taking such liberties with their history. As the *Bay of Plenty Times* has revealed to me they were keen on amateur dramatics, I think they'd approve.

Joe eventually did all right for himself as an accountant, founding a practice later headed by his son Fred and then by my own father Peter.

Joe always had a soft spot for Tauranga, however. A Bank of New Zealand branch still stands close to the corner of Wharf and Willow Streets where he once bent over his ledgers. Despite the disappointments of his time there, he was certain that one day the town would flourish. Imagine if he could see how mightily it thrives today as New Zealand's largest port.

* Quotes at the head of each chapter are taken from newspapers and journals published in the era covered by this story, from the late 19th to early 20th centuries. I found them at New Zealand's online resource, paperspast.natlib.govt.nz, and in Australia's Trove archives at https://trove.nla.gov.au/newspaper

ACKNOWLEDGMENTS

I had help from many good people in researching this novel. Firstly, I'm grateful to my great-grandpa Joe for writing the letters that sparked me off on the writing journey, and other family members who kept them for more than a century so that I could get my own hands on them.

The late Stephen Stratford delivered sharp assessment, excellent editing and kind encouragement. Nikki Crutchley and Eva Chan were also solid helpers in copy-editing and proof-reading.

Many friends were good enough to read early drafts and give me feedback, including Jane Francis, John McCrystal, Glenda Law, Deb Turton, Maria Carlton, and the late Dorothy Vinicombe who awed me with the warm encouragement she offered even as she faced up to grave illness.

Staff at libraries in Auckland, Tauranga and Rotorua are immaculate keepers of records and photographs, for which much thanks. Librarians Karen Craig at Auckland City and Helen Woodhouse at Takapuna gave me Auckland Heritage Festival venues at which I could sound off at the mike about great Victorian stories which were only marginally connected to this one, but all of which gave me a grip on the mood of the late 19th century.

Gratitude also to Tee Carroll of the volunteer team at Athenree Homestead, who gave me a great welcome when I visited the house and even dressed me up, for fun, in Victorian finery. It was lovely to see a Bay of Plenty house that stood in my ancestors' time now being so carefully restored and cared for.

ABOUT THE AUTHOR

Lindsey Dawson is a former journalist and magazine editor who has also worked on TV and radio. She lives in a small Auckland, New Zealand, apartment where she struggles to find enough room for her two creative passions, writing and abstract painting. She authored eight earlier books before this one, including two previous novels. It was while doing research for Scarlet & Magenta that she discovered stories about an old Victorian scandal that led to a new non-fiction book about a tale of passion and tragic death — *Poisoning on Parker Road: One Family, Two Deaths and all the Secrets in Between*.

www.lindseydawson.com
www.amazon.com/author/lindseydawson

ALSO BY LINDSEY DAWSON

Fiction

Angel Baby

Lipstick in the Dust

Non-fiction

The Next Book of Decorating

Pearls: Let Out the Wise Soul Within You

Wise Up: How to be Fearless and Fulfilled in Midlife

The Elemental You: Discover and Delight in your Primal Personality

Crack Your Life: How to Write Memoir That Rocks

The Answer: How Nature Can Help You When Life Seems Too Hard

Poisoning on Parker Road: One Family, Two Deaths and all the Secrets in Between.

www.ingramcontent.com/pod-product-compliance
Lightning Source LLC
Chambersburg PA
CBHW011115100726
47898CB00011B/3092